"The details...all ring true, especially Yvonne trying to prove herself in a man's world... Overall, this is an interesting treatment of a little-known aspect of WWII."

—Historical Novel Society

"Fast-paced, often heart-pounding... What makes this novel all the more powerful is the fact that [the protagonist] is based on a real person."

—*Library Journal*

PRAISE FOR
ALL IN HER HANDS

"A lively, heartfelt novel following one woman who will do anything to realize her dreams. Historical fiction fans will love this."
—Julia Bryan Thomas, author of *The Kennedy Girl*

"Audrey Blake has crafted a masterful work of historical fiction! *All in Her Hands* sweeps you away with its richly drawn cast—characters so vivid and beloved they feel like old friends—and its stirring collision of a deadly London epidemic with the battle for women's place in medicine. It's one of those rare novels that transports you entirely—both in time and heart."
—Amanda Skenandore, author of
The Medicine Woman of Galveston

"An ode to female doctors, nurses, and medical professionals everywhere, *All in Her Hands* is a compelling story of a brave woman facing down the prejudices of her time in a London not yet welcoming to her hard-won expertise. At times tender and others thrilling, Audrey Blake's latest novel sweeps you along to a satisfying and breathless conclusion."
—Heather Webb, *USA Today* bestselling author of
The Hope Keeper

PRAISE FOR
THE GIRL IN HIS SHADOW

"In *The Girl in His Shadow*, Audrey Blake takes the reader on an exquisitely detailed journey through the harrowing field of medicine in mid-nineteenth-century London. Nora, the ward of the eccentric and brilliant surgeon Horace Croft, learns far more than any woman is allowed. Bravely saving lives while risking her own, she defies the law to pioneer breakthroughs in medicine."

—Tracey Enerson Wood, international bestselling author of *The Engineer's Wife*

"A suspenseful story of a courageous young woman determined to become a surgeon in repressive Victorian England. Fluidly written, impeccably researched, *The Girl in His Shadow* is a memorable literary gift to be read, reread, and treasured."

—Gloria Goldreich, author of *The Paris Children*

"With its strong woman protagonist and authentic period detail, this is the best kind of historical fiction, transporting readers to a place and time peopled with memorable characters. Readers who enjoy medical drama will gravitate to this book."

—*Library Journal*

"Assured, engaging, and full of fascinating detail and richly realized characters."

—Historical Novel Society

PRAISE FOR
THE SURGEON'S DAUGHTER

"I tore through Audrey Blake's *The Surgeon's Daughter* without pause. This richly detailed, expertly paced saga of the only female student attending a prestigious medical school in Italy brought into crystal focus the many obstacles a nineteenth-century woman faced—at either end of the scalpel. In Nora Beady, Blake has created a truly captivating heroine, for then and for now."

—Sally Cabot Gunning, author of *The Widow's War* and
Painting the Light

"History comes to life in the dramatic account of Nora Beady's ascension in the medical world of Bologna… The depiction of women earning their place amongst the medical community and the everyday concerns of young professionals will appeal to lovers of historical fiction, and the dash of passion and yearning will appeal to romantics."

—*Booklist*

"This is an intense, suspenseful, and insightful read about the challenges both women and doctors faced in the nineteenth century… Our heroine rises to the challenge with courage and determination."

—Historical Novel Society

PRAISE FOR
THE WOMAN WITH NO NAME

"You will feel like you know Yvonne Rudellat from the start. Rather than a superhero, she's an ordinary woman who makes extraordinary sacrifices for her country. A mother. A spy. A saboteur. Yvonne becomes who she needs to be in order to help her country during WWII. Her story is as fast-paced as it is well researched. Authenticity shows itself on every page. It was a pleasure to read, as well as an education about the heroics of the French Resistance."

—Diane Hanks, author of *The Woman with a Purple Heart*

"An enthralling, based-on-truth story about a remarkable woman whose courage and determination to create a new, meaningful life at a time when she feels invisible to everyone, including her estranged husband and grown daughter, which is as heartrending as it is inspiring. Rich in detail, action, and emotion, *The Woman with No Name* breathes life into the legacy of one of many women whose lives demand celebration. Bravo, Yvonne and Audrey Blake!"

—Penny Haw, author of *The Invincible Miss Cust* and
The Woman at the Wheel

"Resilience, courage, and bravery outshine the enemy in this fast-paced, historical read."

—*Booklist*

Also by Audrey Blake

The Girl in His Shadow
The Surgeon's Daughter
The Woman with No Name

ALL
IN
HER
HANDS

A NOVEL

AUDREY BLAKE

sourcebooks
landmark

Published by Sourcebooks Landmark, an imprint of Sourcebooks
1935 Brookdale RD, Naperville, IL 60563-2773
(630) 961-3900
sourcebooks.com

Library of Congress Cataloging-in-Publication Data

Names: Blake, Audrey, active 2020 author
Title: All in her hands : a novel / Audrey Blake.
Description: Naperville, IL : Sourcebooks Landmark, 2026.
Identifiers: LCCN 2025037976 | trade paperback | epub
Subjects: LCGFT: Fiction | Medical fiction | Novels
Classification: LCC PS3602.L3415 A77 2026
LC record available at https://lccn.loc.gov/2025037976

Printed and bound in the United States of America.
SB 10 9 8 7 6 5 4 3 2

CHAPTER 1

August 14, 1849; London

ONLY FOUR STEPS TO CLIMB TO THE GLOSSY FRONT DOOR of 43 Great Queen Street, but Nora's strength unraveled further with each one, dropping completely from her shoulders the moment she slipped inside the dim entrance hall.

The house was quiet. Nora let out a sigh and plucked at the linen rag covering her chest. It had been a pressed blouse just this morning, before she'd had to sally out into the late-summer heat. But the air inside was almost as stifling.

She had one goal—to sit in the ice room with closed eyes until the waves of heat stopped radiating off her skin. Then she could finally open the letter she'd received yesterday but hadn't had time to read. Navigating past a pile of newly arrived crates in the hallway, she glanced at the labels—India. Horace must have gotten word of some exciting specimens. Detouring around them, she stepped into the parlor and stopped, letter and ice room forgotten. A tall, slender man was stretched across the sofa, slippered feet hanging off the edge. The newspaper draped over his face lifted ever so slightly with each of his languid breaths. Daniel was sleeping.

Though her sore arms begged her to drop her heavy bag with a thump, she lowered it carefully to the floor so as not to startle him. Besides, it held too many precious medicines and instruments to treat it with anything less than the utmost care.

She tugged at her bootlaces to free her tired feet. Leaving the dusty boots in a heap, she tiptoed closer, studying her new husband. The newssheet, rising and falling with each exhale like the gentle swells of a calm sea, bore an article about American gold prospecting in California.

A trained surgeon, she lifted the paper with remarkable care and transferred it to the sofa arm, revealing his face—his sideburns trimmed with her usual precision. Daniel could have done as well himself, but she enjoyed shaving him. She liked any excuse to touch him, particularly those opportunities requiring a battle between deliberate motion and reckless proximity. The first time, she'd gotten carried away and actually nicked him. Daniel had teased her for weeks.

Nora grinned, nudged her way onto the edge of the cushion, and bent, kissing his cheek. He looked younger than his thirty years when he slept.

"You're home," he said before he managed to open his eyes. His arms found her and tugged her close as he turned to his side and burrowed into the sofa to make room for her. "You missed supper. I hope it was an interesting case."

"Nothing exciting. I was treating a girl with a fever in a rookery. When word spread a doctor was there, I had a line down the hall all the way to the front door. I opened a cyst, removed a dead fingernail, and tomorrow I have a child coming into the clinic. He's tongue-tied and needs to have it clipped."

The poor didn't mind so much when their doctor wore skirts. Since returning from Italy six months before, the clinic here had grown more and more empty. Most middle-class men simply refused to submit to her care. Nora took a deep breath. "How was your day?"

"Three surgeries. An amputation, a bone excision, and a bunion removal."

Nora tamped down her jealousy, diverting her attention to Daniel as he pressed his lips into her hair, sending a rush of electricity over her scalp.

"Let me squeeze you for a minute, and then you can go eat."

"I can't eat yet. I'm still too hot. I meant to go to the ice room."

A throat cleared behind her. Nora sat up. "Hello, Mrs. Phipps. Did you want something?"

The housekeeper wasn't normally inclined to interrupt, but as general manager of the chaos contained in their household, specimen room, hospital ward, surgery, and clinic, she often needed to. "I *want* you to be able to eat, perhaps sleep, and freshen your clothes." Her presence was always more forceful than her rail-thin, diminutive stature justified. "But I'm afraid a messenger's come to the clinic. Mrs. Franklin is asking for help. She's on Milk Street. It's urgent." Her voice softened. "I'm sorry, Nora. Cook is packing you a sandwich."

Untangling himself, Daniel sat up, too. "I can come with you." Mrs. Franklin was a skilled midwife, but if she needed help—

Nora glanced at him, his cheek red and indented where it'd been smashed against the button of the tufted pillow. He must be tired, even more so than she, if he'd done three surgeries this afternoon. And he was scheduled to work at St. Bart's, one of London's enormous teaching hospitals, again in the morning. "You need to sleep. I'll manage fine."

"Don't walk," he said. "Take the carriage and rest your feet for a few minutes."

"The driver is already bringing it around," Mrs. Phipps said as Nora wrestled her boots back on, her feet magically sorer than when she'd stripped them off only minutes ago. "I'll have the sandwiches and your vaporizer put in."

As she disappeared, she kindly closed the door.

Daniel came up behind her, resting his hands on her shoulders and working at her knotted trapezius muscles. "Are you certain, Nora? I'm happy to help."

"Go up to bed." She rummaged through her bag, opening the protective case of her newest acquisition—a beautifully crafted glass syringe. No cracks. Good. "I'll join you as soon as I can."

She hadn't meant any innuendo, but he gave a complaining groan and kissed the back of her neck. "Not soon enough."

She swallowed and waited for her stomach to return to its rightful place, then turned and placed a pert kiss on his head. "No fair making me regret going when I have no choice. And just so you know..." She paused at the doorway. "I'm going straight to sleep when I get home."

"We'll see." The sound of Daniel's laugh chased her down the hallway, the feel of his hands on her shoulders lingering until she was in the carriage, rolling toward Milk Street.

She wished she could have stayed home.

But she was needed, and this promised to be today's most challenging case—probably the most demanding work she'd do all week. A humbling thought. Six months ago, in the midst of the furor she'd caused by registering with the medical association as a surgeon free to practice in the city of London—without letting them know N. Beady was a woman—she'd conducted a successful cesarean section, something no other English doctor could claim.

But the victory of her one incredible feat was fading, and she couldn't make a career out of dangerous and rare surgeries. If she kept doing only the work no other doctors would take—and no male patients would give her—next time she needed to do a cesarean, she'd be out of practice, dangerously so. She couldn't collect enough fees or keep her mind and fingers sufficiently trained dressing burns, treating bunions, and removing ingrown toenails.

Nora took another bite of her sandwich and extracted the letter in her pocket. With traffic clogging the streets, she ought to have time to read it all. And she was anxious for news of her teacher and mentor, Magdalena Marenco, a surgeon and professor of obstetrics and midwifery at the University of Bologna. Magdalena would have good advice for her, whether she knew Nora's current troubles or not.

Nora broke the letter's seal with a quick flick of her thumb, smiling as she studied Magdalena's handwriting. It was so like her—flowing, bold letters that dominated the page. Another bite—Nora shook some fallen crumbs off the paper—and she started to read, chewing as she devoured her former teacher's words.

My darling Nora,

Yes, I'm sure your husband is excellent, but I also know that you have no real yardstick by which to judge. After all, you never did sleep with Salvio Perra, which on the whole I think was wise. He's generous, but so easily offended. That becomes tiresome. However, I'm glad you are happy and glad that Daniel makes you so. I told Salvatore, and he looked like he'd bitten a lemon.

Nora huffed. Magdalena tended to be even more forthright in her letters than she was face-to-face. Wrenching off another bite of sandwich, she chewed furiously.

The recipe Dr. Croft sent for the primrose tincture is very nice. Please offer my thanks.

No, I'm afraid I have no female students since you left, excepting the midwives, of course.

At the mention, Nora saw the faces of her friends. The midwife nuns had been separate from her, of course, by their vows and customs, but they'd worked hand in hand, nursing and bringing children into the world. Here in England, most doctors considered a midwife as little more than a woman with a water bucket and some ragged towels. They were certainly not trained to work in hospital like their Italian counterparts. Licensed doctors, known as accoucheurs and obstetricians, now claimed the world of English childbirth, leaving midwives to attend to the impoverished and those too frightened of high mortality rates to go to charity hospitals.

I worry over it. In my mother's time, the university had four women attending classes. At present I am the only female, if I don't count the nuns. I want to train others — other women, I mean; there are enough men enrolling in my classes — but I have found no one willing to try. Once I'm gone, what of the girls who'd like to learn then? Who will help them, or show them that this is possible? That women are not just capable of this work, but meant for it?

You must think of this too. I know in England right now there isn't a way for them —

Nora swallowed, looking blindly through the carriage window. There truly wasn't. Unable to remove her from the medical register once she'd qualified, the college had instead made a new rule, barring women applicants entirely. They might not be able to get rid of her, but they'd stop every other woman who tried.

Her stomach twisted with familiar guilt. She'd snuck her way in, unintentionally damming the way for any other woman to follow, though none had tried, yet.

It's the college's doing, not yours, she reminded herself and returned her attention to the letter.

You must think of the future, Magdalena continued. *For the women who would and will work with you. For the sisters you will care for and save.*

Throat tight, Nora refolded the letter. Magdalena meant well. She was fierce and uncompromising in her beliefs, but what exactly did she think Nora could do about this? She'd barely clung on to her license. She had practically no patients, certainly none who could afford to pay her. The clinic stayed afloat only because Horace still attracted enthusiastic—and paying—crowds at his lectures and demonstrations.

She was tired, hungry—even after the sandwich—and probably destined to spend all night tending a woman in labor. And next week and next month, she'd do more of the same, waiting for the rare, sporadic cases to keep her mind and hands from rusting.

The driver stopped, and Nora scrambled to swallow one last bite as she hoisted up the delicate vaporizer and her kit bag. Wriggling from the carriage, she almost bumped into a thin young woman twisting her hands anxiously. "Are you Mrs. Gibson?" she asked. "Mrs. Franklin told me to wait for you."

"Yes," Nora answered, glad to have extra help. She passed the girl her instrument bag. "Careful with that." She'd carry the vaporizer herself. It had just been recalibrated and repaired, and was every bit as fragile as her new glass syringe. "Take me to her."

The girl rushed through an alley to a crooked staircase that clung to a filthy, soot-stained building with doors and landings at intervals leading to even dirtier flats.

"Mrs. Franklin's worried," the girl said, her words separated by breathless pants. Nora struggled to keep pace—the steps were steep, and she didn't trust the rickety railing. They ducked inside a door, three floors up. "Just in there." The girl handed Nora her bag and retreated, only too eager to flee. Nora didn't blame her, but she didn't understand, either. Whenever Nora heard screams of pain, her blood quickened, propelling her toward the crisis, not away.

Her adoptive father, Horace Croft, renowned for his work in surgery, medicine, and science, was just as intrepid, luckily for her—and not only because he'd dared to develop and make use of her skill, once he'd seen that she shared his curiosity. First, he'd plucked her, nearly lifeless, out of a flat not much better than this when her entire family perished from cholera. His heedless rush into every undertaking had saved her life.

It had been a searing experience for an eight-year-old girl—losing her family to cholera, nearly dying, then awakening in the home of a strange surgeon with sobbing patients and specimen-filled shelves. But since she'd nowhere else to go, she'd done her best to stay by trying to make herself agreeable and useful. It took Nora years to trust the gruff stranger and even longer to approach his exacting trade with anything other than horror.

Unfortunately, Horace attended fewer surgeries since his stroke last year. His weakened left hand might be just as dexterous as the average man's, but Horace was a renowned surgeon and not accustomed to being average at anything.

Nor did Nora aspire to the commonplace. Squaring her shoulders, she hurried toward the growing moans, willing her eyes to adjust to the dark and her nose to air that already smelled of blood and birthing.

CHAPTER 2

"THANK THE LORD," MRS. FRANKLIN BREATHED AS NORA burst into the back bedroom. "You're here. It's happening now."

"What's the trouble?" Nora asked, searching out a safe spot to store her vaporizer and already fearing whatever made the stoic Mrs. Franklin look so anxious.

"Breech. Which is no great problem, usually. I just have a feeling." The woman's wrinkled brow glistened with exertion, but she forced a smile onto her face as she turned to the patient. "You'll be fine, Betsy. Dr. Gibson's here to help."

"Let me take a look." Nora knelt at the end of the bed. As Mrs. Franklin had said, this birth was well underway. And breech. Instead of a bit of scalp, she caught a glimpse of baby buttocks crowded against Betsy's opening—still small, which was a concern. Nora had no idea how long Betsy had been laboring, but big babies and little pelvises always flooded her with dread.

"Blood loss?" Nora asked as she unbuttoned her sleeves.

Mrs. Franklin jerked her head. "No. But poor Betsy's worn out. This is her first. I usually wait for the babe to make his own way through, but we've been here for hours."

A moan mounted, ending in a scream that tore at Nora's

chest. Patients coped with pain differently, but as Nora added up factors—breech presentation, primigravida, unproductive labor, maternal exhaustion…

"It's good that you sent for me." She glanced at the vaporizer, then turned back to the patient. "Betsy?"

No response. She was too lost in her suffering to register anything.

Mrs. Franklin gripped Nora's arm and angled her away from the bed. "Betsy's my niece. My sister died three weeks after giving birth to her." Her jaw clenched, and Nora noticed her drenched collar and glistening neck. "I can't let it happen again."

Nora scrutinized the scene with new eyes. Everything changed when family was attending. The baby's buttocks inched forward with a contraction, then slid back again. At least the child was prone—*face to the tail*, as the midwives said. "It's not the worst position," Nora reassured Mrs. Franklin. "We'll take care of Betsy together."

Nora yanked out her jars of wine and olive oil and threw some of the oil over her hands just as Magdalena had taught her.

Never force your hand into delicate tissue. You must be as slippery as the child itself. And for the sake of everything holy, keep your nails short. Slow down and think!

Betsy screamed again and the buttocks slid forward, far enough that Nora could see the hip joints.

"That's progress," Mrs. Franklin cried.

Nora was about to lower into a better position, but Mrs. Franklin was already there, weathered hands poised and a mask of fierce concentration on her face. "Bear down, now, Betsy. It's a boy. We're almost through it."

"You continue," Nora said, shifting sideways. "I'm here if you need me."

For all her earlier anxiety, Mrs. Franklin was confident now. Nora understood the sudden change. Frequently, an oncoming crisis simply forced uncertainties to vanish, compelling you to succeed. And sometimes that swift, blind courage worked, but it was hell when it didn't. So as Nora leaned back, crouching on her heels, she watched carefully.

Betsy groaned and panted as the baby's body slowly emerged, his legs pinned up, unable to fall loose. Betsy's thighs shook with pain and pressure, and Nora longed to pull the child out and make the suffering stop, but birth required faith and restraint. The progression stopped, and Nora and Mrs. Franklin leaned in closer. The tiny feet had wedged behind the vulva like bolts in a lock, impeding further descent. Nora started to reach forward when, with practiced movements, Mrs. Franklin hooked her fingers behind the baby's knee joints and flexed upward, freeing the feet to pop out and dangle as she held up the child's belly.

Nora smiled. Most doctors would have tried to stretch the opening laterally, but someone had taught Mrs. Franklin this gravity-assisted technique—one Nora had seen only in Italy. Nora spared a glance at Betsy's purple face, swollen from hours of exertion, her eyes tormented slits.

"Nearly there," she said, reaching up to press the mother's tightly clenched fist.

The baby's back slid into view, tilting to take advantage

of every sliver of open space. Screaming, Betsy grabbed her bedcovers, so Nora jumped to her side, rubbing Betsy's upper arms and shoulders with hard, grinding strokes as the nuns had taught her.

"I'm going to die like my mother," Betsy sobbed.

"You'll do no such thing," Nora promised as she tried to massage some courage into her. She glanced at Mrs. Franklin, who hadn't responded to her niece's cry.

"What?" Nora asked. Something else was wrong.

"One arm is pinned up by the head. I've seen breeches like that where the child was palsied all their life."

Nora nodded. Nerve damage at the neck and shoulder could be crippling. "Let me look."

The vaginal wall quivered. There wasn't a centimeter left, no give for the bulging weight of the baby. "I need to cut." Nora spoke softly, only for Mrs. Franklin's ears. "Can you get the surgical scissors from my bag?"

Nora didn't hold with cutting, though many doctors favored the procedure—which they called episiotomy.

Mrs. Franklin answered with a grim frown. "You need to hurry." She knew, better than Nora, that delay was dangerous.

"I assume these are the ones you want?" Mrs. Franklin passed Nora the blunt-edged scissors. A quick nod—they were the right ones for this, though not specifically what she'd requested. This midwife had good instincts.

Nora exhaled. She liked to have a little more time to select her spot, but this would have to do.

She closed the blades and Betsy jerked, letting out a piercing scream. "Sorry," Nora whispered through grinding teeth. Blood ran from the wound as Nora inserted her hand, working her fingers carefully between the baby's sternum and Betsy's pelvis, the contractions crushing her hand painfully. She waited as the pain mounted, her fingertips numbed from the pressure. She could just brush the baby's chin, but not yet reach his mouth.

"I need gentle pressure from outside. Extremely gentle," Nora warned as Mrs. Franklin applied her hands to Betsy's swollen abdomen. The extra push worked, and the head slid toward Nora's fingers. She hooked her pointer finger into the baby's mouth, blinking when the tiny tongue flickered against her.

"He's moving!" She sighed, relief sweeping from the top of her head and rolling over her shoulders. At least there was that. But he wasn't having a better time than the rest of them. There was no reaching the arm. She had no room at all. How a man with larger fingers ever navigated this…

Giving up, she carefully withdrew and reached her bloodied hand into her bag for the forceps.

Mrs. Franklin's eyes went wide from her position above Betsy.

"These are short forceps," Nora explained. "Some doctors treat them only as leverage to pull harder, but we're smarter than that. They can reach where we can't. Every tool is a good tool in the right hands."

"No!" Betsy screamed at the sight of the large metal clamps. "I can't."

"It won't increase your pain," Nora vowed. "It will help it end sooner."

Betsy didn't seem to hear, protesting even louder. Nora

wished momentarily for the vaporizer, but there was no time to ready it, let alone administer a dose of ether.

"Stand there."

Mrs. Franklin repositioned herself as Nora slipped one forcep into the inferior opening near Betsy's tailbone and eased it into position on the right side of the head. "Hold this one in place here," she explained over Betsy's hysterical screams. "Then we do the same on the left side. I extend the handles beyond the head, so the curved bits help push instead of pulling on the neck."

Necks were so fragile.

"Try and keep her still."

Murmuring incomprehensibly, Mrs. Franklin leaned in and grabbed her niece's knees, holding her fast while Nora clamped the forceps together and rested the tiny body on top of them to support his weight before she guided the head downward. Horace had often warned her of the unique times you needed to ignore a patient in order to save them, but today, Nora couldn't manage it. "We're almost there, Betsy. Try to hold on to something."

She turned back Mrs. Franklin. Flushed, sweating, she also looked at the point of breaking. "As soon as the chin appears—" She grunted as the nape of the neck and the mouth began to emerge. "You stand and draw the child up and out, toward the ceiling, decreasing the circumference for the mother."

Almost as soon as she spoke, it happened. The head escaped, the rubbery cord dropping nearly to the floor as Betsy gave a shuddering cry.

Nora dropped the forceps and collected the baby from Mrs.

Franklin's trembling hands. The midwife rushed to clutch Betsy's shoulders. "Well done, love. Well done. We've got him out."

Nora turned the baby over, wrapping him in her billowing apron. He was limp now—the suck she'd elicited moments ago absent when she thumbed his tiny mouth. She rubbed his chest, waiting for the first gasp.

"Come on, dear," she whispered, opening the mouth and sweeping it with her finger. Still no response. Nora rubbed harder, angling the baby's head toward the floor.

"Is something the matter with him?" Betsy asked urgently.

Mrs. Franklin, moving like lightning, reached for the child with hands so demanding and certain that Nora relinquished him, the slack limbs flopping as Mrs. Franklin swiped his face with a towel. She opened his lips and placed her mouth over his, then gave a steady blow. The tiny chest swelled.

"Pinch his foot," Mrs. Franklin ordered, then lowered herself for one more puff. Nora obeyed, and his limp fingers opened like a five-pointed star bursting to life in the sky. He sputtered indignantly, purple face reddening as he let out an objecting wail.

"Oh, my heart." Mrs. Franklin exhaled, her head dropping in relief. "He's fine, love," she reassured Betsy as she wiped away the white coating of vernix. "Sometimes they're too stubborn to take their first breath and we have to make them."

She delivered the child into Betsy's arms while Nora pulled out her threaded needle to suture the cut. In her experience, if she worked quickly now, the mother's exhaustion and joy dulled the pain.

It took another hour to deliver the placenta. When all was

settled, and the nervous father and grandfather brought into the room to watch over Betsy and bestow extravagant praise on the baby, Mrs. Franklin steeped some tea and pushed a cup toward Nora across the rickety table in the sitting room. The room was too hot and stuffy for it, but Nora accepted the cup gratefully, if only as an excuse to quiet her nerves.

"You did well," she told Mrs. Franklin. "I know it's harder with someone you know and love, but blowing into the lungs worked."

Mrs. Franklin closed her eyes. "A fair mite better than swinging them around. I swear on my life I once saw a doctor take a babe by his feet and swing him like a cat."

Nora lifted an eyebrow, praying the unnamed doctor wasn't Horace. He was never afraid to be unconventional. No, it couldn't have been him. His favorite maxim was to treat things quietly. "Did it work?"

Mrs. Franklin's nose twitched in disgust. "Aye. But I thought the head might snap off. Not to mention the baby could have slid straight out of his grip and gone flying across the room. I'd never let anyone try that on a baby in my care, especially not my sister's grandson." Her eyes lowered and her words slowed. "I felt like my sister was watching today, and I suspect she was as terrified as I was."

"It was a difficult birth," Nora agreed, collecting her thoughts as she indulged in the sweeter sips at the bottom of her cup. "Betsy will have a slow recovery, most likely."

"I want to know more about those metal instruments you used," Mrs. Franklin said, cocking her eyebrow. "I've only seen one doctor use them, but it was on a dead child."

"They can save lives if you're trained, but they're dangerous in the wrong hands. I learned the use of these ones in Italy and taught Dr. Croft and my husband."

Mrs. Franklin turned her cup around in her saucer. "Could you teach me?"

Nora stopped mid-sip.

She lowered the teacup, her mind racing through scenarios, laws. She'd have to study the restrictions. Doctors and surgeons were protective of their privileges, and certain methods were only allowed to be taught in hospitals and universities by instructors approved by the Royal College of Surgeons. She could lose her license if she misstepped.

Three years ago, she'd nearly cost Horace his, so she knew better than most the consequences of medical experimentation. She'd conducted an emergency surgery under anesthesia to save a man's life. But she hadn't been licensed. And she was female, so how could she possibly be considered a pupil or an apprentice?

It didn't matter that she'd begun making anatomical drawings while still a child. (Horace found her talent a convenience, but Mrs. Phipps, who'd largely taken charge of orphaned Nora's upbringing, was the one who'd brought in a drawing master.) By the time she was twelve, Horace was using her as an assistant in preparing cadavers and, soon after, as an extra hand on living patients. By the time she was twenty-two, she'd received as deep and full a medical education as any of his students. If any other aspiring doctor had repaired that man's hernia, he'd have been celebrated, but because she'd done it, the surgery was, in the words of one newspaper, "a travesty and a scandal." The doctors of London had called for everything from censure to fines to stripping Horace's licenses. Some had even argued for prison. Luckily, Horace's prestige and her hasty escape had deflected these scenarios.

She'd dodged their ire by absconding to Bologna, Italy, where they allowed females in their university, and earned her own medical license. She now worked quietly among the grudging London surgeons, winning a few over with her obstetrical expertise. But she needed to tread carefully.

"I'd very much like to teach you," Nora said slowly, returning to Mrs. Franklin. "But…" She forced a smile. "I could get in trouble training you outside of a hospital."

But then, she possessed a hospital owned by the most respected surgeon and lecturer in London. While she studied in Italy, Horace had enlarged and renovated his home, building a small but modern hospital that he'd turned over to Nora the moment she returned to London. He knew it would be the only place she was allowed to practice in peace—if one called the continual criticism and censure she received *peaceful*.

Horace's name and reputation had always provided considerable protection. Even with her license, she relied on it every day. There might be a way to train Mrs. Franklin without getting either of them dragged into court, but only within the walls of her hospital at 43 Great Queen Street.

Her thoughts flashed to the letter tucked away in her instrument bag.

Magdalena knew. If they didn't train more women, the door Nora had forced open for herself might be closed forever. Magdalena had complained about fewer women training in medicine, but here in London, Nora was the sole female representative of the profession, and there were fewer midwives working every year, largely because of male doctors advocating that they were better skilled for the job. Midwives were scorned by the scientific community as uneducated nuisances, useful only for poor patients who couldn't afford real physicians.

As patients turned increasingly to doctors, midwives' unique and undervalued skills—like Mrs. Franklin blowing into Betsy's boy's lungs—might be lost.

Nora looked away from Mrs. Franklin's sharp brown eyes, frustrated by the latent intelligence crouching there. Mrs. Franklin had safely brought more children into London than scores of doctors combined. She'd performed flawlessly today. If she wanted to learn to use short forceps, she deserved to.

Magdalena would teach her, so why couldn't she? While Nora intended to be careful, this looked like an instance where she needed to stick her foot in a door, forcing an opening again. "You know, I happen to be giving a demonstration lecture tomorrow at my hospital. I'd be happy to have you join."

"Hospital instruction?" Mrs. Franklin straightened her shoulders, a grin creeping over her mouth. "If it were a lecture by some doctors I've seen at work, I'd save my time. But after seeing your forceps, I think you may have some tricks to teach me."

Nora smiled, recalling the quick release of the baby's tiny feet freed by Mrs. Franklin's capable hands. Her fearless exhalation into the child's mouth. "Perhaps we have things to teach each other."

CHAPTER 3

N ORA STIRRED, FLUTTERED AN EYELID, THEN WINCED, reconsidering. The morning light seared her vision—much too bright to bear. But if it was this light already, she ought to get out of bed. She pried both eyes open and, after the initial shock, shifted her head to peer past the bulk of her pillow.

Daniel's cheek and handsome nose—only inches away—glowed softly in the strange yellow-gray sunbeams of a London sunrise. She liked waking first and watching him sleep.

Gloating, really, that after years of waiting, he belonged to her.

He sighed, maybe sensing she was awake. They'd not yet grown accustomed to sleeping through each other's stirrings. His lips hitched into her favorite smile, and she could almost see the dreams behind his eyelids. She leaned forward to wake him, lips parted with words half-flirtatious, half-mocking—when she froze and cocked her head.

Scratch. Scratch. The distinct animal sound came from somewhere inside the room, similar to, but not exactly like, the fast scuttle of a mouse. It sounded…bigger.

Nora's hands tightened on the sheets, and she turned her head to check the door. Still firmly closed. "Daniel." When he didn't stir, she prodded his shoulder. "Daniel."

"What—" He pushed up on an elbow, sensing her tension.

"Shh," she commanded. "Did you hear that?"

"No," Daniel said through a yawn. "What did you hear?"

"Scratching." They both listened, Nora dimly aware he was awaiting a more affectionate greeting. He leaned closer, but she pushed firmly against his shoulder. No distractions yet. She sat up, scanning the perimeter of the room. "There's something in here, but our door and window are closed."

"Maybe we're haunted like the neighborhood children say," he mumbled, flopping back onto his pillow. "Some dissected soul coming back for us."

When she ignored him, continuing her survey of the room, he moaned and pulled himself off the pillow again, wiping the sleep from his eyes. "All right." He pushed back the blanket and started to swing himself off the bed when she gripped his striped sleeve.

"Check the floor! Remember the boa?"

Daniel raised his eyebrows and ruffled his overlong dark hair. Time he visited the barber.

"Remember?" Daniel shuddered. "I'd rather not."

The Egyptian sand boa, gifted to Horace by another avid naturalist, was luckily nonvenomous. Last month it had escaped and found a temporary home in Daniel's slipper. London, apparently, was much colder than Egypt. And though sand boas were supposedly harmless, the confrontation had not been pleasant for man or reptile.

Daniel swept his eyes across the rug. The heavy drapes rustled, and Nora tightened her grip on Daniel's nightshirt. Definitely bigger than a mouse, whatever it was.

"Over there," she whispered. The scratching started again, this time accompanied by moving fabric.

"What has he brought home lately?" Daniel whispered.

Nora frowned. Mrs. Phipps had a dog, but Duchess couldn't get into a closed room. "Nothing I know of. Please tell me it's not a giant rat."

"Could be a bird down the chimney," Daniel offered.

Hardly any better.

Jaw set, Daniel gingerly donned his slippers as Nora leaned forward, body tipped over the edge of the bed like a child peering over the rail of a ship, searching for sea monsters. Warily, Daniel plucked up a folded newspaper and brandished it in front of him, feet springy, ready to retreat. He poked the curtain with the newspaper, keeping his distance, but when nothing erupted in surprise, he gripped the draperies and yanked them aside.

"What the—"

Nora squeaked and recoiled to safety in the center of the bed. A fuzzy brown ball, nearly as large as Duchess, darted around Daniel's legs. The fur was short and coarse, but the creature had no hairless tail, so it couldn't be a rat. Besides, it was far too big. "What is it?" she demanded, clutching the sheets.

"I'd tell you if I had the slightest clue. It doesn't seem aggressive," Daniel said hopefully, peering at the animal hunched beneath the writing desk. It had a comical face—beady black eyes and a shining nose, all set close together.

"Is it a bear?" Nora gasped.

"A ten-pound bear?" Daniel shook his head and inched closer, craning his head to get a different view. "Lords and ladies, what did Horace get his hands on this time?"

"And why is it in our room?"

Daniel shrugged, and Nora had to admit, even if just to herself, that there were plenty of things in this home defying belief, reason, and description.

The animal swiveled its head back to the wall, making her jump, but it merely commenced an unhurried scratching on the molding with thick black claws. "I'd think it was a beaver, but it's got the wrong kind of tail," Nora said, curious now. Horace had a beaver pelt in his collection, and this creature clearly lacked the spade-like, scaly appendage.

Daniel reached his long arm toward her. "Hand me a pillow cover, will you? I'll bag him in case he bites."

Nora pulled the case off Daniel's pillow and threw it to him. Hiding a smile—whatever he pretended, he liked Horace's creatures—Daniel nudged the fur ball into the pillowcase without much resistance. "Got him!"

Nora flopped back onto the bed, rolling her eyes to the ceiling. "Quite the battle."

He chuckled, regarding the wiggling bag. "Our mystery guest doesn't seem to mind it in here, but I think we'd best take it back to wherever it belongs."

"But how on earth did he get in our room?" Nora demanded.

"Loath as I am to correct you, we don't know it's a he. Snooping around inspecting the drapes sounds more female, if you ask me."

"Why not take him out of the bag and check," Nora grumbled.

"Not the body I was hoping to examine, but—" He side-stepped as she lobbed a pillow at him.

"Let's take him to Horace." Nora stuffed her feet into

slippers after a quick check for snakes, spiders, and sundry, and tugged on a dressing gown, all the while surveying the room. The windows were closed, and though it was possible the beast had come in by the chimney, she didn't think—"*Oddio!*" The interjection sprang from her mouth in Italian, just as she'd learned it from Magdalena, her volatile mentor. "That thing must have come in with Julia's linens!"

She waved at a wicker basket, lid askew, and leaped back a good two yards. "It probably urinated in there!" Nora grimaced. "I thought that basket was heavy." She'd carried it into their bedroom herself yesterday afternoon. "I—"

"I think she's friendly," Daniel announced. "Not saying I want her in here, scratching at the new wallpaper and getting ideas about climbing into the bed—"

Nora's muscles seized.

"Downstairs," she commanded. "Now."

Daniel usually dressed before breakfast, though occasionally he took a quick cup of tea wearing a fantastically embroidered silk dressing gown he'd purchased as a joke in Paris during his medical-student days. Arriving in the breakfast parlor in only a nightshirt, with Nora clad in nightdress and wrapper, was singular enough that Horace nearly dropped his spoon.

His bushy eyebrows shot up, eyes widening, as a bit of egg fell from his mouth and lodged in his full gray beard. "Good morning?" he offered hopefully.

Nora felt her cheeks burn scarlet. "Not particularly," she snapped.

Mrs. Phipps locked narrowed eyes on the pillowcase from the opposite end of the table. "What is that, pray?"

"Delivery for Horace," Daniel announced.

"And what is it?" Julia spoke coolly, but she had a white-knuckle grip on her fork. She was the newest member of the household and wife of Harry Trimble, resident surgeon and Daniel's closest friend. Her conventional upbringing made these episodes something of a trial. Nora wished she could manage that tone—and that look. Julia was beautiful and flawlessly put together, as always.

Meanwhile, Nora's rumpled nightdress and hastily tied wrapper did nothing for her dignity.

"That's precisely what I asked," Daniel said.

The pillowcase wriggled sharply, and Mrs. Phipps yelped. Horace leaped to his feet, almost upsetting his chair. Julia dove for the tea set, sweeping the tray of Meissen porcelain to the relative safety of the sideboard.

"You know what I say about specimens at the table," Mrs. Phipps snapped. "What *thing* do you have in there?"

"Sorry, Mrs. Phipps, but the old man deserves this one," Daniel apologized.

Horace poked at the bag before opening it and peering inside. "What are you doing with my wombat?"

The strange name made Julia retreat, pressing against the wall. It didn't mean anything to Nora, either, but she was more used to this kind of predicament—and Horace's bewilderment that anyone might possibly be discomfited by something new, strange, or of interest to science. She lifted her eyebrows. "What in the world is a wombat?"

Horace glared; he never approved of ignorance. "Marsupial

from Australia. Egg-laying mammal. I've never handled one. Evans from the Linnean Society sent it over."

"When?" Nora insisted. "You said nothing about this new guest."

Horace shrugged. "Last week sometime. I've been experimenting with her food. She won't take leaves, she won't take berries, but I've got her onto vegetable roots."

"She," Nora mumbled, irked at Daniel's triumphant grin. "But why was *she* in my room?"

"They produce cubed droppings," Horace added, his low-pitched voice humming with excitement.

Julia twitched. "There was an odd little square three days ago…in my embroidery."

Mrs. Phipps scowled.

"Cubed, you say?" Daniel leaned in for another look. "How precise of a cube? Actual squared edges?"

Looking upward for strength, Nora almost crossed herself—another habit that had imprinted during medical school in Bologna. "Why was she in my room?"

Horace waved his hand, brushing off her question as he did all boring inquiries. "She's not dangerous in any way. I haven't seen her for a couple of days."

Nora's mouth dropped open, and Mrs. Phipps made a strangled sound.

"Lord save us, Horace," Daniel scolded. "You might be a genius, but you're no true naturalist. You must *care* about the specimens you work with. She'll die at this rate." Forgetting breakfast, he tucked the cotton-wrapped wombat under one arm and retreated for the door.

"Where are you going?" Nora asked. "You've got to get ready for hospital rounds." Daniel seldom worked at the hospital and clinic in the basement of 43 Great Queen Street, but he'd agreed to look in this morning. Most days he was too busy assuming the care of Horace's private patients, making house calls, and supervising a ward at St. Bartholomew's teaching hospital.

Horace lectured at Bart's as well, but Harry had too many enemies there. Working in London, amid so many competing egos and theories, wasn't easy for anyone.

"I'm taking my first patient right now," Daniel said. "She and I are going to the kitchen to forage for suitable nutrition. Then I'm putting her in one of the cages outside. It's warm enough for a tropical animal. She'll be more comfortable there than in our room."

Nora approved of removing the wombat, but said, "I must prepare for my obstetric lecture, and I can't cover rounds here. I invited a guest to attend."

"We've got a bone spur removal at noon." Horace sniffed huffily into his tea, probably smarting over Daniel's gibe at his failings as a naturalist. "What guest?"

"Harry can tackle the bone spur," Daniel said, shifting his struggling burden. "And yes, what guest?"

Harry wasn't at breakfast. Most likely on a call. He'd love this, though, so Nora faithfully committed the details to memory to share later.

"Harry bloody well cannot!" Horace snorted. "He'll take the whole heel off."

"Horace," Nora said in the level warning tone normally

reserved for their carriage mare when she pinned back her ears.

"Harry was out half the night with *your* patients," Julia told them, and the unusual sternness in her voice turned Horace's belligerent face contrite. "And he left early this morning to rebandage the Thompkins girl. If you speak of my husband, I expect your tone to drip with gratitude."

Nora's smile quirked on one side as she waited for Horace's reaction. Horace conveniently forgot his truce with Harry at least once a day.

Harry Trimble—Daniel's best friend since they had met as students at the Sorbonne—had joined their household along with his wife, Julia, the previous year. Horace never liked reminders of how close they'd been to losing this place follow-ing his stroke, or how much he owed to Harry's timely financial investment. Without Harry's money, they'd never have been able to stave off the banks.

The past was a crooked, thorny road when it came to Harry. Presuming on their friendship, Daniel had lied and named Harry as his assistant in a hernia surgery that Nora had per-formed. He'd done it to protect her. If anyone had discovered Nora had cut into a living man, she'd have been at the mercy of the courts. Under normal circumstances, Harry would have happily, perhaps theatrically, taken credit. Tragically, he'd been performing a different illegal surgery the same night—an abortion on a seventeen-year-old girl named Julia who had attempted to kill herself when she discovered she was pregnant. Harry could only protect one woman, and he chose the woman who would later become his wife.

Harry had been forced to reveal Nora to the medical community, driving her to Bologna and nearly costing Horace his
career—a debt difficult to pay off in money alone. But he had
managed it by taking over much of the work Horace could no
longer do—long days of patient calls and surgeries, in addition
to seeing a large caseload of district patients.

Humbling himself—something he never did for anyone
other than Julia—Horace ducked his head. "Quite right. I'm
sorry, Julia."

Nora and Daniel exchanged a silent laugh.

"What guest did you invite, Nora?" Horace asked, pushing
the focus away from his own surrender.

"Mrs. Franklin."

"The midwife?" Julia's head snapped up. "To a medical lecture? With the physicians and surgeons?"

"Yes."

Perplexed frowns and silence all around.

"And what's wrong with that?" Nora demanded.

"Nothing," Daniel offered. "But will she be able to make
sense of the terminology? Midwifery is not scientific—"

"Precisely," Nora shot back. "Think of what she accom-
plishes with experience and intuition alone. And think of
what she could do if trained. She wants to learn to use short
forceps."

Horace's teacup landed with a clatter. "You put those tongs
into the wrong hands, and you'll have a headless baby."

"You always say Mrs. Franklin is more skilled than most
doctors," Nora argued.

"She is," Horace agreed. "And I'd take her over nearly any

student at Bart's. But you said yourself she works by good sense and long experience, not science."

"Maybe it's time we combine them." Nora exhaled, disappointed in their responses.

"It's an interesting idea. You can tell us about the results at supper," Daniel conceded, without relinquishing the wombat. "But we need to sort out a meal for this creature."

Nora frowned skeptically. "You don't have time to play with the wombat." There were nine women, three children, and one elderly man waiting in the two wards on the other side of the house.

Daniel's eyes widened. "*Play*? I'm saving a life."

"And your human patients?" Nora tilted her head.

"I don't think you can pass off rounds here to Harry when he gets back," Julia said. "He's been out all night."

"I'll do both," Daniel promised. The delay would almost certainly make him late to St. Bart's, but there he did have the luxury of a team of student apprentices—dressers—who'd manage things in his absence. "There aren't that many to tend today."

Since Nora's return from Italy, the patient wards here had never been full—not like the crowded wards in London's teaching hospitals. But she wasn't permitted there.

That didn't mean she could manage everything on her own, though.

"Daniel, my patients—"

"They'll have to wait while I attend to an important foreign ambassador."

The bag gave a low grunt. "It will be fine," he promised, grinning so widely that the knot eased in her chest.

It will be fine, she repeated to herself as he hurried away to the kitchen. Mrs. Phipps rose and followed him with rapid steps. "Don't you put Cook out. If we lose her, we'll starve."

Unable to resist, Julia followed, sounding her own warning. "And don't put it on the butcher block, Daniel. We're rolling out pie crusts today."

"I'm the one who found she likes roots!" Horace shouted after them.

"Yes, you're brilliant," Nora placated, taking a seat at the almost empty table with a sigh. "But I'm glad you never tried to be a locksmith. Could you keep your wards under better watch? For their sake and ours."

"Keep my wards locked up," Horace grumbled, his whiskers quivering. "That's what they said about you, you impertinent little—"

Nora burst into laughter, almost dropping her bread. "It is, isn't it?"

Horace's eyes flashed blue lightning. "I kept you alive, didn't I?"

Sobering at once, Nora laid light fingers on his wrist. "You certainly did." Before he grew embarrassed, she added, "But no more animals rummaging through my wardrobe, or I'll send you my dress bill."

He shrugged and turned back to his plate, dismissing her threat. Horace paid little attention to money, and lately that had almost undone them all. *Thank God for Harry and Julia*, Nora thought. They were solvent again—house, hospital, practice, and clinic—but only just. So everyone worked, and Daniel kept a close watch on accounts. Her obstetrics lectures brought in some much-needed money. Another reason she had to do well today.

But first she needed to put a measure of fear into Horace. That wombat in her room was the outside of enough. "I recommend a little more caution with the creatures, Horace. You never know what I'll put in your room as revenge."

Horace looked up and grinned. "You know, I believe you would."

Nora's lips quirked. Serve him right if she did.

CHAPTER 4

NORA PEEKED THROUGH THE RED CURTAIN BETWEEN THE hospital hallway and the lecture room. Horace had hung velvet instead of installing a door because it was much easier to roll cadavers through curtains than to maneuver them through solid oak.

She didn't like entering the lecture theater while doctors were still settling in. Something about standing in the bare circle in the center, surrounded by rows of rising benches, made her feel as exposed as a menagerie animal. Horace and Daniel usually finished straightening their instruments and tying their smocks while exchanging news with the students and doctors readying notebooks and pens. Nora took a different approach— waiting for all attendees to settle before making an efficient sweep into the buzzing room and diving headlong into the subject without pause or greeting. It was how Magdalena always corralled students' attention, and it worked well enough that Nora had adopted the technique.

She straightened her apron and reviewed her meticulous notes in the dim light from the window at the end of the hall. Daniel and Horace attended her lectures whenever they could, but the bone spur surgery kept them away today, leaving her without allies if anything went awry.

You wouldn't think academic lectures would get out of hand, but she'd seen all kinds of horrors at them, and not just on the dissection table. Shouts, insults, accusations, brawls—they weren't particularly uncommon. So she peeked again, careful not to move the curtain enough to alert anyone to her presence. She wouldn't for the world be caught cowering outside her own theater.

Seventeen attendees. A good number, though not nearly as many as at one of Horace's lectures. Everything appeared hazy through the slit between heavy velvet panels as the gentlemen moved about. That should be nearly everyone, and her watch said—

Some change in the buzz of conversation caught her ear—a sudden easing of syllables and then the distinct tones of a female voice. Mrs. Franklin had arrived. Nora had almost given up on her.

Abandoning her carefully planned entrance, Nora emerged through the curtains. Up in the risers, Mrs. Franklin's usually phlegmatic face shone pink with excitement. Beside her, two other women in work-a-day wear stood uncertainly, scanning the room.

"Mrs. Franklin?" Surprised by the additional women, Nora couldn't keep her greeting from sounding more like a question.

"I've brought Mrs. Bailey and Mrs. Howell. They've been in the business for over twenty years, both of them. We're all interested."

Nora caught the unfortunate expression of the doctor closest to Mrs. Franklin, and her face heated as she tried to rein in the situation before it stampeded away without her.

"All interested students are welcome," she said, forcing a smile to remind everyone that this was indeed true. It was not uncommon for learned men to visit medical lectures on a whim. Even ladies had been known to accompany their curious escorts to enjoy the horrors of dissection or view natural spectacles, like the wombat. But the attendance of female practitioners at this sort of lecture was something Nora had never seen in London before.

"Please be seated, everyone, and we'll get started." One man opened his mouth but swallowed whatever he'd meant to say when she continued. "I will be expounding on the use of forceps, as taught at the University of Bologna."

Nora smoothed the sheet covering the dissected body she and Horace had spent two days pinning and preparing. Though the decedent was past child-bearing age, she would still do for demonstration purposes. Nora knew the impressive specimen would enthrall them—the abdomen was wide open from pubis to sternum, each pale organ displayed in strange stillness. In the cradle of the hollow pelvis, the shrunken uterus lay almost invisible—only a strip of unimpressive tissue when not in miraculous use. Imagining their admiring gasps, she clutched the corner of the sheet and whisked it aside with a snap.

No gasps. Instead, one of the midwives squawked in dismay and recoiled.

The doctor next to her gave her a disdainful look and moved farther away down the bench. Of course, none of these women expected a body opened like a cupboard, while the doctors expected nothing else.

Should have left the theatrics to Horace.

Hurrying on: "We'll use the cadaver to demonstrate possible fetal positions and how the forceps can help us access areas our fingers cannot reach."

"I've tried forceps on occasion," one doctor spoke up. "If the va—" He hesitated, no doubt remembering the women seated behind him. "If the passage is tight enough to need them, they do naught but push the baby's head higher into the birth canal."

"A problem we'll address," Nora promised. "As you see, I have the short forceps, with which all students in the obstetrics course—physicians, surgeons, and midwives"—she nodded at Mrs. Franklin and her friends—"are trained at the University of Bologna."

That ought to give the skeptics something to think upon. Smiling, Nora plowed on, using a cloth model of a baby to show positions within the pelvis and the careful placement of the forceps to turn the child when necessary. She was demonstrating a mento-anterior presentation when Mrs. Franklin raised her hand.

"I don't know what words you're using," she stated baldly.

A hum of discontent rippled through the doctors like the uneasy revolution occurring simultaneously in Nora's middle. Ignoring it, she hurried to explain. "It's quite simple. Our cadaver is in the supine position, facing upward. If someone is lying on their stomach, that is prone..." She made it through *cephalocaudal*, but before she could define *anterior*, an unfamiliar doctor rose, making a show of looking at his pocket watch. "Back at primary Latin? I have patients to see, if we're not getting on to something helpful."

Nora's eyes flashed to the spot where Daniel usually sat, filled today by a pockmarked young student.

"I think she's trying to say 'face-first,'" one of the midwives interjected, attempting to be helpful.

One student laughed, and the doctor beside him threw his hands up in exasperation.

"Yes, I was," Nora said. "I was referring to a face-first presentation. Something most of you have never seen, I assume."

"I've heard they right themselves before they come out that way because it's not possible to fit," a smartly dressed young man offered.

One of Mrs. Franklin's companions (rather round, and she'd already giggled twice) burst into laughter. "Right themselves," she repeated, shaking her head as if relishing the punch line of a joke. "Wouldn't that be lovely?"

"I beg your pardon," the offended man said with a deep frown.

"Don't worry, love. You're pardoned. But it's perfectly possible to deliver them. We've all brought children into the world face-first. And we did it when the mother were neither up nor down or sootin—supine? Whatever you call it."

Nora had seen two face-first presentations in Italy, but the nuns had managed to rotate the child before bringing it through.

"The baby emerged face-first?" she asked Mrs. Franklin, wanting to verify this rather spectacular claim. "And lived?"

"Came out looking right at me," Mrs. Franklin confirmed. "Alive as you and I." The other midwives nodded in confirmation.

"How did you overcome the symphysis pubis?" Nora glanced at the open cadaver, trying to understand the methodology. If the child could not be rotated, the common solution in London was to collapse the head and bring it through piecemeal before it killed the mother. In Italy, where doctors refused to kill a living child, it demanded a cesarean surgery.

The midwives stared back blankly. "The pubic bone in the front," Nora clarified. "Didn't the chin get stuck?"

"Excuse me," Dr. Impatience and his watch interjected. "Is this lecture going to be taught by common midwives?"

Mrs. Franklin frowned, her face hard and offended. "I'd hate to be accused of teaching you anything."

Nora raised her arms, hoping to draw the man and Mrs. Franklin's attention away from each other. "I'd listen to a horse if it could tell me how to deliver a mento-anterior presentation. If I were you, I'd stay and listen."

"Hmm. I'm afraid I'm slightly more selective. Good day, ma'am." He bowed and left the room, wafting dissatisfaction in his wake.

"It seems a waste of your time and entrance fee to leave before she's even had a chance to answer my question," Nora called after him.

He didn't reply, and it was easy to see that others were thinking of following. She lived with enough doctors to know their minds were not solely scientific. They were all painted with a vivid streak of drama. Perhaps herself included.

"Mrs. Franklin. Would you come show me how the child presented and how you delivered? As well as explain the after-effects." She held out the crude doll in invitation.

Mrs. Franklin hesitated, starting to refuse.

"If you're telling the truth," Nora goaded.

The woman's face went from pink to crimson. Just as planned, Nora had struck her pride. Mrs. Franklin climbed down the risers and opened the gate to enter the demonstration floor. "Lying on the back is fine for some deliveries," she said with a serious frown. "But all the doctors I know dismiss the other birthing positions."

"Good Lord, are we going to discuss medieval birthing stools next?" one man complained.

Mrs. Franklin's brow contracted. "You haven't brought hundreds of women through. A stool is a necessity for some of them."

The doctor stood, sputtering. Nora raised her hands for silence. "We are here to learn something new, are we not? We'll return to my lecture, but first I'd very much like to hear Mrs. Franklin's account."

Of all days for Horace to be gone. He'd have shouted them down by now, and they'd have listened, cowed and silent in their seats.

"The face were pointed this way," Mrs. Franklin proceeded, gingerly placing the model baby above the open cadaver, her voice shaking as she let slip poor grammar that only made the men scowl more.

"Right mento-anterior position," Nora announced for the doctors taking notes. No one did.

"Did you tip the chin down or rotate the head?" Nora asked.

"Neither. I rotated the mother. I rolled her to her side and brought her knees up, keeping pressure on the bottom of the mother's—" She hesitated, as if suddenly aware of the critical men looking on. "Her—" She was searching for a term that wouldn't embarrass herself.

"Her vulva," Nora finished neatly.

Mrs. Franklin nodded.

"She doesn't know the simplest terms," one man pointed out. "This isn't a lecture. It's a story hour. Fairy stories, as far as I can tell."

Heat rose from Nora's stomach into her chest, pulsing with her heartbeat.

"I might not know your foreign names," Mrs. Franklin retorted, "but I know where to apply pressure so the mother doesn't tear clear through, and how to bring a baby face-first without using your lethal hooks."

Nora shivered from a bleak and poisonous memory. She'd once been with Horace when he was forced to use the blunt crotchet for a mother who'd labored for two days without the head descending. Afterward, he'd stumbled home and drunk himself into a stupor, saying he feared the child was still alive when he'd done it.

"What are you saying?" A portly doctor stood, his mustache bristling. "I've been begged by midwives to use the crotchet to save a woman." He pointed his quill at Nora in a threatening manner. "It's surgeons who step in when midwives are out of their depth."

"Physicians attend more births than surgeons," a bearded man shot back.

Not this.

She couldn't afford any more fractures in this audience. Surgeons and physicians in England hadn't made peace in the last fifty years. Neither group cared much for apothecaries, and all of them judged midwifery most inferior of all.

Nora raised her voice. "Regardless, we have an opportunity to learn—"

"From them?" a man mocked, gesturing at Mrs. Franklin and her companions.

Nora gritted her teeth and closed her eyes. "In Bologna, doctors work side by side with midwives and nuns, consulting them, often deferring to their years of expertise. They are women dedicated to the science of childbirth, always amassing new experience."

"What science?" one medical student asked timidly. "Birth is natural. We certainly didn't invent the procedure, and indigenous women give birth with hardly any trouble, according to—"

"You'll know how important education is the first time you're faced with a placenta previa, or breech delivery, or—" Nora tried to regain order, but they were all speaking over one another now.

"Maybe some midwives are skilled," the bearded man admitted. "But there is no licensing. No regulation. No exams. Think of the damage a rogue woman—"

"It's not so different for us." Nora cut him off. "The current guidelines for physicians and surgeons suggest we attend two lectures on midwifery. That means you could leave here today half-finished with your education on childbirth."

One of the midwives burst out in a humorless laugh. "I was called to a birth last week after the family realized the *qualified* doctor had no clue what he was about. He knew nothing about turning the child or lessening the pains."

"We are not in the business of abating pain. We are in the

business of keeping mother and child alive," an older man called from the back.

"Sometimes that's the same thing!" the midwife retorted. "Sometimes easing the pain is a matter of life and death. If the mother is frightened, she cannot obtain the correct positions—"

"The pains force her into the correct position eventually." The man crossed his arms as if the argument were over.

It wasn't. Shouts from both sides only mounted.

"Stop!" Nora's voice snapped sharp and clear in the commotion. She scanned the men in varying states of agitation. "If you want to leave, please do so now so we can get back to work. I need to know how to bring a child safely through a mento-anterior birth, and if none of you can answer my question, I have a woman here who says she can. I'm sure Dr. Horace Croft will be thrilled to hear her account."

Not even the name of her mentor could persuade them all. Three more men gathered their papers and exited in a cloud of grumbles and discontent. To Nora's surprise, the rest stayed, their skeptical eyebrows raised and curiosity twitching the edges of their mouths.

"Perhaps we can get on now," Nora continued, smoothing the sides of her skirt to dry her palms. She gestured the midwife forward. "Mrs. Franklin?"

CHAPTER 5

DANIEL LIFTED THE EDGE OF A YELLOWED BANDAGE, assessing the degree of drainage. The slightest disturbance of the wrapping released a putrid odor. Dying flesh. Gangrene.

He looked up, met Horace's eyes, and gave an infinitesimal shake of his head.

Horace frowned, pushing past Daniel and his best dresser, Bernard Jeffers. "Don't be hasty. You haven't taken a full look. Hand me the scissors."

Daniel had mastered human anatomy and a dozen different sutures, but he was most proud of his hardest-earned skill— not rolling his eyes at Horace. "I can smell gangrene from here. You can too," he whispered, keeping his words from the resting patient, a sixty-year-old man, half-deaf, who'd been knocked down last week by a slow-moving engine in a train yard. His demolished fibula normally dictated immediate amputation above the knee, but this unfortunate man had already lost his other foot in childhood. Horace declared him the perfect case for a risky procedure to save the broken limb, since conventional treatment would prevent the patient from ever standing again. "If we cut the leg off now, we can still get it all," Daniel pressed.

Horace tsked and waved Daniel back.

Under Horace's direction, Daniel had stifled his own pro-tests and attempted the novel surgery, aligning the four pieces of bone and wrapping the limb in plaster. Plaster that, four days later, was yellow, soggy, and foul.

"The leg has to go, Horace," Daniel insisted. "Now. Before it kills him. Clean up his leg for surgery, Jeffers."

"Don't be a fool. And don't touch him." Horace's command carried fierce authority.

Jeffers looked between them, unsure which to obey. Daniel was about to repeat his order when another wave of stench rose up, forcing him to cough and turn away. The fetid odor was as bad as a week-old cadaver.

"Here you are." Jeffers offered a handkerchief liberally anointed with menthol. Daniel thrust it under his nose, the fumes blurring his eyes with tears.

"Give me a moment. All I want is a thorough look." Horace continued his steady cutting, dropping the sodden plaster into a bucket at his feet. Daniel circled his shoulders, sore from the work of today's earlier surgeries. The heel spur removal was delicate work, not terribly taxing, but he'd also amputated an arm, set a fractured femur, and supervised Jeffers in three small procedures.

With practiced discipline, he inhaled through his mouth and closed his eyes. The sooner this leg came off, the better. Horace chuckled, and Daniel whipped his head around despite the smell. *He* saw no reason to laugh.

But Horace grabbed a pitcher of warm, weak tea, one of his favorite anointings for wounds, and flushed the leg. "Granulating!" Horace crowed once the multicolored pus was rinsed away.

"What are you talking about?" Daniel stepped closer, peering at the sutures.

The flesh around them was angry, red—and healing—not a putrid black, gray, or yellow. Daniel pressed one hand to the skin above the knee and the other to the ankle. Warm. "Dammit," he muttered.

Horace chortled. "Feeling foolish?"

The patient shifted, angling for a look. Catching a whiff, his face went pale. "What's appenin' to my leg?" he moaned.

"Fair question." Daniel turned to Horace. "It looks much better than I expected, but you have no idea what's happening beneath the skin." He touched the leg again, aching to see inside and know if the bones were knitting. "We have no way of knowing if there is infection in the bone or if it will ever hold weight. We both smelled it!"

Horace leaned close to the patient, ignoring Daniel. "Your leg is healing very well so far."

"Then what's that awful smell?" the old man demanded.

"That is the smell of genius," Horace said.

Daniel had to look away and cough again.

Jeffers leaned in for a look, the mint fumes of his handkerchief forcing tears from his irritated eyes. "May I?" he asked, waiting for a nod from Daniel before touching the skin. "I don't understand," he said, pressing gently. "We can smell the gangrene, but there's not a trace—"

"Rinse with more tea and then plaster him again." Horace adjusted his spectacles, cheeks pink with amusement. "You smelled old, foul bandages. Not necrotic tissue. That was rotting pus and blood, not flesh and bone."

"How did you know?" Daniel asked, happy for his patient but nettled by Horace's self-satisfaction.

"I didn't," Horace said with a shrug. "*I* was just patient enough to check. Go call in the others so we can educate them before we throw the bandages away."

Jeffers stuffed his handkerchief into his pocket, clearly relieved to be sent on an errand and escape the sickening smell, however briefly. He paused at the door. "Dr. Croft, how does the smell not affect you?"

Horace looked at the young doctor in training. "You learn control with time. Then you can command your hands not to shake. Your head not to doze off after a night without sleep. Your nose to overlook upsetting smells. But I must have filled buckets with vomit when I was your age."

Jeffers smiled, his shoulders loosening. Daniel hadn't realized they'd grown so tense.

"It was good of you. To give Jeffers some encouragement," Daniel murmured once his dresser had left the room.

"They all need it," Horace said. "Besides, it's no fun showing them up. Much more satisfying to do that to you."

This time, Daniel did roll his eyes. "Get ready," he said. "I can hear them coming."

Right on cue, a half-dozen doctors and dressers filtered into the ward, surrounding the patient's bed. Several handkerchiefs appeared, but Jeffers resisted the urge to employ his again.

Horace held up the putrid, sopping bandages, explaining the case in theatrical style, with gestures and embellishment. Then, mercifully, he ordered the bandages removed from the room to be burned with the other diseased dressings and linen.

After Horace washed the leg thoroughly, only the echo of the former smell remained, replaced with the strong fume of soap.

The students began to disperse, revealing two colleagues conferring a short distance away, arms crossed, brows furrowed. They frowned at Daniel.

Whatever for? While he wouldn't mind taking credit for this, the discovery—and the ensuing theatrics—were Horace's. Ten minutes later, the last student was gone, off to observe another case, but Adams and Howe remained, still casting dark looks in Daniel's direction.

Leaving Horace to examine the next patient, Daniel approached. "Is there a problem?"

"We've just come from your wife's obstetric lecture." Adams insisted on an absurdly pointed little beard that made it difficult for Daniel to think of anything else, but he perked up at the mention of Nora.

"And?" Daniel crossed his arms, all too accustomed to complaints about his surgeon wife.

"Oh, stop bristling," Howe sneered. "We paid to go, didn't we?" He fumbled his pocket watch in his loose fist. "The lecture would have been fine if she taught it."

"What do you mean?" Daniel demanded.

"She had a trio of common midwives there. Halfway through, she invited one of them to explain a case—just because the creature had been lucky enough not to kill the woman. Once your wife let that hedge witch take over the lecture—"

"Take over the lecture?" Daniel echoed. That didn't sound like Nora, with her careful notes and rehearsed presentations. And three midwives? This morning, she'd said there would be one. "There must have been a reason." Though what it might be, he couldn't imagine. When midwives had "interesting" cases, they sent for her or Horace.

"Indeed," Howe said. "Even if the woman's claims are true—and I don't believe them for a second—I won't attend another lecture from your wife, no matter how impressive her résumé. And I certainly can't recommend them to my students or anyone else. Deferring to midwives!" He shook his head.

"Nora doesn't defer to them," Horace said, drying his hands as he joined the conversation. "She uses them. As do I. The good ones are valuable."

Howe frowned. "For fetching water and cleaning babies. Perhaps for uneventful cases when the child needs merely to be caught. But one never knows which births will be uneventful."

"Your wife was supposed to be instructing doctors on delivering with short forceps." Adams's dark eyes glinted. "I've been using them for five years and—"

"You never thought of teaching anyone," Horace said. "Why not? Didn't want to cut into your own business?"

Adams flushed. "If she thinks she can put tools like that into the hands of illiterate women—"

Daniel grunted, a heavy weight in his stomach. Nora wouldn't hand a midwife a pair of forceps. It sounded like a sure way to decapitate a child. "I'm sure you misunderstand. My wife wouldn't—"

Beside him, Horace shifted in a way that sent warnings along Daniel's spine. Surely she hadn't—

"Nora is more concerned about knowledge than her

pocketbook," Horace spoke up. "She shares her skills—unlike you, trying to guard secrets."

Adams barked a mirthless laugh. "And every dressmaker should publish her most desirable patterns for anyone to use, though she worked her entire life to develop her skills?"

"A dress is hardly the same." Horace fastened his cuffs. "We're in the business of treatments and cures, not silks and pearl buttons." He glanced pointedly at Adams's fine coat. "Or haberdashery."

This conversation wasn't headed anywhere productive. Daniel exhaled. Adams and Howe had influence. Horace might not mind quarrels, but it would be better for all of them to avoid one. Better still if he could convince Adams not to criticize Nora's lectures.

"My wife is always curious. If she was intrigued by something this midwife said, she would have wanted to know more. What's the harm in listening? A doctor should be able to hear and judge claims."

"A doctor should know better than to give ear to every quack and chatterbox," Howe retorted.

"I'll ask her for the full story tonight." Daniel calibrated his voice. Better to beat them in calm than in temper, though far less satisfactory. "She has enthusiasms, I know. But that's what makes her so brilliant. None of us have managed a cesarean section."

"Yet," Howe said.

"If you don't wish to hear her teach, I'm sure there are other doctors who will enthusiastically take your vacancies," Horace said.

Adams raised his eyebrows into incredulous arches. "You can't forever provoke everyone, Horace," he warned. "Your days of stunning everyone in the surgical theater are already over. You will not always be untouchable, you know."

Horace surprised Daniel by settling his weight onto one hip, his mouth falling into a relaxed grin. "And with good luck, you will not always be an ass, Adams."

Daniel bit his lip and looked away.

Adams sputtered. "How dare—"

"Oh, come off it." Horace waved a hand. "There's very little in your medical repository I didn't teach you. Stop putting on airs, and come look at this leg. I'm particularly proud of it, and you couldn't have had a good look back there."

"I'll do no such thing," Adams announced and stalked from the room. Howe lingered only a moment longer, casting one look at the man who, thanks to Horace, would keep his leg.

At least for a few more days. It was dangerous, sometimes, to hope.

Daniel shook his head. "I don't blame you," he said to Horace. "Adams is insufferable. But you've never had an ounce of tact."

"With luck," Horace said, "I'll never need it."

Daniel closed his eyes. "You're going to teach my students to be as impossible as you are."

"You know what Nora says," Horace countered. "Impossible doctors are the best ones."

Daniel inhaled. A bit of conventionality might do his life good now and then.

CHAPTER 6

THE BALANCE OF NORA'S LECTURE FINISHED WITHOUT any brawls, for which she could only be thankful. Mrs. Franklin managed a clear-enough explanation—she'd persuaded her patient into a lateral fetal position (curled onto her side with one bent leg held in the air) and coaxed the child slowly between the pubic and tail bones without incident.

There were few questions after Nora returned to her original subject, and none of the doctors took the opportunity to come forward and inspect her meticulously prepared cadaver more closely. One left shaking his head as if dazed by a heavy punch.

The experience hadn't been much different from a bout of fisticuffs for Nora, either. She peered, tight-lipped, over her tools, which lay beside the waxy, pale body.

"Your doctor students might not come back," Mrs. Franklin noted with a worried frown as she brushed off the model baby and laid him gingerly beside the open cadaver. Her two friends hovered uncertainly several feet behind her. "They didn't much like us being here."

Nora stopped arranging her instruments on the table. She was as particular about the order of her scalpels and retractors as ladies-in-waiting vying for position behind a queen. "It's a foolish prejudice. We shouldn't be at such odds."

"But we are," Mrs. Howell said with a sniff. "There's some doctors I don't want anywhere near my women." She stopped abruptly and her eyes darted away. "I wouldn't mind you, of course," she corrected.

"No offense," Nora reassured her. "But there are as many good doctors as there are midwives. We need to find some way to work together."

Mrs. Franklin scoffed. "Work together? They don't want us *working* at all. Ten years ago my patients were well-to-do women. Now the upper class think I'm a danger because their doctors say so. They won't hire any of us, no matter how many women and children we've brought through." The afternoon light from the high windows turned the woman's dark eyes to a defiant amber as she spoke.

"I know." Nora studied the three midwives who'd remained behind. Mrs. Bailey, the small, sharp-nosed one, hadn't spoken, but Nora liked her keen eyes and furrowed brow. She'd not missed a word. Mrs. Howell was plump and motherly and placid. The sort of woman who'd calm a frightened patient merely by her presence. And Mrs. Franklin was as redoubtable as a general, according to Horace. She'd been with Daniel and Horace years ago on a particularly tragic case when they'd lost a mother to a massive and sudden hemorrhage. He said she'd performed like a seasoned surgeon.

"I know there is enough resentment to go around on both sides, but I've seen it accomplished—midwives and physicians helping one another. If we don't show them the value of what you know, women will suffer at their most vulnerable moment—giving birth."

"The doctors don't—"

"I know they don't care." Nora cut Mrs. Howell short. "But this is women's work. It always has been." If only they could see Magdalena sweeping through the hospital wards, the students deferring to her expertise. "You understand a woman's pain and needs in ways no man ever will. You can't let them push you out of your place. We must make them care."

Mrs. Bailey tightened her arms against her chest, doubt in every movement.

"Why don't you have a look at our hospital?" The thought formulated as Nora spoke it, unfinished and unsteady. "I could show you our facility and offer you some tea."

Mrs. Franklin accepted with a smile, but the other women exchanged glances.

"I've a newly delivered mother I need to visit. The child is a lazy one, refusing to suck unless I help, and I haven't seen them since breakfast." Mrs. Bailey's words slurred with a gentle lisp—perhaps why she spoke so little.

"Would you like me to examine the child?"

Nora didn't realize she'd blundered until Mrs. Bailey stiffened.

"I can manage."

"Of course. I didn't mean… Well, sometime I would love to see you work," Nora rushed on. "And to show you around here—"

"We shared a hackney," Mrs. Howell interjected, "so we should leave together. Perhaps we can see your hospital another day, love." She gave the cadaver a doubtful look.

She's not coming back, Nora realized, and the weight of the failed lecture doubled.

"You two go on," Mrs. Franklin said. "I'd like to stay. I'll find my own way home. It's no trouble."

When the other women left, Nora glanced at Mrs. Franklin. "Do you really wish to stay?"

"Very much. I'm interested to see what a hospital looks like with a woman such as yourself in charge. I learned the trade in my aunt's lying-in house, you know, and she kept that place beautifully. I don't know anyone now with enough work to keep that sort of place afloat." Mrs. Franklin passed her eyes toward the door, unable to hide her curiosity.

"Well." Nora quickly covered the cadaver with a sheet. Magdalena was right about needing more women beside her, and Mrs. Franklin was ideal. "I need to return this body to the ice room. I'll show you about along the way."

She unlocked the wheels and used her hip to get the cart rolling, but paused just before the curtains, realizing this room deserved some explanation. "Here in the theater, we do both live and cadaver demonstrations. There's another smaller surgery in the clinic for routine procedures, which don't have an audience." Horace had designed the theater, and it was his pride and joy. Along with the laboratory and the conservatory...

"I had no idea it would be so spacious," Mrs. Franklin said.

"Most days, we have a larger audience," Nora admitted.

The theater had been built on the ground level, conveniently close to the clinic entrance and the ice room, with a drain set in the middle of the demonstration floor. The room was two stories high, to accommodate the rows of seating and high south-facing windows, which provided the best light while keeping out curious glances from the street.

Nora grunted as she pushed the heavy cart through the red curtains into the dim hallway. "There's a lift just there. We use it to move cadavers like this one to the ice room and bring patients from the theater or the small surgery to the first-floor ward. We've ten beds there, but could accommodate twenty if necessary."

Mrs. Franklin stepped onto the lift uncertainly. She jerked as Nora started the drum and the contraption slowly ground its way down. "It's quite safe," Nora assured her. "A winding drum. It's run by a very small steam engine in the basement."

"I see." Mrs. Franklin fiddled with her cuff. The lift landed with a rattle, and Mrs. Franklin jumped out as soon as Nora slid open the gate. "Never been in a lift," she explained.

Nora wheeled the cadaver into the ice room. "We've no lights in here because it is only for storing bodies. We keep it lined with ice year-round." Mrs. Franklin peered into the dark room, where one other body lay—an elderly patient whose enlarged heart had given out yesterday. Nora closed the door, deciding to skip the adjacent dissection room. Medical students loved it, but Mrs. Franklin was in the business of living patients.

"Our dispensary," Nora announced, showing her instead the organized cabinets and shelves of gleaming bottles, the center table for measuring and compounding. "Dr. Croft gave me charge of our hospital—"

"Because of his hand?" Mrs. Franklin asked.

Nora pressed her lips together. She didn't like others speaking of Horace like an invalid. "He still oversees everything," Nora said. "There are four doctors working here. Myself, Horace, my husband, and Dr. Harry Trimble, though they're often out attending patients in their homes or at other facilities. Dr. Croft's practiced medicine for nearly fifty years, since he was sixteen. Most people today go to the Royal College, or some other college or hospital to get a diploma in surgery or as a physician or an apothecary. But Dr. Croft is licensed in all three."

Mrs. Franklin's eyes widened. "Are you as well?"

Nora shook her head. "My husband and I are both trained in medicine and surgery. He studied at the Sorbonne, and I trained at the University of Bologna, but we each had to get a license from the Royal College of Physicians of London to practice here." Such tidy words to summarize a nearly impassable road. Flashes of breathless surgeries and hateful faces whipped through her mind before she returned to Mrs. Franklin. "I still have my troubles. Few male patients let me practice on them. Even many women are reluctant."

Mrs. Franklin grunted, uncannily in the same pitch Horace used to denote disapproval.

"I knew Dr. Croft was up to something with all the construction on the home, but I never imagined anything on this scale. A lift, a dispensary... My aunt compounded some remedies in her lying-in house. Still-room recipes, mostly, but women swore by them. She was a fine hand at it, but her house..." Mrs. Franklin shook her head. "Her house was nothing like this." She looked directly at Nora. "He thinks the world of you, doesn't he?"

Nora blushed. "We did keep patients here before." There'd been a laboratory and surgery here when she'd arrived as a sick and dying orphan. But when she'd left for Italy, Horace had truly outdone himself constructing the current facilities.

"This is our new exam room." Nora took a few more steps and opened another door. Three faces spun toward her in surprise, and Nora realized, in her embarrassment, that she'd ignored the muffled sounds of conversation that ought to have warned her away. "I'm sorry to interrupt," she apologized, closing the door.

"Don't go. You're just who we need," Julia called after her.

Nora leaned into the room, still hesitant. The place was crowded, with Julia and Harry bent over a seated female patient.

"You can prevent a disaster," Julia said. "My husband is trying to cut this lady's hair."

"She needs sutures," Harry said, scissors poised a few inches above the patient's long, brown hair.

"Please don't cut it off," the woman pleaded.

"Mrs. Parley," Harry said with exaggerated patience. "I am holding a bandage to your bleeding head. Your husband will not appreciate me sending you home in this state to spare a few curls."

"You don't understand." Julia blocked the scissors, hands spread protectively over Mrs. Parley's tresses. "If you take off that entire piece, she can't put her hair up at all. You need to take locks from the middle so she can use this piece to hide it."

"Do you often get this kind of trouble?" Mrs. Franklin whispered to Nora.

Nora grinned, holding in a laugh. "More often than you'd think." Julia was the real expert at these impromptu hairdressing consultations, even if she was less skilled at wielding the curved needle.

"She's bled through this one," Harry said, tossing aside a wad of folded linen and reaching for another. "Nora, can you interject some reason?"

"This is Dr. Trimble and his wife, Julia, who assists us in the clinic," Nora whispered to Mrs. Franklin. "I'm afraid I—"

"Go right ahead," Mrs. Franklin said, obviously highly entertained by the scene already. "I can wait."

Harry removed the soaked bandage, revealing a gaping cut at the base of Mrs. Parley's occipital bone—which Nora could see glistening white—flowing with unstanched blood before he quickly covered it again. The woman flinched as Harry pressed hard on the back of her head.

"What happened?" Nora demanded.

"It was stupid of me. I was just down the street when I dropped my package. I stooped to get it and didn't see the railing above me. I saw stars for a moment."

"That will do it," Nora agreed. "Dr. Trimble's right. We'll need to cut the hair for him to close the wound safely."

"Thank you." Harry huffed.

"But we don't need to make a hack job of it," Julia objected. "Let Nora cut it."

"Please let her," Mrs. Parley begged. "I'm proud of my hair."

"Proud enough to bleed to death," Harry grumbled.

"He's teasing," Nora reassured as the woman's eyes went wide. "But it won't stop bleeding on its own."

"Just trust me," Julia said, taking the scissors and passing them to Nora. "I'll be certain no one ever knows until it grows back."

Harry relented and looked on skeptically as Julia directed while Nora cut and shaved until just the straight split was bare.

"This is a novel one," he muttered in mock complaint. "If you'd like to consult on all my head wounds, there's plenty to be found in local pubs."

"Those wounds are all yours, dear," Julia said, her white teeth on display. "But you should take a hairdressing class from me." She turned her attention to Mrs. Parley, who sucked in her breath as the needle entered her scalp. "I'll show you how to pin it when he's finished," Julia promised, distracting the woman from the burn of the silk sliding through her skin.

When the last knot was tied and Mrs. Parley sent on her way, Nora drew Mrs. Franklin back into the hall. "I didn't mean to interrupt the tour." She shook her head with a silent laugh. "But as you can see, it's never dull in clinic."

Mrs. Franklin's eyes crinkled. "Certainly not."

Nora pointed across the hall. "Here's our newest addition—a ward for patients who require longer care. It used to be the kitchen and pantry of the neighboring home before Horace joined the houses together. We left the stove and hearth to heat the large room." Nora opened the door into the long room lined with beds, a few guarded by dressing screens. "We've only four patients now." She thought of Mr. Lampley lying in the dark, frozen ice room. The undertaker was supposed to collect him tomorrow.

"We don't often have funds or time to keep ten patients, plus run the clinic, so Dr. Trimble is a district doctor as well. Dr. Croft and my husband also work at St. Bart's Hospital. That leaves me most days to manage this." Nora gestured to the large room—chamber pots that needed to be emptied, bandages to change, patients too weak to feed themselves.

"You need more hands," Mrs. Franklin stated.

It was as precise a diagnosis as Nora had ever heard. "I say that every day, Mrs. Franklin," she admitted.

"My name is Ruth," the midwife said after a pause. "Mrs. Howell and the others call me that. I'd like you to as well, if you will."

Nora's eyebrows lifted. "Happily."

"I don't stand on formality," Ruth continued. "When you work with people in their most intimate moments—"

"You needn't call me Mrs. Gibson. Or Doctor," Nora added. "Nora will do."

"Good." Ruth pinched her lips in thought as she surveyed the room. "You have as fine a facility as I've seen. Why don't you advertise it more?"

Nora paused while their consumption patient gave a mighty series of coughs from the far end of the room. "As things stand, looking after the patients we have takes nearly all my time. Until we've paid off more of the debt we accumulated building it—"

"Aye," Ruth said with a nod. Her brown eyes slid to where John, the orderly, was dozing in a hard chair. "You need more hands."

CHAPTER 7

NORA NUDGED THE THICK PILE OF STRAW AT HER FOOT, prodding a sharp stalk away from her ankle. The overturned bucket she sat on dug uncomfortably into the back of her thigh, but that was a minor detail compared to the relief of resting her feet for the first time in hours. A single struggling candle burned away just enough darkness to illuminate the shape of Mr. Lampley lying atop the stone table to her right. The ice room remained as dark and cold as a cave even in the unrelenting summer heat. So long as she was quiet, no one would suspect her hiding spot.

She nibbled away at her beef sandwich and cast another look at the corpse. He was in the moderate stages of rigor mortis, limbs tight and rigid but not yet stiff as bone. He'd passed quietly, his weak, whistling heart finally wheezing out its last slow thud.

"This is the nicest part of my day," she confessed to him, aware of the pathos of that truth.

After saying goodbye to Ruth, a string of loud, demanding patients had managed to descend on her all at once just after Harry departed, leaving her the only doctor home. Horace had promised to return after the bone spur surgery at Bart's, but he'd done what he did best—vanish without a trace, with no warning or note. She'd expected him three hours ago.

Most likely he'd caught wind of some interesting case at another hospital or across town and followed it like a will-o'-the-wisp across London, forgetting Nora entirely.

"He doesn't mean to be inconsiderate," she reassured the deceased man, as if he'd noted her complaints. "He would have done the same to anybody. There is no priority in his life above curiosity." She took a minute to bite and swallow, noticing the play of warm candlelight on Mr. Lampley's white hair. "As much as I'd love to stay and have dessert with you, I have patients."

Nora carefully blew out the candle and felt her way to the door in the blackness. She caught the handle and took one deep breath, bracing herself for the work ahead.

As soon as she entered the hallway, she heard the plaintive coughs of her next patient, a young woman named Meg, afflicted with consumption. At least the humid misery of London this August was good for one person. Nora had never seen Meg's color this good. Some doctors swore brisk, dry air aided consumption recovery, but Nora's patients all breathed easier in the summer months.

She wished she could prescribe all her consumptives a month or more of fresh sea air, but Meg's family could hardly scrape together the small fee to pay for her food and linen washing while in hospital. A stay at the seaside was out of the question.

Meg's chest rose and fell evenly, pulse steady and slow enough to indicate restful slumber. Satisfied, Nora continued on to the next occupied bed, where a middle-aged woman stared blankly at the aisle, probably too overcome with heat to read the book abandoned in her lap. Nora had done Mrs. Hooper's surgery herself—a hernia repair, one of her specialties, since it was the first internal procedure she'd ever attempted.

"A little feverish," she said, feeling Mrs. Hooper's brow and noting the flush on her cheeks. "Nothing alarming. Let me examine your dressing."

Still draining. The gauze needed changing. She'd have to fetch more bandages from the supply room.

She slipped into the shadowy hall, grateful clinic hours were over and no one had pounded on the door with burns or broken bones, when the sound of hurried footsteps on the stairs warned her of her mistake.

Shouldn't have even thought it.

"Nora?" Daniel strode into the hall, looking almost as starched as when he'd left that morning. Nora glanced hopelessly at her stained apron and limp, rolled sleeves.

He gave her a fleeting smile. "I came to see if you needed help so you can freshen up before dinner. Where's Horace?"

Nora huffed. "Lord knows. I thought he'd be back with you. I'm changing Mrs. Hooper's bandages and then I need to give her a dose of laudanum. I think we can safely decrease the concentration. I probably won't have time to come to dinner. You can tell Mrs. Phipps to leave me a tray." She stepped into the dispensary and opened the closet where they stored all their sheets and bandages.

"Don't forget to write those down for Mrs. Hooper's bill." Daniel nodded toward the open book that she'd pushed to one side of the nearby work table. He was constantly urging Nora and Horace to use it more faithfully.

She displayed her heavily laden arms. "I can hardly write with my hands full," she pointed out.

"I'll put it on the ledger for you," he offered.

"Or—" Nora tamped down on her words, certain it was the heat melting her tolerance into a thin puddle, not her husband. "You could help me change the bandage and I'll record it when we're done."

Daniel lifted an eyebrow in acknowledgment of her tone but said nothing. Nora thought longingly of the cadaver's ice room. She'd happily eat her dinner with him instead.

"How was the lecture?" Daniel asked, his voice maddeningly calm as he recorded the supplies in his precise handwriting.

She'd been trying to forget. "Hardly my best," she admitted.

"I heard." He put his hands into his pockets and looked at her expectantly—too much like a schoolmaster who'd asked for an explanation.

You're just prickly today, she told herself. *He's not criticizing.* "What do you mean, you heard?"

"Adams and Howe came to Bart's afterward. They were discussing it. Energetically."

Her chest seared as she held her breath—the same paralyzing heat that gripped her whenever she'd failed.

Had they discussed it privately with Daniel, or broadcast their complaints to a room full of doctors?

It wouldn't be the first time this had happened. "And?" she asked stiffly.

Daniel's brow creased. "They claim you turned the lecture over to a midwife."

The heat reached her face, a torrent of words coming with

the rush of blood. "I did not *turn it over*. I asked a question, and she answered."

In her mind's eye she replayed Mrs. Franklin at the dissection table, explaining the birthing position as she held the crude model of the baby. *Perhaps it was more than just an answered question...*

"Might want to tweak your methods," Daniel suggested. "Adams, in particular, wasn't happy deferring to untrained midwives."

"Adams isn't happy deferring to anyone," Nora pointed out, though she hardly knew the man. She knew only that he refused to discuss his methods—including the use of short forceps—selling them exclusively to a tiny selection of high-paying students, while she worked endless hours in a charity hospital.

She glanced at the open ledger—nothing entered yet today. She ought to remember to charge for things. "I assure you, Mrs. Franklin is well trained in the matter under discussion."

Daniel held back a reply, doubt in his eyes. "Adams did attend your lecture and pay for your expertise. Wouldn't you say that was liberal of him?"

"Should I write him a thank-you note?"

Daniel glanced up at her, the air growing almost as hard as the brass mortar and pestle resting between them. "Don't be like that." He sighed. "You have doctors willing to listen to you because of your expertise, but asking them to attend a lecture from a neighborhood woman—"

"I didn't—"

"They seemed to think you did."

"And what did Horace say?"

Daniel shifted his head. "He reminded them the value of a good midwife."

"As you should have done!" Nora sensed tears marshaling along her eyelashes, threatening to charge.

"Nora." His voice softened. "I'm not trying to make you cry. It's just...you don't need to make enemies, especially of doctors willing to listen to you. I'm certain if you reach out and explain to Adams that it won't happen again—"

Her head snapped up, a strand of hair falling loose and sticking to her perspiring face. "You weren't there. Did it ever occur to you to defend me like Horace did? Why do you assume I was in the wrong?"

"Nora!" It was the closest thing to an outburst she'd heard from him. "I defend you day and night. You have no idea. And I never said you were wrong. Just that this isn't the place—"

"*This* isn't the place?" she demanded, pointing at the floor. "For whom did Horace build this hospital?" She dropped the bandages onto the table, one rolling away and falling to the floor.

"For you, Nora. I haven't forgotten."

She thought guiltily of the ledger, then quashed the emotion. "Just checking that you remembered. You can finish here. I'm changing for dinner."

She wasn't one to storm away, and Daniel wasn't one to sympathize with displays of temper, but a moment later she was mounting the stairs like a thunderstorm, promising herself she'd reach the privacy of her own room before she let the rain fall.

She didn't count on blundering full force into Horace as

she turned the corner at the top of steps. He grunted, and she instinctively clasped his coat to keep him from falling.

"I'm sorry." The impact loosed one rogue tear. It tickled the top of her cheek, but if she wiped it, he would notice. "I had no idea you were home."

"Quite right. Or you and Daniel wouldn't be carrying on like that."

Nora released his lapel and brisked her hands over her face. "You heard?"

As he flicked one eyebrow in answer, she noticed an uncharacteristic hollowness to his eyes. His usually animated face was stiff with distant thought.

"What's wrong?"

"Horace, where have you been?" Daniel's voice made them both turn. His hands, deep in his pockets, and his heavy tread told Nora he dreaded finishing their quarrel, but he wasn't the type to turn away from a fight. Not an important one.

"I was near the docks. Dr. Berry wanted a second opinion."

The tension in Nora's spine wavered. Interesting cases took precedence over personal matters. Just now, she'd welcome a new topic.

"Anything unusual?" Daniel pressed.

Horace sighed, leaning on his cane. Sensing a longer answer, Nora pointed to the study down the hall. "Sit down." She could do with a moment off her feet, too.

Horace waited until they were all seated before speaking. "They took Berry and me out on a dinghy. Didn't want to berth the ship until they knew what to do with the body."

Nora's eyebrows shot up.

"When I saw it, I thought he'd been dead and drained a week already—a dried husk." Horace's jaw flexed, as if fighting against the escaping words. "He only died last night."

"What killed him?" Daniel asked.

Horace gave a long blink and shifted his eyes. "Cholera."

With breathless speed, Nora's vision jolted from the well-lit study to a dark, closed room. A woman's shrunken hand—her fingers weathered ropes, the skin leathery and tough—hung over the side of a soiled bed. She willed herself not to peer at the woman's motionless face. She'd died with her eyes open and Nora didn't want to see the lifeless rings of color, the same color as her own.

"Nora?" Horace barked.

She turned her head, and the dead woman disappeared like vapor.

"Are you all right?"

"How many?" she asked. A jade bowl filled with roses sat on the nearby table. Mrs. Phipps must have changed the flowers today.

"Just the one. The ship came from Rotterdam, and apparently the sailor took sick almost immediately. None of the other sailors showed symptoms. They would have put the body overboard last night, but he's the first mate and has family in London. The crew thought they'd want a proper burial."

"Are you certain it was cholera? There's other illnesses that cause purging... What about dysentery?"

Horace inhaled deeply, shoulders rising. "I have no doubt. They described him passing what can only be rice water stools. Death came in less than two days. And the condition of the body... Berry already knew. He just wanted confirmation. They're bringing the body along soon. You can see for yourself before the family comes for it." Horace tugged on his beard. "I wish families would believe me when I tell them they don't want to see someone in that state. They always insist."

Nora closed her eyes to push out the memory of her mother's shriveled arm and open eyes. It didn't work. She shuddered. And yet... "I want to see it." She wouldn't believe until she assessed it herself. If there was anything else plausible... Horace had been wrong before. *Rarely, but still...*

Daniel steepled his fingers. "I need to study it as well. I haven't seen a case in years. I only saw one body at the Sorbonne. Never the disease in action. I was far from London in '32—" He cut off abruptly, his eyes dropping to his fingertips.

1832, the year Nora had lost everything. Most of the time she didn't think of it—concentrating instead on her new life. Practically a rebirth. But the description of the withered body dredged up an old despair.

The tears she'd reserved to shed over Adams and the idiotic doctors threatened again—but this time for more visceral pains. She swallowed hard and stood. "I'm washing up now. Send for me when the body arrives."

"Nora, I'm—" Daniel started, but she waved his attempted solace away.

"We should try to arrange a lecture—let as many students as possible see it so they recognize the signs. You'll ask if the family will let us keep the body until burial?" That was usually Horace's job—to coolly overlook the human suffering in lieu of science. Her words lined up in such an orderly fashion, as if they weren't broken shards of glass in her throat.

Horace knuckled his chest—*his angina again*—and gave half a grimace. "One thing at a time. For now, let's count ourselves fortunate there's only one body."

"So far," Daniel said, then glanced carefully at Nora.

They'd laid her father to rest first. He was only one body. *Until*—

Horace glared at his fist, clenched tight on the handle of his cane. "I'll write to doctors I know in Rotterdam, find out if it's spreading there. But I haven't heard anything. And it doesn't seem to have survived the sea crossing."

"Thank God," Daniel whispered.

Nora glanced at his relieved face. He had no idea. Whatever he imagined cholera to be, she knew it was worse.

CHAPTER 8

"A REN'T YOU LISTENING?"

Nora snapped her eyes up, realizing too late Julia was waiting for a response. She couldn't even recall the original question. "I'm sorry. My wits are wandering today. What did you ask?"

It was Sunday afternoon, and she and Julia had escaped outside to enjoy a bit of quiet, seated on the lawn.

"Nothing. I was only saying how surprised I am that you've made friends with Queenie."

Nora smiled and returned her gaze to the wombat sitting on her lap. Queenie—she had a name now, bestowed by Mrs. Phipps—looked up, clearly expecting Nora to resume stroking her back. The sun, sifting through the leaves of the nearby plane trees, struck glints in the marsupial's dark fur.

"I also said you've been quiet the last two days," Julia said with an amused smile. "But you didn't hear that, either."

"I'm sorry." Nora pushed Queenie off her lap and watched her amble to the herb border, where she began digging with her enormous front claws. Maybe hungry? At least she wasn't meddling with Mrs. Phipps's roses. Nora didn't think any of the animals would last here after trying that.

"She's grown bigger," Nora said. "Must have been a baby when they caught her."

Julia dipped her head. The sunlight did lovely things to her too—gilding her bright hair—but now her features were in shadow. "Poor thing."

They'd tried a cage on the lawn—Horace kept them ready for any interesting acquisitions—but Queenie preferred a shady stall in the carriage house.

"Nora."

Julia probed with her blue eyes. They shamed the London sky. Nora had only seen that color in Italy, over the burnished hills—

"I'm sorry. I'm doing it again. My mind is wandering," she apologized.

"I expect some quiet from you when you're researching or preparing for a difficult surgery, but you've hardly spoken this week, even at meals. What's troubling you?"

Nora ran her hand over the cool, shady grass, letting it tickle her palm. She wished she could untangle the knot of thoughts snagging in her brain. Dr. Adams, Daniel, the wasted body of that dead sailor… "Daniel and I are in a bit of a standoff."

"No." Julia crossed her arms and refused Nora's explanation. "Not possible."

"What do you mean, *no*? We are." Nora leaned against the tree's rough bark. "We've barely spoken more than civilities today."

Julia pursed her lips. "What did you do?"

"What did *I* do?" Nora's eyebrows vaulted skyward.

"Daniel would turn the world over to find a grain of sand you wanted," Julia continued calmly, one dimple peeking out of her otherwise smooth cheek.

"And I wouldn't do the same for him?" Nora demanded, surprised by the sting in her chest.

"Of course you would." Julia held up her hands. "Perhaps you've been a bit sensitive?" she added more gently.

Nora tamped her rising temper and settled against the tree again. Even if she wanted to deny it, Julia had just proved her point. Something she was terribly good at. "Just because you and your husband never quarrel—"

Julia's eyebrows interrupted her. "We've been married over two years. If you really think we've never argued—"

"Not that I've ever seen," Nora amended. "Harry's never grumpy with you."

The obvious rejoinder—Julia was never, to Nora's knowledge, grumpy with him—sounded loud in the silence.

Nora muttered, "And Daniel hasn't exactly been grumpy with me." She picked a bit of grass off her skirt and tossed it aside. "What he *has* been doing is injecting his opinion into my work."

Julia frowned. "You work together. All of you. All I hear all day is four doctors sticking their noses into one another's work. I thought you liked it that way. What's different now?" Julia waved a leaf at Queenie. The round wombat peered at her through impossibly small eyes.

Nora rearranged her legs, but that didn't ease the growing discomfort in her back. Daniel was usually supportive of her ideas. But the way he'd looked at her when he talked about Dr. Adams… "This *is* different." She started slowly, finding her way through the words. "He took Dr. Adams's side over mine before he'd heard my account of it." The memory still stung.

Julia scratched Queenie on her round rump. "I know a bakery—it's in Clerkenwell. Serves the best pastries I've ever eaten, but you can hear the husband and wife bellowing at each other before the sun comes up. Perhaps blending marriage and a business is difficult for everyone?"

Nora wrinkled her nose. Poor comfort, being compared to the screaming bakers of Clerkenwell. She had no interest in bellowing at her husband and no tolerance for being bellowed at, either. "But we love collaborating. At least, we always have before." Given her current feelings, some qualification was necessary.

"And I'm sure you always will," Julia hastened. "Most of the time. But differences are bound to happen—and that's often how you push each other forward. Horace is beastly to Harry, but—" She licked her lips. "Harry's much more confident in his work than he was two years ago. And he's not ashamed of his mistakes. They don't get in his way anymore.

"Some conflict can be helpful, I think. And from what I see of you and Daniel... Well, you are so connected because of your work. This is a tiny wrinkle."

"Julia."

They both turned toward the sound of Harry's voice. He had a fine one: deep, with a warm Scots burr. Walking out from the house toward his wife, he wore a matching smile. "Are you trying to get your fingers bitten off by that savage thing?"

"Queenie's about as savage as your slippers," Julia scoffed.

Harry swooped up the unresisting wombat, careful to aim her claws well away, and kissed her on the top of her head. "I've missed my girl all day," he said with a teasing look at his wife over the furry bundle.

Julia pretended coolness. "Well, you can promenade round the park with her if you like, but you'll need to buy her a fine dress first." Harry worked long hours, but Julia insisted on a stroll with him every Sunday.

Nora shifted onto her knees. She ought to leave them alone.

Harry squinted at Queenie's face. "No dress could help this homely thing. Still, I can't help adoring her."

He dropped to the grass with a tired groan, and Julia lifted her hands, making room for him to put his head on her lap. "What a day," he said. "I had to put a man's shoulder back in place. I swear he was eighteen stone. It felt more like a wrestling match with a bear than a medical consultation."

"Sounds dreadful." Julia ran a finger through his short, ruddy hair, and he fell silent.

Nora studied the picture of utter contentment before her, unable to leave just yet. Perhaps she'd try to paint it from memory later and give it to her friends as a gift. There was something so complementary about the angle of Harry's face and the turn of Julia's shoulders. A purple smudge on his sleeve, from the shadows of the thick branch overhead, and a yellow stroke across Julia's jaw where the light slid down her face...

She didn't know where Daniel was today. They'd just nodded at each other this morning. He'd left before breakfast.

She sighed. Her trouble with Daniel was nothing compared to what Harry and Julia had overcome in order to sit contentedly together. Nora didn't like to think of it, but it was heartening to see no trace of unhappiness left over. There certainly could have been.

Years before, Julia had been raped at a house party while away from her family. When she'd discovered she was pregnant, she tried to kill herself, cutting her arms to ribbons. Miraculously, she'd missed her arteries, but she'd come perilously close to bleeding to death.

At the time, Harry was a mere acquaintance, but one Julia's father had trusted enough to summon for this emergency. Anxious lest she try again, he'd begged Harry to end his daughter's pregnancy, though she was still unconscious and performing abortions was illegal and highly dangerous for the patient.

Harry had done as asked—uniting them with a terrible secret.

Now, beneath the gilding light of late summer, with Harry's head cradled in Julia's skirts and her ragged scars concealed beneath her violet sleeves, Nora could hardly imagine something so dark or terrifying touching either one of them.

Queenie rooted at Harry's knee, nudging his trousers with her stubby black nose as if begging to be included.

Nora sighed inwardly, the air trapped against her sore heart. The worst part was knowing the rigid distance between her and Daniel was of her own making, reinforced every day this week by her clipped words and averted eyes. But until he understood what it meant to blindly support Adams over her… Her blood rose unbidden once more. She thought the anger had burned out, but it was smoldering beneath the ashes.

Daniel doesn't trust my ability. The fact that he'd assumed her wrong from the start… But it was more than that. She hadn't confided her plans to him, either. Perhaps they'd stopped trusting each other. "I should go back to the clinic," Nora announced. "Will you make sure Queenie gets put away?" She didn't wait for an answer as she started resolutely across the lawn, her chest heavy and sore. The two lovers likely preferred to be alone anyway.

CHAPTER 9

N ORA MEANT TO SIT ACROSS FROM HER HUSBAND AT DIN-
ner and attempt some form of rapprochement debating
the merits of a report on a cesarean section (not hers, but by a
foreign doctor who'd consulted her) in the latest edition of *The
Lancet*. Unfortunately, the consumption patient on the ward, Meg
Prather, had suffered another hemorrhage, coughing up an alarming amount of blood. John, the orderly who slept in the ward most
nights, came with the bad news in the middle of their soup. It was
Daniel's turn for emergencies, but this one required at least two
sets of hands. Instead of finding amity over the latest journal and
roast lamb, she and Daniel passed each other water and bandages
as Daniel applied a menthol plaster to the girl's chest while Nora
gave her a small dose of ether to calm the throat muscles.

"We can't let her choke on the blood while she's not able to
cough," Daniel said as the girl succumbed to the fumes of the
vaporizer.

"I know," Nora agreed. "But if we let her keep coughing at
this rate, she'll open a fresh hemorrhage."

They met eyes over her motionless body. The girl was only
eighteen, but she looked even younger than that. Nora told herself the girl's pale face was peaceful and sleeplike, but the stillness reminded her too much of death.

"If she stays in the city, I don't see her lasting much longer."
Daniel spoke low so other patients wouldn't overhear.

"They can't afford to send her anywhere else. Our hospital
is a spa compared to their flat."

Meg's chest spasmed, and Nora used a rubber tube and
bulb to draw more secretions and blood from her throat.

"We need to roll her," Daniel said, pushing Meg's left
shoulder upright.

Nora flinched as he pounded Meg's shoulders. Even his
attempts to help felt like criticism.

"We could take her out to the garden during the day and let
her take a sunbath. It's not the seaside, but it might do her some
good," Nora suggested as she packed away the ether mask. But this
lingering summer heat only magnified the stench of the Thames
and the filthy streets. Sewage and sour river smells wouldn't have
the same benefit as clean sea air with the tang of salt.

"Maybe she's not the only one who needs to leave the city."
Daniel dipped his eyes as he listened to Meg's chest through
his wooden stethoscope. His voice carried softly to Nora's ears,
something vulnerable in the words.

"What do you mean?" she asked as she measured the pulse
in Meg's thin wrist.

"Perhaps you and I could get away from patients and papers
for a bit. We could visit my family's house in the country, go
riding, walk the woods."

She saw it for a moment—the picture he painted. Bluebells
in the shady ferns of the forest, rowing across the small lake
as trees burst into autumn color around them, and listening
contently while Daniel demonstrated his expansive knowledge

of flora and fauna. She'd never learned to ride, but Daniel had offered to teach her. "With your surgery schedule at Bart's and the clinic—"

"I know." He sighed, putting away the stethoscope. "There's fluid in the lower-right lobe. That must be where the hemorrhage originated." His face resumed a businesslike expression, the supplication gone from his tired voice.

Nora thought of Harry's head in Julia's lap. "You're right, though." Her words were quick, lacking her usual confidence. "We should go. Before winter. Perhaps next month when the worst of the heat is over?"

Daniel lifted his head, and she was startled by the relief softening the corners of his eyes. He'd been as troubled by this standoff as she.

"I'll ask Harry and Horace to cover the clinic. Is she waking?" It had been ten minutes since Meg inhaled the ether, and Daniel was impatient with the anesthesia. He worried over the prolonged sleepers more than Nora did.

"Not waking, but her pulse is normal and strong. The sleep will do her good. You finish your dinner. I'll stay with her."

Daniel carried his chair to Nora's side and set it down with a soft thump. "I'll wait with you, and we'll eat together."

They hadn't discussed Ruth Franklin, Dr. Adams, or the midwives at all, but Nora didn't want to. She wished only to sit here with their shoulders pressed together and their fingers interlocked as they waited for their patient to awake.

Besides, this compromise might break if she mentioned Ruth would be visiting here tomorrow. *I'll be more careful this time*, Nora told herself. Adams and the rest wouldn't be here.

"I like the notion of learning for myself." Ruth Franklin's lips pursed. "But I'm afraid it's likely to stir up trouble."

"I'm not worried about that," Nora lied. "I'm thinking of the good it will do. You were so eager to learn to use forceps. I'm sure your colleagues—"

Ruth shook her head, and Nora exhaled away the mounting pressure in her chest. Some, at any rate. "You don't think they'd be interested? Even in a class of just women? No doctors?"

After the challenges of her last lecture, Nora was convinced a separate class was the answer, and better than what she'd originally envisaged. Ruth and the other midwives wouldn't be sneered at for their lack of Latin, and their years of practical experience wouldn't be dismissed. Men like Adams would be more receptive to their ideas if they were filtered through her. Or even Daniel. Grating as that was, Nora was used to adjusting to practical realities. The result was what mattered.

But judging from Ruth's uneasy frown, it might not be possible to coax other midwives to come back. "Mrs. Bailey says it'll anger the doctors. When she needs to call one, she sends for Frederick Brown, and he apprenticed to Dr. Adams. She doesn't want to tread on any toes."

Nora chewed the inside of her lip. Maybe that was her problem; she never meant to, but she'd flattened a few feet already. "How would Dr. Brown—or Adams, for that matter— ever know? I'm not inviting them to your class. It would be exclusively for women, all experienced midwives."

"You know I'll learn whatever you're willing to teach me. But..." Ruth sighed. "I'll ask the others. They might be keener if the class were held at night. They could come without being seen."

"Of course." She'd done her share of hiding, but it rankled that these women felt they must, too. Most were at least a decade older than her, and Ruth had begun apprenticing to her mother when she was twelve. "If the fees are a problem..." Nora had decided to keep them low, only a quarter of Horace's one-pound fee. Even the reduced amount would be helpful. But it wasn't her motivation.

With trained women beside her, she wouldn't be alone. An aberration. She longed for the day she'd turn her head and see an encouraging smile from a female colleague.

"It's not the fees," Ruth assured her.

Nora sighed in relief. She hoped to at least reimburse Horace for the expensive supplies she'd ordered.

In her enthusiasm to defend the use of midwives through formal training, she'd already written to Italy, asking Magdalena to arrange the purchase of teaching models like those she'd trained with in Bologna. The local craftsmen were experts at anatomical replicas, largely because of tighter restrictions on cadaver dissections.

These were necessary aids, especially if she wanted to run parallel lectures for men and women, and over time, they'd save her plenty of hours in the dissection laboratory, but the expense was considerable. Even Horace had blanched a little.

The cost was even more staggering if she was teaching only a class of one.

But given enough time and students, she could make a name for herself and her hospital.

"Nora?"

She turned. It was Harry, sticking his head through the laboratory doorway. He had his hat and overcoat on, so either coming or going.

"You've a fancy visitor on her way down. Julia offered to entertain her in the drawing room, but the visitor insisted she wasn't going to stand on ceremony. Or something to that effect."

Nora glanced behind her, but the bones she'd been wiring together were safely concealed beneath a sheet. If any bodies had arrived in the night, they'd been stowed safely in the ice room.

"Who is it?" Nora asked.

"She said to tell you Ben Bee's mother is here. Bye the nou." He touched his hat, grinned, and vanished, hurrying out the side door.

Nora rubbed her forehead. She couldn't remember Ben Bee. And the surname didn't sound "drawing room."

"Do you want me to go?" Ruth asked, but Nora had no time to do more than shake her head. She had plenty of persuasive arguments left and intended to use them.

"Dr. Gibson, how good to see you."

Nora started at the sight of the lady in the doorframe. She was beautifully attired, her bonnet a masterwork of asymmetric japonais motifs, with a parasol slung over her arm.

"Lady Woodbine?" Nora hadn't seen her aristocratic patient in several weeks—not since determining that she was conclusively recovered from her surgery, the cesarean section that had brought Nora so much attention and acclaim.

"I thought you were in the country."

"Came to visit my cousin. Little Benby is still at home, but you'll be glad to hear your namesake is thriving."

Ah. Lady Woodbine's slightly different inflections explained the mysterious name. The child Nora had delivered safely via cesarean, Charles Benedict Beady Rawlston, owed the *Beady* in his name to her, though naturally Nora had traded her last name for Daniel's after her marriage. She'd not expected Beady to figure in his everyday moniker, however, and flushed at the unexpected tribute.

"Of course I am. That's wonderful news. You look very fit yourself, if I may say so."

Lady Woodbine smiled. "Thanks to you. Motherhood agrees with me."

"But what brings you? I…" Nora hesitated. Gratitude seemed a poor excuse for this surprise visit, which could only be counted as a significant honor.

"I'm afraid I want your help," Lady Woodbine said. "And it's a bit of a crisis, so I came myself, hoping I could carry you away with me." She paused, and Nora noted the anxious bobbing of her throat.

"It's my cousin. She's expecting, but it's still six or seven weeks before her time. She started having pains last night. We sent for her doctor, but he's been called away to see his sister. If you know any way to halt her pains…" Lady Woodbine licked her lips. "I would hate for her to lose this child," she whispered.

Nora glanced at Ruth. Many women had false contractions. Hopefully… "Of course I'll come," Nora said. "Ruth, are you—"

The midwife nodded. "I can help, if you want me."

"I do," Nora said firmly. "But I understand if you are called away." She turned to Lady Woodbine. "This is Mrs. Franklin. A very skilled midwife. We'll come at once."

"Thank you, Dr. Gibson." Lady Woodbine's whole body—face, shoulders, hands—softened with relief. Her tension had been well hidden by her manners and fancy trappings, but it was plain now. "My carriage is waiting outside."

The house was an imposing one, at the end of a row shaded by plane trees, but there was no time to admire the facade or the architectural symmetry of the street. Nora pushed her shoulders back, alighting from the carriage and mounting the steps in long strides that would have done credit to any hurdler. Ruth followed, toting Nora's bag since Nora was carrying her medicine box in one hand and the vaporizer in the other.

"This way." Lady Woodbine ushered them through the hall and up the carpeted stairs, a housekeeper and two maids falling in behind her.

Ruth glanced at Nora and raised her eyebrows. Though she'd helped many women, Nora realized Ruth might not have attended any in a home like this.

"I'll leave you here." Lady Woodbine stopped just outside a stately double door in the upstairs corridor. "Green, the housekeeper, can provide anything you need. My cousin, Mrs.

Roland, has her maid, Gladys, with her, and she'll help answer any questions."

As Nora hastened forward, Lady Woodbine touched her arm. "Please." She blinked twice. "Do what you can."

"Of course. We'll take a look, and that should tell me what we're up against."

"I'll be just across the hall."

Lady Woodbine retreated, and Nora followed Ruth inside. "Mrs. Roland? Your cousin fetched me. I'm Dr. Gibson, and Mrs. Franklin and I are here to help."

Mrs. Roland didn't seem to hear. She grimaced—one eye closed, her face a mask of concentration—and held up a hand, signaling Nora to wait.

"She's having another pain," the maid, Gladys, explained unnecessarily.

"When was the last?"

Gladys gave her a blank look. Nora set down her burdens and hurried to the bed. She couldn't see anything of Mrs. Roland's body. Everything but her face and hands was concealed beneath a billowing, ruffled nightdress clinging to her in damp patches. Her hair, too, stuck to her neck and forehead. "I need to feel your belly," Nora said, but as she placed her palms, Mrs. Roland squirmed miserably.

"The pains are getting stronger. My back never hurt like this before," she said.

"You have other babes, then?" Ruth asked.

Mrs. Roland panted, her face screwing up in concentration. "Two."

Nora eyed her patient, not her watch. But even so, false

contractions didn't last this long. None of her medicines would stop this.

"How long have you had the pains?"

"They only grew stronger this last hour. I hoped they were phantom pains, because it's too early. And my waters haven't come away, so—"

Ruth picked up Mrs. Roland's hand. "Don't fret yourself. You just need to rest and let Dr. Gibson have a look at you."

Mrs. Roland settled back on the pillows, and Nora quickly ran her hands over her patient's distended belly, feeling for the top of her uterus.

Not yet, not yet—there. She glanced at Ruth. "Too high." She frowned. "Mrs. Roland, your cousin told me you are only seven months along."

She nodded. "Yes, that was when I last bled, and—"

Nora leaned closer. "But Dr. Adams has examined you?"

"Yes, he calls every week, pays particular attention to my sleep and my diet." Her face twisted, and her hand clutched tightly around Ruth's, provoking a wince.

Ruth didn't draw back. "Squeeze my fingers. It'll pass."

But Mrs. Roland was biting her lip hard enough to draw blood, writhing against the sheets.

"You don't need to be quiet, love," Ruth said, and Mrs. Roland let out a piteous gasp.

"Everything's wrong. I feel all wrong." Her voice rose, high and panicked.

"Not everything," Nora said wryly, but only Ruth could hear. "Check her fundus...I mean, the height of her womb."

The contraction passed, and Ruth's hands traced the same path Nora's had, her eyes widening.

"Seven months?" She snorted. "This babe's full grown."

"When you bled last, was it the same? The usual amount of blood, the same number of days?" Nora asked.

Mrs. Roland looked at her helplessly, her breaths still coming fast.

"No," Gladys filled in. "The bleeding was milder, both times."

Nora nodded. She was confident in her assessment, but just in case… "When Dr. Adams came, did he touch you? Inside or on your belly?"

Gladys looked horrified and vigorously shook her head. "That wasn't needed. He listened for the babe's heart, but there was no reason to put his hands on her."

Ruth barked a laugh. "No reason?" But she stopped, intercepting Nora's look.

"I didn't wish it," Mrs. Roland confirmed. "So uncomfortable." She was too red and sweaty to blush, but shifted uneasily against the sheet.

"Well, there are certain things we can verify by feeling your middle," Nora said gently. "Such as how far along you are."

She rested the edge of her hand at the top of the uterus. "So unless you're carrying twins, I'd say this baby is coming right on time. You are just the right size to be nine months along."

"Sometimes there's still some bleeding early on," Ruth added. "Doesn't mean your child isn't there, growing."

Mrs. Roland licked her lips. "Then—"

Gladys intervened, pressing a glass of wine to Mrs. Roland's lips. "You're thirsty, ma'am. Wet your throat first."

She complied, downing two quick sips. "You're saying my baby's ready? I don't need to stop it?"

"You couldn't even if you tried," Ruth said.

"And we're going to help you," Nora said. "This is the right time."

While Gladys ran to share the good news with Lady Woodbine and alert the household, Nora used the intervals between contractions to complete her exam.

"How many fingers?" Mrs. Franklin asked Nora.

"Five or six. She's very elastic. Hard to say."

Mrs. Roland's nose flickered, and then she squeezed her eyes closed, the muscles in her neck tightening. After a long minute, she breathed again. "That was the worst one. Lord, my back is going to break." She raised a hand to her mouth, the color draining from her face.

Ruth moved to her side with the chamber pot just as she vomited.

"It's the exam," Ruth explained, moments later, as she sponged Mrs. Roland's face. "Some women's bodies react more to being touched during labor."

Mrs. Roland whimpered and collapsed back onto her pillow, eyes half-closed in the misery of nausea and blinding pain. "I can't do it," she said, starting to cry. "Even if the baby's ready."

"We can help you feel better," Nora said, straightening and smoothing her apron. A low dose of ether might slow the birth, but Mrs. Roland was in such distress… She glanced across the room to where she'd left the vaporizer.

"Nonsense." Ruth leaned close, pressing the cold cloth to Mrs. Roland's chest. "You're doing as splendid as I've ever seen a woman do in twenty-five years."

Mrs. Roland groaned as another contraction racked her muscles and bones. "My back," she gasped.

"Roll to your side and we'll help with that," Ruth said, already coaxing her onto her left side and pressing her hands into the curve of Mrs. Roland's lumbar region.

"It hurts," the woman wailed, her voice half-smothered by her pillow.

The familiar smell of peppermint reached Nora's nose. She hastened to the bed and picked up the cloth that had fallen aside, placing it on the back of Mrs. Roland's neck.

"Peppermint water for summer births," Ruth said quietly. "It cools the skin and helps with the nausea. Just avoid the eyes."

Nora hadn't noticed Ruth getting the solution ready—but then, she'd been preoccupied with the exam. And along with the lumbar pressure, it seemed to be helping. After several violent contractions, Nora checked again but the cervix and baby's position hadn't changed at all. Nor had they an hour later.

"She's not progressing," Nora whispered to Ruth, wiping sweat from her own hairline. "The head is low enough to reach with forceps, but her cervix isn't fully open yet—"

"She's been on her side too long," Ruth said with a frown. "We need to help her stand."

Nora frowned doubtfully. Mrs. Roland was exhausted. "In her state? Why would she stand?"

"Because her waters haven't ruptured yet. But if she stands, they will."

Nora shook her head. "I'd rather use the ether. When she's able to relax—"

Ruth squared her chin. "I think she's nearly there. Just a few more minutes. Let me try."

Behind them, Mrs. Roland cried out again.

"Just a few more minutes," Nora conceded. She was fast with the vaporizer, but it would take time to warm the water and the ether to the right temperature. If Ruth was right, and they managed to help Mrs. Roland's waters rupture, it might be worth it.

"It'll work, you'll see," Ruth said, and quickly slipped her arms around Mrs. Roland. "All right, love. We're going to get you up. Baby can't come with you on your side."

Mrs. Roland shook her head. "My back."

"I know something that will help," Ruth promised as she began leveraging Mrs. Roland into a seated position. "Slide your legs over like that." With a grunt, and Nora's assistance, she managed to help Mrs. Roland until her feet met the floorboards, but just as she was perched at the edge of the bed, Mrs. Roland cried out and clung to the mattress.

Nora's grip tightened. Mrs. Roland was tall. If she went down, they'd have a terrible time lifting her. Besides, she'd never, ever dropped a patient, and didn't intend to now.

But before she could lay Mrs. Roland back on the bed, Ruth offered her a corded forearm, helping her take several steps to the foot of the bed. "Thank goodness you like poster beds. These are dead useful for births." She guided Mrs. Roland's hands to the ornate post. "Now, keep a firm hold, and when there's a pain, lean over as much as you want. I'll take the weight of your belly."

Mrs. Roland cried out again, legs shaking beneath her. Ruth pressed one hand into the small of her back and bore up her inflated belly with the other.

"What can I do?" Nora asked Ruth quietly, beneath Mrs. Roland's low moan.

"Help me hold her up." Ruth checked the floor. "You must have a water bag made of iron," she announced to Mrs. Roland. "It still hasn't come apart."

"Let me check again. Stay right where you are," Nora instructed. She crawled into position, reached to check…

Her earlier misgivings left in a rush. "I can still feel the edges, but we're nearly there." It was working.

Mrs. Roland leaned forward, grinding her face into the hard wood of the bedpost. Nora put out her hand to stop her, but her teeth were gritted in supreme concentration. Then, without warning, Mrs. Roland shifted backward and squatted toward the floor, her mouth opening in a keening wail.

"What—" Scrambling out of the way, Nora had no time and insufficient strength to right her. But Ruth didn't look anxious, and that steadied Nora's nerves. With one smooth, practiced movement, Ruth took the spot behind Mrs. Roland and crouched low so it looked like their patient was sitting in her lap. Her forearms bulged as she squeezed the suffering woman's hips.

"That helps," Mrs. Roland gasped.

"Pressure right here, with me, as hard as you can manage," Ruth said to Nora.

"Supra pubic pressure," she said reflexively. She'd used it often enough, but never holding a patient like Ruth was.

"Make it stop," Mrs. Roland pleaded, her face red and swollen.

"It will stop. And you'll be holding a beautiful babe," Ruth promised. "Sit down on me. I won't break."

Nora would have. She didn't know how Ruth bore up the weight of a straining pregnant woman.

Mrs. Roland writhed through several more pains before she closed her eyes and announced, "It's coming."

"Almost," Nora said, panic fraying her voice. Last she'd checked, the cervix hadn't expanded enough. The pressure of pushing could damage it permanently. After taking her hook from her bag, she massaged the top of the baby's head, finding a safe spot...

Mrs. Roland screamed as the amniotic fluid burst from the ruptured membrane, dropping the baby's head and eliciting an immediate contraction. Nora was ready with a towel. After this, they wouldn't have much time. "Get her on the bed," she commanded. "She'll be ready to push in one or two more pains."

"No. No. No," Mrs. Roland repeated, shaking her head. Instead of staggering onto the bed, she dropped to the floor on her hands and knees.

"Mrs. Roland—" Nora hooked an arm under her shoulders. They must get her off the floor. She heaved upward, but Mrs. Franklin stopped her with a firm hand.

"She's in a good place right where she is. She can deliver like this."

"But she—"

Mrs. Roland moaned through clenched lips. Her body

shook, her face bright red with the effort of pushing. The baby's black hair slid into view and then vanished again.

They couldn't let her birth on the floor. Nora bit her lip, then told herself there was no point in considering her patient's dignity. Nothing was going to move Mrs. Roland now. She'd been in such pain, but as soon as she'd dropped to all fours, her screaming had stopped.

With the child already crowning, it wouldn't be long.

Ruth bent low and pressed her fist into Mrs. Roland's aching back with such strength her arms quivered. "You bring out the baby; I'll help her through the pains."

Mrs. Roland leaned onto her forearms, her bottom thrust up as the baby's face emerged, bloated and purple. Out of arguments and time, Nora supported the stretching tissues and watched the slick body turn on the next contraction, expelling more fluid and blood. Mrs. Rowland had stopped screaming and was pushing silently, no strength left for sound. The shoulders emerged and Nora took hold of the infant, who blinked, fingers splayed wide, then squalled indignantly.

"I need another towel."

Ruth was already beside her, taking the baby and swabbing her off. "Do you see how easy that was?"

Easy seemed hardly the appropriate word.

"What is it?" Mrs. Roland asked, voice muffled against her arms.

"A girl," Ruth said, and carried the baby to her mother's side. Mrs. Roland laughed shakily, dissolving into tears.

"Let's get you and your mama up to the bed now," Ruth said, setting the baby in the middle of the mattress. The infant stopped crying and scrunched into a tight ball, eyes refusing to let in the offending light of day. Nora helped Mrs. Roland to her feet.

"I thought I was going to die," she said, wiping tears from her eyes.

"No, no, love," Ruth said. "There was never any danger, but those kinds of pains might make you think so. But you're finished now, with a beautiful daughter."

"Not even a tiny tear. No stitches," Nora said, smiling.

"Most of mine never do," Ruth said, busy arranging the bedcovers. "My aunt was a great midwife. She taught me the hands and knees."

Nora chewed on the inside of her cheek, replaying the birth. Unconventional. Visually disturbing, but effective.

Lady Woodbine sent them home in Mrs. Roland's coach, their ears full of praises.

"I've read about that technique, but it was different from anything I've seen," Nora said quietly.

"Some women, like Mrs. Roland, will find the position their babe needs by themselves," Ruth said.

"It does work against gravity." Nora pursed her lips. "The baby was coming out uphill."

"But less swelling after—in the nethers." Ruth scrambled for her recently collected knowledge. "The vulva."

Nora nodded. It made sense. Less continuous force against the perineum. "There's something about it," she mused, gathering her thoughts, "that's a bit medieval. Like a squatting stool."

"Medieval?" Ruth frowned. "You sound like those ignorant doctors. Squatting is one of the best ways to give birth."

The carriage jarred with a quick stop, and Nora tightened her grip on the vaporizer beside her. "Squatting and bottom up?"

"If Dr. Adams had attended that birth, he'd have kept her flat on her back in agony," Ruth pointed out. "Some even hold women down. I'm just glad they sent for you and me."

Nora swallowed guiltily. She'd have turned Mrs. Roland to her side but never allowed her out of bed.

"It would have kept all the weight and irritation right on her back, and she'd have been too frightened to push when the pains came." Ruth shook her head. "I've seen it. Women refusing to push when the pain is too unbearable. It can have terrible effects."

"I always roll them to the side." Nora's voice dropped. "But I've never encouraged crouching or kneeling." Or permitted it, either.

"You pushed on her back. That was well done."

A sop. Like when she was sixteen and fearful, but needed by Horace to help some patient with something.

Ruth inhaled. "I don't have the things you have. Vaporizers and such. But I do know how to help in a case like this. You must let the baby drop away from the spine completely. Otherwise—"

"The nerves remain compressed," Nora finished, the anatomical picture forming in her mind, like a landscape coming into focus as the fog lifts.

When Mrs. Roland dropped to the ground, the child had swung forward. And when Mrs. Roland had lowered her head and leaned on her arms with her bottom in the air, the child had shifted even farther from the spine. "That makes excellent sense." She smiled at Ruth and fanned the heavy summer air. "When we get home, I can show you what happened inside her body after you let her get on the floor."

Ruth's eyes narrowed in confusion. "I already know what happened—"

"I mean the medical explanation. When you can see the actual nerves and spinal structure, you'll be even more impressed with yourself and be able to explain the process more convincingly." Nora was already selecting which anatomy books she'd pull off the shelf. Only three blocks from home, and she nearly sat on her hands in impatience.

"Who would I need to convince?" Ruth asked.

Nora gave a tight-lipped smile. "All those doctors who are too pompous to sit beside you in a lecture, so proud of their degrees and Latin. They have a lot of learning to do." Her lips softened. "So do I."

Ruth shook her head. "I can't tell them. They'd never listen."

Nora frowned. "Maybe not." She tapped her fingers against her opposite wrist, remembering Dr. Adams stalking out of her lecture, chin high, nose almost scraping the ceiling. "But I can."

This was an intriguing case. She'd write it up and submit it to her favorite publication, the *Provincial Medical & Surgical Journal*. She'd had letters and papers published in there before. It would give her colleagues something to talk about. Perhaps even change a few minds.

CHAPTER 10

NORA STIRRED AND RELUCTANTLY PULLED HERSELF FROM bed, her mind a confused blur of the twins she and Mrs. Howell had delivered the night before. Working alongside Ruth, and now also Mrs. Howell, she'd attended five births these past two weeks.

Last night's, though… The blur was fading, and the case, unfortunately, was the kind that was hard to forget.

A living child behind a dead one. Not a rare anomaly, but Nora had never been able to simply keep on when a life expired before it even began. These infants sat in her thoughts for days, and even once they faded, they'd reappear in her memories years after. She'd breathed for this baby just as Ruth taught her—tried to rub animation into her back and limbs, only giving up when her hands cramped, leaving Mrs. Howell to bring out the other child.

Nausea crept over her chilled skin, but that was probably just this elixir of grief and failure and fatigue. She stumbled to her washstand and splashed her hands and wondered what particular brand of crisis had kept Daniel out of their bed. By the time she'd returned last night, he was gone.

The door creaked behind her.

"I missed you. How was—" Halfway into her turn, she

stopped. It wasn't Daniel. It was Mrs. Phipps, bearing a tray with toast and eggs. "Breakfast? On a tray?" Nora asked.

"You had a terrible night."

Nora flinched. "How did you know?"

Mrs. Phipps balanced the tray on the bed and turned her attention to fluffing the pillows. "I'll sit a bit." Her elliptical response—more a sidestep than an answer—settled in the quiet room.

"Watch me eat, you mean."

"These sad cases. They always put you off your food," Mrs. Phipps said. "I know you had one because you tend to forget to remove your boots downstairs after you've lost someone." She nodded toward the tangle of leather and shoestring on the floor. "Mother or child?" Nora saw in her face the hope it wasn't both.

"One of a set of twins," Nora confessed.

Mrs. Phipps folded her hands. "Eat some breakfast. You've plenty of time. Harry already checked the ward patients, and Horace is in the theater doing heaven knows what. You can give yourself an hour or two."

Nora managed a sideways smile. "I've taken a couple already." The clock showed that the time was terribly late.

"The world won't break if you take another."

Like a child, Nora sank onto the rumpled blankets and took a sip of tea. Mrs. Phipps was right. She had no appetite whatsoever.

"The toast," Mrs. Phipps commanded, as crisp as the browned crust.

Nora relented. She didn't want it, but Mrs. Phipps would stay until it was gone, and if she was stealing an hour, Nora wanted at least some of it to talk to Horace. It helped on days like today.

⁓

She found him alone in the surgical theater, working with a corpse, not a patient. Lingering at the threshold, she took a moment to observe him unseen. Usually at least one person shadowed him, listening and learning. Today he mumbled alone, his back insufficiently broad to hide the miniature body before him.

A child. Nora's mouth drooped, even as her nose twitched at the smells of early decay and something else in the air. Singed hair. Burnt flesh.

Her frown deepened.

Today's lecture subject must be a burn victim. Nora turned up her cuffs, wondering if she really ought to help with this one. Burns were especially distressing, even on the dead, but more so on a child.

Horace glanced over his shoulder, his face unreadable. "You coming? Or are you going to dillydally some more?"

Of course he'd known she was here. Silly of her to think he was too distracted. "The burns surprised me."

"Never be surprised; it is an unattractive quality for a doctor. Treat every case as if it were precisely what you expected." Horace bent and peered at the small raw stub that remained of the child's left ear.

"What happened?" Nora asked. His commands, though brusque, always helped steady her.

Horace tsked. "She was home alone, cooking for her younger

siblings when her clothes caught fire." He pinched his mouth together, a sign Nora recognized as his own concession to grief. "It's a wonder the whole building didn't go down. Every year, I'm amazed there isn't another Great Fire that turns the entire East End to rubble."

Nora studied the hopelessly disfigured face before them. Nothing could have saved her. "What are you doing with her?"

Horace pointed his thin probe at the burnt face. "I want to attempt to reconstruct a nose with skin from her leg. See if we can update Professor Bünger's method. Should be a well-attended lecture."

Her stomach tightened. Sometimes Horace wandered too far into the realm of madness. Rhinoplasty on a burnt child, however interesting it might be, seemed a callous experiment.

"Do you really think—"

"I want your help with this," he said, cutting her off. "There will be others, which you know very well. Not so burned as this, of course, but unless we try and practice some cure, they will be doomed to live and die in disfigurement."

With a sigh, she picked up a damp sponge and wiped a smear of ash from the girl's blackened arm. The small limb rested stiff and cold in her hand.

Horace studied the skin of the upper leg, looking for the least affected area, before marking a spot with a charcoal pencil and drawing a precise ellipse, pinching the skin. "It's similar to nose skin. Or perhaps the stomach?" He moved his inspection to her abdomen.

"Daniel said you lost a wealthy woman at Bart's to burns last week." Nora felt like she'd hardly seen her husband since he'd told her about the case, and that was days ago. "Why do burns almost always befall the girls?"

Horace grunted. "I've told you not to wear silly costumes, haven't I?"

Nora blew out a breath. Flowing gauze skirts and voluminous sleeves caught fire much more often than narrow trousers and heavy work coats.

"Don't know why you bother with all that." Frowning, Horace waved his scalpel at the ruffled collar and neat pintucks peeking above the top of her apron.

Nora rolled her eyes. "If I dress too fine, I'm silly. If I dress too plain, I'm unwomanly."

Horace sniffed.

"I know you don't think it matters, but it does," she argued. "I can't treat anyone unless they come to me in the first place."

"They don't come for your wardrobe, my girl. And I don't think she cares one whit for this conversation." Horace motioned to the lifeless corpse. "How cruel to make her listen to such vacuous fluff."

"And what would you discuss with her instead?" Nora crossed her arms, waiting.

"I've been telling her about useful plants. Ironweed. Heal-all. Goldenrod."

Nora hated that her mouth dropped open right after his comments about not being surprised. "You haven't." Nora scanned him for signs of bluffing.

"I certainly have," he murmured. "It's what I did when I thought you were as good as dead from cholera. You weren't awake for most of it, but we discussed the making of paint pigments. I figured you'd be interested due to the supplies in your family's flat. I was right, wasn't I?"

"You never once told me…" She'd seen him muttering away over corpses for more than a decade, but always assumed he was taking mental notes of anatomy—not carrying on conversations.

Horace glanced at her with his sharp eyes. "There are thousands of years of human knowledge to cram into a mere sixty or seventy years of mortality. Might as well review every fact we can, when we can, with whomever we can." His nose wrinkled. "You're getting sloppy. If I see another novel in this house—"

Nora colored. "I hardly read any. They're mostly Julia's."

"*Hardly* isn't none. If you've spare hours, you should be studying. You'll have plenty of time to rest during your confinement."

Nora's gaze jerked from his careful fingers to his face, which betrayed no emotion.

"My what?"

Horace lifted the girl's arm to clean her tiny fingers. "Your pregnancy."

Nora's nostrils flared, his words ricocheting through her brain. "I suppose when the time comes—"

"You truly don't know?" He looked at her over his spectacles, mildly curious.

She pressed her hand to her hip. "Horace!"

Redipping his sponge, he wrung it out again. "I'd say you're four or five weeks along. Check your dates."

"You can't possibly—" Her voice rose with warning.

Horace shrugged. "You've overslept twice. You eat less. You cover your nose more frequently here in the theater, and there's some slight edema around your nostrils—"

Nora's hand flew to her nose, relieved to feel it the exact size and shape she remembered. Edema indeed!

"And I used the water closet after you," Horace added, as if a detective with a case tidily solved.

"What does the water closet have to do with it?" she asked, instantly regretting it.

"I could still smell your urine. I've never been wrong about this before."

"Lord give me strength," Nora muttered. She shook her finger at him. "Don't start any rumors, Horace. If I were expecting—and I'm not—I'd certainly know before you."

Horace shrugged, conceding. *Too easy.* He never gave up a bone without a growl.

Nora continued washing the cadaver, her thoughts numb. Despite his claim, Horace was wrong every day. He'd mistaken Lady Gallatin for a shopkeeper just last week. He'd told the family of a girl with an abscess on her foot she'd likely die— because he'd confused them with the relatives of a man suffering from heart failure (they looked nothing alike). And Mrs. Phipps had caught him eating off a Wedgwood serving tray he'd confused with a plate.

But.

None of those were medical diagnoses.

"When do the students and doctors arrive?" she finally asked when she found her voice again. Anything to change the topic.

"Just after one. Will you sit in?"

Nora sighed. "I better. You can't be the only person in this house who knows how to build noses."

He gave an approving grin. "I'll let you try it yourself tonight after they leave."

Good. She needed more time with the scalpel. Already her fingers felt overlarge and fumbling at the thought of parting skin and muscle. She'd done too much gross motor practice lately and too little of the fine movements required by a surgeon.

"I need to see to the clinic." She excused herself, but didn't exit the corner door to the back staircase. Instead, she slipped into the parlor and paused in front of a mirror. The one above the Japanese table, where the light was best. She tipped her head carefully, scrutinizing her profile.

"What are you doing?" Mrs. Phipps asked, appearing in the reflection over Nora's shoulder.

Nora continued her inspection of the ball of her nose. "Checking to see if my nose is swollen."

"Did you hit it?" Mrs. Phipps's brow creased with worry.

"No. But Horace says it's bigger. Do you think it is?" Unconsciously, her hand wandered to her waist. Her skirt fit as well as ever, but it would, even if he was right.

Mrs. Phipps pursed her lips until they nearly disappeared. "What did he say to you?"

"Absurdities, as usual. He diagnosed me with—" Nora blushed. Mrs. Phipps had never been married, and speaking of such things seemed insensitive. But Mrs. Phipps waited, frowning, for Nora to finish. "He thinks I'm with child."

Choking, Mrs. Phipps forced out a strangled cry. "I'll thrash him. He *told* you?"

Nora's mouth dropped open. "He told *you?*"

"That man!" She flung up her hands. "I ordered him to let you figure it out on your own."

Nora stumbled backward. "What do you mean?" There was no reason to think—

Mrs. Phipps's frustration melted into an appeasing smile, and she stepped closer to Nora, dropping her voice into a confidential tone. "I know you've been distracted, but I oversee the laundry, dear. You're a week late."

CHAPTER 11

MUCH AS SHE WANTED TO, NORA COULDN'T AUTOMATICALLY reject Mrs. Phipps's evidence. Some women kept rigid accounts of their monthlies. And apparently, some—like Mrs. Phipps—kept rigid accounts of *other* women's monthlies. Nora, however, had never been one to count days. There was too much work to get done without worrying about something that inevitably came on its own, whether she expected it or not.

You don't know anything for certain yet, she told herself.

And—this was hard to do—there was no point in thinking about it until she did.

She stumbled over simple tasks and took two wrong turns on her walk to the Roland house. Once arrived, she wasn't ushered immediately to the sitting room of her recovering patients, as she had been on every other visit. The haughty butler instructed her to wait in the hall. Instead of Gladys or Lady Woodbine appearing, she was startled by a harsh voice coming down the stairs, matched by an equally heavy tread.

"Mrs. Gibson, is it?"

She looked up—and willed her face still. Dr. Adams, affronted in every look and line, paused on the stairs, taking advantage of the height to glower down at her, as intractable as the heavy-chinned woman glaring from a massive portrait behind him.

"I prefer 'Doctor,'" she said with a warning edge.

His face spasmed into a frown. "My patient is not in need of your assistance," Dr. Adams said. "I returned to London yesterday and was informed of Mrs. Roland's delivery—and your treatment."

"Yes, it was fortunate Lady Woodbine thought to consult me. Otherwise, Mrs. Roland would have been quite unattended." Remembering what he'd said to Daniel, and what Daniel had then said to her, it was impossible to keep the acid from her voice. But she checked her tone, adding, "I'm here to assess her recovery."

"Unnecessary," Adams declared. "And unwise."

"Unwise?" Alarms jangled faintly in the back corners of her mind.

"I do not think Mrs. Roland needs to be reminded of the way you conducted her birth. I haven't been fully informed, but what I've heard was damaging enough."

Nora stiffened. "Damaging?" She needed to do more than parrot his insults. "I thought you'd be more concerned with the error in your calculation of Mrs. Roland's dates. You've seen little Lily?"

His eyes narrowed over his pointed beard.

"Then you know she wasn't a seven-month child when I delivered her."

He smoothed his face, waving away the evidence of his negligence like a mosquito. "Yes, that does sometimes happen. Clearly there was no need for Lady Woodbine to go into a panic."

"There was every reason, based on what you'd told them. If Lily were that early, she wouldn't have survived."

His brow lowered. "I have something very particular to tell you."

Her blood, heating with each of his words, scalded her chest and face. "Whatever it is, there's no need to proclaim from the stairs like some second-rate stage actor."

He practically flew down the stairs, stopping a mere foot in front of her. Her momentary burst of courage wavered under his scowl. "It would be best for everyone if you left."

"I'm here to follow up with my patient," she said. "Just as I have been for these past three weeks in your absence. She's been nothing but pleased with my care."

"That hardly matters now. *Mr.* Roland has dismissed you from his wife's case."

Nora held her breath. "Why?"

"He was very *dis*pleased by an unnamed account published in the *Provincial*, which I showed him this morning." Adams rocked on his heels. His voice held a note of suppressed satisfaction. "Have you seen the piece?"

Nora blanched, her eyes darting to his. She'd written a detailed account of the labor. Such articles were for doctors only—not patients, and certainly not their family members. The words she'd used—entirely necessary in medical journals— would sound sordid and ugly to anyone other than an investigating doctor. Because Mrs. Roland was a gentlewoman, Nora had withheld her name. She wouldn't have, though, for a working-class patient.

Adams gave a small smile, no doubt reading guilt in Nora's

consternation. "Yes. You see, it matched many of the particulars described to me by Mrs. Roland's maid, Gladys. When I put it to Mr. Roland that the published case could only be referring to his wife"—Adams stepped back, glancing into the hall mirror to adjust his collar—"he said you were not to be readmitted to his house. He was most disappointed at the description of his wife, laboring in a way that you compared favorably to indigenous methods from Africa and the Amazon."

Nora's teeth locked together. Because she had omitted names, Mr. Roland might be upset, but no matter what Adams suspected, neither of them had proof.

"I was particularly concerned," Adams continued, "that you appear to be championing—what was the phrase?—'the reservoir of experience among midwives.'"

"Articles in the *Provincial* are not for laypeople. Any husband would be shocked by an account of his wife—"

"In a public paper? Yes, indeed."

Nora swallowed back a rush of bile. "It's not a newspaper. It's a medical journal for professionals only. As you well know. How dare you make him think I paraded Mrs. Roland in the public—"The words cut off in a rush of nausea.

"You brought in a midwife to treat a distinguished and wealthy woman." How did Adams manage to sound like he was yelling the more he lowered his voice? "You let a midwife put my patient on her hands and knees, like a dog littering puppies."

"That midwife caught your mistake within minutes," Nora retorted, her voice higher than she wished. "If you had bothered to properly examine Mrs. Roland, you wouldn't have erred in your calculations. You might have been here to attend her when she needed it—"

"Be very careful, Mrs. Gibson," Adam said.

"I am." She drew herself up, determined to feign strength, even if she couldn't feel it. "That's why Mrs. Roland is in such excellent health."

"You are not your guardian. I doubt our colleagues will let you voice things they only tolerate from Horace. I certainly will not. Not when you actively propound the virtues of folk remedies and midwives. Are you a doctor, Mrs. Gibson, or a neighborhood woman peddling cures?"

"I'm a doctor. And at least in Mrs. Roland's case, a better one than you."

"You—" He twitched, forcing control on his face. The effort rippled over his features, carrying down his arms and shoulders until at last his hands uncurled. "Things will go badly for you, Mrs. Gibson, if you don't step in line." He reached into his chest pocket and drew out a folded document. "After reading your letter, I started a petition."

He spread out the paper and held it up, inches from her nose.

"Mr. Roland, though not a physician, is a man of considerable standing. He has signed his name. He agreed that you could visit with his wife—one more time, under my direct supervision—if you add your name to this list and never discuss Mrs. Roland's case again, in conversation or in print." He unfolded the paper, already half-filled with signatures—some tight, some looping, in black, Prussian blue, and sepia inks.

Nora scanned it, heart sinking. She knew so many of these

names: Silas Vickery, her old nemesis, who'd probably die
before allowing her or Harry into St. Bart's, where he presided.
Dr. Thompson, who'd once been her ally. Seagrave and Traffett,
who'd both attended her last lecture.

Her eyes narrowed. Clark...Milford. Adams had allowed
dressers to sign their names here, beneath his lines of absolute
drivel.

> *Dangerous precedent steeped in folklore and
> tradition... Need for consistent standards...
> Aim to stop the abuse of vulnerable women
> afflicted by unskilled midwives.*

Abuse? Her hands shook.

"I was there. You weren't, Dr. Adams." Nora snatched the
paper, folded it closed, then handed it back, afraid she'd tear it
in pieces if she kept it even a second longer.

This thing belonged in the fire. Maybe she should have
shredded it.

She could handle criticism. She was used to it.

"I know my work, Dr. Adams, and I know that Mrs.
Franklin did very well with hers. She is neither dangerous nor
unskilled, having been trained extensively by experience and a
medical doctor—"

"You?" Adams mocked.

"Yes. And Mr. Roland should be grateful for her careful
attention to his wife. Neither of us have any mistakes to apologize for." The hot queasiness had passed, and Nora found her
feet firm beneath her. "You should be ashamed of manipulating

her husband into thinking that article would ever be read by his associates or that the nameless patient would be recognized as his wife."

It had been too hasty, writing the case so soon. Adams might not have realized if she'd waited a year or even six months. Nora cursed herself silently and fervently. She'd let regret overtake her later, but not in this man's presence. As for signing his petition—she'd not be blackmailed into anything.

"So you'll not be adding your name with the other physicians?" He paused, about to return the paper to his pocket.

"No. I disagree with every point."

"Once again, setting yourself apart from the profession…" His voice dwindled like someone dangling a string for a cat. She'd not bat at it.

"If signing your absurd document is necessary, I'm afraid that prevents me from seeing my patient today," she said with a coolness she didn't feel.

"It is necessary," Adams said stiffly. "It is essential."

"Well." Nora smoothed her gloves. "Please give Mrs. Roland my regards. She is welcome to consult me again at any time."

Unfortunately, Nora knew she probably wouldn't. That decision had been taken from her.

CHAPTER 12

D ANIEL ROLLED A SHOULDER AGAINST THE TIGHT KNOT forming in his trapezius muscle. The operating tables at Bart's were not designed for tall men, and though surgeries were kept as short as possible—often under twenty minutes— his neck and back squeaked out their complaints.

"You'll notice Mr. Jeffers is constantly checking the vaporizer and mask to ensure the patient is getting the exact dose calculated for his weight. Dr. Croft has not lost a single patient to ether." He angled his voice toward the four students huddled on the other side of the table. "I'd rather you not take notes during the procedure," Daniel said evenly. "They go so quickly. It is more important to observe and feel the techniques."

The student lowered his charcoal pencil right away.

"When retrieving a ball from a gunshot, you want to follow the path of entry as cleanly as possible to avoid extending the injury," Daniel said, indicating the wound on his sedated patient, an older man who'd set off his pistol accidentally and shot himself in the calf. Instead of making a clean exit, it had traveled down his leg and lodged inside.

"Doesn't Croft recommend leaving balls in place?" one of the students asked as Daniel selected a rounded metal probe.

"Internal balls, sometimes. But this one is close to the surface and would likely cause considerable pain before it encapsulated itself in a cicatrix."

The newest student shifted and frowned.

"Scar tissue," Jeffers supplied kindly. He'd been a mere student himself two years ago.

Fortunately, the retrieval went smoothly, and the patient woke without sputtering or confusion as the medical students applauded quietly, their smiles relieved and admiring.

"Now Mr. Jeffers will show you the correct way to dress the wound, which will be especially important to those of you who pursue the work of a military surgeon." Daniel hung his smeared smock on the wall hook and slipped out of the room to rinse the blood from his hands.

"Successful surgery?" Dr. Adams called. He'd spotted Daniel's stained hands, held up in the distinctive pose of doctors protecting their shirt cuffs, as he strode down the hallway.

"Uneventful, yes. Just removing the ball from an accidental shot." Daniel nodded to the two doctors with Adams. He knew them only obliquely, as neither were surgeons.

He stepped forward, but none of them moved aside to let him through. "I should clean my hands before the blood dries," Daniel said with a smile.

"Of course." Adams smoothed his beard. "We were just discussing the petition."

Daniel's fingers curled toward his palms. "What petition?" He'd been involved in more than his share of hospital infighting. If something was brewing, he intended to stay far away— didn't want even a whiff of it.

"There was an article in the *Provincial* about an unusual delivery..."

Daniel's stomach sank a good six inches. The article must be Nora's. He'd read it just the other day. "Forgive me, gentlemen. I really must look after my hands." He wiggled his itching fingers impatiently and started walking.

"We'll accompany you. I'm anxious to hear your thoughts."

"Wonderful." The word sounded pleasant despite his grinding teeth.

Leaving the others behind, Adams followed Daniel into the washroom. Daniel located a clean basin, pumped it full of water, then dipped his hands. The water was cold and soothing, but though it was tempting to pause, he reached for the soap and began working up a lather.

"I'm no Silas Vickery." Adams hooked a thumb on his trouser pocket.

Daniel raised his head just enough that Adams could see his raised eyebrows. "That's good."

Vickery, the head of Bart's board, was twice Adams's size and three times as vicious. He was less known for medical innovation than for his extreme dislike of Horace Croft. Daniel avoided him at all costs.

Adams held up his palms. "I have no desire to start a feud with my colleagues."

"Nor I," Daniel agreed cautiously.

Adams waved a piece of paper as Daniel dried his hands, paying scrupulous attention to the spaces between his fingers and his nails. "This petition argues that innovation in obstetrics must come from doctors. There can be no safe experimentation by the unlearned."

"Like midwives," Daniel said levelly.

"Exactly," Adams said.

"One could argue that there is no true safe experimentation at all," Daniel said.

"Yes, but a physician—a well-trained one—can assess risks, determine if an idea is—"

"My wife is a physician," Daniel announced flatly.

Adams balked. "But the women she's working with certainly are not."

"Our degrees hardly make us immune. Whose idea was it to transfuse Mrs. Colman with milk?" Daniel asked, and Adams flushed.

"Her acute postpartum bleeding required immediate action."

"And her immediate reaction was most unfortunate," Daniel said dryly. Heart palpitations, rashes erupting all over her body, acute nervous shock were all quite unfortunate. Together, they'd nearly been fatal.

Adams continued, his voice as pointed as his sharp beard, "Physicians must present a united front to effect change. Look how long the last medical reform bill took. If we squabble among ourselves—"

"I'm not squabbling." Daniel folded the towel and laid it next to the basin. "I'm in favor of training midwives. I've no wish to attend every delivery in London. You know we can't. There are not enough doctors, and many patients can't afford our fees anyway."

"But they can't be allowed to displace physicians. I make little money from deliveries and lying-in fees when you consider the time involved, but they keep families loyal to me and bring in new generations of wealthy clients."

Daniel knew well enough how happy surgeons would be to forgo obstetrics all together, but it was expected for family doctors to attend to every birth or risk losing the household's business.

Adams continued, "Not to mention, it will stunt discovery. Procedures like your wife's cesarean will never be adopted if she ties herself to mere midwives. And the regulation of doctors, surgeons, and apothecaries is of prime importance. Charlatans and impostors have no place practicing medicine."

"Are you talking about regulation or restriction?" Daniel asked. He had another surgery waiting. He should have been back before now, and his bladder was protesting that it, too, needed attention.

"Aren't they one and the same?" Adams asked.

Daniel shook his head. "No. And you're proposing a completely unworkable solution. What will you do? Prosecute women who have their children at home? Prosecute their mother or sister for helping them?"

"Hardly." Adams somehow managed to straighten his already impeccable posture. "But we can make it clear to the public there is no such thing as a qualified, professional midwife. If the women would only come here where there is an abundance of doctors and surgeons, then—"

"They won't come," Daniel countered. "They're afraid of the hospital. Many more die here."

"They die here because they come as a last resort after a meddling woman with no medical knowledge has done permanent damage."

"That's not true." Daniel kept his voice even. "And your protest needn't be so extreme. Many experienced midwives—"

"Help us modify it, then. We must be united as licensed professionals. And when Vickery's article comes out in the *Provincial*—"

Daniel's eyes narrowed. "What's Vickery saying now?"

"He and several physicians are countering your wife's *position*—ironic play on words, isn't it?—on childbirth and the education of midwives in this field. Cordially, of course."

Daniel closed his eyes for a long blink, savoring the darkness and the break from Adams's meticulously groomed face. First a petition, now opposing articles and papers. "He needn't witch hunt my wife. She merely reported on the results of an unusual labor."

"It certainly was," Adams agreed solemnly. "A wealthy woman who gave birth like an animal in the woods, under your wife's supervision."

"What would you have done, Adams?" Daniel crossed his arms, hoping to hide the thumping in his chest. "If your patient dropped to the floor as the child crowned? Would you have forced her up? Would you even be able to? The laboring woman was larger than my wife."

"Precisely." Adams searched Daniel with a bottomless gaze. "She hadn't the strength or ability. But if *you* or *I* had been there…"

The possibility hovered in the air, as heavy as the grim clouds darkening the window. Daniel shook his head. "Mother and child are safe. Let it be, Adams. I have no desire to brawl with you."

Adams tipped his head in courteous acknowledgment of the compliment. "And I respect you. Enough to give you advance warning that opposition is rekindling against Mrs. Gibson." He brandished the paper again. "Mr. Roland is disgusted over the rumors that the article is about his wife, you know. Your name on the list will appease him."

Daniel frowned. Mrs. Roland's husband was a wealthy man. An influential one known for his caustic temper. He'd make a terrible enemy.

"I haven't even read the thing." Daniel dried his hands with unnecessary violence.

"It's all here." Adams pushed it so close the thing was impossible to ignore.

With a sigh, Daniel read the rambling introduction. He begrudgingly agreed with the language—the consistency of standards, the licensing of those who collected fees for medical procedures. "Be practical," he said with a shake of his head. "Under these conditions, most of our students couldn't attend a birth. Some doctors as well."

Adams lowered his eyebrows. "Nonsense. Any doctor or student well versed in anatomy—"

"The standards should apply to all—not just midwives." Daniel tipped his head back, stretching the painful muscles in his neck as he squeezed his shoulder blades together.

"We need to start somewhere." Adams studied him carefully. "Your wife is once again defying the profession she petitioned so hard to join. It won't end well for her, Gibson."

"Are you threatening my wife?" Daniel tilted his head, eyebrow lifting.

"Not at all. I'm merely warning you out of respect. Right now, I haven't spoken with a single doctor opposed to this petition except her. She'll be excoriated if this keeps on. But if you add your name...I'm giving you a chance to do something to prevent it."

Daniel's eyes narrowed. "Whose name do you really want? Mine or hers?"

Adams laughed. "Well, they're the same, surely. Either way, you'll be setting the example."

Dammit. "I want Nora left alone," Daniel said. "No more articles or rumors."

"Of course." Adams offered his fountain pen.

Daniel gripped the metal cylinder and scrawled a hasty, crooked signature. Nearly unrecognizable. Let these idiots think whatever they wished, as long as they stopped harassing Nora. "There." He thrust the paper and pen back at Adams. "I agree no one should impersonate a doctor or undertake procedures for which they are not trained."

"You see? We are of precisely the same mind." Adams tucked both items back in his pocket. After bidding a good afternoon, he vanished with remarkable speed, leaving Daniel uneasy in his wake.

As he readied his instruments for his next patient, the conversation replayed in jagged fragments, almost nonsensically.

He'd agreed only to safe standards. If anything, it was an argument in Nora's favor—to train more midwives. He fumbled placing a retractor next to his scissors.

Focus, he told himself. *Distraction is dangerous.*

CHAPTER 13

Nora held her breath as Daniel pried at the crate with a crowbar, the thin wood splintering in protest as the nails held stubbornly.

"Careful," she urged.

Daniel pressed the crate against the wall to give himself extra leverage, steadying it with his foot as he wrestled the hardest nail.

"Maybe try another nail first," she suggested.

"It won't matter," Horace said. "The lid won't open until that nail is out. Think of it as a displaced shoulder. Firm, steady pressure until it overcomes the lip of the glenoid and snaps into place."

Now Nora was picturing a patient screaming as she wrenched his arm back into its socket, which didn't calm her nerves at all. There was fragile, finely fired pottery inside this box, sent all the way from Italy at great expense. She'd spent money the household couldn't afford to order these obstetric models, turning the faint black ink of their ledger back to red.

Even Harry had joined them in the surgical theater for the delicate dissection of the shipping box. He leaned against the granite operating table with an amused grin. "Do you need a strong man to help?"

"I'll ask Horace, if it comes to it," Daniel muttered, heaving upward as the nail gave way with a screech. He set the splintered lid on the floor, well away from them.

Horace rubbed his hands together the same way he did before touching a feverish patient to avoid chilling them with cold fingers. "Let the men lift it," he said as Nora reached into the open crate, terrified she'd find only shards wrapped in cotton and paper.

"I can help," she argued, but Daniel and Harry were already grappling with the oddly shaped bundles.

"Wait." Nora grimaced at the stone table. "Don't move it yet." She rushed to the dispensary and snatched several wool blankets and hurried back, fearful they would proceed without her. The three men watched as she arranged the blankets on the polished slab to cushion the newly arrived treasures. "Go on."

She held her breath as Daniel lifted a large bundle and, with Harry's help, hobbled it to the table. "It's bigger than I imagined."

With the care of a woman who'd dissected beetles and houseflies beneath microscopes, Nora unwrapped the fragile prize, peeling away the packing paper one layer at a time. How did anything this fragile survive an ocean voyage with careless sailors and bumpy cart rides through washed-out roads?

A mountain of discarded packing gathered at her feet—up to her knees—before she finally unearthed something with the sheen of white ceramic. Nora held her breath.

Intact.

"Quite the contraption," Daniel said, steadying the strange apparatus on the table—a hollow, headless, limbless torso with a giant, curving glass uterus resting on the tops of the truncated legs. The maker had even created dimples of fat in the thighs. She'd expected terra cotta, burnished, like the color of the Bologna hills, but the clay was fired to an immaculate white.

"*Bellissima*," she whispered.

"Not quite the *Venus de Milo*," Harry said.

Nora gave him an incredulous look. "It's not—" She stopped. This was art, just another kind.

Horace lifted the glass dome and stuck his great head into the empty belly, assessing the accuracy of the size.

"Horace, she's not meant to be worn like a hat," Harry pointed out.

"There's a hole at the bottom, dilated to ten centimeters," Horace said approvingly, voice echoing inside the model.

"Let me see," Harry said, nudging Horace's shoulder. Daniel steadied the apparatus, making sure their movement didn't upset the precious sculpture.

"Both of you, step back," Nora ordered. "We need to lay it down on its back. It's designed to sit upright or be laid down for lectures." She oversaw the careful shift in position as they placed the model on her wool blankets. The sculptor had done his job with care, ensuring the piece was sturdy enough to withstand lectures and demonstrations, and yet gracefully crafted.

"If only births were this easy," Harry said, staring at the yawning hole between the sculpted hips. "So clean and silent."

"Poor Harry." Nora gave him a scathing look. "Are the women too loud for your delicate ears?"

"Sometimes, yes," he grumbled. "I'd rather cut a man's hand

off than listen to a woman suffer like that. I haven't the spine for it."

Nora laughed as Daniel began working to open the second crate. "Are you saying it's best left to women—like the midwives?" she asked with a wicked grin.

Daniel paused and looked at her, face alert. She'd meant only to continue the banter.

"Good Lord, yes. Please let the women do it," Harry said, tugging at his collar. "You won't find me signing that blasted petition. The less births I attend, the better for all of us." He stepped away from the model and began riffling through the rest of the crate.

Horace grunted. "Let's see the rest." In the past, he'd have grabbed the wrapped packages himself, but he still didn't trust his weaker left arm. They arranged the smaller wrapped goods on the table and each began unwrapping. It was better than Christmas Eve.

"It's a boy," Harry announced, holding up a delicately sculpted five-month-old fetus, displayed in situ, in an appropriately sized womb. "He's got some growing to do yet."

Nora's ceramic child was a girl. Full term, the eyes pressed and swollen with meticulous wrinkles in the skin, presenting headfirst—but she'd ordered models with various breech presentations as well.

"Mine's only three months along," Daniel said, holding a tiny baby in one hand. "Not even big enough for the mother to feel yet."

Nora squirmed inwardly. She hadn't confided Horace's and Mrs. Phipps's suspicions to him. Her courses hadn't come, so each passing day suggested they were right. But she'd been irregular before…

She shook her head. No point in saying anything until certain.

"Take a look at this one," Horace said.

He held up a red silk womb, sewn with a placenta that unbuttoned, per Nora's instructions, as well as a long, ropelike umbilical cord. He whistled low. "How much did this all cost me?"

Nora shook her head. "Don't ask. Less than your conservatory."

Daniel continued his inspection of the sculpted child he'd unwrapped, its head obscenely big compared to the tadpole-like legs. "Are you going to sign the petition, Horace?"

Horace looked up from the quilted placenta. "Not a chance. It's too broad. Yes, there are some women calling themselves midwives who should be hung for the damage they do, but you can say the same for several medical students. Some doctors, too."

"It's a farce," Nora stated. "Adams is just using it to get back at me for writing up Mrs. Roland's case. For being right when he was wrong." Now that he'd so obviously targeted her with his petition, if she spread stories about his mistakes, other doctors might think she was making it up out of sheer pettiness.

"Did Adams talk to you?" Daniel studied her too intensely.

Nora bit her lip. "I went to check on Mrs. Roland. Adams was there. Said I couldn't see her unless I signed his petition. I didn't like his tone."

"Did he threaten you?" Daniel demanded with a worried frown. "He's gathered over a hundred signatures now."

So many? "Well, he's not getting mine."

"Did you read the entire petition?" Daniel pressed on. "It said only that we need safe standards."

Nora's nose wrinkled. "But it's using those standards to push midwives out of practice."

Daniel sighed. "You've only been practicing a few months. It doesn't seem the time to incite the entire college of doctors against you."

"You know I've been practicing far longer than that. I'm not worried," Nora said, but this wasn't strictly true. Adams's animosity did concern her, just not enough to back down. What worried her more was Daniel's troubled expression.

"There's a letter with this one." Harry cleared his throat theatrically and held up a folded paper and a model of a six-month fetus, its head nearly proportional but its body too small to survive an early birth.

Recognizing Harry's cue, Nora dropped the discussion and lifted the letter instead, the envelope made of heavy, expensive stationery. "Magdalena," she said without needing to look at the name. She opened it quickly, eyes greedy for the Italian words she hadn't seen in so long.

Her smile broadened as she skimmed past the news of the Grand Hospital of Life and Death, where she'd worked with her mentor and the nuns. She'd savor it later, when the three men weren't watching her every expression. She turned to the second page, dropping her eyes to the last paragraph.

"She says she personally inspected every model and made corrections before they fired them in the kiln. She says the fat baby looks just like her Humberto." Nora smiled, knowing the jokes meant nothing to the others. Humberto had been born two weeks late and, according to Magdalena, had quite over-stayed his welcome.

"You must tell her we approve," Horace said, tracing his finger along one of the smaller fetuses. "I've never seen a model like it."

Nora's eyes misted and she stopped scanning the lines, slowing to read each exquisite word in Magdalena's unhurried script.

"She's telling me to disregard whatever the"—she stopped to find an equivalent word in English—"fussy doctors say. She says I must forge on because mine is not an occupation, but a calling." Nora swallowed, holding back the tears. She didn't translate the next part.

Rimani al tuo posto.

Stand at your post.

It was Magdalena's call to courage and fortitude, as con-vincing as any order ever given to a soldier by a general.

Daniel broke the quiet, jarring her from her thoughts. "These models are incredible. But I still think it might be easier for you to attract students if you signed the petition."

"I think—" She broke off, troubled by the deep furrow between his eyebrows.

Maybe it was better not to answer. If they had been alone, she would have reached out and touched his sleeve, showing she was only opposed to Adams, not him.

"I don't think a single person in this household consid-ers ease when making decisions." Harry sighed. "Look at this ludicrous lady, shipped all the way from Italy. We'll need to

name her. Best do it now before Mrs. Phipps overrides you."
Bestowing names on random creatures, living and stuffed, fell
typically to her.

"I like Mara," Nora blurted out. Daniel gave her a baffled
frown, and she shrugged. It seemed to fit.

Horace was now probing the vaginal opening, measuring it
with his fingers and nodding appreciatively. "It would be nice
to make a cloth one to have a bit of stretch. Do you think we
could find a seamstress—"

"A London seamstress? To re-create a vulva? No, Horace, I
truly doubt we could." Nora let his daydream shatter into shards
as he sulked in disappointment. "But we'll make some cloth
dolls with softer heads to demonstrate births and allow the
mi—our students," she corrected hastily, "to practice turning
babies, placing forceps, and delivering different presentations."

Horace's eyes lit up, and he and Harry began rattling off
ideas about jointed limbs and how to make the dolls slippery.
Nora caught remnants that included cod liver oil and vulca-
nized rubber.

Daniel was quiet, busy sweeping up splinters from the crate.

"Are you worried about Dr. Adams?" she asked quietly,
trying to catch his eye.

"He works at St. Bart's. I have to deal with him."

"You know I can't sign it. It's completely against my prin-
ciples. I'm right in the middle of trying to train the midwives. I
could never lend my support to anything that bars women from
birthing rooms." Until the college decided to admit women (a
possibility that seemed more impossible every passing week),
working as a midwife was the only option if a woman wanted

to practice any field related to medicine. Nora couldn't rest until she made others see the absurdity of the arrangement.

Daniel nodded, refusing to look at her, and untied his apron. "Of course not."

CHAPTER 14

Daniel returned to the house on Great Queen Street an hour earlier than usual, knowing he'd need the extra time. He and Nora were expected for dinner at his parents' home in Richmond. His family was prickly at the best of times, but he felt as much enthusiasm for tonight's event as the salmon that would grace the table.

Daniel had managed to avoid speaking any more to Harry or Horace about the petition, but he'd soon be confined to a small carriage with Nora, and she was far more discerning. *Stupid to have signed it.* He needed to explain soon, but if she took the news badly, he didn't know how he'd manage to socialize for hours in front of all his family, like nothing was the matter. What would they think if she shot dagger eyes at him all evening?

Best to explain to her after the dinner party.

As it was, any exposure to his family put her on edge. Facing his disapproving mother was enough anxiety for one night.

Daniel checked his watch. They must leave by five, and it was already past four. By now, Nora would be in the middle of wrestling with her hair and dress choices. He'd reassure her, calm her nerves, and be a faultless husband the entire evening. It would smooth the blow when he told her he'd signed Adams's petition. Hopefully.

Upstairs, Nora's one fine dress—ruffled green taffeta, which she'd worn to meet his parents and to their wedding—hung silent and limp on the door of the wardrobe. No sign of her. Daniel checked his watch again.

"Nora?"

No answer. He crossed the hall, but she wasn't in the bath. He gritted his teeth. She must have forgotten. He'd meant to remind her this morning before leaving for the hospital, but when he'd checked on the wombat, the creature rooted hungrily against his hand, so he'd spent his last few minutes at home pulling a few tulip bulbs from pots in the conservatory to feed her. When he remembered their dinner plans this afternoon, while writing patient notes for the surgical ward, it was too late to send a message.

Perhaps she'd attended a long case.

On purpose.

Not that he'd blame her. No one could sniff as effectively as his mother. And she possessed a gift for inviting whatever guests made the evening least enjoyable. With her talent, she could very well have invited Mae, his one-time fiancée, no matter that she was also newly married. Or Silas Vickery, who hated Daniel only half as much as he despised Nora but would be an impeccable dinner guest. Daniel closed his eyes, dispelling the thought. It wouldn't be so bad as that.

Unlike Nora, Daniel didn't mind time with his family, despite their stuffy mores. Particularly his sister Joan, still without any prospects of marrying, but who refused to quell the wicked humor his mother blamed for her failures in love. And his widowed aunt, who had no children of her own but carried on several ambitious charitable and social projects. She was fierce but kindhearted, rather like Horace in some ways—not that he'd ever dare make such a comparison aloud.

Despite his parents' dismay, Aunt Wilcox had supported his medical ambitions, and she made no secret she intended him to be her heir. She was a formidable woman, whom he respected. They had an austere and enduring affection for each other.

Daniel returned downstairs, peering into the drawing room, the consulting rooms, and the library, where he stopped.

She wasn't attending a case.

Nora filled Horace's favorite chair, dozing with a book in her lap, her work smock still tied over her dress and a pencil skewered through the listing knot of her hair.

She was not a woman who put much store in flattery or useless compliments, but her smooth cheek against the wing of the chair was pink with sleep, and the wayward curl catching her eyelashes...

"Nora?" he whispered gently and knelt down, suddenly tempted to press his lips on hers in a way he hadn't for days.

"Hmm?" She stirred.

"I forgot to remind you this morning. Dinner tonight. At Whitewood." It was easier naming the house than his family. "It's already quarter past four."

Her face spasmed into a frown, and she muttered something indecipherable in Italian as her eyes shot open. "Sorry. I remembered. I just lost track of time. It'll be all right, though, so long as we hurry."

The book thudded to the floor as she stood and plucked at the ties of her smock with bleary eyes and clumsy hands.

"Let me," he offered, using the excuse to bend close to her neck, grazing her hair with his forehead. Tiny static shocks ran over his scalp.

As soon as he freed her from the apron, she hurried for the stairs, unaware of his longing. "My dress is laid out already, and if I don't wash my hair…" Nervously, she reached for the loose knot. Daniel could almost see her rapid assessment, weighing the lingering smell of pungent medications with the hours it would take to soap and dry her thick tresses. Last month she'd actually suggested cutting it, but he'd averted that tragedy, bombarding her with so many lines of archaic poetry that she'd collapsed with laughter and sworn to give up the idea.

"I'll brush it with that rose-scented powder," Daniel offered. Cracking a smile, he requoted one of his earlier arguments in favor of keeping her hair long:

"Hir hair displayit as the goldin wyre,

Aboif hir heid with bemys radient…"

Nora snorted. "I'm glad you think so." But the smile she sent over her shoulder betrayed her pleasure.

Now if he could just keep her grinning until the end of the evening.

His mother's dining room was at its best that evening, attired as elegantly as the guests gathered around the table. None of them controversial, to Daniel's relief: a neighboring member of Parliament of the Whig persuasion—which was perhaps why he appeared so glum, as they'd had little success with Peel in power—and a country doctor from Berkshire and his wife.

Candles and silver and crystal shone, and it was evident his mother had taken some trouble in selecting the menu, including the salmon Daniel had predicted, wrapped within an exquisitely crafted pastry case and decorated to look like it had scales and fins. Even more remarkable was the degree of congeniality shown to Nora, who was seated in the place of honor between Aunt Wilcox and his father. A smile lurked in the corners of her mouth, and the only time her brow puckered was between bites when she glanced at her dull knife—adequate for cutting the venison on her plate, but a much clumsier tool than the scalpel she was used to. Daniel took an amused sip of wine and returned his attention to his mother.

"I'm glad to see Aunt Wilcox tonight," Daniel murmured. As usual, she appeared entirely ageless—chin firm despite the deep creases around her mouth, silver hair as thick and becoming as it had been when he was a child. To him, Aunt Wilcox had never been young and would never grow old.

When his parents had balked at Daniel's proposal to marry Nora, it had been Aunt Wilcox who frowned imperiously and insisted they all calm down. "She might not be from a fine family, but she is the sole heir to the most famous physician in England. That counts for something." Daniel's cheek flickered as he fought back a smile from the memory.

"She's missed you," his mother said, swirling her wine. "You know she still has hopes you'll take up the role of a private physician—"

"Does she still intend to visit Germany?" Daniel interjected.

"Not this year," his mother said, lace cuffs swaying as she replaced her glass. "Your aunt is very caught up in the concerns of that society of hers. Next year, when she is no longer the vice president…"

Mother had a habit, recently acquired, of not finishing her sentences. Perhaps it was meant to be fashionable, but Daniel's smile stiffened. His aunt was involved with any number of *societies*, and he didn't feel magnanimous enough to give his mother the pleasure of asking which one.

"And Joan?"

"I may have to take her myself." Mother would be pleased to see Joan form an attachment to an eligible gentleman met at a foreign spa town. Happier still if she returned home engaged to be married. Daniel was warier of the idea, but—"We must make sure she is in good company," his mother finished.

There would be no doubt of that.

Daniel glanced along the table, his mouth hitching upward as he caught Nora's eye.

Still smiling.

CHAPTER 15

AFTER FIVE COURSES SITTING BETWEEN DANIEL'S FATHER and his formidable aunt, Nora craved Daniel's easier company. As the remains of a cream tart congealed on the fine china, Daniel's aunt pushed back her chair and stood. "Shall we?" She pointed the question to the women.

Tea with the ladies first in the drawing room, while the gentlemen remained at the table for tobacco and port. It wasn't a custom they kept at home, and longing for her dressing gown and bedroom slippers already, Nora held in her sigh. This was easily the best evening she'd spent in her in-laws' company, and she couldn't ruin it with waning enthusiasm. Tacking an agreeable smile to her lips, she stalled until Joan reached her. As they fell into step, her sister-in-law sent her a mischievous look.

Before Nora could install herself safely next to Joan on the sofa, her mother-in-law captured her arm in a soft grip. Hiding a start, Nora turned with raised brows. "Yes, Sarah?" Though Daniel's mother had asked her to call her *Mama*, Nora simply couldn't bring herself to do it. She'd called no one by that name since she was eight years old. Replacing *Mrs. Gibson* with *Sarah* had been hard enough.

"Are you eating adequately? I'm not sure my son is taking sufficient care of you..." Sarah Gibson's eyes spanned Nora's waist, measuring the inches. The secret possibility she'd still not confessed to Daniel made her wary of attention on her figure.

"Dinner was excellent," Nora returned, smoothing any crispness out of her voice.

"You know, you and I haven't exchanged a word—"

"Not easy, all the way across the table," Nora said.

"You must sit with me now," Sarah commanded, steering her across the drawing room, where Aunt Wilcox was already ensconced in an armchair. A satisfied look passed between the older ladies, sending a frisson of danger tiptoeing up Nora's spine. She glanced back—but the doctor's wife had persuaded Joan to seat herself at the piano. No escape. Lulled by food and kindly chatter throughout dinner, she hadn't prepared herself for a private conversation with the other significant women in Daniel's life.

Unbidden, she thought of Horace, who was probably back at home, reading in the library beside his stuffed zebra, Enzo. She wished she could trade him for her current company, or have him suddenly appear—wombat in one hand, medical journal in the other—and startle this sedate company into commotion.

Nora held back a snort. If she could manage Horace, she could surely find a way to satisfy Daniel's relatives for another hour. Daniel's mother deposited her in a cramped little chair angled between herself and Aunt Wilcox, and the familiar sensation of preparing for a surgery washed over Nora: lungs filling, ears tuned to every sound, her eyes alert and focused. "What a lovely dinner," she began. "Thank you so much for having us."

"Lord Parkins was dull as soup," Aunt Wilcox countered in a voice too flat to travel to any other ears in the room. "Joan teased him all night and he didn't even realize." She pursed her lips and cast a small glare across the room at her niece.

"I'm sorry I missed that." Nora gave a small, conspiratorial laugh that died under the weight of Sarah's disapproving frown.

"The girl is incorrigible. I wash my hands of her."

Nora swallowed, rearranging her face to the proper soberness. She could do with a sip of port like the men.

"I was seated with Dr. Russell and his wife." Sarah's lip twitched almost imperceptibly, but the negligible movement sent a twinge through Nora's stomach. "He suspects that you are the doctor mentioned in some medical articles of late." Her gray eyes looked cold as river rocks, despite her demure smile. "Do tell."

Nora froze, sensing a trap.

"Hardly interesting," she lied. "Only a scientific discussion on childbirth. I'm sure it's not pleasant conversation for your drawing room."

"Dr. Russell appeared very interested. He said that you've put yourself at odds with London physicians."

Nora resented the familiar heat and panic that overtook her whenever someone ambushed her. It made it impossible to speak intelligently. "I'd rather not—"

"Don't be defensive, dear. This isn't an attack." Aunt Wilcox possessed the most agile eyebrows. They angled down as if looking at Nora from a hundred feet above.

Sarah tittered, fussing unnecessarily with her bracelets. "You're my daughter in-law. I'm trying to know you better."

"I didn't know you followed medical debate," Nora asked more than stated.

Sarah plucked again at a bangle, but Aunt Wilcox, made of sterner stuff, snorted instead of dithering. "We hardly follow it. But it does seem to follow you. It must be exhausting to pit yourself against the world so relentlessly."

Nora schooled her face, refusing to show Aunt Wilcox how her arrow had landed. "I'm afraid it comes with the calling of medicine sometimes," she said cautiously.

Aunt Wilcox folded her hands, wrinkled fingers rearranging around her large collection of rings. "I'm quite impressed with your intelligence," she said. "I'm very modern myself, as you know."

"Of course," Nora choked out.

"I have friends intrigued by your experience and ability," Aunt Wilcox informed her. "Members of my society."

"It's a service society," Sarah put in. "The British Ladies' Society for Promoting the Reformation of Female Prisoners." She stopped to draw breath.

Nora's spine stiffened. Every sentence of this conversation was a blind turn. She'd already lost her balance several times. "I've heard of them. And of course, I'm familiar with the reputation of the late Mrs. Fry. She was fighting for separate female prisons, I understand? It's a brilliant idea."

Aunt Wilcox bowed her head solemnly, pausing a moment, as if silently joining a prayer at church. "A remarkable woman," she said.

"Remarkable," Sarah echoed. "And your aunt—"

Daniel's aunt, Nora silently corrected.

"I'm quite involved in the work," Aunt Wilcox said. "Progress has been made, but there's much to be done. Prison conditions are only half the battle. Once the women are released, there is the need for teaching work skills, schooling for their children, obtaining respectable employment—not to mention inspecting prisons across the kingdom and petitioning the Crown when they are not complying with the Gaol Act." She paused, gauging Nora's reaction. "I was with Mrs. Fry, you know, when she addressed the select committee of the House of Lords, but that was probably before you were born."

Nora worked some moisture into her mouth as Joan's piano music lifted its plaintive notes. "How incredible," she said. "I didn't know."

Aunt Wilcox acknowledged the compliment with the smallest of nods. "Please don't take it unkindly if I say there is much you don't know, being brought up as you were. I would never dispute Dr. Croft's genius—he's endorsed by many distinguished persons—but I think it a shame you were raised so far from ladies' influence."

Nora opened her mouth, ready to spring up in defense of Mrs. Phipps, who was as principled and genteel as any woman in the room.

Aunt Wilcox cut her off with practiced efficiency. "However, it's not too late for you. We've lost our treasurer. I put your name forward, and in spite of your unusual credentials and the fact that you'd be a brand-new member of the society, the board members are disposed to consider you for the position."

"As society treasurer?" Nora frowned, glancing between the two women, unable to hide her bafflement. "You see, I've never kept books." *At least, not well, according to our ledgers.* "That's very kind of your friends, but I'm afraid I'm unqualified." Their magnanimous smiles melted, morphing into affronted frowns. Nora tried again, tripping over her clumsy words. "It's obviously very important work, but I'm responsible for a private hospital and lectures…"

Daniel's mother wore her offense visibly on her pinched lips and stiff cheeks.

Nora scrambled for a peace offering. "I could apply for membership. It's a worthy cause."

Aunt Wilcox frowned deeply, but Nora couldn't tell if it was in thought or disapproval. Nora held her breath, the seconds expanding in the perfumed air of the drawing room.

Aunt Wilcox leveled her heavy gaze. "You see, child, we had hoped to persuade you to put down some of your other causes and adopt this one."

"What other causes?" Nora asked, bristling at the older woman's tone.

Aunt Wilcox pursed her lips. "There's no point pretending. We know you've earned the displeasure of most of the respectable doctors in London. You cannot fail to realize some of that disapproval taints our family."

"A discussion is hardly censure," Nora countered.

Aunt Wilcox snapped her fan open. "I came here with hopes you'd put your intelligence to work in ways other than the brutalities of medicine. You can be exceptional and renowned by other means. Like Mrs. Fry."

"I wouldn't call my work brutal—" Nora objected.

"There will be children eventually," Sarah pointed out, confirming Nora's fears over her earlier interest in her waistline.

"Aunt's society would give you an outlet for your considerable talents, as well as a level of respectability."

Nora coughed, searching for air. "Do you mean to say I'm not respectable?"

Aunt Wilcox silenced them both with an upraised hand. "If Nora joined our society, we could channel her talents in a more"—she gave Sarah a knowing look—"admirable direction. If she took up the cause of women with us, she could be an inspiration instead of a singularity."

Singularity.

Tears gathered, but not only in her eyes. She felt them in her shaking chin. Her burning skin. *Too emotional. Too weak.*

"Sarah misspoke," Aunt Wilcox soothed. "You are certainly respectable. She meant to say we could give you a level of protection."

The loose curls around Nora's ears wavered as Aunt fanned the air. "Protection from what?"

"That's an odd question for a woman who is the object of a circulating petition," Sarah's quiet words sizzled like the air before a lightning strike.

"I've heard patients have been slow to accept you, and Dr. Croft's usually successful clinic is struggling financially," Aunt Wilcox added. She left the last words unsaid—*because of you.*

Nora fixed her eyes on the drawing room door, willing the men to enter.

"I have plenty of female patients," she defended. "Only the males are reluctant."

"Of course they are. As I'm sure we all predicted." Aunt

Wilcox had a way of pushing you through your worst pains briskly and efficiently. "But if we could win over some influential women, we may be able to help fund your clinic so you can hire other doctors to do the menial work. You can run it as you would a charity."

"Abandoning surgery?"

Sarah's eyes rolled upward as if she were praying for strength. "Lord, yes. You'll have to, once you have children, so I don't see—"

They didn't see at all. Had no concept of the elation of freeing someone from pain or even closing the door against death with a resounding thud. They were done prancing around the truth and it emboldened Nora. "I can't be a treasurer," Nora said. "I don't have the time or training."

They didn't see at all.

"That's no obstacle," Aunt Wilcox said impatiently. "If you can run your small hospital, surely you can learn to keep financial records. Every good housekeeper can manage that."

CHAPTER 16

H EART THUDDING, LIPS PINCHED TIGHT, NORA CAST HER eyes over the room, searching for an escape, when the far door opened, revealing her father-in-law at the front of the short parade of men, ringed in a cloud of fragrant smoke.

Nora exhaled.

Daniel. He was used to his family's meddling and would handle them expertly. She nearly sprang to her feet but held herself in place, drawing up whatever shreds of dignity remained.

Daniel's relaxed posture proved he'd endured no such interrogation. He took his time locating her, unaware of the hammering in her chest. With a languid wave of the hand, he crossed the room. Too slowly. Sarah and Aunt Wilcox awaited her answer with pointed looks.

"What are you three gossiping about?" Daniel asked as he leaned over them. He'd not yet picked up on her tension.

"We've only touched on the gossip." Aunt Wilcox stopped her slow fanning. "I've offered Nora a distinguished position with the British Ladies' Society for Promoting the Reformation of Female Prisoners."

Daniel laughed. "Dear heavens, that's more of a mouthful than my anatomy tomes."

Aunt Wilcox narrowed her eyes. As did Nora. The name of

the society was the least of her worries. And he'd had more than one glass of port.

The older doctor from the other end of the dinner table approached with his wife.

"Dr. Russell"—Aunt Wilcox shot one last glare at Daniel before fixing a welcoming smile to her face—"volunteers with our society. He's treated several of our women after their terrible ordeals in the jails."

"Dreadful conditions," Dr. Russell agreed. "But my wife wanted to come see the lady doctor this evening. Rumors reached us in Berkshire."

Mrs. Russell was heavy-jowled, her skin sliding down her aging face like a landslide. She dipped her head at Nora.

It gave Nora a chance to stand. She'd been a bird perched between two cats for too long. And perhaps the woman's admiration would quiet Daniel's relations. "I'm Mrs. Gibson, surgeon."

The woman took her fingers in a weak grasp. "Surgeon? I thought you were only a physician."

Dr. Russell laughed. "Not that conversation tonight. I've witnessed two scuffles at the Athenaeum Club over the regulations for each royal college." He wagged his finger at Daniel and Nora. "You mustn't join ranks against me because I'm only a physician."

The cutthroat debate continued as always, well known and fraught with casualties. Beside her, Daniel grinned. "We run a charity clinic and see our fair share of all three branches of medicine. Nora specializes in obstetrics."

"Midwifery." Mrs. Russell sighed with relief and smiled at Nora. "I imagined you…" Her face pinked. "Well, never mind."

"Yes, I saw Adams's petition to outlaw unlicensed midwives and send business to trained doctors like yourself." Dr. Russell nodded with a satisfied grin. He thought he was complimenting her. "Of course, I live outside of London, so I cannot sign it, but I certainly would."

Nora dipped her eyes, following the curving red line of the Turkish carpet beneath them.

"Petition?" Aunt Wilcox asked. They were speaking her language. She'd pitched complaints before Parliament and gathered signatures the way other ladies collected china figurines.

Dr. Russell lowered his voice and straightened his vest. "Everyone was howling over an anonymous article where a midwife forced some duchess onto the floor on hands and knees to deliver a baby."

Nora ground her teeth. He'd gotten it entirely wrong.

Daniel's smile fled, his lips parted as if searching for words.

"What in the world was a midwife doing with a duchess?" Sarah demanded.

She wasn't a duchess. Mrs. Roland held money, but no title.

"The doctor brought her," Dr. Russell said with an incredulous lift to his voice. "Apparently the midwife took over when the doctor panicked."

Aunt Wilcox gasped. "No."

Nora opened her mouth but caught the shake of Daniel's head, barely perceptible but enough to freeze her. Russell was as errant on the facts as the many doctors who'd been published in the paper this week, decrying her case. She didn't mind now that Daniel had insisted she sign her article only under her initials.

"Fortunately"—Dr. Russell panted a bit breathlessly from the port and the excitement of a captive audience—"the doctors started a petition to prevent any such error from occurring again."

"Daniel?" His mother looked to him for both confirmation and apology for not telling her such salacious news.

He gave the slightest shrug, his color decidedly more yellow than when he'd first approached them.

"She wasn't a duchess and the doctor didn't panic." Nora couldn't resist.

"Did you sign the petition?" his aunt asked, ignoring her.

Now he would explain the true facts of the case. Nora waited, forgetting to exhale.

"There's always more than meets the eye…" he began reasonably.

Aunt Wilcox scoffed in exasperation and dropped her fan. "You didn't sign it? Why must you always make unnecessary difficulties?"

"Don't scold your nephew," Dr. Russell said, looking pleased to once more command the center of the conversation. "I'm sure he signed the petition. And certainly his signature counts for his wife as well."

"No, he didn't—" Nora blurted out.

"Yes." Daniel spoke over her, covering her words. "I did."

It didn't make sense the way the notes of the piano continued drifting across the room when everything else froze. Words tripped over Nora's paralyzed ears, falling before they reached her. She saw only the purple shadows under Daniel's cheeks. He mottled when embarrassed.

She would have demanded an explanation if she'd been able to find her tongue. Her feet shook, strangely disconnected from her legs.

"Thank the good Lord." Aunt exhaled in relief. "I'm sorry I accused you. You're growing some sense at last." Her blue eyes marched over her nephew, showing a glint of pride that made Nora inexplicably despondent.

Void of other ideas, Nora fixed her eyes on Daniel's married sister carrying on what looked like a painful conversation with the doleful Whig MP. "I believe Lillian needs me," she murmured, not at all concerned how her abrupt exit would be perceived. She felt Daniel's eyes track her across the room, as firm and sure as a touch.

A memory clutched at her throat. The same difficult breaths, her vision fuzzing at the periphery, her feet unable to feel the floor beneath her. She'd walked like this before.

The Stabat Mater Hall.

Visions arose of the vast room in Bologna where four professors had interrogated her for hours with medical questions before reluctantly signing her surgeon's license. The stifling air. The red curtains. The curled lips and narrowed eyes. She drew up silently to Lillian's side with a show of composure she didn't feel.

"Excuse me, Mr. Briscoe," Lillian said to the MP. "I've not seen my sister-in-law in months." She took Nora's arm in a grateful crunch of fingers and led her to a solitary sofa in the corner. Nora's eyes flitted to the mantel clock. Half an hour until she could escape to the dark, quiet interior of their carriage and sift through the wreckage of their conversation.

Had he said yes only to deflect their ire?

The possibility allowed her to take a full breath as she closed her eyes for a moment.

Lillian gestured to a deck of cards. "Shall we?"

Nora nearly turned her down, but that would require an explanation. However, she needed something that required less concentration than whist. "Snap?"

"Why not?" Lillian giggled, adding in an undertone, "What did you talk about with Mama and Aunt Wilcox? They had you cornered from the first moment. They looked like they were plotting a revolution."

"I—"

"No, I didn't mean it," Lillian interrupted. "And you don't have to tell me. They'll both be moaning about it later. I'll hear it all then."

Charming.

Lillian dealt out the cards and smiled at Nora. "Poor dear. I know they can be fearsome." Her eyes traveled slowly from Nora's face to her skirt, and a line of concern burrowed between her eyebrows. "We need to get you another gown. I do love that one, but I've seen you in it three times now. Don't you own any other dresses?"

Joan's music came to a pounding stop, the echo ringing through the room. Nora glanced at the clock again, waiting for deliverance. Whoever called surgery brutal had never suffered through such a dinner party.

CHAPTER 17

Nora glanced at the clock. The immovable minute hand had mysteriously twined itself around her spine like a vise, her muscles tightening with every tick. She strained to carry on two conversations at once—one outward with Lillian and Joan, the other internal as she reviewed several versions of explanations from Daniel. Infuriatingly, mercifully—despite her need for explanations—he kept his distance, half-concealed by an urn filled with palm fronds, carrying on with his parents and his aunt and the Russells. But Nora read his discomfort from fifteen feet away, betrayed by the small twitch at the bottom of his jaw.

Stalling.

He lingered half an hour later than they'd agreed upon. By the time he finally brought Nora her shawl, her tendons were carved from stone.

They ducked into their carriage in a stiff, icy silence. Their driver was half-deaf, but Lillian was not, and the house windows were all open. Nora waited until they exited the drive before she attempted any words at all.

"What did you mean when you said you signed the petition?"

Daniel inhaled. "I got cornered by Adams soon after he started it. I've meant to tell you, but… I was going to tell you tonight."

She stared wordlessly, so many questions battling for dominance that none emerged.

"He makes a decent point, Nora, and any medical laws take ages. That's to our advantage. It would be a miracle if anything actually passed Parliament in Mrs. Franklin's lifetime, and signing helps you avoid a row with the other doctors." He looked so confident in his explanation. "I just did it to silence your detractors."

"You signed it and disagreed with it?" This from a husband who'd stood up to his parents and warded off the entire medical establishment to protect and marry her? Afraid of Adams?

"I told him I disagreed with parts of it. I only agree that women—and men," he added quickly, "who aren't trained shouldn't be able to pretend to have skills they don't. The same as barbers who are still taking out teeth and setting bones."

The driver took a side lane, and the rhythmic clopping of the mare's hooves turned into a dull squelch as the carriage settled into the heavy ruts.

"*Dannazione,*" she muttered under her breath. Cursing worked much better in Italian.

Daniel didn't ask for a translation.

"Did you think for a moment how it will appear, signing a petition opposing their practice just as I'm starting classes to enhance their training?" Nora demanded. "We'll look like fools."

"Classes? What are you talking about?" Daniel crossed his arms, and Nora realized she was doing the same, locked in place.

"It only makes sense if doctors are fussing about licenses. Give midwives classes and lectures so people know the good ones from the bad."

"The Royal College of Physicians will hardly take kindly to that."

"That's why we need examples to help them see—"

"I only knew you had invited them to your open lectures. When were you going to tell me this plan?" The shadows were too deep to see his face, but she didn't need to. Accusation rang clear in his voice.

"When?" Her voice climbed and sharpened. "You want to know when, after you didn't tell me you signed a petition written by a doctor who's maligning me to everyone he knows? Mr. Roland won't even let me speak to his wife anymore. He threatened to write a letter—"

"I know," Daniel said heavily. "He's still submitting it. But he agreed not to expose you by name because I signed. He's only going to refer to you by initials, like you did with his wife." He had the audacity to look relieved.

"Daniel!" she snapped. If only he could hear himself. "You knew he was writing to oppose me and you still—"

"Did the reasonable thing," he finished curtly.

She nearly yanked the bell to stop the carriage and leap out. "I'm being perfectly reasonable. *I* haven't signed anything we agreed not to."

"I never said I wouldn't sign it," he blurted out. "You never asked my opinion, Nora."

She froze as if struck. "You agree with Adams?"

The pain in her voice unlocked his arms, and he held up a

hand in supplication. "Partly. When caring for patients, everyone must be accountable. We must be sound and scientific."

"And I'm neither?"

Even in the darkness of the enclosed coach, Nora saw Daniel roll his eyes. "Please don't do this. I'm trying to have a fair discussion."

"I'm not fair now, either?" It seemed much more unfair to take the enemy's side with no warning. "I put up with your impossible relatives all evening. Your mother and aunt attacked me, pushing me to renounce medicine, after all my work, so I could keep their books!"

"Attack? I thought it a generous offer. And it doesn't mean you have to accept."

"What a relief," Nora spat out sarcastically. She needed air, but hard darts of rain had begun smacking the side of the carriage, and she couldn't open the window.

"I only mean that they meant it as a compliment," Daniel said finally, rubbing the back of his neck.

Nora released a strangled scoff.

"Our world is so distant from theirs. They're trying to find a way to reach you." He glanced at the roof as the sound of the rain increased. "You've hardly made any effort to befriend them."

Nora pressed her lips together. "Would you find it a compliment if they offered you the position? If they tried to rip *you* from medicine? They want me to give up my own hospital."

"Words, Nora." He sighed. "You needn't load them with such powder. They're not *ripping* anything. They offered you a prestigious position that would help women."

Something crept into his weary voice that sent jolts of warning through her stomach.

"Do you agree with them about that as well? That I should stop practicing?"

Daniel gave an evasive groan. "That's an absurd question. And I don't think we should discuss it now."

She stared at her husband—a person she'd known when she woke up this morning. Tears dove onto her lashes, hovering at the edge of a cliff before plunging down her face.

He sighed again. "Of course I don't want you to give up the clinic and hospital. We've all worked too hard. I only meant they were trying to honor you in their way. You're not used to them."

Indeed, she was not. And apparently, she wasn't entirely used to Daniel. As her silence stretched thin, he continued.

"Someday, when we have children, you'll need a way to channel your talents."

She jerked her head up, panic spinning in her chest. *Had Horace told?*

Oblivious, Daniel went on, "A prestigious society would let you keep your influence even when you're not practicing. It is just something to think over. For the future."

He blurred into the periphery as she followed the raindrops twisting down the window and catching the orange fire of the streetlamps. She wanted Mrs. Phipps and Horace to be right about the pregnancy, but when she thought of abandoning her patients, her calling…

His hand landed on her leg, and she flinched. He stubbornly kept it in place despite her frown. "I never wanted to argue with you. You know I adore you."

Her eyes flashed to him, dull question marks.

He pulled his hand slowly back into his lap.

"When we have children, my medical career will be over?" Nora's voice tasted like lead.

He looked at her as if peering at a stranger.

She knew the feeling.

"How could you perform surgeries with infants at your feet?" It wasn't an angry question. Only a baffled one.

Magdalena. She has a son.

Nora's eyes twitched.

Out of wedlock and raised by her lover's wife. Humberto had never interrupted Magdalena's career because she'd never done more than hand him off to others. Somehow, Nora had forgotten.

"Mrs. Phipps and Julia could watch our children. Or a nurse."

Daniel kept staring, his eyes mirrors of her own disappointment.

The ride home would take the better balance of an hour. Nora closed her eyes, fighting against the headache mounting behind her left temple. Silence and dejection wedged themselves between her and Daniel, burrowing their sharp elbows onto the cramped bench. Such crushing intruders made speech impossible.

After a drive as painful and prolonged as the time spent in the Gibsons' drawing room, the familiar silhouette of 43 Great Queen Street finally loomed out of the humid night. The driver dropped them off at the covered side entrance.

Where the cadavers arrive.

Something in Nora felt lifeless enough to make it appropriate.

"Nora." Daniel's voice pricked the back of her neck as she stepped inside the shadowy corner giving access to the lift and back staircase. Mrs. Phipps had decorated every square inch of the renovated home and hospital except here. The new tiles the workmen had laid were blank—white with small black diamonds scattered in gloomy intercessions. It was hardly Nora's favorite place to pause. No matter how much soap and lime the maids used, the lingering smell of rot tinged the air.

"Let's not be angry with each other. We can each forgive—"

Her bowed head shot up, blurring the room. "Have I offended you? Do I owe you an apology?" She hadn't used this acidic tone with him since the early days of meeting him—before she loved him—when he was simply a trespasser in the established routine she'd built with Horace.

"You won't speak to me." His mistake was the stern bite at the end of his sentence. "Yes, that is unkind." When he was sad, she had no defenses whatsoever. But she could resist anger. Match it. Surpass it.

"Not speaking is the kindest thing I can do at the moment."

She mounted the back stairs and pushed through the hanging curtain to the surgical theater.

"Nora," he called behind her. Just as she emerged into the hallway off the parlor, Julia appeared in her wrap and slippers.

Nora rearranged her face so Julia knew the ominous glare was not for her.

"A messenger came for you a few minutes ago." Julia lowered her eyebrows in concern as Daniel appeared, his expression equally perturbed. Her words slowed to a crawl. "The midwife, Mrs. Howell, asking for assistance. Harry's getting dressed."

Nora glanced at her taffeta dress. "Tell him not to bother. I'll go right away, as soon as I change my clothes. And tell the driver not to untack the horse." Nora could pack her bag in the dispensary and hang her dress on the linen wardrobe there. No need to even go upstairs if Julia fetched her work clothes.

Julia sent her a questioning look before hurrying off.

"Harry could still go, if you want to talk."

She hadn't forgotten Daniel, though she'd angled herself to avoid seeing any part of him.

"Were you going to apologize?" She bit into the words like a hard apple.

Quiet. With her face pointed away from him, she had no idea what expression he wore.

"I was." The courtesy in his voice made her close her eyes. She needed headache powders before she left.

"How benevolent of you."

He sighed.

Whatever either of them did or said at this point would only damage things further. "I'm going to pack my bag." She swept past him, her stiff chin wavering a millimeter.

If she let herself feel or think, she'd dissolve. She'd walled off the terrible truth all evening—that she harbored a secret that now felt as disloyal as his. Even as she accused him, she felt the hypocrisy burning a slow path through her soul, like a flame inching along a wick. With stiff shoulders, she descended the dark stairwell to the back of the hospital, treading quietly to avoid waking any patients or drawing the orderly's attention.

He'd pepper her with questions, and she could barely manage her own breathing.

When she left ten minutes later, Daniel was nowhere to be seen.

And when she returned in the murky hours of dawn, he'd been called away to his own case.

The late-October air stalked Nora into the parlor, where she dropped into the oldest chair in front of the hearth, the usually delicious smell of dank woodsmoke filling her only with foreboding. Despite the fidgety flames, she couldn't warm herself.

CHAPTER 18

NORA MOVED THROUGH THE ROUTINES OF THE CLINIC
the next day, recording pulse rates and tongue color, chest
sounds and pupil size. She changed bandages while carrying on
short conversations with Julia but remembered none of them.
Work pulled her past tea and into the soggy autumn evening.

By eight, gas lamps burned in the surgical theater, the precisely angled mirrors directing the steady light onto a nervous
patient with a stiff chin, wrapped tightly in a robe. Miss Rawly
had insisted on waiting until after factory hours for her surgery so she wouldn't lose additional pay. Now her eyes riveted
on the tumultuous evening sky, visible through the high windows. Each flash of lightning cutting through the dark made
her flinch.

There were reasons why Nora scheduled most surgeries for
daytime—other than better light. The hoots of pigeons and
ruckus of the busy street outside reassured patients with their
mundane normalcy; the patter of rain on a black window and
the noise of distant thunder did not.

"I know the table is hard, but you'll be sleeping soon and
won't notice," Nora reassured her. Daniel had agreed days ago
to administer the ether for tonight's procedure. Though he'd
been present at Horace's lecture last night, they'd each kept

to their own sides of the room. Once Miss Rawly was unconscious, they'd be alone together for the first time since their
quarrel. But for now, he waited outside in the hall.

"We'll remove the robe, and I'll inspect the tumor once
again before we begin."

"It doesn't cause much pain," Miss Rawly said, her finely
lined skin in contrast to her thick sheet of hair, as if her body
couldn't decide whether to remain in youth or sink into age.

"I know," Nora said, probing the red streaks in her left
breast above the tumor. The size of an almond and just as hard.
She used a wet charcoal stick to mark lines to guide her cuts.
"But it is much safer to remove it now. I've treated too many
women who never did."

It was a delicate dance along a spider's web to convince a
patient of the need for treatment without terrifying them. As
she settled Miss Rawly onto the table, Nora silently worked
ahead, choosing the angle of incision. "I'll go get the other surgeon now. He'll be administering the ether."

The patient's eyebrows sank in dismay. "Will the other surgeon be doing the cutting?" The hope in her voice did nothing
to bolster Nora, who drew in a breath.

It was always worse when women doubted her.

Nora forced a smile. "I've done many surgeries. And I'm as
careful with my stitches as you are sewing in the factory."

Miss Rawly supported herself by sewing men's trousers day
in and out. Slightly comforted, her brow loosened.

"She's ready," Nora whispered to Daniel through the curtain.

He swept in quietly, arranging the vaporizer on the small
table at the woman's head. He'd tipped a kettle of boiling water

into the steel basin to keep the ether warm and the vapors consistent. "This will be much easier than some people say," Daniel reassured her.

Nora looked away, trying to ignore the petulant flame in her stomach when the woman turned trusting eyes on her husband. Whatever *he* said, she took as gospel.

Daniel coaxed and explained as he lowered the mask to Miss Rawly's face. Nora had to admit his bedside manner was meticulous and authoritative, yet unfailingly soft and cajoling. She could do the exact same if patients didn't look at her the way they looked at the floating eyeballs in Horace's specimen jars.

Miss Rawly never even coughed as the ether overtook her. Daniel increased the fumes so slowly she noticed nothing except the eventual shuttering of her eyes.

"Well done." Nora couldn't help but praise.

"Thank you." So stiffly polite, like nervous colleagues.

Nora probed the lump with her fingers and laid the scalpel to the charcoal line. The skin parted, globules of yellow fat blooming as she drew the blade nearer to the offending tumor—encapsulated in tough, stringy fibers but clearly outlined from the healthy tissue.

"It will take a minute to free it from this web." She adjusted her head so she wouldn't block the light. Before his stroke, Horace would have extracted this tumor before Nora had even breached the subcutaneous tissue. She never understood his speed. But then, thanks to ether, she'd never operated on a screaming, pleading patient. For better or worse, ether had slowed down operations considerably.

Daniel left the vaporizer to sponge the wound and hold the retractors for her as she ligated a blood vessel in the way. "I can see the lesion," she said. "But it's buried deep."

"Just keep tying off the blood vessels and working your way down," he coached. She hated to admit she would rather operate with Daniel than work alone. Was she as bad as her patients—unconsciously seeking reassurance from the presence of a male doctor?

When she finally freed the mass, she drew it out, trying not to worry over the copious flow of blood.

Daniel gave a low whistle. "That's a large one. It looks like a river rock."

Nora dropped it into a bowl for later examination as Daniel swiftly sponged and ligated the severed veins. "Look how smooth it is," he marveled. "The last one I extracted was a mess of tissue."

"Did the woman survive?" Nora asked.

"Hale and hearty today." Daniel smiled, almost erasing the past twenty-four hours with one dimple in his chin. "But then, the surgery was only a week ago."

Nora waited until he'd finished suturing the muscle before she stepped in and brought the lip of the wound together. The scar would be small compared to the tumor she'd coaxed out from the breast. She commenced with straight, careful stitches.

"What's the news from Bart's?" she asked as she worked, her shoulders tightening when she realized this might lead back to the petition and the fight against midwives.

Daniel was smarter than that. "Jeffers had the latest *Provincial* today. Have you read it?"

"Haven't seen it. I suppose Horace is hoarding it." Nora leaned closer to her work, carefully maneuvering a stitch so it wouldn't pucker.

"An article by a Dr. Conway," Daniel continued as he monitored the vaporizer. "He claimed he's seen cholera cases in London. He classified the cases as Asiatic."

Nora's eyes flitted up. "How many? Where?" Horace had seen the one on the ship, but no other sailor had contracted the terrible blight.

"Only two. Last year Conway reported six, and nothing came of it. Horace says he's an alarmist."

Nora's shoulders rounded with relief. "Two cases doesn't sound like cholera." Though immune to the common fears of corpses and dismembered limbs, if Nora had a monster that haunted her, it was the sallow, yellow cloud that had swept over her childhood like the grim reaper, only to lose its grip on her collar as it bore her family away.

"Horace is going to the club to talk with Conway tonight," Daniel said, watching her face. "I'm sure it's an isolated case, like the sailor."

Nora's teeth found the inside of her lip. Horace would find out the truth. She'd watched him lure, cajole, flatter, and intimidate his way to information before.

Daniel took Miss Rawly's pulse. "Pulse fifty-five beats per minute. Respiration slow and deep. Tongue pink. I'm removing the mask." He glanced over Nora's work. "What stitch is that?" he mused. "I would have used simple continuous, but yours look stronger."

Nora didn't let her warming cheeks show as she dipped her head. "A variation of herringbone."

"Herringbone?" he asked in confusion.

"Particularly useful in needlepoint for making cross-hatches," she admitted.

Daniel gave a laugh. "No fair having all those womanly arts to draw on."

If he was being gracious, so could she. She anointed the sutures with wine and olive oil—a practice Horace, Daniel, and Harry had also picked up, more as a good luck talisman than anything else. Horace was even testing the effect, inflicting sutures on dozens of sedated mice. *I do believe the wine diminishes inflammation*, he admitted. *The red perhaps better than the white.*

But she was stalling. She rubbed her hands together, trying to strike up the flame of courage. With the wound cleaned and Miss Rawly sleeping peacefully and painlessly, there was no better time to tell Daniel what Horace and Mrs. Phipps suspected.

What she herself was beginning to suspect. Her stomach quivered mercilessly. She had no doubts he'd be giddy with joy. But her work—her future as a surgeon—existed in a dark mist her searching eyes couldn't penetrate.

Her lips parted, words stirring like seeds reaching for the sky, until she recalled Daniel's face on Friday evening. He'd looked confused, almost appalled, that she'd want to continue working after having children. If he didn't sympathize with her goals, who would ever be on her side?

Nora surveyed the smooth, hard tumor glistening in the bowl. She'd made clean work of the removal in less than ten minutes, possibly saving a woman from future torment. And yet, even with such skill, Mrs. Phipps surely wouldn't approve of her cutting away with an infant in the nursery. Daniel's family would be freshly horrified, though she could accustom herself to their tantrums. Julia adored babies. She'd be baffled that anyone would put one down in order to take up a scalpel.

Perhaps only Horace would understand. And Magdalena.

Nora blinked, hiding a long second in the darkness.

An eccentric genius and a philandering single woman to back her. That hardly buttressed her argument.

"Are you well?" Daniel asked as she continued her careful stitching. "You're quiet."

Nora swallowed. "Just concentrating."

As soon as she told—if there was even anything to tell—there'd be a hurricane of opinions swirling around her. She'd be ordered off her feet, away from sick patients, forbidden to attend strenuous births. But it had been almost four weeks now, and the longer she waited to tell him, the more hurt he'd be.

Nora pulled the sheet up, covering Miss Rawly's exposed breast. "Let's hope we got it in time," she said. "I didn't see or feel any others."

Daniel carefully poured the hot water from the vaporizer down the floor drain and buffed away a stray drop from his glossy shoes. "If you didn't, no one would."

He glanced at her, relief plain on his face that had nothing to do with the patient. Nora understood instantly. He'd expected another row—thought she'd demand an explanation and apology for his cowardly act of giving in to Adams. At least, she chose to believe it was temporary cowardice and not a true endorsement. She knew it well—the fear that kept one from telling the truth.

She wiped down her instruments, replacing them in their leather sleeves as she tried again to construct an opening sentence that stubbornly refused to form in her brain. Everything in her shouted to delay, at least a little longer. There were too many patients counting on her. Ruth and Mrs. Howell were beginning to trust her more, and both had so much to learn.

"Thank you for assisting me today," she murmured just as Miss Rawly began to stir.

Soon, she silently promised.

CHAPTER 19

A RARE OCCURRENCE TO HAVE THE ENTIRE HOUSEHOLD AT the breakfast table—or any meal, for that matter—but no one had been called urgently away this morning. Horace, eyebrows twisted in worried contemplation, reached for another sugar cube and dropped it into his tea with measured care. "Conway said he's seen eight cases, but all in the same household. It doesn't seem to have traveled."

Forks stilled as everyone listened with concentration too profound for movement. Horace continued, "He found it where you'd expect—down at the docks. Probably came in with a ship." Horace looked out the window to the steel sky, trees glazed with morning dew. "If we must see cholera this year, it's as tame as you'd want, and still—"

"Any deaths?" Harry prodded.

Horace pressed his lips together as if tempted to keep the truth to himself. "Five of the eight."

"Good Lord," Daniel whispered.

"The weather's been terrible," Horace pointed out. "Floods all over the city through a sweltering summer, and now a cold start to autumn. I believe sickness in general will be amplified this year."

Mrs. Phipps maintained a stiffer pose than the painting of

Lord Nelson behind her. At last, she released her thin lips. "If it is cholera, will it be as bad as the year Nora took sick?"

Horace's frown deepened. "I don't see how it could be." His mouth twitched and his eyes burned with thought. "'32 was…" He shook his head. "We're jumping ahead."

Mrs. Phipps exhaled, relief in her breath.

"My district work has me down in the docks," Harry reminded them. "I'll keep an eye out and report everything."

Beside him, Julia's pale, pinched face betrayed her worry.

Horace gave a satisfied nod. "That's good. Everyone on alert. If you do see it, isolate the patient immediately and keep your distance." He raised his spoon like a saber and jutted it at each of them. "I don't want to expose our household."

Julia shifted in her chair. "It's bad enough thinking of Harry being surrounded by disease. To bring it here—"

"Horace brought me here," Nora quietly reminded the room.

"You were one little girl," Mrs. Phipps replied after an uncomfortable pause.

"And she barely allowed me in the front door with you, as I recall," Horace huffed.

Mrs. Phipps's face reddened. "It was a risk."

"Hopefully, we'll hear no more of it. But extreme caution, nonetheless." Horace put down the spoon with finality.

Across the table, Julia brushed Harry's hand with relief. Nora and Daniel still hadn't melted back into easy warmth. Nora's stomach dipped, and she pushed the food on her plate farther away from her.

Daniel lowered his lips close to her ear and asked in a gentle aside, "Aren't you eating?"

"I'm not very hungry. I still have to prepare for my lesson with Ruth today," she whispered while the others kept discussing. Three other midwives were now expressing interest. If Nora could develop a curriculum that satisfied men like Adams…

"Don't forget to keep your strength up," Daniel whispered.

Nora startled. It sounded too much like pregnancy advice. "Why do you say that?" She forced the words through numb lips.

Daniel frowned. "What do you mean, why? You stay so busy. You can't forget to eat." Confusion burned brown rings in his eyes.

Nora resisted the urge to squirm. "I'll be hungrier at teatime."

Mrs. Phipps cleared her throat. "If sickness is more pronounced this year, I propose Julia, Nora, and I take a holiday in Suffolk at my sister's house."

"But who would run the clinic?" Harry pointed out, his cup paused in the air. "Without Nora, we'd have to close it."

"Then we close it," Mrs. Phipps finished smoothly.

Nora dropped her fork with a clatter. "I have patients with nowhere else to go."

Mrs. Phipps narrowed her eyes at Nora, a familiar precursor to a scolding. "And a sick doctor cannot treat anyone. You, particularly, should be cautious."

Nora blanched. They were coming too close. Mrs. Phipps knew Nora hadn't told Julia yet but assumed she'd told Daniel. Most likely because of Nora's vague inferences that she had…

"Wait." Harry held up his hand, his brow wrinkled. "Cholera aside, if you expect sickness will be worse this year, how do we handle the patients with one less doctor? It seems the worst time for Nora to go away."

Julia nodded. "And even if there are a few cases of cholera, don't you all believe she has immunity from her childhood infection?"

"Yes, but we don't know if the baby would have the same immunity," Horace said, doling cream into his tea.

Nora's hands dropped to the tablecloth, carved of lead.

Daniel opened his mouth.

Harry's leg hit the table as he uncrossed it too quickly, and Julia released a yelp of surprise. "Baby?"

"Nora?" Daniel's face was white, unreadable.

"Horace!" Nora reprimanded, tears boiling viciously along her lower lashes.

Horace looked up, bewildered by the commotion. "What?"

"They hadn't told them, you dolt!" Mrs. Phipps pursed her lips in such anger Nora feared she'd smack him with her teaspoon.

"Why not?" Horace asked.

Daniel repeated her name, and she caught the whisper despite the tumult of other voices. She turned to him, tears sliding. "I wasn't sure yet," she lied, wishing he would turn his shocked eyes anywhere else.

"You didn't tell Daniel?" Mrs. Phipps asked, horrified.

"You knew?" Julia asked Mrs. Phipps, her voice leaking betrayal.

Nora didn't even attempt speech. She couldn't untangle the questions, and time had grown so heavy and fast that she could barely thread a breath through the tight seconds.

Horace shrugged. "It's nature's way, isn't it? No need for all this fuss."

Mrs. Phipps brought her fist down on the table, making the china bounce. "There is a way things are done, Dr. Croft."

"So, you are?" Even Horace stopped moving at Daniel's plaintive, restrained words. She'd never heard him sound so small.

"I think I might be." She must soften the blow. "I was going to tell you as soon as I knew for certain. I didn't want to get your hopes up." Her cheeks burned from the lie.

Daniel's frown relaxed, his eyes darting, gathering thoughts. "But that's wonderful." The words came out choked and strangled. "Even if Horace ruined your surprise."

He pulled her to him, an embrace different from the ones they'd exchanged lately. He waited until she molded in to him before releasing her.

"I thought we'd hear the same news from you two by now," Horace said, pointing his fork at Harry and Julia.

Julia jerked to her feet, her golden hair catching the bleak morning sun. "How happy for you," she said without meeting Nora's eyes. "Excuse me." She dropped her napkin and slipped from the room.

Nora looked to Harry for an explanation, but his face wore a stone mask. He said nothing as he followed in his wife's wake.

"Julia?" Nora asked, far too late.

Mrs. Phipps rose and aimed an angry sigh at Horace. "I'll speak to her. Give us a moment." The housekeeper was angry with Horace, but Nora could tell—she knew Mrs. Phipps far too well not to—that she was also disappointed by Nora's evasions.

She couldn't blame her. Daniel deserved better.

Within seconds, the once-busy table was half-empty, only Horace continuing with his toast.

Nora pressed her fingers to her sternum, the sting of Julia's abrupt departure spreading through her. "I'm sorry, Daniel."

"Sorry?" He smiled in earnest now, the way he did when he discovered some new animal or medical anomaly. "I'm ecstatic." His hand hovered over her stomach, knowing there was nothing at all to see or feel. The magic of new life was entirely concealed within her.

Unruffled, Horace folded his paper in half and smoothed it on the table. "I agree with Mrs. Phipps, Nora. If we do see cholera cases, you should leave town."

"If I do have immunity, I'm the only one who should see cholera patients," she countered, livid he'd returned to his conversational tone after setting off an incendiary at the table. She considered it a sound hypothesis. Few argued against the effectiveness of Edward Jenner's smallpox vaccine, and Nora knew from her own practice that children who survived measles, diphtheria, and other ailments could expect to be spared those diseases in later years.

"Seems a foolhardy time to test any theory." Daniel pointed to Nora's stomach.

Nora stiffened at the set of Daniel's jaw. He was formulating arguments already. Everything was unfolding just as she'd feared—everyone joining ranks, urging her to stop working.

"Fortunately, we don't have to," Nora said swiftly. "Two cases—or eight, however many Dr. Conway claims to have seen—are not an epidemic."

Neither man could argue with that, but Nora wasn't about to count it a victory. She had bigger problems than obscure cases and theories. Daniel's excitement over her pregnancy proved he felt no qualms about becoming a parent. His life would change, but not as radically as he expected hers to.

Horace's surprise disclosure had opened a new struggle for her, one only just beginning.

CHAPTER 20

Ruth's hands, as sure and nimble as any Nora had ever seen, fumbled over the cloth doll Nora had ordered from a perplexed seamstress.

"Supine?" Ruth asked uncertainly.

"No," Nora said, trying not to sound discouraged. "Supine is face up. Most babies, as you know, are born in the prone position." Nora twisted the doll to a supine position on the table. It stared up at them with its stitched eyes. The seamstress had jointed the shoulders, elbows, hips, and knees, just as Nora had requested. She wished there was a way to make the neck as malleable as a real baby's.

Ruth sighed. "What's wrong with saying 'face up'? Everyone knows what that means."

"What's wrong is that you won't understand lectures or articles when a doctor describes a position as supine or prone." Nora pitched her voice into something more patient. "When we know the Latin terms, it helps us communicate with doctors and scientists around the world. I'd never have managed in Italy if I didn't know Latin."

"Yes, well, I'm never going to Italy, and Mrs. Kelly won't be yelling Latin while she's giving birth. She'll bawl me out in plain English." Ruth cocked an eyebrow at Nora. She'd agreed to weekly lessons, eager to learn about the forceps, but hadn't expected to begin with Latin.

"We can't be at odds," Nora pleaded. "There's enough opposition to both of us to waste disagreement on each other." Flecks of iridescent gray in the marble table glinted in the sallow midday light. "You know about the petition. If Adams has his way, I worry any midwife who takes pay for her work could be prosecuted. You could go to prison just for practicing."

Establishing a training program, and licensing if necessary, was the best defense Nora could think of—and the way to communicate standards was in the language doctors had made their own.

Ruth's glare deepened. Nora never knew if the woman was seeing a fellow woman or an enemy doctor. "We never had this problem before."

Before I came along. Nora rolled her shoulder backward. "They feel threatened. But we can prove to them that midwives, educated in the latest practices, achieve better outcomes, and that will sway opinions. We've enough women's clubs to take up our cause if we can make a stirring argument." Nora looked over Mara, the model. She'd carefully removed the glass dome that enclosed the yawning cavity of the abdomen.

"Once you get used to the sound of it, the Latin terms are no harder than English," Nora promised, handing the doll back to Ruth. "Button on the umbilical cord and placenta, and we'll practice delivering different presentations. You'll see."

Ruth did as she was told, pausing to glimpse around the

cavernous surgical theater that doubled as a lecture hall. Outside, the rain drenched everything into a soggy mess. London hadn't seen the sky in over a week.

She placed the baby into the ceramic body, the top of the head protruding through the vaginal opening. "Vartrix."

"Vertex," Nora corrected with a smile.

Another sigh.

"We call it the crown," Ruth grumbled.

"Now, keep the vertex presentation and let's change the body position. Show me an anterior presentation."

Ruth's hands shook as she fumbled the doll into position.

"That's right!" Nora cheered. "When the occipital bone is in front of the mother." Nora picked up the small skull she'd placed on the table and stroked the shapely bone that rested just above the neck on the back of the head. "We name the position by the child first, orienting using his occipital bone. Then we name where it is facing. *Anterior* means *forward*. So occiput anterior means his occipital bone is pointing the same direction as the mother's navel."

Excitement heated her cheeks, but Ruth's expression... No excitement there.

"You're understanding it just fine," Nora half laughed. "You're only annoyed with me."

"It seems a waste of breath," Ruth confirmed. "But go on, try another one."

They went through posterior, transverse, breech, until Ruth couldn't be tricked.

"Just think," Nora said, stretching out a kink in her lower back, "when you attend my lectures and some doctor boasts over his occiput posterior birth, you can ask if it was a right or left presentation and leave them all gawping."

A light glinted in Ruth's eye. "I do like the sound of that."

Nora laughed. She'd make a medical marvel out of this midwife. At least, she would if she had enough time. Now that the entire household knew about her pregnancy, she found herself scrutinized at every turn, three doctors and two women piling on so many opinions that it nearly buried her.

But Ruth knew about women and childbirth, more than Julia or Mrs. Phipps. In her own way, more even than Nora or Horace or Daniel. She might be the best source of advice. But suppose she agreed with them? Nora couldn't afford to leave her work yet.

"Have you seen cholera in any of the places you've visited?" Nora asked, composing her words carefully.

Ruth's eyes widened. "Not seen any of that in years," she answered. "Has it come?"

"No," Nora reassured her. "There was one family that went down with an illness resembling it, but there's no other cases."

The way Horace described it, rapidly transmitting infection was a hallmark of the disease. So it was still possible that these cases were something else. Nora licked her lips. "I just don't know how cholera would affect a pregnant woman."

"I hope you don't have to find out." Ruth began tidying away their lesson materials, packing the cloth baby into a wooden box. Her calm expression and large, expressive eyes rested on Nora, inviting confidences.

Easy to see why other women came to her time after time.

Nora sighed, preparing to nudge some especially weighty

words across the table. "Have you ever seen a woman four weeks late who wasn't pregnant?"

"I see pregnant women who haven't had a season in years. And some who spotted so much they didn't know they were with child—rather like our Mrs. Roland, if you recall. Haven't you seen the same?" Her eyes crinkled at the corners. "Or are we talking about yourself?"

"My courses have been fairly regular," Nora admitted. "But I'm four weeks late now."

Ruth was too acclimated to true surprises to fluster or hop about with such news. Her eyes sharpened as they surveyed Nora from top to toe. "How's your appetite?"

"Less?" Nora still didn't know if she was imagining it.

"Vomiting?" Ruth marched on.

"No."

"At least you're spared that so far." Ruth shifted her weight and pressed her fingers onto the stone tabletop. "There was an older woman—over thirty—pregnant for the first time. I cared for her until a doctor took over her case. He didn't worry over her extreme sickness because he thought women were designed to be sick when expecting. She passed away at month six. Her husband never went right after that."

Nora slid her hands along the limp linen of her skirt, hiding them in her deep pockets. Magdalena had never mentioned morning sickness killing her patients, but that didn't mean she hadn't seen it. Nora must write and ask. "Dr. Croft said my nose looked swollen."

Ruth tilted her head and pinched her lips in assessment. "I don't see any difference."

"And he said my urine smells different."

Ruth's forehead folded into perplexed wrinkles. "You had him smell your urine?"

"Not intentionally," Nora hastened. "He used the water closet after me. He's particularly"—there were many words to choose from, but the one she wanted didn't exist—"olfactious."

A scrunched nose revealed Nora's explanation hadn't helped at all.

"He's sensitive to smells."

"Then how does he stand sticking his nose into all the…" Ruth waved a hand, struggling for a word to name the cadavers.

"Bodies," Nora supplied. It was kinder than corpses, and Ruth was particularly resistant to learning from the deceased. "He's adjusted somehow."

"What about you? Most of my…my patients"—she was resistant to adopting other doctor words too—"are troubled by smells. It's often one of the first symptoms."

"I've had a harder time working with the bodies. Lately, I seem more susceptible to strong smells."

Ruth nodded, her hair the color of a field after gleaning, when streaks of silver glistened on brown stalks. "You probably are, then. Some women seem to know instinctively within days. I'm surprised you don't have a sense, with all your training."

Nora smoothed the top of the box, watching the gray light from the windows play over the glossy wood grain. She still had smudges of watercolor paint on her hands from an earlier project. "Everyone says I'll have to abandon my work after I have a child."

"You'll need a good lie-in, for certain," Ruth confirmed. "You can't be standing for hours and running all over town."

Nora dipped her head.

"Not for a good two months," Ruth continued. "Some mid-wives say less. And I won't fib and say I haven't seen mothers back at work in less than five days, but that's only the ones who would starve without it."

"Yes, but," Nora fumbled, "some say I mustn't practice at all after I'm a mother."

A deep frown pressed itself onto Ruth's face. "I have five children. I work every day."

Nora's eyebrows flexed, something coming into focus. Somehow, she had never considered Ruth's work as…work.

"You can't be a midwife unless you've had your own." Ruth crossed her arms against her lean chest. "The more, the better."

"What do you mean? Surely there are women—" Her thoughts moved faster than her tongue, listing the midwives she knew: Mrs. Howell, Mrs. Bailey, Ruth…

"Nah." Ruth shook her head emphatically. "No one will come to you until you've endured it yourself. I had a skilled aunt who never married, and no one would go to her. She had to assist my grandmother."

"Do you mean there are prerequisites?" Nora pinched the cloth foot of the infant doll tightly, rolling the lumpy batting between her fingers. She'd assumed they came to their careers by necessity or happenstance, but if there was some sort of reg-imen, wouldn't that evidence help in the coming confrontation with London's doctors?

"Aye. You can't be a midwife until you're married, and you must be taught by someone with a reputation. My mother could coax a child out of anyone. She lost far less than other midwives she knew."

Nora checked the windows to see if the storm had lifted, but rivers of water still twisted down the panes. The dawning light was in her mind and nowhere else.

Motherhood is a prerequisite for them—a qualification no male doctor could claim. Obstetrics was a fully recognized branch of medicine, and shouldn't it function hand in hand with midwives, experienced women who knew all the facets of pregnancy, birth, and motherhood?

"You'll only be better once you're a mother yourself," Ruth pointed out, still perplexed.

Nora shook her head. None of this should have been news to her. She'd seen midwives hustling about their work for years, but in Italy, most of the women she'd worked with were nuns. She hadn't stopped to think that here…here they were all married women with children.

She squeezed her hands into fists, the dig of her nails inside her palms reassuring and welcome. She could confine her work to obstetrics and still practice surgeries. Complex ones. Hysterectomies. Cesareans. Hemorrhages. A thrill careened up her back, raising the hairs on her neck. Horace and Daniel never objected to Mrs. Franklin doing her work, so how could they object to Nora practicing women's medicine?

The other physicians might not recognize it, but she was about to become even more qualified. No longer would "contractions of the muscles" or "compression of other organs" be illustrations in an anatomy book, but her own experience. What the men said in theory, she would know viscerally, with the scars and stretch marks to prove it. She could advocate for the midwives more effectively once she had benefited personally from their expertise, and advancing the cause of mother-midwives also allowed her to take on Magdalena's charge to improve opportunities for women to work and study.

Protecting and training midwives wasn't just a cause for her. It was her future, and Ruth's, and—

Don't get ahead of yourself, Nora cautioned silently.

Her mind might be reeling with possibilities and precedents, but she must be wise. If Adams was determined to oppose her, she'd face him, one move at a time.

If only his petition didn't bear Daniel's name.

CHAPTER 21

T HANKS FOR COMING WITH ME. I KNOW YOU'VE PUT IN A
long day already."

Harry's voice—low, mumbled, half-buried under the clamor
of the busy street—breached Daniel's cluttered thoughts. It was
true. He'd had a taxing day, but not as many in a row as Harry.

"What do you think it is?"

Harry frowned, his ginger whiskers catching the bleak
sunlight. "Strange presentation. Strong man, only twenty-four,
delirious and fevered. No rashes."

"What's he doing?" Daniel nearly trod into a foul brown
puddle on the pavement. But then, everything looked foul
and brown. Even the autumn leaves were painted with paltry
dark hues and muddled colors. At least the rain had ceased
momentarily.

"Hallucinating and frantic. We can't get him to lie still for
anything."

Daniel frowned, puffing through his mouth as they passed
a courtyard with leaning privies. Ten feet above him, a silent
child in a rag of a gown peered at him from a window, face
pressed mournfully against the dirty, barred glass. Daniel studied the little prisoner until Harry's words called him back.

"He's entirely out of his mind. It started a couple hours

ago. I came home to get you because I was too tired to think through it alone." Daniel abandoned his other thoughts—fuzzy images of Nora sleeping with her back to him and Adams grinning at him in the hallways of Bart's as if they shared a secret.

Harry never admitted defeat or asked for help unless... No, Daniel couldn't remember an instance. "After we see him, you should get a cab home and have supper with Julia. I can finish your calls."

Harry didn't respond for a long beat, his eyes shuffling through the huddles of people sharing the pavement. "Julia left yesterday to visit her parents."

The words came out stiff, starched and ironed with some emotion Daniel couldn't place. Perhaps Harry was wading through marriage troubles himself and could commiserate. "Did you two have a row?"

"Nothing like that." Harry transferred his bulging doctor's bag to his other hand and dodged a sour-faced woman to step up to a black door coated in greasy finger streaks. He knocked once and entered, for the door, like most in this collection of rookeries, was left unlocked. The daylight, however thin and stifling as it had been on the narrow street, died as if enclosed in a coffin the moment they stepped inside. Tenement air. Dull, soupy, teeming with the accumulated smells of sweat, cooking, rubbish.

Harry navigated the shadowy hall into a back room, where a young woman huddled with a whining child on her lap, shadows in a cell of disorder and darkness. Daniel's first instinct was to treat the pair and tend to whatever had made their faces so haggard and hopeless, but the true patient swayed behind them, a thin, unshaven man kneeling on the bed, jabbing a wooden spoon erratically in the air.

"What's he on about now?" Harry asked.

The woman answered in a voice flatter than paper. "He's crimping pipes. Thinks he's at the factory. Apparently, I'm another worker, one he doesn't get on with. He's threatened to crack my head several times."

Harry sighed. "I'm so sorry, Mrs. Healey. I've brought my friend to help, as promised. This is Dr. Gibson. Your husband still hasn't slept?"

She shook her head. "Between him and her…" She looked at the child, features twisting in anguish.

"Sam," Harry called as he approached the bed. The man didn't respond to his name. "Sam, it's Dr. Trimble. You shouldn't be up."

Sam flourished the spoon, and his lip twitched up like an angry cur's. "I didn't take a break. You'll not be docking my pay, Robbins!"

"Thinks you're the foreman, Mr. Robbins." Mrs. Healey winced as Sam swung his arm at Harry, but Harry caught the spoon easily, arresting it in a muscled fist.

"Don't you take me in!" Sam screamed, and lunged forward, coming at Harry with yellow teeth.

"Daniel!" Harry called. "A little help!" But he was already in motion, grappling the crazed man's shoulders. Together, using every hand and elbow they had between them, they wrestled Sam Healey to the filthy mattress. Daniel's elbow pressed into something damp, the smell of excrement stifling.

Mrs. Healey set the crying child on the floor and tried to come to their aid.

Harry waved her off. "We've got him. We won't hurt him."

"What started this?" Daniel asked over the commotion, bracing his feet against the floor as Sam tried to wriggle free.

Her words shook. "Lost his job and didn't eat or go to the pub for two days, trying to save it for me. He only took water and nothing else." Her face crumbled, falling into the disorder of terror and regret.

"Delirium tremens," Harry huffed as he pressed his knee into Sam's back.

"Are you sure?" Daniel asked.

Harry rolled his eyes. "You've not spent much time in Glasgow, I take it." He grunted out the sarcastic words as Sam writhed beneath his grip. "Two days of no liquor. And now an attack of shaking, puking, and hallucinations. It's delirium tremens. Got to be. He needs a weak draft."

"Not just vomiting," the wife interrupted timidly. "He's been running from the other end since last night."

Daniel's grip loosened slightly. "Diarrhea?"

Healey flailed. "Don't let him move," Harry snapped.

The wife nodded. "I can't keep him clean, but he's passing…well, it's scarcely more than water now."

Daniel traded glances with Harry, but Harry spoke first.

"His color. Look."

There was no window, and the paltry lamplight made it difficult to distinguish colors, but Harry was right. Sam's skin bore a strange gray tint.

"When's the last time he ate or drank?" Daniel asked.

"I gave him stew an hour ago, but it all came up and out again." As she spoke, the struggling man whimpered and went limp at last. Harry released him, smoothing down his crumpled jacket. "Keep still, now. We don't want any trouble." Though his voice was calm, Daniel recognized fear in the man's eyes as he bent close, searching inside his open bag.

"Think it's a double diagnosis?" Harry whispered.

Delirium tremens and cholera at the same time? Daniel exhaled in a sharp burst, desperate to believe this was all caused by hunger and a lack of alcohol. But he couldn't tell, and they needed to know for certain. "Show me his chamber pot."

As Harry made to move toward the wife, Sam Healey turned his head, face twisting into submission in a grotesque smile. "Are you taking bets? Half a crown on Voltaire." He reached up and pushed the wooden spoon against Harry's coat.

"Dear Lord, he's at the races now," Mrs. Healey moaned. "He's not usually like this," she promised. "He drinks away his wages, but he's never deranged."

Daniel studied the man, imagining his face calm instead of wearing this mask of mania.

"We can't allow him to get agitated again," Harry muttered. "After two nights of no sleep, his heart might give out."

"If he won't sleep on his own, we'll have to make him." Daniel looked at Harry's bag. "You carry chloroform, don't you?"

Harry nodded. "Just a bottle. I don't drag the whole vaporizer about. Even if I did, we'd have a hell of a time getting the mask on him."

Lying on the bed, Sam began cheering on his hallucinatory horse race.

"Get on, Voltaire. Two more lengths. Come on, boy! Whip

'em!" His hand swung madly, urging on the phantom rider, but then he curled in with a cry, clutching his stomach.

Cholera cramps were said to be excruciating.

Daniel swept his fingers through the depths of Harry's medical bag, identifying bottles by feel: paregoric, with its flared, broad outline; quinine, with its flat metal stopper; and then—*yes*—he located the chloroform, with its sloping shoulders and tapered neck. He pulled it out and handed it to Harry.

"No!" Sam grunted in dismay, holding his stomach and groaning as if he'd ruptured his appendix. "He lost. I'm out 'alf a crown. We'll starve, all of us!" On the floor beside him, not to be outdone, the child competed with a passionate scream, and the ceiling above thundered with someone stomping for quiet.

"Poor fool," Harry muttered. "He can't even win in his delusions."

"I'm mixing the chloroform with port wine. That will get alcohol and the anesthesia into him at the same time." Daniel had to lean close to Harry's ears to be heard.

But before he'd completed the mixture, Healey stopped wailing, turning rigid, his face frozen.

"What the hell?" Harry darted forward, searching for breath and a pulse, jostling Daniel's arm and spilling a trail of wine. "He's starting to seize."

Daniel thrust the spoon of medicine at him. "Give it now."

Harry tipped the spoon into Sam's mouth, then recoiled as Sam gasped and gagged, spewing the mixture into the rank air.

"Too late," Daniel muttered. "Help me roll him."

The coughing increased in violence as they pointed Sam's

sputtering head to the floor. Harry pounded his back. The child hunched her head in fright and cried fit to undo a saint. As soon as Healey's trachea was free of the offending liquid, tight gasps burst from Sam's lips and transformed to guttural whispers. "I'm a dead man."

"Should we restrain him?" Daniel asked, pulling straps from his bag.

"Dead man," Sam groaned, keeping up his tearful tirade.

"Take your little one into the hall," Harry commanded Mrs. Healey, waiting while she hauled her resisting daughter through the doorway.

"We've got to calm him," Daniel said as he fumbled with the restraints.

"If you tie him down, he'll only fight more." Harry gripped the man's shoulders. "Sam." No response from the fixed eyes and large pupils. "Sam." He modulated his voice, making it level and low. "Mr. Robbins sent me."

Sam jerked, searching for the voice. Harry leaned closer, putting a hand on his sweating, shivering cheek. Daniel reached up for a wrist, finding the thundering pulse. Too fast to count.

"Mr. Robbins says you can keep your job as a crimper. He sent over a bottle of wine to celebrate."

Sam's nostrils flared and his eyebrows lunged together. "What?"

"Yes, a bottle of wine to celebrate your job. He'll be that upset if you don't toast him."

A glowing ember of hope ignited in Sam's pupils. A fragile flame, but still...

Daniel was ready, grabbing the half-filled glass of port and chloroform mixture. "To Mr. Robbins," he said. "And your job as a crimper."

Sam stared, the terror ebbing from his face. "I keep my place?"

"Yes, of course." Daniel smothered a twist of guilt in his gut as Harry pressed the bottle into the man's hand and guided it firmly to his mouth.

With a strange smile, Sam accepted the dose and swallowed. Instantly, Harry's stiff shoulders lowered in relief. Another sip. Another swallow. Sam's shaking limbs slowed, quieted. So did his pulse.

"You need a good night's sleep," Daniel prodded. "This will help."

"Sleep," Sam repeated sloppily, his furrowed brow relinquishing its fear. His gaze slid across the ceiling as if watching a seabird slowly circle the room. After a quiet minute, Sam gave a loose sigh, and his eyelids fell.

Daniel planted his wooden stethoscope against Sam's thin chest. "It's slowing down," he announced.

Harry exhaled. "It was going like a steam engine about to blow." He looked the man over, watching as the mottled purple faded from his face. "He'll need a dose of spirits every hour until the shock wears off. The only remedy for putting down the bottle too fast is to take it up again, in moderation."

"You saved his life," Daniel reassured him, troubled by the profound weariness in Harry's voice.

Harry looked beyond the door to the hall where the wife waited, out of earshot. "For now. Is it cholera?"

Daniel found the chamber pot beneath the bed, dread rising when he saw the small white pieces floating at the top.

Once cholera tore all the bile from a body, it continued to strip away the intestines themselves until the only thing expelled was water and tissue fragments. "Dammit," he whispered. "We need to get out of here. Now."

But could they go home? If infected, they risked the entire household—Horace, Nora. Daniel took another step back, holding his hand over his mouth and nose, keeping his inhalations shallow.

"What about his poor wife? The little girl?" Harry whispered urgently.

Daniel chewed the skin of his cheek, face grim. "We'll give them instructions and check back when we're prepared. We need clean handkerchiefs and something to fight the miasma."

"And in the meantime?" Harry stared accusingly.

"We can't save them all," Daniel reminded him.

"I'm not talking about *all*. I'm only talking about one mother and a baby girl. They deserve better than this."

Daniel knew not to argue. Turning away, he stoppered and tucked away the bottle of chloroform. Mrs. Healey stepped back into the room, the child only whimpering now. Her eyes riveted to her motionless husband. "Is he safe?"

Anything but.

Before Daniel could share the diagnosis, Harry spoke up. "He's going to need constant nursing with a small sip of wine or beer every hour, along with a cup of tea. Absolutely no milk or cold water. Do you understand?"

She nodded with startled eyes. "What is it?"

"The hallucinations are alcohol withdrawal. That's why he

needs the spirits." Harry paused, his eyes shining in the low light. "But he has..." The word wouldn't form.

"He has a case of cholera," Daniel finished quietly, clinically, hoping to ward off her shock.

He didn't. She let out a torn wail and covered her mouth.

"When did his evacuations begin?" Daniel asked.

"Yesterday afternoon."

He nodded, pressing his lips. Some patients died within hours. Perhaps Sam's was a tamer version of the disease. He told her as much and repeated Harry's instructions before backing out the door quickly as Harry repeatedly promised to check on her. They escaped the oppressive darkness of the tenement, back to the wet street.

Daniel concentrated on filling his lungs with the cool fall air, but Harry slumped onto the neighbor's front stoop, leaning his head against the railing.

"Harry?" Daniel bent down, unable to keep the trace of panic from his voice.

"Took it out of me, is all." Harry closed his eyes. "The smells and the noise, and I was certain he was going to drop down dead when he started hacking. And now..." He took a mournful breath. "The cholera really is here."

Daniel frowned. "Do you feel faint? Headache?"

Harry shook his head in a way that didn't convince Daniel at all. They'd need to change their clothes before they went into the house. John, the orderly, could bring what they needed to the stable. To be safe, these things should be burned.

But Harry looked too haggard for comfort. Daniel restrained his hand from feeling for a temperature. The gesture was as likely to get him slugged as anything else. "You don't look well."

Harry stared ahead with unfocused eyes, the usual ruddiness of his cheeks gone. "Three nights I've been called out, and even when I could have slept, I…" He looked toward the intersection ahead, where a group of factory girls crossed the street, chattering on their way home.

"You aren't sleeping?" Daniel pressed.

"Doesn't matter." Harry's shoulders straightened and his face went blank and closed, a maddening habit he used for ending a conversation. Useless to pry when he wore this expression.

"I'll take your calls tonight," Daniel offered. "Nora can help, too. You can send some to the clinic."

Harry shifted his bag to his other hand and shook his head. "Nora's expecting. Even if she weren't, she can't wrestle wild patients like Sam."

No, she couldn't. Daniel slumped onto the step beside Harry.

"When she can't work, we'll be underwater," Harry lamented.

We are already.

Daniel turned his head away. "If it were up to her, she'd never stop. She's angry at me for signing Adams's petition."

"It was idiotic," Harry confirmed.

A sigh ran from Daniel's lips and joined the passing breeze. "I'm trying to spare her a firing squad of angry doctors."

"You put yourself in her line of fire instead," Harry pointed out, accurately. "And it's all about to get worse."

Daniel cocked his head. Harry was too tired or discouraged to even open his eyes.

"The *Spectator* had an article today."

Daniel stiffened. Why hadn't he taken the time to scan the papers today?

"A woman claiming to be a midwife in Surrey was arrested for murder." Harry rolled his head toward Daniel and opened his worried eyes. "She apparently made a mess of it, and the mother and child both died."

"What do you mean, claiming to be a midwife?" Daniel pressed.

"She knew nothing about it. Wasn't trained at all. Doubt she'd ever seen between a woman's legs. Thought it would be a quick pound, perhaps." The iron bar of the railing indented Harry's whiskered cheek.

"Dammit," Daniel spat out. It strengthened his argument in the fight with Nora, but he didn't enjoy the victory, not when it bolstered Adams's cause. He turned back to Harry's absent gaze. His friend was miles away.

Harry shook his head. "I can't tell up from down anymore. But the Surrey case—it's a tragedy. Perhaps I was wrong and I should sign the petition, too."

"You saw how well that worked for me," Daniel said.

"You and Nora will find a way to work through it. You always do," Harry said, a shade bitterly. "Disagreements aren't immutable."

Daniel raised an eyebrow, tempted to ask how well Harry thought he knew Nora. Her stance on this issue was harder than he'd ever seen—and they'd sparred plenty of times before.

"You have Nora and a baby on the way. Even if you can't see eye to eye now, that will pull you back togeth—" Harry stopped. Swallowed.

Daniel was trying to navigate a bog. One false step and he'd be swallowed in the muddy swamp. But Harry was his oldest friend, so Daniel ventured, "Is there something troubling you and Julia?"

A small bead of water slid from Harry's eye. His first words were an indecipherable mumble. "What it's like to never have a child."

Daniel swept his eyes over the distant walkers, grateful no one had strayed within earshot. "Have you and Julia—"

"It's been over two years, Daniel. Nothing. And when Nora revealed her pregnancy, something happened to Julia. I lost her."

Daniel reviewed the past week, searching his memory for Julia. He'd hardly seen her.

"But…" Daniel closed his mouth. He couldn't bring up that Julia had once been pregnant. Reminding a husband of his wife's rape, even in the most elliptical terms, was no way to offer comfort.

Harry read his thoughts anyway. "I know. She could carry a child once, before I mutilated her. Why did I ever let her father convince me to do it?" Harry's voice rose and broke, and he buried his head in his hands.

Daniel scanned the street and the windows behind them. Confessions like this could get Harry hauled to prison. This wasn't the place for this conversation. But he wasn't sure he could convince Harry to move. "She was your friend's daughter. She'd tried to kill herself. Her parents were begging for your help. You did it to save her life. You don't know it was what you did—"

Harry's blazing eyes cut off Daniel's sentence.

"She was healthy until my surgery. I've never told you, but my God, how she screamed. She woke in the middle of it, but I kept on." Harry's already ruddy face turned crimson as he choked on the memory. "I deserve whatever I get, but she doesn't."

He needed sleep. A bath. Food. Nothing would help, remaining here. "We're going home," Daniel insisted. "We've got to tell the others about Sam."

Harry's face shuttered, almost as blank as their sedated patient's. The sight turned Daniel cold.

"You're right." Harry stood. "Don't let Nora stay here in the city, Daniel. I know she has ideas about immunity, but if your baby is lost..." He licked his lips. "She won't want to live with being wrong on this one."

CHAPTER 22

NORA WAITED UNTIL SHE HEARD THE FRONT DOOR CLOSE and counted several beats, until certain Mrs. Phipps was down the steps and around the corner. Then, safe, she swung her feet off the ottoman and got up. Horace, reading a letter about lacewing butterflies from an Austrian entomologist, didn't notice, but even if he did, she doubted he'd tell Mrs. Phipps that Nora wasn't, in fact, obeying her stern command to rest.

At the doorway, Nora twisted her head, listening for sounds from the floor above, even though she knew Julia was still away at her parents' home, and Daniel and Harry were both out on calls. She hadn't had a chance like this for days.

"I'm making calls on Broad Street." She smoothed her wrinkled skirts. "Care to join me?"

Horace looked up, his eyes sliding into focus on the world outside of poppy fields bursting with flying insects. "Are you supposed to?"

Nora wrinkled her nose. She'd counted on him to be oblivious. He was the only one who never fussed. "Would you rather I embroider you a flower?"

If anyone could sympathize, it was Horace. His weakened left hand had stripped away his ability to do his most delicate surgical work. Rarely did the two invalids find themselves alone.

Horace grunted. "These calls of yours. Anything good?"

Nora hid a grin. They weren't her cases. The requests had come while Daniel and Harry were away. She usually didn't make blind calls to strangers; it was too much of a battle to convince them to let her in. But accompanied by Horace...

"Your guess is as good as mine. But we're sure to see something exotic and inexplicable at some point." She'd meant it sarcastically, but he nodded and straightened in his chair.

"One can only hope."

She rolled her eyes as he went to collect his coat. His insistence on daily walks in every weather had strengthened his recovery. While his hand still trembled, his legs stood straight and strong as ever. If he clipped along with his cane at a less brisk pace than before, at least he still clipped.

Nora adjusted her grip on her kit bag handle and tried to judge from Mrs. Phipps's meticulous written notes which home to attend first. "A stomach ailment. Sounds severe. One child sick and one already dead in the same family."

Horace's chin rose sharply. "What else?"

"A young woman with failing vision." Nora scanned the list. "Jaundice and black lung."

"Jaundice *and* black lung?" Horace sniffed as if smelling something tempting.

"No. Two separate cases."

He grunted in disappointment. "Child first."

"That's where I was headed." She squinted at the notes, deciphering the address. She lowered her brow in concentration. "I feel like I've been to this address before."

Nora glanced outside. The rain had halted, the clouds

hovering benign and cold. "We can walk," she determined. The fresh air would brush away the lingering strands of nausea that clung to her.

Nora recognized the place even before they arrived at the house. It stood at the end of a row of grimy buildings, walls streaked black with coal dust. The odor of a nearby tannery drifted on a teasing breeze beyond the confines of poverty toward the nicer shops and neighborhoods. She had been here before, but she couldn't remember for what. It must have been years ago.

A young woman paced the front steps, wringing her hands. "My brother's inside with my mother. We"—her voice caught as she beckoned them into a claustrophobic hallway—"need help."

Mrs. Morse. Nora remembered the name once she stepped inside the family's quarters—a single room with a potbellied stove and narrow beds stacked three to the ceiling, weighed down with filthy blankets. It was more crowded than the last time she'd been here. A table took up the entire walking space and left only room for a pile of bedding. Nora had delivered a baby boy here before she went to Italy.

Horace didn't wrinkle his brow; he'd started his career aboard navy ships that barely fit an extra thought, but he'd spoiled Nora with stately dissection rooms and a spotless lecture theater. She crowded in close to a woman who had one child in her arms, another at her side, as she sat on the pile of bedding.

"Age?" Horace asked without preamble.

The woman looked up at the two strangers without

expression, her forehead creased with suffering. "Five. You…
Are you the doctor's girl? The one who delivered me years ago?"

Nora fought to keep her face smooth. The family had been
poor then, but not so poor as this. "Yes. And a doctor myself,
now. I remember you and your boy. He arrived quickly, as I
recall. Too quickly for Dr. Croft to attend you. It was just you
and me. You were one of my first deliveries." Nora took the
small bundle from her arms. "But I haven't met this newest
one yet."

She pulled back the blanket to reveal waxy blue skin and
mottled cheeks—a dead infant.

"Oh." Dismay tinted the shocked word as Nora stifled an
instinctive recoil, unable to set down the tragic bundle.

"He was fine yesterday," Mrs. Morse said brokenly.

Nora tried not to let her eyes film with moisture. The
mother's sunken face spasmed with grief before turning back
to the child in the bed.

Horace had the living boy's wrist in his hand, measuring
the pulse. "No fever. Weak pulse. Sunken eyes. Has he been
vomiting?"

"A few times," the mother replied in an empty tone, more
like the echo of a living voice.

Horace pulled back the blankets, and Nora saw at once the
bedding was soaked as if doused with a bucket of water.

"I try to clean, but it keeps coming out," the mother said.

Nora leaned closer, unwilling to believe her eyes. White
grains scattered across the sodden sheets. "Rice water stool," she
murmured woodenly, her thoughts congealing into an opaque
paste. "Cholera."

Horace narrowed his eyes. "What have you been giving him?"

"Milk with oats. Water."

Nora shook her head reflexively, reviewing what she'd nearly memorized over the years—tersely written case notes Horace had published in the *Provincial Medical & Surgical Journal*. Other than the dim shadows of her memory, it was the only account of her family's demise. "We need brewed liquids. Fermented ones. Tea, weak wine. Put the kettle on," she commanded the sister. Horace and Mrs. Phipps had plied her with these, day and night, when she was eight years old, and she'd survived. It might work for this child.

For this *family*, she corrected herself, surveying mother and daughter again. Both were chalky pale.

"Are you feeling unwell also?" Nora drew closer to study the color of the woman's eyes and skin. The mother shrugged, and would have denied it if not for Nora's delving gaze.

"A bit." The words were mouthed, barely spoken.

"Nora." Horace took a firm grip of her arm. "We must go. We'll send—"

"We can help." She swallowed. Then she shook him off.

"We'll make sure the kettle is full. We'll fetch tea and coal," Horace said, lifting the dead infant from the bed gently. "And we'll send for the undertaker. You can't stay here," he whispered.

Nora ignored the command despite her thudding pulse. "Where is your husband, Mrs. Morse?"

"At work. He's a tub man. He does the roping." An unpleasant job, but a well-paying one, shoveling out cesspits. The rope man on the team hoisted out the tubs and unloaded them into carts to be driven out of the city.

"Is he ill?" Nora asked.

"He was sick first, but he's doing better. He went back to work two days ago."

"You should stay inside until you're entirely well," Horace said with a wrinkled nose and a glimpse at the small window. He always preferred sick patients to convalesce outside, but in this crowded street, that would only expose the neighbors. "We'll come and check on you at least once a day, but we'll speak to you through the window." He fumbled his handkerchief from his pocket and tied it over his mouth and nose. "Nora," he said, ordering her to imitate him.

She complied but didn't let his frown push her out the door. The sick boy's black hair clung to his forehead, plastered in place by sweat and suffering. "I brought this boy into this world. I want to make sure he stays here," she said stubbornly, voice muffled by the handkerchief. She'd tied it hastily, squashing her nose.

The sister let out a small sob. "His name is Elias."

Nora spared her a long look. She looked twelve but could have been as old as sixteen. The undernourished ones always looked younger.

She'd had two dying brothers as well, once. "I'm staying," she whispered loud enough for Horace to catch.

If Elias couldn't swallow, they'd need a spouted cup or a tea-soaked cloth for him to suck. But with others sickening, they might not think of such things or have the strength to carry on tending to the boy, hour after hour.

Horace's chest swelled as he straightened his shoulders, leaning forward on his stick. "Think, Nora." He dropped his voice even lower. "You should at least talk to your husband."

Nora raised her eyebrows. They couldn't argue here, but once she followed him out into the street, it would be that much harder to gather enough resolve and fight her way back in.

The kettle shrieked, saving her from replying. "Where's the tea chest? We want it brewed as strong as we can make it."

Wordlessly, the older daughter gestured to the cupboard. Nora bustled to gather up pot, tea chest, and strainer, trying to forget the unsettling gray hue of the girl's wraithlike arms. *Her color will be better once she's downed a cupful*, Nora told herself.

Cracked lips and perishing thirst, a pounding head that overpowered everything else…one by one, the symptoms came back to her. She remembered sharing the care of her younger brother, Peter, until her mother lay down and didn't get up. She thought she remembered crawling across a threadbare carpet for a dipper of water, finding the pail empty, and knowing it was impossible to fetch any more. The recollection was so cloudy it might have been real or made up, pieced from bits in Horace's carefully edited account. He was right. It was dangerous to stay.

"I'll work fast," she promised.

Behind her, Horace sighed. She heard him unclasp his bag and rummage through the contents. "I've a spouted cup here and a clean cloth." He grunted. "It won't be nearly enough."

"We'll send a messenger to Great Queen Street," Nora said, blinking her eyes clear as she measured tea leaves and dropped them into the pot of steaming water.

"Staying here is your foolish decision," Horace warned. "Not mine. I can't force you out the door, but your husband will be…" He'd never spoken this cautiously before. Arteries might burst, bones might shatter, he might desperately pray for luck or divine intervention, but his voice and his face never betrayed it. Revealing anything but optimism and robust confidence was bad form.

And she couldn't afford his uncertainty, not with her courage wavering so much already.

"Tell Daniel I couldn't be stopped."

"I will. But what will you tell him?"

Nora paused. Daniel wouldn't understand, no matter what she told him. Even though a year ago he'd treated highly infectious children with diphtheria when no other doctors would.

It was different, when you were responsible to guard your own child. Your own family.

Nora bit the inside of her lip and studied Horace, too frail after his stroke to be exposed to any virulent disease, let alone cholera. Her hand went involuntarily to her stomach. Daniel and Horace may have treated countless dangerous diseases, but they'd never done it while harboring a stowaway.

"*Cazzo*," she muttered, the familiar Italian curse escaping before she could stop it.

Horace blinked, reminding her that cursing wasn't safe in any of her languages, at least not from him.

"We should go. But someone must check back here soon," she insisted.

Horace bowed his head in relief. "Yes. We'll do that."

Nora turned back to the older sister. She couldn't stay, so she passed her as much as she could from her bag. More wine. A packet of tea. "Rest as much as you can," she instructed. "Drink often—but only tea. As much as you can swallow. A bit of wine, too."

The girl nodded as Nora led her and the mother to their

beds. "Keep Elias undressed unless he gets cold. He'll only mess his clothes and lay in it."

Still throwing instructions over her shoulder, she allowed Horace to take her by the arm and lead her out.

When they reached the pavement, he stopped and turned to meet her eyes. Nora noticed she no longer needed to look up at him. He'd shrunk considerably. "I've no doubt they are sick with virulent cholera," he said gravely.

"But the father is better," Nora argued.

"Lucky," he shot back. "Some are. But the baby died in less than one night, and the boy's organs have shrunken already."

Nora raised her eyes to a cobalt circle of sky breaking through the dingy clouds. Broad Street was a good distance from the other reported cases, near London's docks. "I hoped the disease would stay contained," she said quietly.

Horace shook his head. "I don't think it can be in cities. People tried before."

He looked over the busy street, filled with people blithely going about their business, mere yards away from a dying family. "It will burn through this district like the London fire." Horace looked at the unending sea of crowded, overfilled buildings. "These people are stacked in here like human kindling."

Nora took a step back, distancing herself from the words. "What do we do?" She turned to the brownstone behind them, the walls hiding the dead baby and the sinking child.

Horace took her by the arm and pointed home. "We dose the living and bury the dead. It's all we can do."

"Horace." His name wavered on her lips. "Is this what my family looked like when you found us?"

The muscles in his cheek flexed as he tapped the nearest basement railing with his cane. "What matters now is a plan. We need to get home, clean thoroughly, and consult with Daniel and Harry."

"Did my brother…" She'd never asked for details about six-year-old Peter. Had he been wrapped in his favorite blanket or sprawled helpless on the floor? How much had he suffered?

Horace gave her the same stern glare that, when she was a child, had wrenched tears from her eyes, eliciting prompt and perfect obedience. "Keep your distance from cholera, girl. We don't know enough."

She opened her mouth to argue, no longer a cowed little girl who took orders. But Horace's expression pushed the words back down her throat.

Written in his indomitable blue eyes, she read the small print of fear.

CHAPTER 23

NORA HAD IMAGINED THEIR HOUSEHOLD CONFERENCE conducted around the dining table, not inside the lecture theater meant to house sixty occupants. Horace had insisted on clearing the air from every common room, beginning with the largest. Smoke from burning pastilles wound thin, white ribbons in the cool evening shadows. The room, designed to pick up a single voice and carry it to a boisterous audience, made their low, anxious mutters echo in the nearly empty chamber.

Daniel and Harry had found cholera patients, too.

"I feel like the pope hiding from the Black Death in his room of fire." Harry snorted, edging the nearest ceramic burner with his shoe to watch the smoke waver.

"We're not hiding. We need to clean the air," Horace answered dully.

Daniel and Harry's case might have spared Nora an argument or a scold, but that didn't afford her any relief. Finding two affected families on different streets on the same day meant the incidence of the disease was higher and more widely spread than they'd thought.

They'd been watching for an epidemic, but it had already come, sneaking up behind them, out of sight until now.

"At least it smells nice," she offered lamely.

"Probably all it does," Horace said wearily. "I don't believe cholera has anything to do with odors."

"Then why bother?" Harry asked.

"It's something," Horace snapped. "It hurts no one, so if there's a chance it helps—"

"We'll use everything we can," Mrs. Phipps said coolly. When Nora and Horace returned, she'd already been in the middle of purifying Harry and Daniel, gathering up discarded clothing with tongs, putting it straight into water to boil with soap. There'd been one awkward moment when she threatened to take Harry's trousers herself if he didn't hurry. She'd ordered baths for everyone in turn, insisting on thorough scrubbings, hair and all.

And now they sat, hair still dripping, bundled in blankets for warmth in the chilly room. The black currant and willow incense almost overcame the pungent tang of lye.

"I still think the wisest thing to do is leave," Mrs. Phipps insisted. "I warned you weeks ago, but only Julia did the sensible thing."

Harry stared at his fists. "Perhaps. But if the disease spreads, I have no way of knowing what's happening in Chelsea. If Julia gets sick, I won't be there."

Daniel leaned forward, elbows on his knees. "And it's not safe for Nora or the baby." He looked at her. "Just think of the poor child you found today."

Mrs. Phipps nodded emphatically.

But Nora would rather not recall the pathetic, discolored corpse. "That child was already born. Perhaps my immunity passes to the womb." She fervently wished that was true. "So there's a chance Horace and I are the safest, wherever we are. I've had cholera. He's treated it. Perhaps you and Harry should leave."

Harry laughed, a sharp, cheerless burst. "Since when do doctors run from sickness? That's like the fire brigades leaving town when there's a fire."

"Fire brigades have water. We've nothing to put out this blaze." Horace dropped his blankets from his shoulders and wiped the back of his neck.

"Are you saying there's nothing we can do?" Daniel demanded.

"Hardly," he snapped back. "I'm only preparing you. We don't have the tools we need."

"But you're better at treating these patients than anyone else." Harry leaned toward Horace, elbows on knees.

"Precisely," Nora agreed. "So we stay?" She steepled her fingers tightly to steady her nerves.

"*We* stay." Horace gestured to the men. "You and Alice are free to go. This isn't pox. We don't know for certain you're immune. And we certainly can't assume the child is."

"Harry just said doctors don't leave. I'm a doctor."

"And a mother-to-be," Mrs. Phipps added.

She wanted to shout that Daniel was a father-to-be, but her throat tightened. He could risk himself without harming his child. She couldn't.

"We will follow the same protocol as in '32," Horace said, sidestepping the argument and pointing his face toward the high windows glowering with the last light of day. "Brewed and fermented liquids in copious amounts. No bleeding. They're losing too much volume already."

"Dr. Stanley says losing so much bile makes a surplus of blood that throws the humors into imbalance," Harry started. "If we don't bleed them—"

"Stanley lost more than half his patients in the last epidemic." Horace removed his spectacles and wiped a film of steam from the nearest burner from his lenses.

"And you?" Harry asked.

"Lost four in ten." Horace sighed. "But when you treat one thousand patients over the course of a year, that's a hundred lives saved." His eyes flicked to Nora.

"Fair enough," Harry conceded with a dull smile in her direction. "No bleeding. Only approved liquids. And food?"

"Only warm beef broth until the evacuations stop completely," Horace instructed. "Be prepared for patients to lose significant weight within days. But we cannot replace it until the disease stops attacking their intestines."

"Enemas?" Harry pressed on. "Powders? Purges?"

Horace scoffed. "They're purged already. In the name of all that's holy, don't take anything else out of their bodies. Feel free to try headache powders, salts, plasters. Whatever gives them a bit of comfort. But don't expect results."

Nora scanned the hollow room, half-convinced she'd conjured all this in a dream. "How do we treat them if we don't get close to them?"

Beside her, Daniel shifted and let out a breath of frustration at the word *we*.

Horace rolled the paper in his lap and brought it down on his leg to emphasize his points. "Wear a scented handkerchief around your nose on every call. You are not to touch soiled linens or clothing at the risk of bringing it home on your own clothing. We will follow the same protocol here for liquids, but until someone is ill, we can eat simple fare—"

"Until?" Mrs. Phipps squeaked.

"Nora," Daniel whispered beside her, the word heavy with supplication and warning.

She turned and watched a chilly drop of water wander from his hair, down his ear. "I'll be cautious. But I am staying."

Mrs. Phipps groaned.

"I'm not being difficult or stubborn. I'm a doctor, too. This is what I must do."

"Horace," Daniel pleaded, "can you—"

"No. He can't." Nora gripped his fingers, though he didn't respond in kind. "Do you think it would be some relief to me, Daniel, if my family perished again and I survived? Once is more than enough."

The sweet-scented room rang with silence, eyes darting to her and away again.

"You all forget that I remember having cholera. I watched the life drain from every person I loved and then lay in a room with their dead bodies. I understand the patients' suffering in ways no one else can. If anyone should avoid the patients, it's Horace, who's still recovering—"

Horace snapped his paper until it creased, his face serious and somber. "You remember one room of the epidemic. One poor family that happened to be yours. I treated a dying city. God forbid it rages like that again, but need I remind you I've survived more cholera than you, without ever contracting it? I stand the best chance here."

Her parted lips froze. "I just want to help," she finished feebly.

"I know," he said with a rare touch of sympathy. "I wanted to help them all, too." His words hung unfinished, balanced precariously over their heads.

She swallowed, the colors of his age-marked face and silver beard the only things she saw now. "But?"

"I failed far worse than you can imagine. You survived, but you don't know the stories of the hundreds I lost. You were the only lucky one who came back from being that far gone." Ghosts—the ones who had expired—traipsed across his face with heavy, silent steps, her parents and brothers and grand-mother gliding among them. "The only one," he repeated.

She dropped her eyes, holding back shadowy memories of her brother, Peter. *Later.* "We'll do better this time," she insisted. "We know more."

Horace chewed the bottom corner of his lip and shifted on the hard bench. "Do we?"

"I agree that it's dangerous for all of us," Harry said, staring stolidly at the empty seats across the theater. "But we are all willing to face the risk. That's why it's only fair that whatever we decide, we all agree."

Nora shifted, impatient at the thought of days of debate, because so far, the only clear thing was that none of them could propose a plan to please everyone. "Deliberation—waiting—is also a decision. I'm not sure it's the best."

Daniel rubbed his forehead. "Haste never helps anyone."

"Cholera will be hasty even if we aren't. If we don't treat them, it will spread faster," Nora argued.

Horace scowled. "It will spread no matter what we do. That is entirely beyond us."

"I'm not leaving." Nora's voice faltered as she recalled her desert-dry mouth, a vise of pain tightening around her forehead. She licked her lips. "We have to stay together. In case." If any of them took sick—and there was far too great a chance they might—who would tend them? She certainly didn't trust any other doctor to treat the people she loved best.

Shoulders tight, she braced for their arguments, but none of them had anything to counter that.

CHAPTER 24

NORA DODGED THE THIN STREAMS OF WATER AS SHE opened a ward window. She needed to keep a supply of fresh air for Meg despite the ghastly weather. Daniel thought the windows were better closed; Horace, open. She traded on and off, depending how strong the rain flowed and how thick the smells of human suffering and nursing gathered in the basement ward.

As if sensing contagion teeming in London's low streets, the autumn sky had refused to close, letting loose a scrubbing downpour that tested the patience of even the hardiest city residents. The roads ran with foul water, sweeping away sewage, manure, and years of coal dust rinsed loose from roofs and pediments. For the first time in her memory, Nora saw the gilded numbers of the Southwark Cathedral clock peeking through the coat of black grime. But the storms didn't cleanse the city of cholera; they flooded it with contagion.

For a few days after their tense discussion in the theater, everyone at 43 Great Queen Street held on to hope that the cases were isolated. When King's College and Bart's received notices of cholera patients from every doctor on staff, they admitted the grim truth—the Blue Death had sauntered back to England after seventeen years' respite. Horace gathered with other fellows of the Royal College for a five-hour-long boxing match of ideas and theories. Amid their squabbling, they managed to organize a count of the cases. One hundred eighty-nine cases three weeks ago. Now, in mid-October, one thousand six hundred.

Nora positioned a bucket to collect the drips and adjusted the nearest pastille burner so stray drops wouldn't catch it and extinguish the sharp smell of cloves. A distant grumble of thunder rattled the sky as she wiped the windowsill. At least her pregnancy demanded little attention so far. At ten weeks, she still suffered nothing other than an occasional burst of nausea or fatigue that passed within an hour. She turned back to Meg to watch her reaction to the windy, wet air. The girl closed her eyes and breathed in gratefully.

"I'm going to leave this open for a few minutes while I go upstairs. If it gets too cold, ring your bell," Nora instructed.

Meg nodded and Nora slipped out, eager for a quiet lunch with Mrs. Phipps to prove she wasn't working too hard. The more Mrs. Phipps saw Nora with her feet up, the less she begrudged her remaining in London.

"I'll pour the tea," Nora said, striding into the dining room. A bright blur caught her eye—a shade of blue silk that would never adorn Mrs. Phipps.

"Julia?" Nora gasped.

Julia rose from the dining chair next to Mrs. Phipps and spun around, her bonnet untied, ribbons streaming in disarray. "My parents' home in Chelsea isn't safe anymore," she blurted out, as if reading Nora's thoughts. "Cholera everywhere. My father's volunteered to come out of retirement and sail a ship to

Denmark. He's taking my mother with him. They want me to go, too—get out of London."

Nora started to exclaim that this was extreme, then dropped her eyes, remembering the short message sent in childish script to her weeks ago. *Elias taken by God.* The Morse family had lost both sons. Taking leave of London certainly wouldn't have sounded extreme to them. If only they'd had the choice.

"I'm not going without Harry. I've been begging him to go as ship's doctor, but he refuses." Julia sat down heavily, and Nora took the empty seat on her other side.

"Try to remember, Horace has had more experience treating cholera than anyone, and he never took sick." She paused and inhaled. "Harry's being very careful."

"It doesn't seem to matter." Julia pressed her hands to her cheeks, a ruby glinting in her wedding ring like a drop of blood. "My mother lost a friend last week, and now her children are ill. It's creeping through the air, whether you're careful or not." Julia lifted off her bonnet and laid in her lap. "There's nowhere to go."

Mrs. Phipps poured out steaming, strongly brewed doses of tea into their cups. "No cases in my sister's town. She wrote just days ago. The three of us can still go."

Nora tried for a reassuring smile. "Daniel and Harry and Horace are overrun with cholera cases, and babies won't stop coming just because the doctors are busy with an epidemic. I have mothers who need me here."

"But I thought..." Julia narrowed her eyes. "Aren't you stopping for your confinement?" A long yellow curl unraveled against her shoulder.

"I'm not treating cholera cases." *For now.* It was an uneasy truce she'd made with Daniel. "But people are sick and hurt, as always." Nora stopped at the dark flash of dismay in Julia's bright eyes before she dropped her head. "What's the matter?"

Instead of answering, Julia gathered her clenched hands into her lap and shook her head, refusing to look up.

"Julia, dear?" Mrs. Phipps ventured.

"She's going to have a child." Her whispered voice fractured, breaking off the rest of her sentence. She folded her shoulders inward, a wall of flesh to block them out.

Nora reached out an uncertain hand. "What is it? Has something happened?"

Something between a scoff and a sob escaped Julia's mouth. "Nothing at all has happened," she finally answered.

Nora's startled glance met Mrs. Phipps's mournful face. How to proceed?

"I'm sorry… Is it about my pregnancy?"

Julia stood, turning herself completely away from her friends. "It's not yours. Or my cousin's. Or my mother's friend's grandchildren. It's not any of the pregnant women or filled prams. Nothing at all to do with a single one of them." She wiped her face with trembling fingers.

"It's me. I'll never have one of my own," Julia whispered.

Understanding spilled over Nora.

Mrs. Phipps dropped her head, but Nora could tell she was not surprised. This was why Julia had fled the breakfast table, then fled this house to visit her parents.

"But…" Julia had been pregnant three years ago when she was only seventeen. She couldn't be barren. Yet there was no way to say it without referencing—

Julia looked at her and pressed a hand to her chest as if suffering from one of Horace's angina attacks. "I know. It makes me want to die when I think *he* gave me a child and Harry can't!"

The burning words scalded Nora's ears until they hardly worked at all. She couldn't let Julia speak of wanting to die. The scars on her arms… "Harry's a doctor," she tried again. "Has he examined you?"

Julia's cheeks went red, and she pressed her lips together. "He said there must be too much scarring from his surgery. That's the only explanation."

"He's not a specialist," Nora pointed out. Harry was an intrepid doctor, but he avoided obstetrics practice, claiming he hadn't the resolve or the temperament. "You should have come to me," Nora admonished gently, wishing she could have eased Julia's pain long ago.

"You've only been home from Italy for nine months, and nearly all of it was wedding plans and setting up your hospital. Besides, I kept hoping…" The strained veins across her temple stood in contrast to her smooth skin. Nora must keep the conversation soothing.

"I was such a fool to not notice. Exactly how long?"

"Two years and four months." Julia's chin wobbled. "We pretended it was normal for so long, but you've only been married a few months and you're already—"

Terrified.

It wasn't the moment to confess the cold distance growing between her and Daniel, or that he no longer wrapped his arms around her on the rare nights they shared a bed. All from their disagreements over the tiny person they'd not yet met.

"I can give you ether to make you more comfortable during the exam," Nora offered, forcing her mind back to the current problem.

Julia closed her eyes and sat down again, as if the brief conversation had wrung her lifeless. "Harry blames himself. For doing the surgery. And I blame myself for trying to kill myself. If I'd just had the child…" She swiped at her eyes. "My father blames himself for demanding Harry get rid of it—"

"Julia—"

"Blame enough to drown us all, and nothing to make it better. Harry and I couldn't let any other doctor know what we've done. That's why I couldn't see one."

Nora waited without breathing. Of course they couldn't consult anyone.

"And I was so ashamed to tell you. Afraid you'd blame Harry for an imperfect surgery. I wasn't the best patient. I was hysterical and fighting until they dosed me with enough morphia to force me unconscious again."

Mrs. Phipps blanched, frozen.

Nora shuddered. Julia had survived that nightmare; they could bring her through this one.

"I have tools that will help me see." She was fairly certain Harry didn't own a speculum. The reasons for his distaste for obstetric work were now painfully clear. "If you were pregnant once, there's hope."

Julia twisted her hands into a mangled knot. "That's what we said for years. But I can't find hope anymore."

"Then we'll find it together," Nora promised. "But I can't treat you if you're in Denmark."

After a quiet moment, Julia motioned with her chin toward Nora's stomach. "If you keep seeing the sick and working all day, you could lose your child. Harry wrote me, saying that Daniel's worried sick about you." She dropped her gaze, staring at her clenched hands. "Is it necessary for you to put yourself in such danger?"

Nora's voice came out too high and forced. "I've hardly any symptoms. And the factory women keep working until they're too large to be seen in public." She had already ordered a higher-waisted dress that would conceal any swelling of her middle, though there'd been none to speak of yet. "I have time."

She didn't add that she wasn't at all sure Daniel was worried about *her*. He didn't seem heartbroken that she'd be forced to watch the war with cholera from a safe perch when she most wanted to help fight; his worry was for the tiny stranger deep in her womb.

"I could examine you tomorrow, if you wish." It wasn't the time to think of herself.

Julia took a staggered breath and looked to Mrs. Phipps, who gave a gentle nod.

"Harry could even help me administer the ether, if you want him there—"

Julia shook her head furiously.

"Are you afraid of the pain?" Nora laid her hand lightly on Julia's, a promise in the touch. "You've never used the ether, but it's strangely pleasant. You'll see."

"It's not that." Julia hung her shaking head, one silver tear plunging to her lap. She exhaled and dropped her shoulders in defeat. "If you examine me and say it's impossible"—her pain hung between them, thickening in the cool air—"I'll believe you."

CHAPTER 25

"T HE SURGERY WILL DEMAND ALL MY ATTENTION," Daniel explained. "A moment's distraction could be fatal, so I need each instrument laid out in order. Neither of us should have to think where the blunt-edged forceps are—and I'm particular with the scissors. The bevel angle of the blade changes depending on the tissue I intend to cut, so I always want them arranged from least to greatest."

Fred Matson, his newest dresser, nodded.

"Exactly like this." Daniel gestured at the tray again, unsatisfied by the younger man's unearned self-assurance.

"Dr. Gibson?"

"What is it, Jeffers?" Daniel spared a smile for his favorite senior dresser, who'd drawn and studied diagrams of the different ways Daniel arranged his trays during *his* first year at St. Bart's.

"A gentleman to see you. I told him you were occupied, but he said I should give you his card. Then I saw his name and thought I'd offended him." Guiltily, Jeffers proffered the white square in his freckled hand. Daniel recognized his father's name and the elegant scrolled letters.

Matthew Gibson, Esq.

Damn. He glanced about, but of course there was nothing

here to wet his throat and stiffen his nerves. The only liquid in sight was a cloudy urine sample he'd examined. His father shouldn't be here—not with cholera filling the hospital.

"I left him in your office," Jeffers said. "And there's—"

"I'd better see him now," Daniel said. He needed to tell his father to get as far from this place as possible. Best to leave London entirely. "Impress upon our new recruit the importance of setting up the trays properly, please."

Jeffers nodded, but before Daniel could quit the room, Jeffers stopped him with a hand on his arm. "Dr. Gibson?"

Daniel waited with raised brows, inwardly wincing. Usually, he wasn't this curt. Jeffers deserved better treatment, but Daniel had been brisk with everyone lately.

"You should know there's a lady with him," Jeffers said in an undertone. "She looks fierce."

His mother would never set foot in a hospital. That left only… Daniel manufactured a ghost of a smile. "I know who she is. Thanks for the warning."

"Would you like me to ask for you in a few minutes?" Jeffers mimed panic. "'Mr. Hamilton's stitches have ruptured, Doctor. Come at once!'"

Halfway through an automatic headshake, Daniel reconsidered. "Only if you hear things breaking."

Though he knew who awaited him, it was still a jolt seeing his father and Aunt Wilcox ensconced in the shabby armchair and the chair behind the desk. His aunt sat imperiously in his place, riffling through a few of the papers left on the desk.

"This is a surprise," he said before either could speak. "I'm afraid I haven't much time to spare." He folded his arms to keep from fidgeting. "And it's not safe for you to be here."

"We've come to see if you've any sense left in your head whatsoever," his aunt scolded as she held up an envelope to read the return address. "Last week it was only in one paper, but today it's in all of them."

"Do you mean the cholera?" They'd lost him entirely and they hadn't even begun.

Aunt Wilcox slammed a newspaper onto the desk and slid it toward him. "Your wife. Praise the Lord, Dr. Adams didn't mention names, but it hardly takes a detective…"

Daniel lifted the paper, Aunt's words blurring as he scanned the headlines.

ROYAL COLLEGE OF PHYSICIANS WARNS THE PUBLIC OF THOSE SPREADING DEATH

His eyes flew through the words, collecting dread like his fingers collected the newsprint ink.

"This is that story Harry told me about. The woman dead from a shamster midwife. That's nothing to do with Nora," he said as he neared the middle of the article. Aunt snatched it and pointed to the next column.

"Well, I was interested in the mention of a *certain unconventional* doctor with *foreign* credentials who refused to sign a petition seeking to disallow meddling midwives. The mysterious doctor even argues these women should be trained and used more extensively." Aunt arched her eyebrows. "What is this, Daniel? Are you a glutton for scandal?"

He looked to his father for help, but worry rested so heavily on his brow there was no place left for sympathy.

"I don't know anything about this midwife case," Daniel admitted with an expression both innocent and cautious.

"A mother and child died in a ghastly manner. But what's just as alarming is the news that your wife seems to be positioning herself opposite the entire Royal College once again."

Daniel schooled the muscles in his cheeks. He'd love to tell her she was wrong, but he couldn't.

Aunt Wilcox huffed, not appreciating his silence. "What a pair you are." She pursed her lips. "I offered her a respected position. A place she could continue her work in more acceptable ways and be a benefit to society. She turned me down, Daniel."

Her voice rose in disbelief, and Daniel nearly shuddered, imagining what she'd say if she knew their secret—that Nora was still performing surgeries while two months along.

"There is a time for a man to put his foot down," Aunt Wilcox said with cold finality. "I noticed you had the sense to sign the petition. Why don't you demand she do the same?"

She'd clearly missed her calling as an army general; she dropped commands as effortlessly as handkerchiefs. "Dr. Adams has volunteered to treat our women prisoners several times. I can't be connected to this controversy. It could affect donations to the Ladies' Reformation Society."

"As I said, I didn't even hear about this case—" Daniel started.

"Now you have," Aunt interrupted. "Tell your wife to accept my offer. It will put her on a path that will draw her away from the unpleasantness of surgery. She can work as a philanthropist instead. Still using her prodigious intellect, of course."

"My wife has a name," he said through closed teeth. "It's Nora, as you well know."

"Daniel!" His father threw off his stony quiet and rose with a scowl.

Daniel held up a hand. "Forgive me. You caught me in the middle of some important preparations. It's hard to disengage my attention from the surgery ahead of me, and for the sake of my patient, I think it's best not to try. My patient's life depends on my clear head."

"Do you think we would come here in the thick of a cholera epidemic for trifles?" Aunt Wilcox asked, her eyes sparking dangerously. "You must get a handle on your wife. I championed you, proud you wanted to pursue a scientific career and marry a woman with intellectual pursuits. But there are limits. Don't make a fool of me, Daniel."

He sighed, the weight of the conversation too heavy for his loaded shoulders. "Surgery is not a mere hobby or intellectual pursuit. She's not bird-watching or collecting seashells, Aunt. And I have spoken to her about the petition. I'm sure she doesn't even know about this criminal midwife. I didn't. And she's not alone in abstaining; Dr. Croft refuses to sign as well. Disagreements are mother's milk to scientists." Daniel spread his hands, hoping to cover his nervousness with an appealing smile.

His father swallowed. Aunt Wilcox stared at him for an agonizingly long moment, then pushed from her chair. "You might choose to ignore me, but I'll keep saying this until one of you listens. Working as a surgeon is dangerous—"

"And your charitable work isn't?" Daniel challenged, talking over her reflexive sputtering. "You inspect disease-ridden prisons, after all. Do your dresses always stay clean?"

"My work is never unseemly," she warned in a hiss.

"You house convicted criminals," Daniel countered.

"I give unfortunate girls another chance by offering employment and sponsoring a house of reform." Aunt's face heated to an ominous red.

"You and Nora are both working for good ends," he insisted more gently. "Surely you've had detractors in your time, Aunt. Detractors you've proved wrong. Nora must have a chance to do the same."

His aunt leaned forward, pressing her thin hands to the desk. "I have no husband. No children. If I die in the course of my work, there is no one—no, don't contradict me—who will really suffer. What will happen when children come, Daniel? Will their claims on you and Nora matter as little as mine?"

A curtain dropped over his eyes. He couldn't afford to give any sign, not when he was troubled by the same questions.

"Consider your future family. Are they to have two parents constantly in danger? I monitor the Soho death rolls, so I know how many doctors die treating patients in this hospital."

Daniel's father raised his eyes from the floor. "Death rolls in Soho?"

Aunt lowered her lids smugly. "I subscribe to the same journals he does. I know every doctor that succumbs to consumption or pneumonia or infection, and now—cholera."

Of course she does.

"I suggest you begin making more intentional decisions about your family—not just because those decisions reflect on ours," she snapped.

"I'm fit as an ox and I've never seen Nora sick a day," Daniel said flatly.

"Don't be dismissive," his father warned. "Your aunt has always been good to us. You, in particular."

Daniel kept in a sigh. True. She'd never denied him a favor, however extravagant—anatomy tomes with beautiful color plates, visits to London to attend botanical lectures. She'd bought his first set of surgical instruments and paid for his room in Paris when he attended the Sorbonne. Since Harry had stayed with him for free, he, too, owed a great debt to Aunt Wilcox.

So he modulated his voice to something gentler. "I'm grateful you care about Nora. Surgery is a fraction of her work. Her days are filled with caring for the sick and injured. You of all people cannot possibly condemn that."

"I condemn nothing. I simply have sense, Daniel."

Daniel let out the sigh this time and looked into her milky-blue irises. Naturally, her gaze didn't waver. He couldn't remember when it ever had. "She will never give up medicine. Whether you wish it, or I." He dropped his eyes at the sudden falling sensation in his stomach. "I'm sure the news of this poor woman dying from an untrained midwife will move her. But I suspect it will move her to act in a different direction than Dr. Adams."

"She goes against the grain, and I can't have anyone saying I support anything unseemly."

Daniel half smiled. "No one would ever accuse you of being improper, Aunt."

"Don't laugh!" Aunt Wilcox clenched her teeth and her cheeks shook. "My causes are not trivial and cannot be endangered! We help women who have no one. Without our aid, they are victimized, oppressed, neglected. Many die, and so do their children."

He was as much taken aback by her emotion as by the truth in her words. He'd given little thought to her work—or how much it mattered. But her work wasn't Nora's, and the more he pushed his wife, the more she'd resist. She and his aunt would never see eye to eye. They were simply too different—Nora an adopted orphan of working-class origins; his aunt, a committed philanthropist but resolutely genteel.

Her loyalty to Daniel had put her at a disadvantage in many ways his family couldn't comprehend. They would never understand that she could have stayed in Italy, been a university professor, and worked in a large public hospital instead of struggling to establish a small one of her own here in London. She'd been made love to, pursued, and pressed to stay by Salvio Perra, one of her professors, and a man of wealth and influence.

Daniel's nostrils flared.

But Nora had chosen England, and him, for love, so Daniel wouldn't—couldn't—whittle away at her. They might be at odds at the moment, but when he thought of that other man propositioning her...

"I am quite aware of all I owe you," Daniel said quietly. "But my first allegiance must be to my wife. She cannot abandon her life's work to be your secretary."

"Daniel..." The rebuke in his father's voice stung.

"I'm sorry. I can't discuss this any longer. My patient is

waiting, and this surgery is a serious one." The air crackled, ready to break. "And please, it would ease my mind if you left London. You may say no one needs you, Aunt, but I cannot agree."

Aunt Wilcox searched him as if studying a stranger, threads of pain knotting her temples. She'd looked at him many ways over the years—most of them stern and daunting—but never with such disappointment.

CHAPTER 26

NORA RINSED HER MOUTH WITH COLD WATER, THEN PAT-
ted her face with a cold towel. She didn't like vomiting in
the mornings, especially since it was hard to hide the occasional
sickness from Daniel. The more she looked and acted like her
usual self, the better she could argue her case to continue her
usual work. But this morning she'd been in such a hurry she'd
barely managed to wait until Daniel left their bedroom, headed
to the hospital.

"Nora?" His voice on the other side of the door wrenched
her upright.

"I thought you left for Bart's," she called back, trying to
sound cheery.

"I heard you." His grim words slid through the door. "Are
you unwell?"

She pulled a deep breath into her lungs, then expelled it
as she opened the door of the water closet. "It's nothing. I'm
perfectly fine."

Daniel looked unconvinced. "Any fever? Chills?" He
reached for her hand and checked the temperature of her skin.
Only after he'd rolled her fingers over in his own did she realize
it had been days since they'd touched. The chills were not from
illness.

"You look pale."

"I'm not sick—not *that* kind of sick," she reassured him. "Just a wave of queasiness. Nothing, really."

"No diarrhea?" When he lowered his eyebrows like that, he looked nearly as stern as Horace.

"I don't have cholera, Daniel." She stepped around him, but he followed her back to their bedroom, close on her heels.

"Effects of the pregnancy, then?" He crossed his arms.

Nora sighed. "Of course it is. You've seen a hundred pregnant women."

"Not in the mornings in the water closet," he reminded her.

How could she want to flee the room and be taken in his tightest hold at the same moment? "Then you know this is no cause for concern. It passes in moments," she said, with more reassurance than truth.

"I'll do your rounds. You should be in bed if you're sick."

"I'm not diseased, Daniel."

He sat down heavily on the chest at the end of the bed, full of books and sketches and the dried flowers from her bridal bouquet. "There was a miscarriage at Bart's yesterday. A woman sick with cholera. I didn't even realize she was pregnant until the blood came."

"Are you sure it wasn't spotting from—"

"She lost the baby. A boy. I suppose I'll find out if we lost her when I arrive there this morning."

She wished he'd look at her. Maybe he couldn't. The distance between them was much more than the scant couple of yards permitted by the arrangement of their furniture. "She could have lost the child even without the sickness. It's a common occurrence." Many women didn't even count a pregnancy until the child quickened and announced itself with timid kicks.

"I don't dislike Mrs. Phipps's plan to take you to Suffolk. Surely it would be better than an awful autumn in London."

She swallowed and told herself he was referring only to the disease and the wet, icy weather, and not their marriage.

She sat in the chair beside the low coals in the fireplace. "I know you're frightened. If you don't want cholera patients here, I won't admit them," she conceded. She knew which point was vital to her, and they hadn't broached it yet.

Daniel narrowed his eyes. She never let him win so easily. "Truly?"

She gave a curt nod, hoping her chin didn't waver. It always gave her away when she was nervous. "I spoke to Ruth, and I think I may have a solution that makes us both happy."

His arms loosened fractionally at her unexpected smile. If she maneuvered skillfully enough… It was like weaving her way through torn ligaments and severed veins to find a healthy bone. "Ruth pointed out something to me that I've been so blind not to realize." She tapped the words out gently, sounding for hesitation, doubt. His face remained impassive, almost curious. "The midwives do have a requirement before they practice."

A slight closing of his expression. Most likely he suspected she was pivoting to the petition. She had to steer clear of it. "No one will hire a midwife who hasn't had a child herself. It's a necessary qualification."

She paused, but Daniel still waited, unaware she'd already shared her news. She spread her hands in appeal. "If I continue obstetrics work after our child comes, I'll be in the company of the midwives—hundreds of married women who help deliver babies. People are already accustomed to the situation of working mothers, especially in midwifery, so why wouldn't they accept me?"

She waited for his brow to loosen with relief, but he only ground his teeth.

"Midwives have no prestige. No training. It's beneath you. You've studied for years. You're a surgeon, Nora."

She drew in a deep breath and plunged onward. "And this way I can continue to perform surgeries. There would be cesareans and torn wombs and cysts of the ovaries." She tempered herself. She shouldn't sound so enthusiastic about calamities. "We know from experience most men won't consent to being treated by me unless it's a trivial complaint, but women surely will. Some might even prefer treatment from me once they know I've experienced motherhood myself."

"A licensed midwife?" he asked dubiously. "What does that even mean?"

"Not a midwife. An obstetrician. You well know the difference. I'm certified. I can practice surgery and medicine. But I can do it in the birth room, where other doctors show little interest. There's a chance they'll leave me alone there."

Daniel huffed. "Very little chance, given our luck. Adams was just telling me all families expect their private doctor to attend births. If you disrupt that, you threaten their livelihoods."

Nora stared at the thin red fissure glowing on a piece of coal. "It's so silly. They hate overseeing births. Harry doesn't like obstetrics, and you are so busy it's a burden." Even Horace rolled his eyes occasionally when called to a primigravida. "And in the meantime, I can't keep my ward filled because no men want me to treat them. We're all working on the wrong cases, Daniel." She sighed out a short blast of frustration. Sometimes seeing a solution galled more than a mystery, knowing there was a serviceable answer no one would accept…

"But if we make the decision to restrict care here—treating only women and children, developing a reputation for scientific, excellent care that's provided by women…"

Why wasn't he nodding? She'd painted a compelling future they could step into together, with satisfying work for both.

"Nora." His low voice vibrated with warning. "Your idea might have worked before, but…" He swallowed and exhaled. "There's been a development. An article in the papers about a midwife."

"What midwife?" Her blood froze. Surely nothing about Ruth.

"A young woman in Surrey. She placed advertisements in the local papers. No training whatsoever. It sounds like…" He hesitated. "She did a few deliveries before branching out into abortions. Apparently, she was doing quite well for herself until last week, when she killed a mother and her child, seven months along. My father and Aunt Wilcox informed me of the case yesterday."

Weight settled on her shoulders: cold, dull, and smothering. Nora forced a quick breath, but it caught in her throat. She swiped at her eyes, embarrassed by her quick feelings. She was so volatile lately.

Death was everywhere, but this news stung. Two tragic losses—and perhaps another coming, because the lawless girl would be prosecuted. Manslaughter was the usual verdict for abortionists and punished by death—or transportation, if the judge felt merciful. But any pity Nora might have felt for her was scorched away by one thing: "She was advertising?"

Daniel nodded. "Not for abortions, not explicitly. The ad promised 'effective treatment for blockages and feminine complaints,' or something like that."

Nora snorted. Clear enough language for luring desperate women. Exploiting them. "She wasn't a real midwife," Nora spat out.

"No, but she claimed it, and some poor woman trusted her. According to Adams, who examined the bodies, both baby and mother were terribly mutilated. The mother died four days later of infection."

Daniel leaned forward, his voice too soft. "Adams is making the most of it, I'm afraid. Drumming up public support for his petition. It's not just an academic issue among doctors anymore; all of London is joining the debate."

Nora straightened. "Understandably. But it's nothing to do with me. I'm advocating for better education. Licensing. Stricter controls." Not this current shamble where anyone could make up an advertisement and promise anything.

Daniel shook his head. "Adams is calling out any doctor who supports midwives. Says they're a danger to female patients who cannot know which ones are safe and which aren't." He turned away, pacing the floor. "He even mentioned—not by name, mind you—a foreign-trained doctor who is misguided enough to—"

"*He* is?" She spoke just above a whisper. "Are you sure *you're* not the one who believes that?"

"Nora." He sighed. "I've supported you in everything. If I had my way, you'd train dozens of midwives and make this hospital everything you imagine. I think your idea is a brilliant one. But Adams is starting a fight, and I can't allow you to set yourself against him when we both know you can't win. We've got to bide our time. Take things slower. In a year or two, circumstances might be—"

"At this rate, in a year or two, things will be that much worse."

"We don't know that," Daniel said. "In any case, we can judge the obstacles now. Standing up to Adams, especially in light of what's happened, is like"—he shook his head—"sending a lightweight against a title champion. You've fought too hard to lose everything now. Adams isn't just looking to give you a bruising, Nora. He'll knock you right out of the ring."

Her shoulders felt rigid enough to break. "I am not a lightweight."

"I meant—"

"I know what you meant."

"I don't think you do," Daniel said.

She wanted to stalk out of the room, but she'd need a walk of several miles in the driving rain just to damp the embers seething in her stomach. And her midwife pupils would arrive in less than an hour.

"My aunt repeated her invitation. I know it's not what you want—I don't want that for you, either. But perhaps if we looked at it more in the way of a strategic retreat? Gathering strength until the right time strikes?"

She sealed her lips in an angry line, refusing to answer.

She wanted to shout at him that now was the only time that mattered.

"What of my proposal about practicing obstetrics after our baby arrives?" she demanded quietly. He'd not even reacted.

"It's interesting," he said diplomatically. "I'll consider—"

"*You'll* consider? I believe it is *my* consideration that matters," she said, biting and spitting out her words like bitter fruit.

"Is it your only desire to fight me?" He looked at her incredulously. "If I'd known that before we married—"

Nora blanched, her legs unsteady. Daniel stopped as if shocked by his own words. He opened his mouth to apologize but the dagger was on her tongue, ready to throw.

"If I'd known how you'd be, maybe I'd never have considered…"

It hit the target. She pictured the blood running down the internal wound, draining the color from his face. They were playing at war, inflicting injuries that couldn't be soothed.

"I'm sorry," she whispered, though it was, of course, too late.

Daniel's disappointment glinted like arsenic crystals in his dark eyes. "I've never wanted to shut you up anywhere, including our nursery. I assumed you'd love our child and want to care for it. Even my mother, with her eccentricities, spent more time with us than our nurses." His stare raked over her. "My aunt wanted you to consider using your talents to help direct her society. You could give input on medical care for female prisoners."

"I'm not a secretary, Daniel." Nora closed her eyes because it hurt less than seeing him. "I don't practice medicine to be a philanthropist. I practice because my fingers ache when I don't. The thought of turning away from someone's cry—"

"And a baby's cry?" He waited, fear in the wrinkles at the corners of his eyes.

Her heart was a stone weight, chipping to pieces like flint. "I love our child already. But I won't stop loving medicine. Please don't ask me—"

His shoulders fell. "Very well. But as I said, the midwife debate is public now. And I'd rather not be in the thick of another controversy."

Nora remembered the last one—keeping the curtains drawn in the middle of the day, waiting for each successive excoriation in the newspapers. When she'd been found out as a woman practicing medicine, Daniel and Horace and even Harry had been seized in the hurricane. Several doctors still avoided the men of 43 Great Queen Street. She'd give anything for a bit of anonymity. But…

"I can't sign it, Daniel. And I can't trade my work for the cheap imitation offered by your aunt."

CHAPTER 27

D ANIEL PRETENDED NOT TO NOTICE AS HORACE EVALU-
ated the neat row of sutures. The patient slept soundly,
blissfully unaware of the careful slices and ligatures Daniel had
employed to excise the rocky tumor from her neck.

"You could have done the surgery easily, Horace. I saw your
dissection work this week. I wish you'd at least join me."

Daniel headed St. Bartholomew's women's ward, which
meant he could only operate on the females in his care, but
Horace was still titular head surgeon and could practice on any
ward in the hospital. Daniel missed the days of watching his
mentor race breathlessly through surgery after surgery.

Horace gave a small shrug. "I could do the routine surgeries, but where is the diversion in that?" He smiled imp-
ishly. "I did receive a note today from a visiting Hungarian
royal. She'd very much like me to oversee the birth of her
spaniel's litter."

Daniel burst into laughter. "Attend the delivery of puppies?"

Horace's face shone with amusement as he instinctively
began cleaning instruments. "So long as it goes well, I believe I
could persuade her to contribute to Nora's hospital."

"Of all the strange—"

Daniel broke off as Jeffers careened into the room. "You're

needed now, Dr. Gibson." His mottled red face and urgent words demanded speed.

"What is it? I'm still with Mrs. Hatfield."

Jeffers surveyed the peaceful patient. "I'll stay with her until she's awake. Wilkins needs you in the delivery room."

"What happened?" Daniel asked as he headed for the door, Horace at his heels.

"He just delivered a baby and he's having trouble with the placenta."

Daniel didn't wait to hear more. One of his most traumatic patient fatalities had come after delivering a placenta. There was no room for error. "Who's Wilkins?" Horace asked as he managed to keep up with Daniel. "Not a doctor here."

"Student. I don't think he's ever seen a delivery."

They reached the room at the same time as Adams, nearly colliding. "What are you doing here?" Daniel asked, not sparing time for manners.

"Wilkins is my student."

"And this is my ward," Daniel returned. "Wilkins should have told me he was delivering." He rushed to the bedside, where Wilkins sweated in a panic as the mother moaned quietly.

"The placenta doesn't look right," Wilkins said, eager to move aside and hand the stippled mass to Daniel. "And it's not coming away."

Daniel slid into position, his blood going cold as his eyes surveyed the scene. The firm, veined flesh was no placenta.

Horace swore. "Inverted uterus. Fully exterior."

"Dear Lord," Adams muttered behind them. "What happened?"

"What's wrong?" The woman yelped, catching the dismay in Adams's voice.

Horace tamed his anger long enough to give her a smile. "Nothing we can't fix."

Horace turned back to Adams, his eyes burning blue flames as his voice dropped to a vicious whisper. "What happened is your student has been tugging this woman's organ out of her body."

Wilkins's eyes reddened desperately. "I did everything they said in the lecture last year. I wouldn't even be on this ward at all, but the other students have cholera and you were in surgery," he said to Daniel as if he was to blame.

"Lecture last year," Horace scoffed. But when it came to midwifery, few doctors started their own practices with more than a lecture or two and, if fortunate, a birth they'd seen from the back of a flock of students.

"What is it?" the woman cried again, trying to sit up for a view.

"Just a displacement of the uterus," Horace said, soothing, coaxing her back down, knowing the words meant little to her. "Get me a long-necked bottle and a pitcher of salt water," Horace ordered, pushing up his shirtsleeves. Wilkins stared, perplexed, until Horace shouted, "Now!"

Wilkins scrambled to obey.

"We need the vaporizer," Daniel said. "If she's awake, we'll never overcome the after contractions."

"Never?" Horace challenged. "Nonetheless, it will be easier when she's unconscious."

When Daniel returned with the device, Horace fit the

mask over the mother's confused face, promising all would be well. "Just a slight complication, but when you wake, it will feel much better."

"Her eyes are closing," Daniel announced after a few frightened jerks of the woman's head.

Horace anointed the inside-out organ with water, which pinked as it collected traces of blood and spilled onto the floor. Daniel watched in confusion. Whatever Horace had up his sleeve, Daniel was as in the dark as anyone else.

"Salt will shrink the engorged uterus, making it easier to work it back into place," Horace explained, taking up a jar of salt and sprinkling grains liberally across the bloody landscape like falling snow. "Just another sprinkle and a bit of wine, as well."

Adams scowled. "Why do all your treatments sound more like recipes, Croft?"

Horace grunted and ignored the man, keeping his eyes on Daniel. "Let Jeffers man the ether for a bit. This part is laborious."

Daniel winced. From Horace, that meant a nearly impossible task.

"Thread some sutures and have them standing by, in case," Horace instructed without taking his eyes from the patient. "There!" Lightning quick, he indicated a spot with a probe. "A tumor. Inside the womb."

Sure enough, a misshapen ball of tissue, the size of a small pocket watch, glistened white and yellow through the membrane of the uterus.

In two minutes or so—twice as long as it would have taken

him before, but still an impressive time—Horace held the offending tumor in his palm. He set it aside and began sliding sutures into place with more care than a tailor. "Now, start easing it back into place," he directed.

Daniel frowned. Easier said than done when everything insisted on slipping through his fingers.

"How in the hell did your student not notice he was tugging out this woman's womb?" Horace growled at Adams.

"I—I was removing the placenta," Wilkins stammered quietly through pale lips.

"And when it came out attached to the uterus, you continued to pull?" Horace demanded.

"I didn't..." The terror of being responsible for someone's demise visibly washed over him. Daniel shivered. Every doctor knew the sensation.

"She needs a hysterectomy. Best to remove it entirely," Adams said, avoiding conversation about his dresser. "You'll never get it back in place intact, Horace. And if you did, it would prolapse again. We can ligate it."

Horace checked the patient's pulse. "We have more time with the anesthesia. She's breathing easily. Proceed, Gibson."

If only he could. Daniel had managed only to prod a few millimeters back into place, but salt was drawing out the bloating fluids, and slowly, slowly, with his finagling, the organ retracted farther inside the birth canal. Horace took a turn when Daniel grew too frustrated, and between the two of them, they finally maneuvered the last bit through the cervix.

Daniel sighed with relief. His shoulders ached with the strain. "Is the patient still stable?" he asked.

"Enjoying a postpartum nap," Horace said. "Let me finish."

Daniel ceded his chair to the older man. Only when he turned did he realize how many doctors had crammed into the room.

"You cannot just leave the uterus in place once you return it," Horace said airily, as if discussing how to prune roses or select a wine for dinner. "The round ligaments are now degraded from pregnancy and injury. Imagine it in a deflated state, vulnerable to prolapse." Horace taught as he always did—conversationally. Even the seasoned surgeons held their breath as they observed.

"Now that Gibson has returned the organ to its rightful place inside the body, we can proceed. This bottle is filled with warm salinized water. I will invert the bottle and release the fluid, effectively inflating the organ to help it hold its shape and position. This will also help the ovaries to return to their place."

The room erupted into boisterous applause as Horace proceeded. One student removed his hat and dashed it against his leg in disbelief. A hurrah sounded from the back of the mob, growing as orderlies and other students tried to cram inside to see what they'd missed.

"I've never seen uterine polyps contribute to a complete external prolapse," Adams grumbled over the buzz of excitement.

Horace stood slowly, unrolling his spine and taking care to plant his feet. "Now you have."

"Where did you learn it?" a student demanded, his young eyes sparking with wonder like train wheels on the rails.

Horace grinned as he rinsed the blood from his hands. "A farmer in Edinburgh."

"Farmer?" Daniel frowned with contracted eyebrows.

"He learned it from his grandfather. One of their heifers pushed her whole sack out with the calf, and they salted it to shrink it and showed me how to use the bottle. Took us three hours to push that uterus back in."

Horace surveyed the incredulous doctors. "You never dismiss a good idea, no matter where it comes from—even toothless, illiterate farmers." He settled a heavy stare on Adams, his soft Scottish brogue more distinct than usual. "We doctors do not have a monopoly on knowledge."

Nora stayed up that night, reading and waiting for Daniel. The clock struck eleven, twelve, then one, before she finally heard the distant groan of the front door. Fifteen minutes passed, but he didn't come upstairs.

Fine.

Putting on her slippers, she tied herself inside her thickest wrapper and abandoned the warmth of the bed, armed with a flickering candle.

She found him in the library with a book. He looked up in surprise and something else—a mixture, perhaps, of equal parts shame and stubbornness.

Setting aside her candle, Nora took the opposite chair, tucking up her feet to keep them warm.

"I was reading, too," she said. "Don't tell me I should have been sleeping. You could also use the rest."

"I wasn't going to say that."

She nodded at the book. "Any good?"

His mouth hitched, then fell as he let out a sigh. "I haven't understood a word."

"Me neither." Nora shifted. "I've been thinking."

Daniel's eyebrows lifted. She could almost see the anxiety tightening around his chest. "Nothing terrible," she promised. At least, she hoped not. "I think...I think maybe there's another way." One that didn't involve giving up. Or giving in, because she was not signing Adams's petition or abandoning midwives like Ruth.

"Adams and his colleagues are right. Unlicensed practitioners are dangerous." She didn't say that she was happy to lump Adams in with the shamsters, although what kind of care was he offering if he didn't physically examine his patients?

But Daniel was right. She wouldn't win a brawl.

"And?" Daniel prompted.

"We're overrun, Daniel. There aren't enough doctors to deal with the sickness in London. What doctor wouldn't be relieved to be spared an eleven-hour delivery?"

"I would," he admitted. "Especially today. If anyone comes—"

"Our hands are full already."

"Yes." He offered a rueful smile. Hope quickened her breathing.

"In Italy, midwives attended the lectures and trained with the doctors."

"Yes, you've told me."

"So we're drawing a battle line where we should be greeting an ally. Abolishing a trade when we could train, license, and partner with midwives instead."

He exhaled in thought, his eyes softening.

"If we could just arrange a discussion," she began. "A public one people could attend."

"You mean a spectacle." He twisted his wedding band around his finger. "That's risky. For all of us."

She couldn't argue. Public lectures and symposia could be volatile events. Her first and last one had been a disaster that spurred her flight to Italy. The discovery that Daniel had lied, taking credit for the hernia surgery that was more Nora's than his so they could publish their findings, had nearly cost him his career.

"It would be different. I'm licensed now, and we aren't trying to hide anything. Everything I'd be presenting is backed by the Italian medical establishment. Once doctors learn of the possibilities—"

"If Horace arranges a lecture, doctors will come," Daniel admitted. "But that would be intentionally gathering a mob that's already against us."

Nora pictured the angry doctors circled around her in the lecture theater. "Adams made this dispute public. Maybe we need to use that to our advantage."

She had another idea, but she was scared to use it. *Don't be a coward.*

"I don't want to keep books for your aunt, but I did think of a way we could collaborate." It was like offering to partner with a bear—a fierce creature capable of lumbering along benignly until it wasn't. Nora didn't want to end up being devoured.

Daniel shook his head. "I don't understand."

"Suppose she arranged the lecture."

He said nothing for a long, long moment. Nora couldn't tell if that was good or bad. "Why do you suggest that?"

"Horace will attract a good number of doctors and scientists. But if the event is organized by your aunt, women will come, too—members of Parliament. And their wives. Women who chair philanthropic societies and—"

"I see what you're driving at."

"Yes. And I can explain how training midwives will help doctors and patients. Especially in times like these, when doctors are overtaxed."

Why wasn't he grinning as brightly as she was? It was a brilliant tack—capturing all the wind of Adams's ire and using it to blow her toward her own harbor.

"And we would get Aunt to agree, how?" Daniel asked as he stuffed his hands deep in his pockets. "She's already offended."

"You're her favorite. Surely—"

"I *was* her favorite. You didn't see her yesterday. I chose you over her, and she felt it keenly." He'd told her about his father and aunt making their terrible appearance at the hospital, but she hadn't realized how deeply it affected him until his dark eyes dropped from hers.

"I'll go apologize." Nora squared her shoulders, pretending a courage she didn't possess. "I'll find a way to win her over."

Daniel raked a hand through his carefully combed hair. "Nora, she's firmly on the other side. Adams is her friend and personal physician. We've lost this one."

Nora studied the two feet of emptiness between them. She'd already sacrificed too much to this argument. Courage might fail her, but stubbornness never did. "I'll find a way."

Nora shortened her steps so she wouldn't miss the rare dapples of sunlight playing through the last bright leaves of the year. She hadn't walked a park on Sunday in too many weeks to count, but her steps fell quietly on the lawn of Green Park as Daniel stepped beside her, his sleeve brushing hers.

"One boy in a family of nine shows no symptoms. Why?" Daniel hid frustration well, but Nora heard it under his controlled words. He'd spent all morning in Lambeth, trying to pry a large family from cholera's ruthless claws.

"Perhaps he's like me and had it before?"

"One of the daughters looks like a miniature version of Julia. I can't stand the thought."

At the mention of Julia, Nora turned away. She'd performed the promised examination Friday. She tried to quell the memory of Julia waking, confused and groggy, demanding answers before she fully knew where she was. Nora had stalled, telling her they'd discuss it when Julia could sit up and gather her thoughts, but she had clutched Nora's sleeve, refusing to wait.

"What did you find?" she'd demanded. "Can I have children?" Her eyes had managed to bore into Nora's soul for a moment before they rolled back from the effects of the ether.

Nora blinked, returning to the dry leaves littering the park lawn. She couldn't relive the crushing despair on Julia's face when she'd told her.

"I hope your patient pulls through," she told Daniel, silently wishing the same for Julia. Her loss and her oppressed mood were as worrisome to Nora as any named disease. And Julia hadn't wanted Nora to confide in any of the men, so for now, the two of them bore the heavy secret alone.

"How do you feel?" he asked softly, without any jagged edges of criticism. His eyes dropped to her abdomen.

She drew in a breath of relief. "Nothing as bad as cases I've treated."

Daniel grinned at the good news. "And you've treated so many. I've almost adjusted to your flock of midwives following you like the students follow Horace."

"The students follow you now, too," Nora corrected.

He nodded modestly and moved on, never one to linger on praise. "I've been trying to share the news from Bart's with you since yesterday, but I haven't had the chance until now. Last night we were occupied discussing the midwives and a lecture—"

"News?" Her arms stiffened as she braced herself.

"Adams made a fool of himself yesterday when one of his students inverted a uterus and nearly killed a woman. Right there in Bart's."

"The entire uterus?" She'd seen small prolapses, but never that. "Did you have to remove it?"

Daniel recounted the incident with the vivid detail she loved, stopping frequently as she posed questions or rattled off exclamations of disbelief in Italian. When he finished, she'd forgotten the stinging chill of the autumn air and their recent arguments.

"Ruth would never have made such a mistake!" Nora declared, pleased by the agreement in Daniel's face.

"The papers are going to sensationalize the murder trial of that fraudulent midwife, but at least now we have an account of a medical student making a dangerous error," he said. "That should give you a bit of ammunition, should they fire shots at your midwives."

Nora couldn't remember the last time relief flooded her. The warmth expanded her lungs, as if she hadn't truly breathed in weeks. "Does this mean you agree with me on the petition?" she asked cautiously.

Daniel laced his fingers together. "We need standards. And we need teachers like you." His voice dropped and his small smile fell away. "The myriad of things that can go wrong…"

Most days, they could walk through the tragedies with a grim and factual acceptance, but on this cold October Sunday, reality fell as lifeless and smothering as the leaves around them.

"What if you get sick and I can't save you?" Daniel asked quietly.

A stiff wind pushed between them, fluttering her lace collar. "I wonder the same about you," Nora admitted.

Sunlight speckled his face as relentless thoughts marched over his forehead. He cleared his throat, fighting visibly for whatever he meant to say.

"I'm on your side, Nora." He groped for her hand and found her. "We have no power over death, but we must stand together in life."

It took a moment to absorb the words, let them travel through her.

She took his face in her free hand and kissed him where his widow's peak swept down his brow. By the time she straightened, the breeze had dried her wet eyes and left her with a smile that felt like happier days.

CHAPTER 28

THE COBBLESTONES ECHOED BENEATH NORA'S BOOTS AS she sidestepped, neatly evading a throng of foreign students spilling from the brightly lit Austrian café. The scent of coffee, woven into the nimbus of tobacco smoke, tugged on her elbow, tempting her inside. A hot, bitter cup might burn off some of the soreness nestling between her shoulder blades—the aftereffect of attending a delivery with Ruth and two new midwives who'd begun her classes.

For the last seven hours, she'd taught medical terms and techniques in the urgency of the moment instead of in a lecture. It seemed to have worked. Discussing pelvic rims and traction during a heated labor cemented the terms into her students' minds. By the end of the delivery, they'd used them with scarcely an extra thought.

There'd been a few moments when Nora had wondered if she'd need her scalpel after four hours of largely unproductive pushing. When the infant finally descended enough, Nora had demonstrated the proper use of the short forceps. After another hour of patient, nearly breathless maneuvering, she'd brought forth a seven-pound boy with downy orange hair and shining eyes—indigo one moment, button black the next.

Fascinating, that particular hue. So common among infants, and so temporary. By a child's first birthday, their eyes morphed into blue or brown, green or hazel or gray—a remarkable array of colors, but none so compelling to her as that glossy, just-born blue-black. She'd tried to duplicate that tint when painting, mixing shades and giving up in disappointment when she couldn't reproduce a color capable of eliciting the sensation she felt meeting the unblinking gaze of a newborn.

Not too much longer, and she'd be looking her own child eye to eye.

A boy, passing her on the pavement, jostled her shoulder, making her drop her bag. She'd thought herself almost to a standstill again.

Before her bag fell prey to watchful urchins, Nora seized it from the ground. Straightening, she glared back at the offending shoulder, but the boy who owned it hadn't bothered to notice and was walking airily away. Grumbling under her breath, she checked the contents. Yes, her mercury thermometer had survived.

She turned her head back to the café, doubly tempted, as she was scheduled to call on Daniel's aunt later today.

That prospect made a few moments' retreat even more necessary.

Nora slipped inside the café and purchased a kleiner brauner. She'd learned in Italy how to nurse one cup for an hour or more, and she used her training well.

If only she could reschedule her visit with Aunt Wilcox for later in the week. But Aunt Wilcox was not the rescheduling sort. She wouldn't understand or sympathize with a long labor, and Nora couldn't breathe a word about her unsettled stomach or groggy head. The pregnancy must be saved for another day—another battle.

She was tempted to burrow her head atop her arms and doze right at the table, but a flock of young men kept up a rowdy banter two tables away. A few more sips and then she'd pay for a carriage. Perhaps fill the extra time by having it circle Regent's Park while she caught a half hour of sleep...

She left her payment beneath her empty cup and ventured into the chill and damp air, waving down a dull-faced driver with a sad, drenched palomino pony. "Just slowly," she instructed, handing him a generous fare. "I'd like to see the leaves in the park before I arrive."

When the carriage halted, Nora lifted her head from the bench, shaking away sleep as she oriented herself. The musty odors and worn fabrics of the cab blurred in a dizzying swirl. Biting her lip—the pain would jolt her awake—she blinked to clear her eyes.

Aunt's house.

She wished for a mirror, certain that her once carefully pinned hair was now fuzzy. Hopefully, she'd have a moment to make repairs in the hall.

Grasping her bag, Nora trudged up the steps. A stern-faced butler opened the door without a word, elastic eyebrows lowering at the sight of her. "Mrs. Gibson?" he asked, though he'd seen her before and knew precisely who she was.

"Yes, thank you." She stepped inside and handed him her bag. "Please see this is kept safe. I'd like to visit the water closet before I see Aunt." She spoke with far more authority than she felt. The butler's cuffs and collars were of finer quality and certainly in a better state than her own.

An older maid showed Nora to a small room, which also happily contained a washstand and mirror.

Nora washed her face, shivering from the cold water, and repinned her hair, smoothing it into place with wet fingers. A pinch to her cheeks, a quick shake of her skirts—thank goodness her billowing apron had protected her clothes throughout the delivery. One smear, the unmistakable brownish-red of dried blood, marred her sleeve, but she did her best to twist it toward the back of her arm, retucked her blouse, and reemerged almost a new woman.

The maid was waiting. "This way, ma'am."

Nora followed obediently, fortifying her confidence by trying out suitable greetings in her mind. Pleasing and convincing Aunt Wilcox seemed the only way if she was to mend things with Daniel and circumvent Adams.

Aunt Wilcox presided over the drawing room from a fireside chair. "You didn't come in your own carriage?" Her eyes swept over Nora, fixing on her arm. "Where have you been?"

"A difficult labor. But the child and mother are safe."

Aunt's nose flared and her eyebrow lifted. "Certainly left you the worse for wear." Before Nora could scrap together a reply, she continued, "I suppose that's to be expected. At least you're competent, not a criminal like that Surrey woman. Take a seat."

Nora had expected more idle conversation before confronting the matter, but perhaps this was fortunate. It was hard, maintaining pleasantries with Aunt Wilcox, and this spared her from introducing the difficult topic. "That case in Surrey is one of the reasons I wanted to speak with you. You are so influential. If that woman is found guilty—"

"She will be."

Nora swallowed. "I know she'll find her treatment in prison more humane because of your efforts."

Aunt nodded. "That is our aim."

"And a noble one," Nora agreed. "I've come to—"

"One moment, please." Aunt raised her hand, then turned to another maid, just entering the room with a tea tray. "That should have been placed before my guest arrived."

The woman apologized with a quick bob and scurried from the room, face red and crumpled.

"She's new. From the refuge," Aunt Wilcox explained. "You must forgive her failings. Margot just started upstairs yesterday. She's intelligent, though. I've no doubt she'll improve."

Nora looked back toward the empty doorway. "That's very commendable." Even if she thought it might be done with a little more kindness.

Aunt waited expectantly.

"I wanted to discuss a scheme I have," Nora began. "For the education and improvement of women. It bears on this recent case and your own work. I'd like to establish a training program for midwives."

"I don't—"

"As you know, there are some unqualified women—"

Aunt Wilcox snorted. "I'd say. My physician, Dr. Adams, abhors the lot of them."

"I'm familiar with his argument. But it is a very limited

view—tainted, I think—because he is a man. If I could impart a female perspective..." Nora held her breath, but Aunt Wilcox didn't object, though her brows lowered.

"When I worked in Italy, it was common for midwives to learn from each other, as they do here, but also from doctors and surgeons. They frequently work alongside them, even. When there are complications, a surgeon is summoned. But when matters proceed smoothly, he or she can confidently entrust a woman's care to the midwives."

Aunt scowled slightly—whether in doubt or disdain, Nora couldn't tell.

"There are extremely skilled and experienced midwives here in London, treating hundreds of women unable to afford physicians."

"The charity hospitals are free," Aunt countered. "They could have a baby with a physician attending, all without a farthing."

"It sounds reasonable," Nora conceded. "But I know a great deal about such hospitals and doctors. The vast majority are students who have seen one or two births. And the close quarters spread disease. Most women, rich or poor, prefer to be attended in their own homes."

The maid returned and lowered the tray to the table with a wobble that made Nora flinch. Luckily, the tea service landed safely. "We'll serve ourselves," Aunt said, dismissing her, and turned back to Nora. "According to Dr. Adams—"

"He does have some valid critiques," Nora admitted, the words grating her throat. "But I think those are best resolved by improving the education offered to women and creating standards like those that govern doctors and apothecaries. If it works for those professions, why not for midwives as well? In Bologna, medical professors train and work beside the midwives, who attend some of the same classes as the surgical students—"

Aunt replaced her cup in her plate with a clink. "The same classes? The men and women together..." Aunt exhaled in a tight huff. "Do you know how long and hard I've worked to have female prisoners given their own wards? The impropriety of the male inmates is beyond description. Mixed company in such settings—"

"The medical setting is quite different." Nora pushed away inconvenient memories of bawdy medical students casting sideways glances at her as they discussed cervixes and birth canals.

"Impossible. I cannot contemplate such a thing. To view and discuss such intimate concerns—"

"I quite see your point," Nora said smoothly. She must switch tacks to ensure Aunt Wilcox didn't dismiss her out of hand.

"That is why I propose teaching midwives at my own hospital, in a setting entirely female. My best student, Mrs. Franklin, is learning the safe use of forceps. She's far more experienced than any student at Bart's."

"But what does any of this have to do with your visit today?" Aunt might have learned to position her eyebrows from the tzarina herself. Nora had never seen such a superior expression.

"You've heard of the petition trying to outlaw midwives?"

"The one my nephew signed and you did not? Yes, I have."

Nora swallowed, ignoring the barb. "Daniel signed it only

because he believes midwives should be trained, not outlawed. And I agree. If Mr. Adams has his way, they will make midwifery illegal, and we will see even more women turning to shamsters out of desperation, just to have someone attend their births."

"I'm sure he doesn't intend that." Aunt Wilcox frowned. "He is not a cruel man."

"No. But I've come for your help. You've championed women for decades. You know every woman of influence and charitable leanings in London. If we could appeal to them..." Nora glanced at the inexpertly assembled tray, thinking of the young woman who'd brought it into the room. "I would like to train some of your former prisoners—give them a job that is respectable. A new start."

Nora couldn't pretend interest in her tea. Her face flushed as she set her saucer on the table. "We must find a way to help all women—the pregnant ones who deserve a qualified attendant at their births, as well as those who must provide for their families. And perhaps give women who are not skilled at domestic service another choice?"

Aunt Wilcox stared at her tea, deliberating.

"I'm not interested in fighting with other doctors," Nora said. "But you know as well as I do how difficult it will be to persuade them. I can't do that alone, but I might succeed with your help."

Aunt Wilcox set aside her cup. "What you say makes some sense."

Nora froze, resisting the urge to laugh. From Aunt, that was practically a fond compliment.

"If your students are especially talented—"

"They are," Nora asserted.

"And the training you propose is rigorous and morally unexceptionable—"

"It certainly is," she promised.

Aunt inhaled as if the action caused her a great deal of trouble. "I could perhaps sponsor a private meeting for you with a selection of acquaintances."

Nora pressed her lips together, her fingers tightening into fists to rein in her excitement. She didn't want to make any movement or speak a word that would change Aunt's mind.

Aunt Wilcox withdrew a small, dry biscuit from the tray and dipped it into her tea as she pondered. She took a tidy bite and chewed interminably before speaking again. "But there is a favor I require of you." She perched at the edge of her ornate chair, much like a hawk considering its prey.

Nora nodded cautiously.

"I associate with a particular set of people—educated, brilliant, refined—and they have high expectations of manners and traditions." Aunt replaced the misshapen biscuit on her saucer, the shape of her strong front teeth imprinted in the sweet. Nora studied it with the same intensity Horace would bestow on a fossil. "They are the people with whom I wish Daniel to fraternize."

The wet October chill fell away, replaced by the warning heat under Nora's skin. How had she not noticed the cloying perfume that filled Aunt's house? She nearly choked on it now.

"They will, I believe, tolerate an eccentric girl educated in midwifery. There are certain allowances offered you because of your celebrated guardian. But they will have little sympathy with a female surgeon. So I must insist you limit yourself to educating your students and put off surgery. For your sake and Daniel's."

The clutch of the talons stole Nora's breath. Her mind blackened and lost the words she'd been readying. Aunt took advantage of her speechlessness.

"It is a more appropriate and useful way to use your talents. Why a woman would ever want to cut into a body... Though truly, I don't comprehend how even a man could consider it. If you give me your word that you will limit yourself to midwifery, I can perhaps arrange a drawing-room lecture and give you a chance to win over people of influence."

At last Nora found her breath. "I can't—"

Aunt Wilcox continued over her, a slow-moving, inexorable current. "But if they are not convinced and continue on with their petition, I expect you to be a gracious loser and sign it."

Nora licked her lips. Obstetrics included some of the most demanding surgeries, ones many surgeons refused to attempt. Apparently, Aunt knew nothing about that.

"I'm a doctor, Aunt. For us, the practice of treating feminine concerns is termed obstetrics."

Aunt Wilcox waved a blithe hand. "Yes, naturally."

Was this loophole big enough? She had to try. "I'll concentrate my efforts on obstetrics—what you call midwifery." Let her think she'd won that point, when it was Nora's plan all along. "But I will not sign that petition. It is an ill-conceived attempt to push females out of a profession that once belonged solely to us. A profession which could help the women you serve. For their sake, I cannot."

Aunt's blue irises quivered. She was not the compromising type. Her lip trembled, as if her next words were particularly challenging to form. "Very well. My club meets every third Wednesday. I will bring up your proposal and see if they agree."

Nora knew better than to smile. With a humble nod, she folded her hands demurely in her lap. "Thank you."

CHAPTER 29

N ORA." JULIA'S BREATHLESS VOICE CONVEYED A TIGHT, controlled urgency.

Nora glanced up from the burnt arm she was bandaging, coating the injury with cold, soft flour that eased the pain as the young boy gritted his teeth. He'd been injured by a blast of steam from a burst factory pipe, and his father was watching her narrowly, still disappointed there was no male doctor available to help his son.

"Yes?" Nora asked cautiously, praying that this interruption was no domestic emergency involving cooks or laundry. If the boy's irate father was presented with one more reminder that she was a woman...

"Mrs. Franklin is here with a child." Julia's eyes darted to the doorway, a clear message to hurry. Ruth had never brought a patient in. One of her newborns? Fragile and on the cusp of life? Nora brushed the flour from her hands.

"Mrs. Trimble can finish bandaging your son." Nora sped through instructions, giving the last ones from the hallway, hurrying to the clinic entrance, racing through possible scenarios. Aspirated meconium? Cord strangulation?

Wheelbarrow.

Nora stopped short at the wooden gardener's cart in the

middle of the reception room. Ruth twisted her hands, eyes red as she pulled back a ragged blanket revealing a filthy young girl curled into a ball of misery.

"What?" This was no newborn, but a school-age child, limp with blue skin.

Ruth's voice trembled as she spoke. "I delivered a stillborn child today. Found this girl—a sister—on the floor in this state. Cholera."

"You brought her in a wheelbarrow?" Nora bent down, taking a frail wrist in her hands. Even her practiced fingers struggled to find a pulse.

"No cab would take her in her state. I had to plead for this rickety thing."

"How far did you come?"

Just as Ruth tried to answer, the incensed father thundered down the hallway, carrying his crying son.

"Mr. Brown, stop," Nora pleaded.

"I'll take him to Bart's. No one told me this place was run by women." He nearly collided with Mrs. Phipps on his way out the door.

"Who was that?" she demanded, scowling after him before her eyes riveted to the wheelbarrow. "And what's this?"

Julia emerged from the hallway, shaking. "I'm sorry," she said through trembling lips. "I was bandaging him just as you said. The father asked where the male doctors were, and I said they were doing rounds at St. Bart's. He just yanked up the boy and left without a word."

"Never mind that now." Nora turned her eyes back to the

softly panting girl. If she examined her quickly and sent her home, she'd not be breaking the agreement to keep cholera out of the hospital. "Julia, I need clean linens and something for this girl to wear."

Mrs. Phipps tossed her bonnet onto the desk. "I keep a small collection of clothes—for emergencies. I'll find her a shift."

For half a second, Nora wondered if Mrs. Phipps had always done so—even when Horace had appeared carrying a feeble eight-year-old almost twenty years ago.

Ruth twisted her skirt in a tight fist. "I probably shouldn't have brought her, but—"

"I wouldn't have left her, either. But I'm not sure it will help." Nora lifted the child carefully, trying to keep the filthiest parts away from her blouse. The girl didn't weigh nearly what she expected. "Heavens, does she have hollow bones?" The motion expelled a small flood of clear water from the girl's mouth. Nora shifted so most of it splashed to the floor. It was the symptom of cholera she most dreaded—when the fluids no longer required a heave to make their way out, but simply flowed like a high river breaching an embankment.

Ruth did a mincing step to avoid the sudden puddle. "Her name is Amelia Dawson. Her parents begged me to—"

"I can't keep her in hospital. If people hear there's cholera here, they won't come." Back in the examination room, Nora swept aside the spills of soft flour and the unused bandages from treating the burnt boy and settled Amelia onto the table. The small body—she could hardly admit there was a girl still inside—sprawled out without resistance or recognition.

A web of blue veins discolored her wraithlike arm, and a warning tinge of lavender suffused her lips. "She's ice cold," Nora said.

There were warming stoves in the patient ward that kept the room toasty against the coldest days. And clean linens. And screens to shield infectious patients.

"Go to the kitchen and get a hot kettle. Cook always keeps at least one ready," Nora said.

Mrs. Phipps returned with full arms. "I brought a blanket from the oven, but we need to bathe her."

"Ruth's getting water. I have sponges in here." Nora took the warm blanket and put it over the girl, willing it to seep some heat back into the frozen limbs. She looked up at Mrs. Phipps's worried face, somehow older than it had been at the breakfast table. "I can't keep her here. We all agreed—"

Mrs. Phipps pursed her lips. "Does she have a decent home to go back to once you treat her?"

"Her mother just delivered a stillborn and is failing herself. The father can't take care of both of them," Ruth answered grimly as she set down the kettle.

"You did the right thing," Mrs. Phipps clipped, always brisker when deeply troubled. "We'll care for her. Quietly," she added when Nora opened her mouth to protest. There was currently a sign on the clinic door announcing *Cholera Patients Seen in Homes Only.*

"We must be adaptable," Mrs. Phipps said reflexively—one of Horace's maxims. "She's a child."

The four women worked together, removing the stained

nightshirt and wiping down the cold, soiled skin. At one point, the girl gave a sigh that sounded so much like a last breath that Nora panicked and searched for a heartbeat. It still slogged on—lethargic and reluctant.

Nora fitted a tube into the girl's mouth, tucking it between her teeth and cheek where the saliva glands were located, and used a funnel to drip a slow stream of tea. Jasmine leaves stimulated blood flow, and Nora's most immediate fear was the small heart stopping.

"A cholera cot would be best," Mrs. Phipps said, speaking of a cot with a hole cut away and a bucket placed underneath so the patient didn't need to be moved and cleaned constantly.

Nora gave her head a small shake. She and Daniel had only just reconciled. If he came home to her cutting up cots and treating a cholera patient in their own home—

But then again, once he saw Amelia…

They'd done everything they could in the exam room. The girl hadn't focused her eyes once. Nora doubted she knew where she was. If she survived, this day would be folded away into the mysterious vaults of her mind, never to be reopened. Nora chewed the inside of her lip and looked to Mrs. Phipps.

The older woman steeled herself. "We'll put up the screens and set her far away from the others." Her eyes dipped to Nora's middle, and her voice dropped. "But perhaps you shouldn't tend her anymore."

Nora stepped forward to tuck the girl's dangling arm on top of her frail chest. Without warning, the weak purple fingers closed around Nora's, the grip fragile and pleading.

Mrs. Phipps knew the answer as soon as Nora lifted her eyes. "This way," Mrs. Phipps said, leading Ruth out the room. "We'll put her on a cot by the stove."

Julia caught Nora's sleeve as she started to follow. "We can let her stay, but Mrs. Franklin said Amelia's mother delivered a dead baby today." Julia's voice lagged as her eyes melted into pools of blue worry. "It sounds like cholera kills unborn children."

"I—I doubt—" Nora stammered.

"You should keep your distance."

With timid hands, Nora smoothed her skirt over her stomach. It was swelling. Though not visible to anyone else, she'd loosened the drawstring on her drawers by several inches. The small person was making its presence known.

"But, Nora," Julia added in a conciliatory tone before she sucked in her breath. "You can still teach Ruth what to do. You could teach the midwives how to nurse all the sick patients instead of only laboring mothers. If you taught them basics like suturing and treatments, they could do work when you can't."

Nora stood still, staring at the striped wallpaper. Had the idea just sprung into existence in Julia's mind? It was surprisingly brilliant. "Horace always says cholera is like an invasion, marching over cities and devouring everything." Nora's words escaped slowly, knitting into solid thoughts as she spun them off her tongue.

Every doctor in London was whittling away with the demands of a sick, teeming city. But the midwives were women with time and talent to spare. Nora had thought only of training them in labor and delivery, but they could do far more. They could help stem the flow of disease and suffering. Women well acquainted with the most afflicted neighborhoods and their tenants.

"If it's true—if cholera is an armed invasion"—Nora's eyes widened—"then we need soldiers."

"The midwives?" Julia asked hopefully, giving a small bounce on her feet.

Nora smiled. She could kiss the brilliant girl in front of her. "The midwives."

—

Between the hackney and his umbrella, Daniel managed to stay mostly dry above his ankles, but he'd spent so much effort getting Horace safely through the swimming streets that he'd not placed his own feet carefully enough. Now the two men were reduced to using the clinic entrance to avoid Mrs. Phipps's wrath. Whatever vile substance covered their shoes, they didn't dare track it into her parlor.

"You're back." Julia froze as they opened the door. She balanced a pillow in one hand, a small pile of clothing in the other.

Horace gestured to the mud on his trousers. "Don't come too close. We haven't washed yet."

"Cholera patients?" she asked, a strange tightness to her face.

"All day," Horace replied. "We'll change into new clothes in the ice room."

Daniel hardly relished even chillier temperatures, but it was certainly the last place they needed to worry about infecting anyone. And unless Nora had had a terrible day, there were no bodies stored there at the moment.

"Would you bring a bucket of hot water and soap?" he asked.

Julia's nervous eyes darted down the hall. "Of course."

As he and Horace shivered through a fast scrub and change, a timid knock sounded on the door. "Yes?" Daniel asked, speeding up his numb fingers as he buttoned his shirt.

"It's Nora. I need to show you both something."

Horace met Daniel's gaze, his eyebrows lowered. "That doesn't sound promising."

"Just a moment," Daniel called through the thick door. Horace hadn't even gotten his arms into his sleeves. But Horace was right—something tense and hesitant hung in her voice.

When they opened the door, she stood across the hall, hands knotted.

"Is something wrong?" Daniel prodded.

Instead of answering, she motioned them to the hospital ward. "Ruth brought in a patient today. She and Julia and Mrs. Phipps are tending to her. You need to see for yourselves."

Daniel's muscles tensed, coiled for whatever sight might meet him behind the screens Nora had positioned. Something dire enough that it required the attention of four women.

"This is Amelia." Nora nudged away the screen to reveal an undersize child that hardly made a bump in the thick blankets covering her. The girl slept on despite the visitors, her large eyelids bulging slightly from her skeletal face.

"Cholera," Horace said flatly.

Daniel glanced quickly between the silent observers and the girl.

"Yes," Nora confirmed, nervously chewing her lip.

"I knew you didn't want the cholera here," Ruth admitted. "Her home was little better than the streets. I couldn't leave her there."

"Of course not," Julia said, giving Daniel a warning glare. "We've agreed to care for her, and Nora will keep her distance."

Horace gave a grim chuckle. "It seems every epidemic brings some dying girl in with the tide."

"Don't be absurd. She's going home after we treat her. She has a family." Mrs. Phipps squared her shoulders, ready for a battle.

"So you all expect her to stay?" Horace scanned the women who sported various expressions of guilt and fierceness.

"There's no choice, is there?" Ruth spread her hands.

"There certainly is," Daniel finally injected. "I could take her to the cholera ward at Bart's."

Four voices rose in tangled arguments, impossible to unwind into separate words.

Daniel raised his hand to stop them. "Didn't we all agree—"

"We agreed not to start a cholera ward," Nora pointed out, her voice so low everyone halted to hear her. "And we won't. But I think we should treat Amelia. If it's going to kill her, it will be quickly. And if she survives, we'll return her home as soon as she's strong enough."

"The outlook is grim," Horace interjected. "There's very little chance—"

"What about the article I came across—from that surgeon, Mr. Torrance, transfusing the vein with solution?" Nora was stretching wildly and they all knew it.

"Haven't read it. Not sure I need to." Horace lowered his

eyebrows in disdain. "I think you know well enough how it goes when we start throwing random substances into the bloodstream. We can't let desperation make us fools."

Daniel looked at the girl's waxy face, her thin hair sprawled across the pillow like straw on a field of snow. He'd already lost the girl who reminded him of Julia. This one reminded him of Nora.

"I'll not treat her, I promise," Nora added.

Horace's lips played with several expressions, one of them clearly surrender. "I fear we're outnumbered."

If Horace wouldn't help him put up a fight, he'd look like a monster, ordering a dying child away. Nor did he have the stomach for it. "I am now." Daniel sighed. "But we'll only take this one."

CHAPTER 30

W E CAN'T AVOID IT ANY LONGER."

The fire in the hearth raged valiantly against the icy night as the six occupants turned their eyes to Horace. He leaned forward in his bedraggled armchair—a strange contrast to the extravagant cut-crystal bowls on the table beside him, gifted by some French royalty. The angled glass collected the orange flames and threw out glittering shards of light over the group.

"Numbers are rising. Harry, what are you seeing on your district calls?" Horace turned his silvery blue eyes to Harry, who lifted his head from his hands at the sound of his name.

"I saw twenty-two cases yesterday. Would have been twenty-four, but two were dead before I arrived."

"Neighborhood?" Horace asked.

Harry rolled his eyes up in tired thought, as if reaching for yesterday's information tasked him to his limit. "Southwark. Thereabouts."

Daniel swore quietly but fervently. "We've had six doctors and students contract it at Bart's. We've lost two already."

Horace glanced at him briefly. "It's getting closer."

"Why haven't any of us gotten ill?" Julia asked reluctantly, as if frightened to tempt fate.

Horace exhaled. "There's no way to know, but it means we keep doing what we have been. We take the same tea and broth regimen as our patients. No milk. No cold water. I want everyone to keep coal and incense burning in whatever rooms you occupy and drink a bit of wine daily."

Harry threw back his head and finished his scotch with a violent grimace. "Or whatever liquor suits you," he teased.

Mrs. Phipps sighed, unaware of the comical picture made by the zebra posed just above her, looking as if he wanted to nibble at her severely knotted hair. "There's no more avoiding it. We might as well set up the ward for cholera."

Daniel paced faster. He'd said the least of anyone. Nora tried not to make eye contact as she glanced at him. She didn't want to provoke him further.

"It won't bring money," Horace pointed out. "Only the most wretched find a hospital better than home."

"And there's nothing to learn from them," Harry added grimly. "We've all done dissections on cholera. We all know exactly what happens. We just don't know why."

"Or how to stop it," Nora piped up.

"No money, no scientific benefits," Horace recited.

"We can save them," Julia said, her cheeks pinking. "Or some. Isn't that enough reason?"

"Not for the grocer or the washwoman," Mrs. Phipps grumbled. "They bill us no matter how many lives we save."

"Daniel, can you stop that infernal pacing?" Harry interrupted. "You're going to drive us all mad."

Daniel jerked to a halt in front of the mantelpiece, glaring at the stuffed falcon. He pulled a crisp piece of stationery from his pocket. "A missive came from Aunt Wilcox just before we gathered in here. We have another problem."

All heads jerked upward as the storm shook the roof. Daniel rolled his eyes. "I could have done without the theatrics of the thunder. Nevertheless…"

He unfolded the letter and read: "Mr. Muller, the renowned comparative linguist, has had to cancel his scientific lecture to be held on Sunday, November 4, due to family illness. He will no longer be able to travel to London. I have secured the vacated event for Nora to present her experiences with training midwives. She will be presenting to the Marylebone Literary and Scientific Institute at 8 p.m., the fourth."

"That's next week," Mrs. Phipps blurted out.

Nora sucked in a small gasp. The Marylebone literary and scientific club was no small gathering of philanthropic women. Nor was it a fraternity of doctors or scientists. It was a collection of the richest, most influential people in London, who took at least a self-serving interest in science, art, and literature. Daniel read on.

"As you are aware, her audience will be exacting, with high expectations of propriety and expertise. There must be absolutely no embarrassment to me or our family." His voice faded. "There's more."

"Oh dear," Mrs. Phipps pronounced, which did little to ease Nora's nerves.

"She includes a list of acceptable clothing, accessories, mannerisms…" Daniel's voice trailed off glumly.

Nora squeezed her hands together. "I was expecting a ladies' circle in a parlor. Certainly, a fine parlor, but not the new

Marylebone lecture hall." Nora hoped for someone to offer bracing encouragement, but Julia's expression fell somewhere between dread and despair. Harry looked like he'd just watched her consume a beetle.

"Well, it seems we've already stepped into the bog. No trying to keep our feet clean now." Horace leaned back in his chair with a small groan. "If we're looking for funding, there's no better spot than Marylebone."

"And if we're looking for enemies, we'll make the most powerful ones there," Daniel countered.

"She'll be addressing MPs and aristocrats." Again, if Mrs. Phipps could have looked a little less distressed at the prospect, it would have bolstered Nora greatly.

"I'm more than capable of lecturing," she reminded them.

Julia turned her eyes politely elsewhere, which only worried Nora more.

"We haven't the best record." Harry didn't have to expound. They all knew what happened the last time she'd addressed London society.

Daniel leaned an elbow against the zebra's sharp fur. "Not to mention, secrecy becomes even more important. If the attendees found out you're with child, it would be a scandal. And with my aunt—perhaps a homicide. She'd surely kill me."

Nora didn't appreciate the dramatic use of words. "How would they know?" she demanded with more bite than necessary. The detail of her pregnancy seemed utterly unrelated. "I don't have any visible signs." She cast a furious stare at Horace, quelling whatever he had started to say about the shape of her nose. "None that normal people would see."

"Eventually, my family will need to know. They might be curious when we appear with a fat infant in a pram." Daniel's eyebrows raised half in surrender, half in warning. "And when Aunt does the math, she'll know we did all this campaigning for the midwives and training while you were pregnant. And there's nothing more dangerous than my aunt when she's affronted. Then what happens to your support and funding?"

"Can't you placate her—" Nora began.

Harry laughed mirthlessly. "He cannot. That woman visited us in Paris when we were in medical school. I've been in navy battles less terrifying."

Nora sighed. "Then do I refuse?"

Daniel sputtered. "Absolutely not. She arranged this as a favor. I only mean we need to be strategic about how we share news of the pregnancy. Perhaps swear we didn't know."

Nora rolled her eyes. "We're both doctors."

"We'll think of some excuse."

Horace made a few excited gestures from his chair. "I once arrived at a home for abdominal pain and delivered a full-term infant to a very surprised mother. She'd already had three children and had no clue she was expecting."

"What about her monthlies?" Harry asked.

"She'd not had them since she started nursing her first child. She thought she had an acute attack of the bowels."

"But her abdomen? How did she not notice a massive belly?" Harry countered.

"Hardly distended at all," Horace announced enthusiastically. "Mind you, I can't be sure the child was full term, but it was nearly six pounds and it lived."

"May we return to the matter at hand? Marylebone, if you recall," Julia chided.

Harry and Horace both looked back to the annoyed group as if they'd forgotten the rest were there.

Daniel cleared his throat. "And we need to decide what we're doing in the ward. We've tried to do the right thing by keeping Amelia. It's right for her, at least. I'm still worried about Meg Prather and her consumption. She cannot survive a bout of cholera on top of it. Nor can our other patients."

Horace cleared his throat, his eyebrows tangled in contemplation. "We have the facilities to handle twenty patients, but not the hands. Not for cholera patients. We need help."

"And the midwives need work," Nora answered. "No one wants to hire them after they found the Surrey girl guilty of manslaughter this week. But Julia had an idea…" Nora looked to her friend, who nudged her on with a nod. "We could offer the midwives a salary to help nurse the cholera patients. They need the work, and it is a ripe opportunity to give them training."

"Who would pay money for a nurse?" Mrs. Phipps demanded. "Every household has a medicine cabinet stocked with essentials, and it takes no training to wipe a forehead. I did it with you."

"Not true," Nora disagreed. "You had Horace to tell you what I should drink and when and how to keep me clean and warm. But we all know there aren't enough doctors and medical students for London on a good year. Harry can't see half the people on his list most days."

Harry inhaled in wordless consensus, and Nora continued

with a nod. "But if we train the midwives in nursing, they would be more useful to the doctors and perhaps earn their respect."

Daniel hung his shaking head like a man about to deliver dismal news. "They'll be useful so long as cholera is overrunning us," he agreed, not looking at any of them. "And if we have the resources, we can pay them to make up for Adams's campaign against them. But the doctors will only be angrier. They don't share their territory."

"It's an absurd stance," Horace growled. "If they stopped being such fools—"

"How can we change their minds?" Harry asked as if he already knew it was a lost cause. "And also, what did the woman—that patient of yours, Horace—think the quickening movements were?"

"Apparently, she never recalled feeling them!" Horace fumbled the pipe he'd been filling, and the tobacco tumbled across his lap and hideous chair. "She dismissed them as stomach complaints."

"*Maria auitami*," Mrs. Phipps groaned under her breath. Nora wasn't the only one who'd learned Italian in the two years on the Continent.

Nora stood and rolled her stiff shoulders as she tried to gather her thoughts. The walls shivered with the wind, and the light from the lamps shook the shadows in a strange dance. "We need nurses. We need money. And the money we need is at Marylebone." Nora pressed her unsteady palms together to hide her doubts. "I have to give the lecture and win them over."

Daniel's eyebrows flexed. "You understand the strings attached?"

Nora straightened her shoulders. "We have no choice. Tell Aunt I won't embarrass her."

She quietly prayed it was the truth.

CHAPTER 31

N ORA'S GAZE CREPT UP THE ORNATE COLUMNS FLANKING the foyer of the lecture hall. She flinched. The size of this place... "Might as well be Parliament," she muttered.

"Not so very large," Horace grumbled. "But I didn't know we were coming to an aviary. Look at the plumage."

Nora laughed, then ducked her head to stifle the sound. No color in the palette had been neglected—dresses, hats, feathers, jewels, clashing in a garish riot of fashion. But what else did she expect from the wealthy attendees of Marylebone Literary and Scientific Institute lectures, who flocked to Grotrian Hall as much to be apprised of the newest styles as the latest news in art and science.

Unfortunately, her midwives, after careful, persistent coaxing to attend, now appeared poised to bolt.

Every attendee had been forced to consult a corpulent physician as they arrived, who checked each wrist for rapid pulse or clammy skin, vigilant in keeping the cholera far from their respected circle. He'd taken one look at Nora's modestly dressed guests and insisted on feeling for fevers, and humiliated the women by looking at their tongues before reluctantly letting them through.

"Good heavens," Ruth whispered over her shoulder. Mrs.

Howell and Mrs. Bailey looked too pale and intimidated to say a thing. "What have you gotten us into?"

Squelching her own misgivings, Nora touched Ruth's arm—less a kind gesture, perhaps, than her attempt to keep the others from fleeing the room. "Don't let that man intimidate you."

"I'll show these ladies to their seats," Mrs. Phipps offered, nodding at the reserved chairs in the front row. Nora glanced to her other side, but Horace had disappeared, wandering off to talk to someone. Unlike her, he relished large crowds. More ears to hear his tales.

Nora scanned the assemblage for Daniel, who was escorting his aunt tonight as a conciliatory offering. She located Aunt Wilcox in the fourth row, appraising the spectacle she'd created. No sign of Daniel, though. Worried, Nora cast her eyes again over the crowd and found him, weaving his way toward her.

"Is everything all right?" she asked, darting a look at Aunt Wilcox.

"She's in a pet," Daniel said. "I think she expected a smaller crowd."

She thinks I'll humiliate her. Nora blew out air slowly. She'd followed Aunt's rules of dressing to the letter—with Julia's help. She'd borrowed a burgundy silk gown and an ornament she could not bring herself to call a hat. It was a scrap of netting, a velvet ribbon, and a flower. She'd thought it too fine for the evening until now, looking over the crowd.

"I wish I'd worn nicer jewelry," she whispered.

"That's not going to help." He stepped close and tapped her temple. "This will."

Heat stung her eyes. Daniel's intellect garnered respect, but Nora had never received the same, not from all her study, practice, and skill. "I wish Horace hadn't abandoned me to discuss his newest fossil or whatever he's on about."

Daniel raised his eyebrows. "You're fine on your own. Didn't need him in Italy, did you?"

No, but now she wished she could look out and spot Magdalena. She turned her glance to Mrs. Phipps and the midwives. *Women on my side.*

Her lips quirked. It wasn't at all the same. None of them had Magdalena's audacity or confidence. Therefore, the confidence— and maybe the audacity, too—must come from her.

"I'll see you afterward," Daniel said, and left after squeezing her hand.

Her stiff, trailing skirts whispered against the floorboards as she half stumbled to the table in the middle of the room, feeling like a girl playing dress-up. But this wasn't a game of pretend. Three quiet midwives, waiting with impassive faces in the first row, and hundreds more across England depended on her to plead their case.

Row upon row of crowded seats surrounded her. It would have felt even more claustrophobic if not for the dark skylights overhead.

The president of the Marylebone society stood and called the meeting to order, giving a complimentary, but anemic, introduction. He hesitated over his notes, especially at the part describing where and in what Nora had earned her university degree. She walked to the lectern like she was making her way across a tightrope.

"Thank you for having me." The words came out weak and scratchy.

"Louder," someone yelled from the back.

Nora's face blazed and she lost her voice altogether. She gave a conciliatory smile to hide the nerves and inhaled as deeply as she dared. "I'm honored to be here," she nearly shouted. She'd give anything at the moment for one of those effortless, booming voices. Hers sounded reedy and thin. Horace made it look so easy. Had he been yelling his lectures all these years?

She continued her introduction. It wasn't hard to talk about Italy. Though she saw numerous skeptical frowns, the numbers spoke for themselves. Magdalena and her physician mother had collected ample evidence to prove the advantages of providing rigorous, lifesaving training to the nuns who served as midwives.

"Most of you came here because you have an interest in improving society or to learn of the latest advances in culture and science. The education of midwives addresses both. While families with means choose to consult doctors and accoucheurs, most expectant mothers rely on their local midwife. And while they have their own expertise, there is much to learn from modern medicine. Rigorous training of competent midwives will save the lives of women and children, and provide worthy employment to women practitioners."

In the front row, a heavy-jowled man thumbed the head of his cane in lethargic boredom, his dismissive attitude so profound that Nora lost her place. The rustle of starched skirts and whispered asides hummed like thunder in her head, making the next sentence even harder to force out.

"There are also skills familiar to practicing midwives that doctors could do well to learn. The records of midwives' lying-in houses speak for themselves, with rates of puerperal fever many times lower than those in hospitals. When we consider it logically, it makes no sense to house expectant mothers, new mothers, and infants with those who are ill. They aren't sick. But they do require expert care, and that care should be provided in a way that doesn't expose them to the risk of infection."

Across the room, Daniel gave a minute nod, his dark eyes shining in the dim light. Her shoulders loosened slowly as her voice deepened to a richer tenor.

This was what she'd come to say. "Decisions about who can and should be caring for babies and mothers must be focused on what is best for them, and that is doctors and trained midwives working together." Nora scanned the faces before her. Unsmiling, but attentive.

"Many of you contribute to charities that educate poor women in dressmaking and millinery and domestic service." Several heads bobbed in the dim light. "What if you also adopted the mission of training impoverished women as midwives? It not only benefits the women; it also frees doctors to attend to other urgent cases, especially in times of epidemic disease. Perhaps helping your own families or servants in their hour of need."

In the second row, Aunt Wilcox lifted her eyebrow expectantly.

"What of doctors who train for years at great expense and sacrifice? Are they to be replaced by hobbyists and amateurs?" a man with a billowing mustache who Nora didn't recognize called out from the midst of the crowd, followed by rumbles of agreement.

"You haven't been listening if you think that is what I'm advocating," Nora said, pressing her hands against the lectern. "A doctor might have extensive training, and many patients generally assume that he does. But the truth is, in obstetrics particularly, only two lectures are necessary to be licensed. A man might not have attended a single birth before he is allowed to go out collecting payment from women patients."

A portly man jumped to his feet. "I've delivered hundreds of children in my career."

She fumbled for his name, snatching it at the last second. "And I hear great things of your abilities, Dr. Gordon. But how many children had you delivered when you first received your license?"

He huffed and sat down, silenced, which Horace took as a cue to guffaw, his amusement audible to everyone in the room.

"I do not disparage doctors. Do not forget, I am one," Nora said. "I mean to point out that midwives have had their own children, so they know from experience the hardships of labor. They have also attended dozens of births before practicing alone."

"Lies!" a man thundered. "What of Caroline Jepson in Surrey?"

"A tragedy and a crime," Nora agreed. "But if a man had pretended to be a doctor and killed a patient, we would not attempt to ban the entire profession outright. We'd insist on requiring licenses and stricter proofs of ability, and that is what I propose. Education and certification that prove a midwife's knowledge and skill." Nora's eyes strayed to the three midwives. Mrs. Bailey's lips were pressed so tightly she might have bitten them off. "Some midwives I've worked with have managed to successfully deliver babies that I was taught were impossible to bring through."

Nora turned the page of her notes, but before she could continue, a man rose from his chair in the back of the room.

"That's all well and good, Mrs. Gibson. But are trained physicians to share their knowledge and fees with meddling women simply because they want it?" Dr. Adams stood near the back on her right side, blocking the light of a flaming gas lamp. An expectant hush fell as his shadow loomed across the wall, towering all the way to the skylights. "I've invested time, money, and years of my working life perfecting my use of short forceps. It has come at great personal sacrifice."

The gentlemen beside him nodded, and someone shouted, "Hear, hear!"

"You would not expect a virtuoso musician or a celebrated portrait painter to simply teach his technique to all and sundry," he finished.

Nora's swallowed against the heat climbing her chest. "I would say we must share our knowledge, not because midwives want it for nothing—and I don't advocate it should come free of charge—but because the mothers of England need it."

Someone clapped, but the sound was too far off for Nora to see who.

Adams stroked his beard, pretending to be thoughtful. "I see. It is now my duty to find every woman in the boroughs and villages who helps fetch water for a birth and force them all to go to medical school." He won several laughs.

Nora bit her teeth together, grinding through her dislike

of this man. "You bring up another compelling point," she said, wishing he'd retake his seat. This was not his lecture. "As you all know, cholera has appeared in several neighborhoods the last two months, with devastating results. We've suffered thousands of deaths. The mortality rate is currently fifty percent. We lose half of everyone who contracts the disease."

"I didn't bring up that subject at all," Adams argued.

The crowd shifted, disturbed by the sudden shift in topic. "In an oblique way. You scoffed at the idea of women being trained in medicine. Which made me think—St. Bart's recently lost two medical students to cholera. District doctors are seeing far more patients than they can manage. Death is only kept at bay by meticulous, continuous tending—something over-worked physicians have no time to provide."

Adams squinted in suspicion, unsure where this new tack was steering them.

"At my hospital on Great Queen Street, I've trained mid-wives to help nurse cholera patients, to great effect."

A murmur ran through the crowd. "If we had more char-itable funds, I could train and employ more." She smiled at Adams. "So could you."

Adams squared his shoulders. "How would we license these women? How do we keep them from making the same disas-trous mistakes as the Jepson woman?"

"Doctors also make mistakes."

Her eyes latched on Daniel, rising to his feet. Even carrying over the crowd, his voice was so even Nora doubted anyone else caught the warning tenor. Beside him, Aunt Wilcox blanched. "Should we review those cases as well? Last week, for example?"

Nora's eyes grew wide. It was the closest thing to a threat she'd ever heard pass Daniel's lips.

Adams smoothed his waistcoat. "It is true that at Bart's we had a woman nearly injured by a medical student. But it was quickly corrected by trained doctors. We are a teaching hospital. That type of correction would have been impossible in a private home."

Horace stood, his gaze bouncing between him and the warring doctors. "*Nearly* injured? No midwife I've ever known would pull a woman's womb from her body." The audience gasped. "That's what was done by your student doctor."

"There were mitigating circumstances—" Adams started.

"There often are, for doctors. But you demand higher standards of accountability from these women," Daniel interrupted, waving at the midwives. "I've worked beside Mrs. Franklin many times. By the time she's done learning to use forceps, she'll be as capable as we are."

Adams's eyes narrowed. "What did you say, Dr. Gibson?"

Daniel's eyes darted to Nora, widening in mute apology. She'd not meant to disclose that—not yet.

Adams rounded on Daniel. "Forceps can be injurious— even deadly—if misused. And you're teaching this woman—"

"Not him," Ruth interrupted, nodding at Nora. "Her. Dr. Gibson."

The electrified crowd hummed with murmurs.

Nora drew up her shoulders. She must regain order. "My training is slow and meticulous. I've done nothing to rush any midwife into a situation she cannot manage."

"Forceps could be argued to be a surgical procedure,"

Adams said, the disgust on his face vibrant and horrible. "You're hardly licensed yourself, but you admit to teaching women off the street?"

"Off the street?" Mrs. Howell jumped to her feet.

"Stop," Daniel put in. "We're growing emotional. My wife only meant to say that more training is best for all of us. Can we all agree on that?"

Three seats down from Daniel, Harry dropped his head onto his arms. This lecture was going exactly as he'd predicted. Nora wished she could reverse the action of the clocks and refuse the invitation, or push them forward and escape. But there would be no relief, not for another half hour at least.

Adams smoothed his waistcoat, a motion belying his anger-blotched cheeks. "It seems we cannot agree at all, Dr. Gibson." This time, he was speaking to Daniel, facing him over the heads of the crowd. "You signed my petition to stop midwives from practicing. Why would you do that if you agree with your wife and believe they should be professionally trained?"

Daniel flinched. "I wished to keep unqualified practitioners from deceiving the public. I still do. But I've reconsidered the best way it can be done. Especially in times like these, we need as many competent—"

"Your wife received only one and a half years' instruction in a foreign country. Do you find that sufficiently qualified?" Adams didn't look at Nora as he referred to her—only threw a lazy hand in her direction.

Nora wasn't going to allow this. "I'm right here, Dr. Adams. I may have been in Bologna for a shorter time, but I'd been studying for years before I went. I passed all the required examinations, and in my first attempt. Not all your students can claim that. I'm not sure you can, either." She smiled at him, and Horace laughed again.

"Got you there, Adams. You faced your examiners twice, if I remember," Horace said. Some members of the audience tittered nervously.

Adams glared, ready to hurl lightning.

The eyes of those in the audience darted from player to player, the performance much more fascinating than anticipated.

"I propose we train as many women as quickly as possible. The cholera, as devastating as it has been this year, is only just beginning. The spread is increasing." Horace spoke slowly, collecting attention and fear with each word. "We've lost well over ten thousand in London already since August. That is two short months. Liverpool reports five thousand, and Glasgow four thousand.

"I know it is thought to be a disease of the poor, but at this rate, it won't be long before it overruns the poor boroughs and spills into every part of the city."

"But cholera has never spread to better neighborhoods," one woman said, her eyes wide with fright.

"I assure you, it has no boundaries," Horace continued. "A justice in Paddington died this week. There are people here who attended events with him only days before he expired."

"It's here," someone whispered, the words carrying unnaturally in the silence.

Two ladies stood, edging their way to the nearest exit. All around, faces jerked left and right, accusing their neighbors with every glance.

"No need to alarm yourself," Nora began, then bit her lip as more people began creeping toward the door. "Ladies and gentlemen, we're scheduled for another ten minutes. Then we'll be opening the discussion for questions—"

Well, that horse was out of the barn. No one paid her any heed.

The club president stood and raised his arms. "If you can please remain in your seats…"

If anything, that seemed to send more people on their way, shoving toward the exits. Even the balance of people still in their seats eyed the doors.

Someone could get hurt if this didn't stop.

"Please remain calm," Nora said. When no one even glanced her way, she shouted, "You don't need to stay. But you must exit in an orderly fashion!"

"Let me through!" a man bellowed, just as someone on the opposite side of the room slipped in the mayhem.

Nora's legs quaked beneath her. She'd never seen a crowd lose their heads this quickly, though she'd read of mass panics in the newspapers.

"Good Lord," she whispered as someone let out a terrified shriek.

Horace and the midwives were safe in the nearly deserted front row, joined by Harry and Julia. Harry stationed himself between them and the fleeing crowd, fists clenched to deter all comers.

Nora's hand flew to her stomach, resting there uncertainly as she searched the crowd. The top row was mostly cleared, but she couldn't find Daniel.

CHAPTER 32

W HAT'S WRONG WITH THESE PEOPLE?" AUNT WILCOX gripped her necklace and glared at the man shoving past her. "Show some decorum, sir!"

Daniel pulled her a little closer, grateful she'd allowed him to hook a hand through her arm. "We'd better move away from the doors." They'd get trampled, trying to exit that way. Aunt's dress had a train, which had been stepped on already as they were jostled down the row to the stairs. "Come along."

He tugged her into a clear space at the end of a row, then recognized his mistake. Someone had seen the opening first. Two women, skirts hitched over their arms, charged toward them, one wielding an umbrella.

"Mildred?" Aunt Wilcox gasped.

"This way!" Daniel tried to move aside, but the women hurtled past, pushing Aunt Wilcox into his shoulder. He crashed against the body behind him, and it gave way with a clatter and a yelp.

An elderly gentleman with a frail, emaciated face lay sprawled at his feet, blocking one side of the stairs. As Daniel dove toward him, a fleeing woman trod on the old man's shoulder with a high-heeled shoe, provoking a scream of pain.

"Get back!" Daniel shouted, but no one heeded. "Let me help!"

The man who'd fallen batted him away, unable to distinguish him from the column stampeding for the nearest door. Ignoring his feeble defensive blows, Daniel wrapped his arms around the man's waist and tugged him into the row, away from the pushing crowd.

"Are you in pain, sir?"

Nothing but incoherent mutterings in response, so Daniel maneuvered him into a chair, noting his dilated eyes and the tremors of his body.

"Mr. Brandon?" Aunt Wilcox said. "Mr. Brandon!"

Daniel hushed her. "Something may be broken," he whispered, unable to explain more as another party, bent on escape, surged toward them. "You cannot pass here," he said, hands extended, using his surgical theater voice, the one that sent dressers and orderlies running. The man in the lead checked, considered, then retreated out the other end of the row.

Aunt Wilcox heaved a sigh of relief. "They've turned into complete imbeciles. After sitting here for an hour, do they think—"

"People aren't reasonable when it comes to cholera," Daniel said.

"So I see. You'd better tend to Mr. Brandon."

His shivering was worse, and judging from the man's age, he was a prime candidate for a fractured hip. Daniel had no tools with him. "Just a few moments, Mr. Brandon," he said, taking the man's hands. "When things clear out a little..."

What then? He had no medicines. No bag. They'd have to carry the man to a coach. If Brandon had broken his hip, there was little to be done. Bedridden for months, the odds of him succumbing to pneumonia were practically certain.

"Here." Aunt Wilcox pushed her smelling salts into Daniel's

face. As he recoiled, eyes and nose stinging from ammonia, she said, "Not for you, boy. For Mr. Brandon."

"Those will not help him," Daniel said tersely, pushing her hand away. "Unless you have any laudanum about you—"

"Afraid not."

A shriek cut the air between them, and Daniel spun around instinctively, because he knew that sound. It wasn't the noise you made when you fell, or were pushed, or couldn't get where you wanted.

"Fire! Fire!" a man shouted.

Dear God. "Stay here. Watch Brandon," Daniel ordered, and vaulted over the rail, plowing into the crowd, chasing the screams rising a few yards away. Someone—perhaps trying to beat a way through with a cane or umbrella—had broken a lamp on the wall.

"Out of my way!" Daniel bellowed.

Beyond the churn of people, he spied curls of smoke and a leaping flame whipping from a wide skirt. He tore off his coat, ignoring the volley of screams as the crowd surged in panic.

One man was already beside the screeching woman, beating the flames from her skirts as she kicked wildly. Daniel shoved forward, flinging his coat at the fire eating its way up her back, and pushed her to the floor. "We must smother it! Your coat! Quick!"

"Here!" Someone tossed him a cloak, and Daniel pressed it over her, smashing down on the burning dress where lamp oil had splashed her. Fire and heat licked his fingers and wrists as her screams wrapped around him.

"Don't check yet," he yelled as the man who'd been working on the flames on her skirts tried to lift the cloak. "Starve it of air!"

If their efforts weren't working, they'd know soon enough. Flames would eat through the cloak, scorching their hands. Another coat dropped on top of him, but Daniel didn't look up, seizing the dark cloth and clapping it atop the other layers.

"It will be all right," he promised over her cries.

When he was satisfied that the flames were extinguished, he peeled back layers of smoldering cloth, revealing a pale, shuddering woman with hair falling sideways and over her face. "I'm a doctor," Daniel told her.

"Not her doctor." He looked up and saw Adams.

She stretched a bleeding hand to Adams. "Help me."

"We must get you home," he said. "Check your burns and dress them."

"Yes, as quickly as possible." Daniel sat back on his heels as Adams and the woman's escort lifted her. He didn't seem needed anymore. Not surprising that Adams had many patients in the crowd. He kept a large acquaintance in this neighborhood.

The few who hadn't panicked remained in small clusters, and though there was still congestion around the doors, no one was pushing or shoving anymore. The screams of *fire* had extinguished with the woman's dress, and the crowd had sobered at the sight of her needless injury. The woman's low moans and the sobs of the elderly gentleman were the only sounds of distress—flotsam on a churning sea of whispers.

Daniel picked himself up, fingering a scorch mark on his sleeve. The elderly gentleman—Brandon—was surrounded by Harry, Nora, and Horace, urgently conferring. Aunt was just as he'd left her, in the same chair, hands folded in her lap, visibly shaken.

"I'll go with you," Harry told the elderly man reassuringly. "As soon as the doors are clear, we'll carry you to a carriage."

"I'll come," Horace added.

"I know how to rig a traction splint," Harry grumbled.

Horace raised his eyebrows.

Nora met Daniel's eyes, and he watched her take inventory of his scorched sleeve, relief washing over her face when she found he was unharmed.

No time to exchange words. They were all hurrying about, making arrangements for Mr. Brandon, assisting Dr. Adams with the evacuation of his patient, and improvising a dressing for a young man with a cut forehead.

But at last the hall cleared, leaving Daniel and his wife nearly alone. Nora leaned in to his chest, her face tired and pale.

"Will you come with me and Aunt Wilcox?" Daniel asked. "I need to see her home." He wanted Nora's company. In the turmoil, he'd been so preoccupied caring for the people in front of him that he hadn't thought of his wife. The omission scared him, and now he wanted her near, within arm's reach, with a comfortable, reassuring quiet lying between them.

He wondered if she'd sought him in the crowd. If she'd noticed he hadn't been looking for her. He hoped she'd been sensible and stayed clear of the melee.

"I should go home," Nora said. "I think my nerves—"

"That's why I want you close," Daniel answered before she finished.

He turned to his aunt, still fossilized in her chair. "It's safe to go now."

She stared at his outstretched hand like she'd never seen

one before. "I'm not going anywhere with you," Aunt Wilcox whispered. Her eyes, he saw, were full of tears, dammed by rapid blinks of her short, blond lashes. Her hands fisted together.

"Aunt, don't," Daniel protested.

"I'll take a cab," she said stiffly. "I'm not—" She shook her head. "This." She jabbed a rapier-like forefinger at the room, a wide black scorch marring the new wallpaper. "This is what you did. Miss Vaughn—the young lady who nearly burned to death—is supposed to marry next week. Mr. Brandon has been my friend for forty years. Can you honestly tell me he will mend?"

Daniel rolled words over his dry tongue but couldn't force them out.

"I didn't think so."

"We didn't start this panic," Nora reasoned.

Daniel tried to catch her attention, to warn her with a shake of his head. This was not the way to comfort his aunt.

"It could have been defused if you'd been just a little self-effacing. If you'd not tried to advance your agenda by scaremongering about cholera."

Nora blanched.

"She was talking about treating cholera," Daniel countered. "Dr. Croft only wanted to show—"

"Your Dr. Croft," Aunt sneered. "You encouraged him."

Nora shook her head. "You know I only wanted to secure funding to help the midwives."

"No one will consider that now," Aunt Wilcox scoffed. "Not if I have anything to say about it. This should have been an uneventful, mildly interesting lecture on the qualifications of midwives—not a riot. I'll be exceptionally surprised if I'm ever permitted to organize anything again. In addition to this evening's casualties, you've pummeled my reputation."

Nora's lips thinned. Before she could answer, Daniel jumped in. "Adams started the battle. What were we to do?"

Aunt pulled her mouth into a severe line. "Respond with dignity and restraint."

"I think I did," Nora said. "My aims—"

"Are finished," Aunt Wilcox interrupted cruelly.

Daniel's heart twisted as Nora bit her lip, but he couldn't think of anything helpful to say. He disagreed with his aunt on many points, but he couldn't dispute her on this one. This lecture, this attempt at enlisting support, wasn't just a failure; it was a catastrophe.

As Aunt Wilcox tried to move past, he stopped her with a hand on her arm. "How do you propose to travel home?" he asked quietly. "I must be sure you are safe."

"I'm safer on my own than near you two." She sniffed. "Leave me alone." On that, she swept out, leaving them to stare after her.

They were not alone in the vast hall. A few remained amid the broken lamps and overturned chairs. But no one felt like speaking, and Nora looked done in, defeated.

"If I ever consider another public lecture again," Nora said quietly, "please talk me out of it."

CHAPTER 33

For a week, Nora avoided the clinic as adamantly as the stacks of mail and the papers delivered twice a day. If the hallboy appeared, she remembered urgent business in the dispensary or notes she needed to review. Only in the evening, alone, could she bear to glance at the news, privately imbibing sensational accounts of the lecture, stampede, and fire.

For days, it seemed like the London papers spoke of nothing else, despite mounting cholera deaths and intrigues abroad. Daniel's tactful inquiries revealed that Miss Vaughn and Mr. Brandon were making slow recoveries, but that was small comfort.

Nora hadn't expected a procession of admirers after her lecture, but a fiery conflagration was abysmal luck, even for her. After days of refusing to see patients, no one—not even Daniel—attempted to ban her from the cholera ward. Instead, they softly coaxed her to return to work, perhaps deeming the risk of infection less harmful than spending her empty hours reliving the spectacular humiliation.

The first time she had shuffled into the large, overfilled ward, Daniel looked up with something resembling relief.

"Here," he had said, passing her a nursery book. "Amelia wants me to read it again, but she'll like it much better coming from you."

Now, in the strange quiet of late morning—she'd overslept again—she stood in front of her washstand, the mirror tilted to reflect the small curve of her abdomen. The oval glass caught a corner of the heavy floral quilt of her empty bed, and she cast her eyes down. Daniel occupied it for shorter spans every week as his nights grew later and his mornings earlier. There weren't enough doctors to meet the cries of suffering across London.

She donned her skirt, concealing the slight evidence of the burgeoning child, determined to help until her condition was noticeable. Despite the horrific failure of her lecture, she could still teach the new midwives, who managed to appear at her door as if conjured from air. Ruth was adept enough now to help with the rudimentary training. Nora had hoped to train dozens of women—more, if possible—and release them onto the streets of the city like angels of mercy, but even the small handful who'd sought her out would make a difference. She could still make her hospital a fit and welcoming place for women to work and seek treatment.

It was much harder without funds, but she wasn't a girl anymore, railing against events that were over and done. She wouldn't let upsets, even ones this large, destroy her. When facing an intractable problem, the only thing for it, as Horace said, was work. There was certainly plenty to be done.

She met Horace in the cholera ward, his face strained after another too-short night and too-full morning. He rubbed his twitching right eyelid with a thick thumb, then handed a rubber tube to Nora. They needed no words in this dance that was reflexive now. She fitted it gently between a woman's blue lips.

"Goring died of an undisclosed illness in Sussex," Horace said as he started a trickle of tea into the tube. "Took him in one night."

"Goring the MP?"

He nodded. "And Gloucester is enduring a violent increase in cases." Horace shifted the stethoscope on the woman's thin chest and listened intently before continuing. "London work-houses are seeing more deaths, and the papers are making it worse, saying people are in such a hurry to dispose of the deceased that no one is adequately checking to see they are truly dead before burying them."

Nora flinched as her eyes shot to their patient. Nothing ter-rified the sick like stories of being buried alive. Unfortunately, there was no need to worry they'd frightened the patient beside them. The gray-tinged woman was in no state to understand their conversation. She stared sightlessly, her lips trembling as if in attempted conversation with beings only she could see.

Nora turned away from the pitiful sight and back to Horace. "Did Goring's death or the newspaper articles start any riots in Mayfair?"

"Don't be bitter. The brouhaha at your lecture was a singu-larity." His critical eyebrows reproved her even more eloquently.

She pressed her lips together. What a fitting word, *singularity*—like herself. *At least for now.* Perhaps someday there would be more women licensed as midwives and nurses—women she understood far better than the ones who pored over dress catalogs and advertisements for face creams.

She held out a hand, and Horace passed her another filled syringe. More broth to slip down this poor woman's dry throat.

"What are numbers like at Bart's?" she asked, dreading the answer.

"Filled to the rafters," Horace confirmed. "It's like a continual water brigade, only we're tossing out buckets of dia—"

"Effluvia," Nora corrected, and Horace gave her another stern look.

"Don't let women like Daniel's aunt make you mealy-mouthed. If you are talking about diarrhea, call it *diarrhea*."

Nora stretched her shoulder blades backward, the ache in the middle of her back spilling down her spine. "All right," she conceded. "At least with you."

She handed him the empty syringe, picturing the overflowing wards of St. Bart's, her husband navigating the aisles of filth and death. They weren't doing much better here, now that they'd filled one ward with more than twenty cholera patients, all women or children. Even with her handful of midwives willing to risk infection to help, they struggled against the power of this violent disease.

Horace pushed their patient's lip aside to check the color of her gums, frowning at the gray flesh beside her yellow teeth. He picked up her hand, inspecting her fingernails. "Have you tried oatmeal to slow this one's stools? Her hands are puckered."

"I know," Nora admitted with a sigh. "I'll try some gruel again. She's done nothing but sink since she stumbled in yesterday."

Ruth appeared at her side with a tray. "I'll get the gruel from the kitchen. No cream," she promised. It tended to curdle in the sour stomachs of the patients, so they avoided it all together. "But there's a new patient in the last empty bed. I brought her in this morning before you came down." She pointed with her elbow down the row since her hands were full.

"How bad?" Nora asked.

Ruth wrinkled her nose for a moment. "The cholera or the stench? I need to clean her."

That was hardly encouraging. Ruth had spent decades working in the poorest neighborhoods and was as accustomed to unpleasant smells as any doctor. Horace followed Nora to the next bed, the odor of old fish ripening with every step.

"Fisherwoman," Horace muttered beside her. Probably one of the poor souls who tried to scrape a living picking mussels and crabs at low tide on the Thames. He shook his head. "She's been in the Thames just this morning. I can smell the dirty water. If we allow the foul air—"

"What do we do?" Nora asked.

Horace motioned to Ruth. "You need to take patients' clothing before you bring them into the common ward. This one ought to be scoured in lime water, before the smells contaminate the entire room."

"What do I put her in if I take her clothes?" Ruth asked, scanning the room as patients leaned forward, vomiting into their buckets.

"Don't worry," Nora reassured her. "We'll find something."

"We can't keep cutting holes in your old nightgowns, Nora," Horace insisted.

She would have smiled at his uncharacteristic concern for her wardrobe, but the smell of sour, rotting fish was turning her stomach…

She took several steps to the nearest bucket, and a burning

flood of bile exploded from her mouth. Several retches later, she realized she'd sunk to her knees, a glaze of sweat gathering in her hairline.

"Get her out of here," Horace barked to no one in particular and hoisted Nora up with a strength she hadn't felt in his bad arm since before she left for Italy.

"I'm not ill. It was just the smell," she whispered.

"Out," he growled. "And straight to bed."

"You're too old to take my weight like this. Put me down."

His arms tightened. "I will if you lie for a bit. I don't want you back in here until you've had a cup of tea. And kept it down."

She glanced over her shoulder. Ruth, her expression just as severe as Horace's, picked up the forgotten bowl of gruel. "Go on. I'll look after this one."

"Very well," Nora conceded. "I'll rest for a quarter of an hour." Her stomach would settle after a piece of toast and chamomile tea.

"Half hour, at least," Horace countered. He nudged the partition door with an elbow and coaxed her slowly into the hall.

"I didn't realize you were this strong again," she said, breathing slowly to fight the urge to vomit.

"The daily walks help. Sometimes I tackle the stairs at St. Paul's."

"Is that wise?"

"What do you think?" He grinned.

"Now you're boasting." She struggled to finish the sentence. She needed to close her eyes. He really wasn't going to release her until he reached the sofa. And he didn't look like it hurt him. "It's just the pregnancy. It catches me unawares." She sighed and reached out for the sturdy armchair.

"I beg your pardon?" a sharp voice rose from only feet away, startling both of them.

Nora whipped her head around, peering past Horace's shoulder. Beneath a trembling ostrich feather was a stylish hat—and a face she dreaded.

Nora reviewed her last words, mouth dropping in horror. "Aunt Wilcox?"

"Pregnancy?" The woman's eyes scraped over her face like claws, leaving her cheeks red and flaming.

Horace tightened his grip on Nora's arm, holding her upright.

"I—I didn't know you were here," Nora stuttered.

"That's quite obvious," Aunt snapped. "Your Mrs. Phipps just went to tell you I arrived." Aunt stood but took a step backward. "You look positively green. Which I would fear was the cholera if I hadn't just heard with my own ears—"

"You shouldn't be here," Horace interrupted in gruff syllables. "We're treating cholera in our ward. None of the patients come into the living quarters of the house, but I'd never put you in danger."

"Only my nephew," she sniffed, her eyes shifting uncomfortably at the mention of sick patients. "And his wife and now his future child…" Her words trailed off in disbelief. "How could Daniel allow this?"

"She's overtired and expecting. Nothing else. She's as safe as any of us." It didn't help that Horace's voice faltered. They all knew that comparison counted for very little.

Cold dread swept over Nora's body like a poison. She wrenched free of Horace's arm and threw up into the nearest fern.

Aunt stepped backward again, almost stumbling. "This looks like cholera," she said in horror, pressing a handkerchief to her mouth.

Horace pressed his hand to Nora's forehead as he helped her into the chair. "She's fourteen weeks along and had no breakfast this morning. It's to be expected. No fever whatsoever."

"Fourteen weeks?" Aunt repeated the words as if they were a foreign language. Her quiet voice grew sinister. "Do you mean to tell me you've known for months? And hidden it?"

Nora shut her eyes and exhaled. Trust Horace to cause a scene. "No, not that long." She shook her head carefully. No sudden movements yet.

"But you're still working? And Daniel—"

Nora's mouth flew open to defend herself, but she choked on her reply at the last second. No need to make Aunt hate both of them. The lie formed as she spoke it. "He didn't know. I only just told him. He was going to travel home this weekend to announce it, but work has kept him away around the clock." She caught Horace's raised eyebrow and his clear, silent warning not to continue down this track. Too late now.

"Deceiving your own husband?" Aunt's cheeks trembled, and she looked at Nora as if she were a dangerous, unknown creature. "You knew you were with child and didn't tell him?" The plume in her hat quivered as lines of outrage dug deeper around her mouth. "I came to tell you how Miss Vaughn and Mr. Brandon were faring after the accident, but I see you are not worthy of the consideration."

Nora fought the compulsion to fight back by inwardly reciting Aunt's twitching facial muscles. *Masseter. Risorius. Buccinator.*

"I cannot countenance this. If Daniel will not make you see sense, someone must. You cannot risk his child, his name, and my family's heir any longer. I'm ordering you stop work at once."

"You cannot order me to do anything, Aunt Wilcox."

Mrs. Phipps bustled into the room and froze, detecting the emergency in one glance at their stricken faces.

"But I can disinherit and disown your husband. So will his parents. You must give this up."

"You would break Daniel's heart?"

Mrs. Phipps's hand went to her mouth, a nervous habit.

Aunt drew her velvet bag to her waist, as if fearing Nora would steal it. "That's your doing, girl, not mine. You've used us all badly and continue to do so with no compunction. My nephew gives you latitude to do whatever you like, and you repay him in lies and deception. He deserves better." She straightened, transferring her glare in turn to Horace and Mrs. Phipps. "I can't pretend I don't blame both of you as well."

As Aunt Wilcox swept past them, Mrs. Phipps mouthed something to her. Nora couldn't decipher the words. But she understood perfectly well that she had to do something. Unfortunately, the older woman was marching away at a furious pace, and Nora stepped on her own skirts as she started forward, stumbling after her into the hall. By the time she caught up, Aunt Wilcox was at the front door, spitting orders at the terrified hallboy.

"Aunt, I'm sorry. I wanted to be sure before telling anyone. To spare Daniel additional worry. There's so much—"

Aunt Wilcox yanked her umbrella from the hall stand like a warrior drawing a sword. She wheeled on Nora, cheeks red with anger, spittle flying from her lips. "There's only one thing you can say to me to show any remorse—that you are leaving town today and finding a safe place to convalesce."

Nora folded her hands at her waist. "No. I can't leave London. No doctor with any kind of conscience—"

"You're a mother now, girl—or as good as one." She flung open the door, pausing at the threshold. "I gave you a stage and a voice. I encouraged my friends to help you. And all the time you were hiding a pregnancy, risking my nephew's child and my future heir. A lady engaging in work for the good of society is one thing, but a woman working during confinement when there is no financial necessity is quite another."

She whisked her skirts outside, as if afraid Nora was contagious, and slammed the door behind her.

When the reverberations died, Nora clutched her waist. "I think I'm going to be sick again."

CHAPTER 34

DANIEL CORNERED HER IN THE WATER CLOSET, BRUSHING her teeth.

"Horace told me to find you," he explained, sidling past the door. "And I heard some of the shouting from the ward. What happened?"

Nora spat into the washbasin and pressed a wet towel to her face. No way to avoid telling him the new problem she'd created. "I had no idea Aunt was here. Apparently, the maid came down the main stairs while I went up the back with Horace." She paused just to spare him the truth a second longer. "Aunt overheard me mentioning my pregnancy."

She recounted the argument as stoically as she could, watching her husband's jaw tighten. When she finished, he passed a tired hand over his eyes.

"How is your stomach?" he asked quietly.

She swallowed, touched by the tender tone. But even if he sided with her now, what about next week? Ten years from now? Would he still think defending her was worth alienating his family?

"I don't know," Nora admitted. "My brain is spinning too fast to take note of anything else."

"I'm sorry. She's… My aunt has a quick temper, but she'll soften in time. By the time our child is born—"

Nora looked up at him.

He shrugged. "I'll talk to her. She'll recover."

"I don't know if she will, Daniel."

"None of us are at our best just now. Especially since the lecture."

"She said she came to tell me about Miss Vaughn," Nora said, wincing at the thought of the young woman's burns.

"She's improving," Daniel asked. "Adams said he saw her three days ago."

"And?"

"Still in a great deal of pain. Sleeping mostly, from the laudanum, but her skin is starting to granulate." As she turned away from the basin, he took her hand. "None of the scars will show. Her clothes will cover them."

Nora bit her lip. Was she supposed to consider that a mercy? Julia's scars, both inside and out, gave her untold distress, no matter how cleverly she concealed them.

"It shouldn't have happened," she said quietly. Mr. Brandon, if he survived the months with his leg in traction, would have to learn to walk all over again. No easy task for a man aged seventy-seven.

"No," Daniel agreed, pulling her close and sliding his arms around her.

She drew back, though not because she didn't want the embrace. "Are you angry?"

His mouth twitched. "I am, some. But that doesn't seem particularly helpful just now."

"At me or at her?" Nora placed each word carefully, as if building a house of cards.

He loosened his hold, studying her with concern. "It's not really a case of—"

"Daniel." She wanted an honest response, not sidestepping.

"Neither." He blew out a resigned breath. "At life in general, I suppose. Every time we try to do some good, it burns down in front of us. And now you're…" Daniel blinked twice, his eyes glossing. At once, Nora understood why.

"Now you're worried I'm sick," she whispered.

Daniel swallowed, then gave a barely visible nod.

"I'm not," she promised.

"You can't be sure." He tipped out the words like coins he couldn't spare.

"If I was, you shouldn't be this close."

He shook his head, pulling her nearer, resting his chin on her forehead. Nora's eyes stung.

"You know perfectly well how smells bother me since the pregnancy."

"Yes." The word was unsteady. "Will you rest awhile?"

It didn't hurt, on a day like today, to be persuadable. "Yes."

He nodded, satisfied. "I don't know what we're in for," he murmured. "I keep thinking things can't get any worse, but the way Horace speaks about the last cholera epidemic… He doesn't think we've even neared the peak of this one."

She shook her head. "You could have been a barrister, you know. Never dealt with any of this."

"No, I couldn't." His hands tightened again. "And you

couldn't, either." He might not celebrate her compulsion for medicine right now, but he understood it.

Maybe he was right and Aunt Wilcox would relent, once sufficient time had passed and their wards weren't full of cholera. But this rupture might just as easily have arisen from something else. She and Aunt Wilcox were like two reactive liquids that should never be combined unless you wanted an explosion. Whether it was this year or next, Daniel would have to choose.

Somehow, she'd have to make this up to him.

So many of their carefully tended patients died that whenever one recovered, everyone looked on in numb surprise, bewildered by the slow transformation from husk back to health. The relentless and unpredictable losses took a toll on all of them, but Daniel was especially irritable, with the date of Aunt Wilcox's Christmas party fast approaching. They were not invited, and Nora knew the sting of it had burrowed into his chest.

Aunt's party was one of his favorite traditions. One of his best childhood memories was the year he was finally deemed old enough to attend. He'd only missed one, when the weather was too wretched to permit him to travel from Paris, where he was studying.

It was easy for Nora to imagine, as Daniel's eyes grew shadowed and dejected, that she alone didn't outweigh the things he had lost.

Aunt Wilcox had never even allowed her to present a defense, and as one day succeeded another, Nora's arguments swelled and rankled inside her. Not that they'd do her any good. Aunt Wilcox would never listen, and that certainty rankled even more, as niggling and impossible to ignore as a chipped tooth. Between rounds, Nora tried to immerse herself in articles, but the words ran away from her and forced her to corral the same paragraphs over and over. A dull ache in her head sanded down her thoughts until they had no handholds.

Finally, she sighed and set her journal aside, irritated by the persistent queasiness brought on by the pregnancy.

"You know, I think there's something to that transfusion idea you mentioned," Julia said from the sofa, making Nora start. The room was so quiet, her bitterness so strongly brewed, that she'd forgotten she wasn't alone.

"Pardon?" Nora straightened in her chair.

"The article you mentioned about transfusions. I took it to Harry, and he explained the terms that were obscure to me."

"Dr. W. Pepper's article? The transfusions of milk?" Nora's brow creased.

Julia shook her head. "No. The other doctor who used that solution. Lady's—"

"Latta's," Nora corrected.

"Yes, that's right. It sounded much more promising than the milk one."

Nora frowned. It had sounded promising, but as Daniel had pointed out, Torrance, the Rugby-based surgeon advocating transfusion therapy in a single, brief article, was referencing cases from the first epidemic, years and years ago. Nora had written to Mr. Torrance, care of the journal's editors, requesting further details but had received no response.

"It did sound interesting," Nora admitted. "But there have been plenty of deaths after putting foreign substances into a patient's veins."

"Yes, I know. But that surgeon…Torrance?"

Nora nodded.

"Says six of his seven cases recovered. It sounds almost miraculous…"

Nora grinned at her friend, calmly conversing as she drew her silk thread into a neat French knot. "Julia?"

She stopped talking, lifting her eyebrows.

"Are you becoming a doctor?"

Julia's cheeks bloomed pink as she bit down on her bottom lip. "It's the fault of living in this house. I have no other conversations to overhear." Her eyes fell, and Nora swallowed the lump in her throat, wishing Julia could have the half-dozen or so children she longed for. Nora knew her friend would far rather hear the prattle of little ones than referee disagreements between surgeons.

"I admit, I like siding with you when the discussion gets heated." Julia's fingers played with the needle. Then she looked up, lips twitching with a faint smile. "The profession is awfully catching."

Nora grinned. "I certainly contracted a lifelong case from Horace."

"I'm enjoying the nursing more than I thought," Julia admitted. "If I could have my own children…" She cut off, pain apparent in her face. "I like that Harry and I have work to do together. I like being able to help and understand the arguments at the dinner table. I enjoy compounding salves and tinctures with you and Horace." Her voice strengthened and grew more pointed. "I certainly have no desire to venture into the surgical theater. You can keep the blood to yourselves."

Nora studied Julia's confident smile. She was a different woman from the girl Nora first met when she returned home. Nora swiped at her eyes. "I'm sorry," she mumbled. "You know what a watering pot I've been lately. I just—" She swallowed. "I'm glad you're here. You keep us all sane."

Julia scrunched her nose. "I would never go that far."

"I should get back to work," Nora said, tickled by the unexpected exchange with her friend. She'd never realized before Harry married, but this house had always needed at least one more female.

Nora returned to the ward, where Daniel was struggling with the drinking tubes, more tired than ever. When one of the recovering women hummed "God Rest Ye Merry, Gentlemen" between spoonfuls of broth, he flinched, making Nora's eyes burn. He shouldn't be cast off from his family right before Christmas; it was needlessly cruel for a man expecting his first child. And keeping him from seeing his sisters… In the past two weeks, the only word he'd received from the Gibsons was a furious missive from his father, dripping with feelings of betrayal. She knew he wanted to drive out and see them, but he couldn't disappear for days in the middle of this outbreak.

"Please go upstairs and get something to eat. Maybe lie down," Nora pressed, and Daniel complied so easily and silently that her worries only multiplied as she watched him drag his feet up the narrow staircase.

Nora closed her eyes, willing away the nausea and aching

head that plagued her. There was no time for pregnancy symptoms amid so many other pressing needs. After a deep breath, she placed her stethoscope on the patient's chest and listened carefully. Miss Bagnell's pulse was improving.

All the patients had been fed and now were sleeping or resting, buckets in hand for the vomit. A catalog of bleak emotions—fear and hopelessness, fatigue and pain—was displayed across their quiet faces.

Silent suffering, commendable here on the wards, was impossible to summon herself. Nora couldn't watch Daniel wither any longer. She had to *do* something. She checked the clock on the wall—half past two. The proper hour for making social calls. She could attempt a trip across town if she took a hackney. It was too cold outside to walk.

Aunt wouldn't welcome her, but if she came with an offering... She could be meek and tractable. For Daniel's sake.

It wouldn't hurt to try. This was supposed to be a season of goodwill. If she failed, she'd at least know she'd done everything she could.

Still frowning, Nora went for her coat, wishing courage was as easy to don as the cloak and muffler that armored her against the December chill.

CHAPTER 35

RELENTLESS COLD HAD DRIVEN THE GREEN FROM THE once-bright holly leaves adorning Aunt Wilcox's door, leaving them tattered and withered like so many scraps of brown paper. They rustled when Nora knocked, and she wondered why no servant had replaced them.

Aunt Wilcox would certainly follow tradition, displaying her holiday greenery until Epiphany, but it seemed unlike her to allow it to look shabby, especially with her party approaching. The wind pushed a smattering of snowflakes against Nora's face.

She brushed them away, pressed her hand to her temple to lessen the ache, and knocked again. She was rewarded with another long silence. Puzzling. There ought to be half a dozen servants in the house.

Perhaps Aunt Wilcox had gone to Richmond with Daniel's parents? As outcasts, Nora and Daniel wouldn't have been informed if she'd decamped and canceled the party. A wise choice, with the current surge in cholera cases.

Nora was about to resign and retreat when she heard footsteps approaching behind the door. It swung open, revealing a stranger, almost. This woman was as unlike Daniel's mother as anyone could be, in a wrinkled lace-trimmed day dress adorned with tiny flecks of blood.

"Sarah?" Nora froze, taking in the sight of her exhausted mother-in-law in the huge doorway. "What's wrong? What are you doing here?"

Sarah's eyes closed for a moment. Nora took her hand. "Are you ill?"

"No. Not me." She swallowed. "You got the message? Come inside."

The dark house was draped in a perplexing silence. "Message?" Nora echoed, but her question was lost in her mother-in-law's fussing with the bolt. "Are you alone?"

Sarah shook her head. "There's five of us. I came for a visit two days ago, but yesterday Fenella fell ill."

Fenella? Nora's moment of confusion vanished in a rush. Sarah must be referring to Aunt Wilcox. Nora had never heard anyone use her first name before.

"Her doctor said it was cholera, so we sent the servants to the country house, not wanting them to contract the sickness. Only her lady's maid stayed, and a footman and cook, but her maid, Miss Pritchard, is suffering a headache and the cook now refuses to leave the kitchen even to deliver broth—"

Nora bit her lip. Headache was often one of the first cholera signs.

"—and the footman, Charles, went hours ago to send word to Daniel and fetch Dr. Adams, but it's been so long I'm afraid he's absconded. He's only been here two months. I said we should keep her butler with us, but Fenella insisted he go with the others because he has a family."

Aunt Wilcox could have ordered everyone to wait on her hand and foot, but she'd thought of her servants first. Nora cursed herself for not coming to apologize earlier. "Why didn't you send for Daniel yesterday?"

Daniel's mother pushed back her hair with a tired hand. "Fenella was still angry at him. But when I saw how severe it was, I ignored her and sent the footman. Hours ago. Isn't that why you're here?"

"There was no message. I came by chance," Nora said, her hand naked without the familiar, encouraging handle of her doctor's bag against her palm. "I don't have my supplies."

The stairs creaked as Nora followed Sarah upstairs, the shadows gathering under the unlit sconces. "So what brought you?" Sarah asked, her voice weak.

Nora grimaced. "Regret, I'm afraid. I don't want Aunt to be angry with Daniel or me anymore. Nor you. I was a fool to try and keep secrets."

Sarah sighed. "I should have told Daniel right away when Fenella was ill."

"If we'd known, we'd have come instantly," Nora insisted.

Sarah shook her head. "It happened so fast. She took ill just yesterday, I think." She paused on the stairs and counted on her fingers as if trying to make the interminable hours of sickness fit into one night. Nora knew the feeling.

"It's so hard to tell. We went to the refuge together, her and I. We wanted to give them a party. She had Christmas presents for all of them. They sang and gave us tea and punch, and the place was neat as a pin. But hours later, we had a message saying some were gravely ill."

Nora's heart sank through the soles of her shoes.

"By then, Fenella had a sore head, so we sent for her doctor.

That must have been yesterday afternoon." Sarah met Nora's eyes as they reached the landing. Nora had no idea which bedroom belonged to Aunt. She'd never been this far inside the opulent home.

"It was so fast." For a moment, Sarah's lips parted, but weariness washed over her, and she closed her mouth.

"Are you certain it's cholera?" Nora prodded gently. It was progressing speedily enough, but there were other quick illnesses.

"Without a doubt," Sarah stated. "Adams confirmed it. He stayed for hours last night."

"What about the blood?" Nora demanded, stroking a finger across a stain on Sarah's sleeve. "If the effluvium is bloody, that's most likely not cholera."

Sarah looked over her crumpled dress.

"That's not effluvia. That's from helping Dr. Adams. He told me to hold the basin."

"He bled her?" Cold crawled the length of Nora's limbs. For a moment, she couldn't speak. Horace had tried bleeding cholera patients initially, seventeen years ago in the epidemic that had killed her family, but soon abandoned it, telling her his patients were so painfully thirsty he simply didn't have the heart to keep on with it. Bleeding might help other things, but it increased thirst. "Show me," Nora said, already in motion again.

Sarah led her into a dim room lit with a low, fidgety fire in the grate. An ornate bed cradled a sleeping lady.

Daniel's aunt was a commanding woman. When Nora last saw her, she'd been perfectly turned out in jet beads and taffeta silk, as straight as a bayonet and fierce as a general. The body before her was shrunken, with hollow eyes and skin the color of a winter sky. Even her hair seemed a different color, dull and drained.

"She screamed most of the morning yesterday," Sarah said. "The cramps in her legs... The bloodletting eased that, at least."

Nora thinned her lips. "How long ago was it? And how much?"

"Yesterday at seven," Sarah said. "When it didn't halt the evacuations of her bowels—"

Or stop the shite, according to Horace, who disliked euphemisms. Lately, even Mrs. Phipps was too tired to reprove him.

Focus, Nora told herself.

"Dr. Adams came back this morning and gave me opium to keep her comfortable, but he said barring a miracle, she would pass today." Sarah's lips trembled and she pressed a handkerchief to her mouth.

"And you're alone," Nora stated with a tongue almost too heavy to lift. Daniel's mother was not built for such a crisis.

Sarah's lips wobbled, threatening to break her fragile resolve.

Nora looked again at the bed and the wasted woman in it, taking inventory of the signs of imminent death and the paltry offerings available on the nightstand: blue pills, calomel, a glass of water that probably contained some grains of opium.

"I'm here now," she muttered, doubtful that would improve the outlook.

She'd brought nothing with her. No medicines. No stethoscope. She'd come for a social call, planning only to say her piece and hopefully patch together some kind of truce for Daniel's sake.

"What about Aunt's maid? What's her name?"

"Agnes Pritchard. She's in the room next door. She's been with Fenella for fifty years. I was just with her. She's still able to walk, but—"

"Give her tea. As much as she'll take," Nora commanded. She would check on Agnes next. "And summon a messenger boy." On a frozen day like this, they'd be scarce. Sarah might not find one in the square, but if she walked to the next street or watched for one from the drawing room window... "We must send for Daniel. And supplies."

"Dr. Adams said to give them both beef tea," Sarah said on a fresh sob. "But she can't even swallow."

At least he'd been right about that. *Probably copying Horace's methods.* "Let's try this," Nora said, pulling out a clean handkerchief and dipping it in the cup. The liquid had cooled, but at this point, the temperature hardly mattered. Ignoring the amber drips running down her hand, Nora pushed the soaked cambric between Aunt Wilcox's withered lips. They closed, slowly, feebly, barely managing that most basic action: an infant's instinct to suck.

"Where does Dr. Adams live?" Nora asked. If he was close by, perhaps she could send Sarah to borrow a rubber drinking tube and a syringe. If she waited for Daniel and her instruments to arrive from Great Queen Street, it might be too late.

"Hampstead Row?" Sarah worried her fingers together. "I'm not certain. Perhaps Havers?"

Nora shook her head. No help there, then. And she didn't

really need him, just his tools. "Never mind. We need to work now."

Sarah looked at her blankly.

"Are there any doctors who live nearby?"

"I don't know. I've tried three of the neighbors, and the houses were shuttered. No one is staying in London this winter..." Sarah's voice rose with each word, climbing octaves toward the high notes of hysteria.

Nora swallowed. "All right. Don't fret. I'll write the note and tell Daniel exactly what's happened. You only need to find a messenger."

In harried strokes, she summarized Aunt's condition— *advanced*—and listed necessary supplies, closing with, *Come quickly*. He would know what that meant.

"The hospital at 43 Great Queen Street," she said, pointing to the address she'd printed in thick black letters. "If you can't find a message boy, ask a carriage driver or a passing stranger." Anyone with legs would do. "Offer a pound and tell them to hurry. Offer ten if you must."

"What about Agnes?" Sarah glanced at the closed door behind her. "She needs someone to tend to her, too."

"I'll check her before you leave," Nora said, glad Sarah had seen fit to put her in the nearest bedroom. There was no time to be shuttling to the servant rooms in the attics and back. Nora slipped inside the silent room to find a woman even older and thinner than Aunt. "Miss Pritchard?" Nora said softly.

The woman rolled her eyes toward Nora, squinting as she focused. Then the lids widened in surprise. "Daniel's wife?" she whispered, her throat too parched for normal speech.

Nora inhaled. "Yes." Somewhere in the list of duties for a lady's maid, between setting out clothes and drawing baths, was the unspoken dictate to carry the same grudges as your lady. Nora saw Agnes's compliance plainly in her distrusting eyes. "I'm here to help you both."

"Is my lady—"

"She's resting at the moment," Nora reassured her as she took up her wrist to feel her pulse. The skin was paper dry, but the palpitation under Nora's fingertips beat steady and persistent. She could wait a few minutes while Nora attended Aunt. "If you start feeling worse, call for me," she instructed. "I'll take care of Aunt Wilcox for you." From the nervous fumbling of Agnes's hands to her wrinkled brow, Nora knew that promise would do more to calm her than anything else. "You did an excellent job nursing her while you could. I'll take over now."

The woman nodded, anxiety sloughing visibly from her face. As Nora stepped out of the room, she left the door open to hear the woman easily. "You can go now," Nora told Sarah, attempting to hide her reluctance. Sending away her only set of helpful hands seemed her worst idea yet, but what could she do without any of her tools or medicines? She needed Daniel. "Be sure to dress warm."

Then she returned to her examination of Aunt Wilcox—no easy task without any of her tools, but Horace had taught her to roll heavy paper into a tube when she had no stethoscope, and her fingers would do, for now, in place of a thermometer.

Aunt Wilcox's pulse throbbed thready and slow, her skin far too cold. In her haste to send for help, Nora hadn't paid any mind to the fire, and it had sunk to embers. She needed hot bricks, but they took time to warm. Nora shoveled coal from the half-filled scuttle onto the grate and blew until flames licked to life again, then stacked the forgotten bricks around them.

She tried again with the soaked handkerchief, but Aunt Wilcox refused to suck this time. Nora squeezed the drops into her mouth, wetting the parched tongue, but it wasn't enough to thin her sluggish blood.

As Nora lifted one eyelid, Aunt's stare was vague and unfocused, her pupil nearly obscuring her blue iris. Far too big. Far too much like the eyes at death, the pupils expanding into black portals as if to let the soul out.

"Aunt." Nora shook her by the shoulders, trying to elicit some response. Not that it would help. None of the patients in her wards who'd sunk this low had ever recovered.

She pictured Daniel's stricken face. If he and his aunt never reconciled…

Nora pressed her ear to Aunt's chest and felt the low vibrations of a weary heart, toiling to move meager amounts of thickened blood.

If she did nothing, this was the end.

She exhaled and dropped her head, ransacking her mind, demanding it give up a solution.

Julia.

The article just hours ago.

Her head snapped up. Mr. Torrance had described patients very close to this. She was still awaiting his reply, hoping for more details and to test the transfusion therapy on some animal first…

Aunt released a weak, broken breath.

Nora scanned the room, willing a syringe to miraculously appear, when her eyes fell on Aunt Wilcox's writing desk and the cut-glass bottle holding half a dozen long quill pens. No doubt there was a penknife, too, somewhere.

Perhaps she could steal a little more time—at least give Daniel a chance to say goodbye if he hurried.

Nora rushed to the basement to find the kitchen and the cook. Unfortunately, the kitchen was dark, a scribbled note on the counter from the woman who'd run away and left several pots of broth to make up for her defection.

"Dammit," Nora hissed as she removed the lids to find one pot of hot water.

It didn't matter that she'd never attempted this before. Sarah should be back in time to help her, and there was nothing else to try except giving up, and that was no option at all. Daniel and the others might not want to risk attempting transfusion, but Aunt Wilcox had nothing more to lose.

Nora threw back the curtains so she could see well enough to rifle through the cupboards, trying to remember details. Instead of transfusing his patients with milk or blood from a servant, Torrance had injected something he called "Dr. Latta's solution" into his patients' veins. While Nora recalled the ingredients, she couldn't recall the exact amounts. And Dr. Thomas Latta himself—well, she'd found no trace of him in journal indexes or medical registers. The only thing she knew for certain about Latta's solution was that she'd find the three simple ingredients here.

Without the supplies and medicines in her bag, and with

Aunt unable to swallow, this was all she could do—get liquid into Aunt Wilcox to ease her thirst and thin her blood, and hope she didn't provoke a deadly transfusion reaction.

After picking up a step stool, Nora emptied the cupboards until she found what she needed—a tin of salt and a carton of bicarbonate of soda. Pocketing both, she scooped some water into a kettle and legged it back upstairs, not trusting Aunt Wilcox's thready pulse enough to leave her more than a few minutes. As soon as Daniel arrived... Nora's brow knit. Why wasn't Sarah back?

She'll be here soon, Nora told herself, and turned up the lamp. She added pinches of salt and bicarbonate to the hot kettle, tasting it, hoping she'd find a good ratio—something close to the subtle saltiness of blood but not injurious to the body— like when shipwrecked sailors tried to slake their thirst with seawater. Prying the window open several inches, she left the mixture to cool in the arctic air, then threw a harried glance at her patient.

If she sat beside her, dripping broth into her mouth and watched her die, no one would blame her. But if she proceeded with this madness, the results would be her fault.

"Stay with me a bit longer," Nora urged, and turned to rifle through the desk. Her fingers shook in protest.

Eight pens. Some would split, but cut and trimmed, Nora figured she could assemble a tube of at least twenty inches. With the pulse so suppressed, the hydrostatic pressure should be enough to force her makeshift mixture into Aunt Wilcox's veins. Though how she would manage, with only her own two hands... She glanced at the window but saw only snow, swirling through the square and collecting on the sill of the open window.

"I'm sorry, Horace," she told the almost empty room; Aunt Wilcox barely counted as another life in this state. "I can't treat this quietly."

She inspected the pens, choosing the strongest, and sharpened it to a fine point. Then she trimmed off the remaining feather, leaving a pointed tube about five inches long. The second quill split, but her third attempt yielded another tube, which she slid into the blunt end of the first. The next quill was too narrow, so she cast it aside, and the fourth split.

"You can slice open a trachea and tie off arteries," Nora reminded herself as she shivered in the current of frozen air from the window. "Pull yourself together." She wasn't clumsy. Maybe the pens were too dry. She could have soaked them first.

No time! Just do it, she scolded, and tried again with the last quill, this time successfully.

Tube ready, she inspected the penknife, testing the point with her thumb. Despairingly dull, but it would have to do.

The mixture was lukewarm now. She slammed the window shut and set the kettle on the bedside table, pulling close beside Aunt Wilcox, her hip pressed to the bed. She had a knife, a makeshift tube made of joined feather shafts, and warm water that, to her tongue, seemed about as salty as blood. Aunt had been using a spouted cup. Nora blessed Adams, assuming he'd left it with Sarah to help coax liquid into Aunt. She poured out the cold dregs of beef tea, rinsed the cup, and filled it with the warm mixture before snatching the shallow dish, still stained, that had been used to collect Aunt Wilcox's blood.

Nora picked up a wizened arm, the skin disconcertingly cool to the touch, and propped it across the shallow basin. Her feeble hopes sank as she compared the shrunken vessels to the width of the first doctored pen. Cursing under her breath, she returned to the desk, snatched up the narrow quill she'd discarded, and whittled it to a fine point.

"Please work," she whispered. And though she had to squint, bite her tongue, and curse, she managed to fold a minuscule pleat into the wider pen, forcing it into the narrower one.

"Don't you dare break," she ordered, then realized the command applied to herself just as well as her makeshift assembly. She surveyed the table. Everything ready, but she tasted the mixture one more time. She was guessing with the solution's concentration, but this would have to do.

Taking a breath, she positioned the penknife with her right hand and angled her quill tube with the left until her fingers stopped trembling. "All right." Swiftly, she punctured the median cubital vein where it crossed the hollow of Aunt Wilcox's elbow, then slid in the tube, letting blood seep into it. It oozed slowly, thick and dark.

When the blood reached the end of the tube, Nora pinched it shut, angling it upward gently, her right hand keeping the point secure in the vein. Quickly now. Blood would seep through the joints of the tube if she didn't hurry. Freeing her right hand, praying the tube would stay in the vein and keeping her left impossibly still, she reached for the spouted cup.

Not daring to breathe, she released the pinched end and began slowly easing the mixture into the tube. The majority of it spilled down the sides, flowing into the basin and across the bedspread, but enough entered the tube to force the blood inside back. Into the vein, though? Nora watched the basin. Pink swirled into the liquid, and her heart stopped until the color faded.

The blood had slid back into Aunt Wilcox's body, chased by the solution, which was now trickling into her. If the point had dislodged, the liquid in the basin would be bloodred.

It's working.

Arms burning from the strain of holding Aunt Wilcox's arm completely still while grappling with the spouted cup, she manipulated the liquid into the misshapen tube. Torrance had administered a quart of mixture at a time, but Nora still didn't trust the unorthodox procedure. She didn't know what she feared most—the solution missing the vein, or flooding inside it. Also, it seemed she'd overestimated her strength. Her shoulders seized, trembling from the strain of keeping both arms aloft. All of it intensified her headache until it throbbed in the back of her skull.

But she didn't dare pour any faster, fearing what might happen when the solution reached Aunt's heart. She had no way to know how many spoonfuls she had pushed into her blood. This wasn't like the controlled press of a syringe. A tremble started in Nora's back. She couldn't hold this position much longer.

Pour out another cup's worth, Nora told herself, biting the inside of her cheek.

A quarter…half… If she had to guess, she'd postulate she'd delivered three ounces into the vein.

She made it to three-quarters, then dropped the cup,

pulled the tube from the vein, and pressed a handkerchief to the wound with burning, aching hands. Heart pounding, she sagged to her knees, leaning against the side of the bed. She just had to keep pressure on the wound, keep every drop of hard-fought fluid inside. Clumsy with exhaustion, she tied the arm loosely with the handkerchief. With luck, Aunt Wilcox would stay alive until she had a real syringe, another batch of mixture, and Daniel to help her. With two more hands and proper equipment…

Nora tried to push to her feet, then realized what she'd ignored while pouring the infusion and binding the wound— black clouds blurring the edge of her vision and ringing ears growing louder every second.

Smelling salts. There were some in a silver holder on Aunt Wilcox's table. Nora fumbled as sparks burst through the darkness veiling her eyes. Seconds ago her arms had burned with pain, but now she couldn't feel them. Breathing in rapid pants, Nora heard something fall to the floor and realized there was no help for it; she was on her way down, too, and nothing could stop her from slumping in a heap.

You choose the absolute worst times to faint, she berated herself.

CHAPTER 36

NORA CAME TO HERSELF SLOWLY, DAZEDLY, UNTANGLING herself from a maze of colors—scratchy reds, blues, and oranges that smelled of camphor. A carpet. That made no sense.

She sat up, head aching enough to make her squint against the low flame of the lamp. Her face was damp, and her hip rested on something hard—an upturned basin.

Dear God.

Aunt Wilcox.

Wait, ought those two be put so close together?

Fighting back a groggy giggle—a worry, because she shouldn't be giddy—Nora knelt and reached across the bed, her breath steadying as her fingers located Aunt Wilcox and then a brachial pulse. Muzzy-headed as she was, she hurried to Aunt's other wrist and found the pulse again—confirmation.

The infusion was working. At the very least, it hadn't killed her.

Nora knelt back onto her heels, breath steadying. Did she imagine the room darker? Or were her fuzzy eyes still clearing? "Sarah?" she called weakly, the words barely making it past her lips. When she spoke, the pain in her head sharpened. Perhaps she'd hit it when she went down. Feeling for bruises, Nora turned to the fireplace to find only curls of thin smoke and ashes. Had she been unconscious for more than a few seconds? The spent coals and fading light outside indicated she'd been out for far longer.

Nora closed her eyes to steady herself as she used the mattress to pull herself upright. Her chest tingled with a strange chill as her stomach lurched. "Aunt?" She prodded the woman's frail cheek with her hand. There was a color resembling human flesh blooming beneath the gray skin. The bed was damp where Nora touched it, still wet from the spilled solution that hadn't made it into the improvised tube.

She started to sigh but buckled as her stomach flipped.

Nora stumbled to the water closet, hardly making it to the toilet in time. She'd suffered from diarrhea frequently during the pregnancy, and tonight was no exception. She made her way back to the bedroom and forced her eyes to focus on the clock on the wall, but the unwound hands had stuttered to a standstill hours ago. She hadn't brought her own watch. She crossed to the window and drew back the drapes.

"Good Lord," she half prayed, half cursed. Thick ice had yanked the heavy tree limbs to the ground, the unlucky ones already snapped, casualties lying in the road. The snow had turned into the worst kind of storm—wet, frozen, and impassible. Where was Sarah? Daniel would never get the carriage through. With so many broken branches, there wouldn't be any hackneys, either.

Was Sarah safe? Guilt roiled her already unsettled stomach, and Nora shivered at the frigid tendrils of air slipping through the casement and curling around her. In her haste, she hadn't fully sealed the window. With one last, desperate look down the barren street, she locked the window and pulled the drapes. Aunt Wilcox needed to stay as warm as possible.

Nora swiped at the hot tears needling her eyes. No time for that. She pictured Horace's fierce scowl and squared her sore shoulders. She'd collect firewood and more coal from the kitchen and boil water for tea. This time she'd raid the larder for anything edible. She hadn't eaten in hours, and the little passenger inside her...

Nora paused midstride, her hand pressed to the small mound of her abdomen. "At least I'm not entirely alone," she murmured with a caress on her belly. At the touch, her muscles tightened uncomfortably, and she hurried to the toilet once more. In the small, dark room, she closed her eyes and breathed against the rising fear.

You're not sick. You're immune to this. It's only the pregnancy.

The words repeated like a rosary prayer, giving her a crust of courage.

Immune.

Immune.

The thought of hiking to the basement and dragging up supplies only multiplied the wet droplets on her eyelashes. Every life in this house depended solely on her, no matter how weak or tired she was. One step after another, she'd go.

"Aunt." Her raised voice brought no response. "I'm going to get you tea and warm bricks." She studied the small figure buried in quilts, still breathing. "But I'm coming back."

CHAPTER 37

S HE'S NOT IN THE LABORATORY," MRS. PHIPPS SAID.

"I haven't seen her since lunch," Julia confirmed.

Daniel rubbed the back of his neck, more worried than he cared to admit. Nora wouldn't leave, not with so many patients so close to the edge. Unless... "No one remembers any summons for a birth or an emergency call?"

Ruth shook her head. "I thought she must be resting upstairs."

Daniel knew she wasn't, because he'd fallen asleep in their bed almost instantly when she'd sent him up hours ago. She'd never come in their room.

"She might have snatched a minute in my parlor," Mrs. Phipps said slowly. "And fallen asleep? It's quiet there." Mrs. Phipps considered her parlor a necessary retreat and allowed few intrusions there, but Nora sometimes joined her. "I'll look now," she said, out the door before Daniel could respond.

"This isn't like Nora," Julia said. "She usually leaves a note. But we're all tired. Perhaps she forgot?"

Daniel hoped so. And once he found her and railed at her for worrying him enough to cause a heart seizure, he'd apologize for being ridiculous.

He paced to the window again. "She didn't take the carriage, because Harry was using it. Where could she be?"

It was nearly time for evening rounds, but attending their many patients was impossible right now. He was as twitchy as an anxious cat. "You're sure there have been no messages?"

"None," Julia said, glancing again at the window. "But that's not surprising. It's wretched outside. I'm amazed Harry got back."

Maybe she had been called out, somewhere close enough to walk, and then been delayed. If the call was for a birth, there was a good chance she wouldn't return until tomorrow, but...

Daniel pulled back the thick drapes of the drawing room to reveal a world obscured by sheets of ice that glinted in the light of the streetlamps. The few people outside were shadowy huddles cocooned in hats and shawls, burrowing against the frozen storm.

She's probably waiting out the weather in a patient's home.

He said a silent prayer that it was a cozy middle-class flat and not a miserable hovel. The thought of her locked in a bleak room with deadly contagions while icy air infiltrated cracked walls...

"She's not upstairs." Mrs. Phipps returned, eyes creased with worry. "I looked in every room."

Daniel slid his fingers through his hair to press out the unwanted, foggy images trying to form.

"Let's not borrow trouble." Ruth's stiff words stood up straighter than the hunched group of worriers. "She's most likely seeing to a case and has no idea we're concerned. It's only five. I expect she'll be home for dinner. If not, she'll send a note."

She must have thought we were too busy to take anyone with her.

But the thought didn't reassure him. Julia was right. This wasn't like Nora. Frowning, Daniel left the parlor. "It's not late, but it's dark. She must be attending someone. Where's her list of cases?"

"She keeps her book in the clinic dispensary," Mrs. Phipps said, trailing him, the others close behind.

Once downstairs, he walked past the books and papers and journals stacked on her desk, and opened the wardrobe. His arms went cold.

"Is that her bag?" Julia whispered.

Daniel nodded and licked his lips. The familiar bag yawned wide, the eclectic contents neatly arranged. "She's not on a call."

The others stared at him as images of his expectant wife clouded his thoughts. Hurt. Sick. Struggling.

"Are you sure you checked the entire house?" he asked. "Every back staircase? Every closet?" If she'd fallen somewhere or fainted...

"We'll do it again," Julia promised. "All of us, together. But I'm certain she's not here. If she's not on a call, she must have—"

But he was already searching, looking behind doors and under tables in the empty exam rooms, like this was some tormented game of hide-and-seek.

—

"Daniel, it's only been a few hours," Julia insisted a quarter hour later. "The patients need you. Let Mrs. Phipps and I search the house."

He shook his head, unable to explain that stopping was impossible until he'd searched every inch himself.

"We'll all be laughing over this tonight." Mrs. Phipps opened the linen closet, though the wobble in her bottom lip betrayed her own unease. "It's surely some silly misunderstanding."

He knew she was right; chances of disaster were slim. Most certainly, he'd be annoyed and relieved by dinnertime. But the possibility of Nora injured dug like a dagger tip at his throat. He couldn't accomplish anything until he'd shoved it aside.

"I'll take the servants' rooms in the attic and work my way down. Should have started systematically. You keep searching down here and work your way up," he told the women.

It was like a case—eliminate everything it cannot be and see what remains. He opened the doorway to the shadowy back stairs. Only after he knew that she wasn't lying at the bottom of some rickety stairwell, he'd consider the possibility that she was at a shop, stocking up on tea or soap.

"I'm sure she's fine," he lied.

CHAPTER 38

A FTER A FRUITLESS SEARCH, DANIEL FORCED HIMSELF TO tend patients for an hour, moving from one bed to the next, alongside Harry, who watched with strained eyes. When the doorbell rang, Daniel started like a rabbit. Normally, he wouldn't have heard it from in here.

"Go. See who it is," Harry said. "I can look after things."

As he ran, a maid stopped him on the landing. "Dr. Gibson, I believe your mother is here."

Heavens, he hoped not. What in the world was she doing, arriving unannounced in a blizzard? Bounding up the stairs, he decided the maid must be mistaken. Perhaps she'd meant a message had arrived from his mother and stumbled over the words.

But when he reached the hall…

"Daniel!" His mother flew at him, clutching him with icy fingers. If not for her voice, he would hardly recognize her— hems muddied, hair rumpled and falling to her shoulders, a stricken expression on her face, her height disguised in layers of clothing and thick furs. Even wrapped within an inch of her life, she shivered violently. Mrs. Phipps and Horace, already in the hall, stared openly.

"It's your aunt," she quavered through chattering teeth.

"What's wrong with her?" Daniel demanded, bracing himself for news of an accident, his feet ready to fly.

"She and I took our luncheon at the refuge yesterday. It was a sort of holiday celebration."

"Yes?" Daniel fought the urge to roll his eyes. His mother had a maddening habit of starting stories far too early.

"I was going to stay and help her with preparations for her Christmas party. But she fell ill yesterday afternoon."

Daniel didn't mean to be impatient, but the words took too long. "Ill? But why did you come now? Why not send someone?"

"Her doctor said it's cholera." She choked back a sob. "Fenella sent nearly all the servants away to protect them. But the ones who were supposed to stay and help all fled. I'm the only one left. Miss Pritchard is sick, too."

Daniel's eyes widened. "How did you get here from Mayfair? Is Aunt alone?"

"Nora's with her," she continued without hearing him. "But she needs help. And she wants her bag."

"Nora?" The buzzing in Daniel's brain sharpened at his wife's name. "She's in Mayfair?"

"If she's treating cholera, why doesn't she have her bag?" Horace demanded.

Daniel's mother had to speak over the sudden snap of ice hitting the windows, and they all looked toward the panes. The sharp sleet threatened to crack the glass. "She only came to call, so she didn't bring any supplies. But she found us just in time." His mother pried a glove from her hand, revealing fingers crimson from the cold.

Daniel shook his head, clearing away questions he didn't

have time to ask. "In time for what? Isn't Adams there?" He'd made such a show of being Aunt's personal physician.

"He bled her yesterday and checked her again this morning, but he said there was no hope and he had other patients—" His mother's composure broke, and she slumped.

"Sit down, now," Mrs. Phipps ordered, and guided his mother to a chair, calling for blankets and tea.

"But Aunt's still alive?" Daniel pressed, kneeling in front of his mother. He placed his hand against her cheek, even though cholera didn't cause fever.

"She was. Only just. Nora showed up like a miracle and sent me to fetch you."

"And you?" Daniel asked, searching her colorless face. "Any headache? Abdominal pain?"

His mother gestured away his concerns. "I'm fine. Only tired. But the roads are unbearable. It was near impossible to find a hackney. No one's risking their horses in this snow. The driver refused to take me all the way, so I came the rest of the way on foot. And I kept falling because of all the ice. I skinned my hands and wrenched my ankle. No one even offered to help me."

It was a wonder she'd made it. "Horace, can you see to her?" he asked, releasing her icy hands. "I need to go."

Horace frowned as he faced the windows. "If you go by horse, you'll have to saddle it and ride. I don't trust any carriage on this ice."

Daniel assessed the thick flakes plastered to the black window. He knew frozen snow like this… Any journey would be pure hell. The mare's hooves would cake with ice, and he'd have to dismount every five minutes to chisel it out, but going on foot to Mayfair in an ice storm was impossible.

Mrs. Phipps reappeared—not that he'd seen her leave—arms laden with thick clothes. "Are you sure you shouldn't wait until morning? The streetlights aren't even burning, and Nora's safe with your aunt, so—"

"She won't be able to do much without her bag." Without medicines and a tube to help ease the liquids into Aunt's mouth... Daniel shook his head. All he'd wanted was to see Nora well and safe for the last two hours. Nothing could deter him now. "I'm not waiting until morning," he announced. He'd never forgive himself if his aunt died while they were at odds. "Tell Harry what's happened and ask him to saddle the mare. If my mother could manage..." He shook his head.

"Walking might be the best option," Horace said. "It would take half the night, but I could come with you."

Mrs. Phipps dropped one of Daniel's boots. "No, you will not. Harry will go, if anyone does, but I think Daniel can get there much faster on his horse. Daniel, put these on. The maid will be here soon with hot stones for your pockets."

"Thank you, Mrs. Phipps."

She pressed his hand and lowered her voice. "Go help our girl."

CHAPTER 39

N ORA LEANED AGAINST THE DOOR OF THE WATER CLOSET, trying to still her trembling.

Not immune.

Years of tedious conjecture answered by one session in the water closet.

She needed fluids. Quickly, because if she sickened further, there was no one to dose her—not until Sarah returned, and she should have come back hours ago.

Nora shut her eyes, unwilling to consider where Sarah might be or what had detained her. She could not allow her imagination to conjure up one more disaster.

Navigating by feel—it was too dark now to see—she slipped back into the hall, took another step, then doubled over, hands clasped at her middle. Her head felt like a grape, squeezed between finger and thumb, ready to burst.

"Miss Pritchard?" she called, voice already hoarse. She hadn't heard a sound from the other room in too long, but she hadn't been able to leave the toilet for at least an hour. Her intestines must be entirely vacated now.

She recalled voices like this—her mother's and grand-mother's, frayed and breaking; a raspy sawing that replaced her young brother's cry. She couldn't remember any of them dying, but their ghostly groans came back, echoing in her pounding head. Her back ran cold and slick with sweat.

"Pritchard?" she tried again, but couldn't muster enough volume to breach the long hallway.

Drink first. You'll be louder after wetting your throat.

Pushing upright, she hobbled to Aunt Wilcox's bedroom, one hand braced on the wall. She'd needed to make more solution. Aunt's color was still better than before the transfusion, even after the passing of so many hours.

Aunt stirred, clutching at the handkerchief in her mouth. Nora wetted it again, then gulped all the remaining broth. The wineglass was empty.

A wave of cramps shook her. Nora dropped to her knees beside the bed, head pressed against the mattress. Even if she mixed more Latta's solution and downed it all, what would this disease do to her baby?

"Don't give up," she rasped, and reached for the washbasin. She'd dipped her hands several times into the cold, dirty water. She shouldn't drink it—cold water was forbidden—but she had nothing else, and venturing to the kitchen was impossible. Hands shaking, she poured in salt and bicarbonate, spilling bits of both on the carpet. Mrs. Phipps had said spilling salt brought bad luck, but it was too late for that.

Her mouth was as dry as dust. No way to tell if she'd managed the ratio, but the solution was wet and cooling against her papery throat. Nora took four gulps, then sat back, leaning against the bed, taking deep breaths, fighting to keep her roiling middle from expelling everything.

"Aunt Wilcox?" she gasped, and was answered with a soft moan.

"I need you to drink something." Nora reached overhead, groping for Aunt Wilcox's handkerchief. She dunked it into the remaining solution, then pushed it, sopping, back to Aunt Wilcox's mouth. Then she lay back on the floor, gasping.

Rest a bit. Drink some more. Then check on Pritchard.

If she felt this thirsty, the other woman's mouth must be—

Another cramp seized her. With a groan, Nora curled onto her side, squeezing her eyes until lights danced at the corners from the pain. They flickered and swirled until the room blurred into nothingness.

She drifted, sinking in the cold black waters of unconsciousness, limbs slack and useless.

———

"Nora? Nora!"

Daniel's voice.

Footsteps, pounding up the stairs.

She turned her head just as a bearlike shape barreled through the doorframe. He was muffled up to his eyes and clad in so many capes and coats that he might have been a peddler.

Nora wanted to cry in relief, but instead a strangled moan escaped her lips.

He charged forward, dropping to the floor beside her, shedding capes and tossing aside the preposterous fur hat that made him look like a hussar. Or a Russian. "What's happened? What are you saying?"

"Miss Pritchard needs something to drink," she told him. "And I have cholera."

Daniel gripped the lantern and held it close to her face, the glare piercing her aching head.

"Your color is dreadful." His eyes strayed to the detritus scattered across the floor: matches, broken quills, the overturned basin and spilled bicarbonate. "What's all this?" he asked, lifting her to a sitting position.

"I gave Aunt a transfusion of Latta's solution." She stopped and closed her eyes, surprised by the violent nausea. "She's still alive. I can't get to Miss Pritchard."

His hands moved, testing the temperature of her forehead and finding the pulse at her neck. He moved closer, staring into her eyes.

"You're making me nervous," Nora said.

He scoffed a humorless laugh. "*I'm* scaring *you?*" His arms tightened, and he gathered her up. "How long have you been ill?"

She leaned into his straining chest, sorry for the burden of her weight as he grimaced. She had no idea whether it was past midnight. "What day is it?"

He only huffed in answer. "Never mind. We need to get you in clean clothes and feed you some broth." He bore her along the black hallway. All she wanted to do was sink back into unconsciousness, where the blackness numbed the agony of the cramps. As he lowered her into chilly sheets, she rolled to her side, cradling her spasming body.

Daniel whispered some prayer or plea she couldn't understand. She pushed one hand forward on the sheets to find him, but he was gone.

CHAPTER 40

HE SHOULD HAVE BROUGHT HORACE. IT WOULD HAVE taken longer to get here, but now he had three patients—four, when he counted his own child—sinking fast and a kitchen two stories away. He needed to focus like never before. As Daniel raced through the frozen house, every heavy exhalation was an entreaty for his wife. He'd never seen the kitchen or basement rooms, and he navigated them crudely, opening doors to storerooms and offices, before he found the pantry.

He cursed when he reached the stove, cool to the touch, the fire long spent. Boiling a pan of water would take far too long. He lit the coals anyway with trembling hands and raided the wine cellar. He could start with that. He loaded a basket with bottles, coal, towels, and linen, and ran back upstairs. Halfway through the front hall, he struck an ornate side table in the darkness and sent it sprawling and splintering. He'd never cared less for any object. He ignored the sharp throb in his shin and continued his blind sprint.

His heart demanded he return at once to Nora, but intellect ordered him to tend the older women first. Nora had been able to speak coherently, which meant she wasn't in the final stages. Yet.

Dropping his armful onto the bedroom carpet, he hurried to Aunt Wilcox's side. *Ashen skin, sunken cheeks.* Daniel thumbed up her eyelids to check her pupils. They responded sluggishly to the light.

"Aunt, it's Daniel. I'm here." He pulled his tube from his bag and fitted it into her mouth, replacing the wet handkerchief. After a brief tussle with a corkscrew, he opened the wine and attached a funnel to the tube, his toes pressing impatiently against the soles of his shoes. Everything with cholera took painstaking time.

He inhaled as he forced his hands to mete out a trickle of wine. His aunt managed to swallow, a bitter pucker to her lips. *Must be a bad vintage.*

He waited until he was certain she'd had at least four ounces and the wine began to dribble out the corner of her mouth before he removed the tube. He took up the lantern and followed its wavering glow into the hallway, his glance ricocheting between Nora's doorway and Pritchard's. But reason had fallen through the anxious chasm in his brain. He needed to see Nora. He promised himself only a reassuring glance, but the skin of her cheeks was dry, crepe-like, as gray as the wings of a dead moth. He coaxed several ounces of wine into her mouth and raised his voice until she finally fluttered her eyelids open, pain and exhaustion in the vacant recesses.

"You can go back to sleep. I'll keep giving you liquids," he promised.

Her eyes closed instantly, but her mouth cracked open. "Latta's," she whispered.

He kissed her forehead with frantic force. "Yes, Latta's," he agreed, though he had no idea who Latta was. He only knew she needed to rest and not worry.

Now for Miss Pritchard, the woman who'd always been his aunt's shadow. Silent, brooding, forever peering at Daniel with disapproval whenever he didn't give his aunt due deference—which, at this crucial moment, he worried had been far too often. He creaked open her door to find an all-encompassing blackness. The lamp had burned out. A cloying stillness clung to the heavy air. Daniel raised his own lamp, throwing shadows across the monstrous bedstead. Not a rustle or whimper like those he'd grown accustomed to hearing from so many suffering patients.

"Miss Pritchard?" he asked slowly, inching forward. It took two more steps before he could discern her small shape in the twisted covers.

He moved the lamp toward her head and closed his eyes. No need to take her pulse. Her dried flesh was frozen in a mask of death, gray and pitiful. Miss Pritchard's prim mouth now gaped open as if begging for a last drop of water, her once-stern cheeks collapsed and creased in surrender.

"I'm sorry," he whispered. He could never tell Aunt or Nora that Miss Pritchard had suffered silently and alone. Neither would forgive herself, even though they'd each been battling the same demon disease. Daniel gently closed her mouth, the leathery skin strange to the touch—just like all the cholera cadavers he'd handled. He didn't need this jarring evidence to know Nora, his child, and his aunt teetered at the precipice.

He shook his head and latched the heavy door behind him.

Only three patients now.

He'd not lose another.

———

Daniel wrestled his watch out of his pocket, from beneath a handkerchief, a thermometer, and hard candy. Half past 10:00 p.m. It had taken him an hour and a half to travel less than two miles. He counted the hours. Nora had been fine at 2:00 p.m., so she'd been sick less than eight hours. But that was more than enough time for cholera to kill.

The water in the kitchen should be seething by now. He'd need it to get through the long night. Horace wasn't coming, not in this weather. Maybe not even tomorrow. And Harry wouldn't think to—not with Daniel and Nora already treating the case. No one else knew Nora was ill.

Daniel reasoned through the possibilities as he filled two kettles and brought them upstairs. He'd divide himself—thirty minutes with Nora and then fifteen with his aunt. He couldn't change their bedding on such a schedule—Aunt would have to burn all three mattresses when this was over—so he'd focus only on keeping their fluids up.

When he returned with the tea, he stripped Nora down to her shift so she could rest easier, and propped her up. She could still sip so long as he held the heavy cup. She drained five ounces of steaming, bitter brew in minutes.

Daniel sighed with relief. "That's good," he praised her. "Can you take any more?"

She gave an exhausted shake of her head, squeezing her face in misery. "The cramps," she panted.

"I know," he lied, and pressed her face to his chest. She resisted enough that he leaned back and realized she was still trying to speak, the words labored and slow.

"I need Latta's solution. And Aunt, too. Just a bit of salt and bicarbonate in the water. The same saltiness as blood." She paused to catch her breath. "Transfuse it into my vein, not muscle."

"Transfuse it?" Daniel startled. He'd assumed she meant a mixture to drink. "Into a vein?" Was she delirious? "You know how badly transfusion experiments have gone, putting anything into a vein."

Nora sank into the pillow, at the end of her strength. "It worked," she managed to whisper. "I gave it to Aunt." Just when he thought she'd gone back to sleep her lips parted. "Aunt? Pritchard? Are they—"

Daniel swallowed. "Doing better."

Not entirely a lie. He believed wherever Miss Pritchard was now, it had to be better than the pains of her deathbed.

Nora's lips relaxed into the ghost of a smile. "It worked."

Daniel's heart twisted. "Did you give the solution to both of them?" He'd repeat nothing with a 50 percent mortality rate.

Nora tried to focus her yellowed eyes. "Just Aunt."

Daniel exhaled. Only if necessary.

He slanted his watch to catch the firelight. After eleven. Time to check Aunt and dose her with tea. "Sleep for a few minutes. I'll be right back," he promised. But she'd slipped under the waves of sleep before he finished speaking.

Daniel returned as quickly as he could, within his allotted fifteen minutes, but he could tell at a glance Nora had declined considerably. Her color had blued in the small span of time, and her heartbeat was so fast and feeble he struggled to measure the beats.

His throat seized, but his hands moved with speed and certainty, plying her with liquids. Barely any made it past her throat. He'd have to spend at least half an hour coaxing moisture back into her mouth just to help her to swallow, and by then... Daniel withdrew the glass-and-metal syringe from his bag and studied it at length.

While he often used it to measure medicines, draw out swelling from afflicted organs or joints, and irrigate wounds, he'd only administered fluids with it orally. He'd certainly never imagined using it to propel foreign liquids into a patient's bloodstream, especially his wife's. And then there were the logistics— he'd need to cut into a vein to introduce the bronze tip of the syringe. Daniel rubbed his eyes, trying to picture the procedure. If he hadn't studied the horizontal slice across his aunt's arm, he wouldn't believe Nora had done anything so foolhardy. It was entirely possible Aunt had survived out of luck or coincidence, but he couldn't trust either, not in Nora's case.

He filled a teacup with water and slowly tipped in some salt, unable to measure because of the pounding of his heart. He'd seen a transfusion experiment in Paris once and witnessed the patient's immediate reaction. She'd nearly died of it.

He'd try to replicate Nora's recipe, but that didn't compel him to put it in her body. He could—no, there was no chance she'd be able to drink it. Everything he'd given her earlier had

gone straight through her, the bed soaked and nearly odor-
less. Her bowels were stripped bare. If he didn't act now, there
wouldn't be another chance.

"Let it work," he prayed. With reluctant hands and disjointed thoughts, Daniel filled the barrel of the syringe. He
turned up the wick and positioned the lamp to throw all its
glow onto Nora's wasted arm. *So thin. It looked normal just this
morning.*

Quietly. That was what Horace always said. To treat things
with the least intervention possible. He'd likely strike the syringe
from Daniel's unsteady grip. And yet his hands kept moving,
ignoring Horace's imagined prohibition, winding a strip of
linen around Nora's arm and pulling it tight. He watched, waiting an age for a vein to emerge. He flicked the hollow of her
elbow, trying to provoke it to the surface. Nothing. He'd have
to go in and find it, then.

He rubbed his eyes until gold sparks scattered his vision.
No more delays. Time for decision.

"Please," he murmured as he pressed the scalpel to her cold
flesh. A bead of blood bloomed slowly, dark and reluctant. He
deepened the cut, searching for the lighter blood of the vein,
and she flinched but didn't wake. Blood started to flow, and
he tamped down the opening until he could fit the tip of the
syringe inside the open vein. He pulled the plunger up to be
certain he was in the vein, watching red blood swirl with the
salty mixture, still tempted at the last moment to divert the
fluid under the discolored skin.

"Please be right," he pleaded with Nora. With trembling
fingers, he depressed the plunger while holding pressure on the

tip to decrease the bleeding. He got through half the syringe and jerked it out, breathing heavily as he bandaged the wound, already regretting his impulsiveness. Sweat moistened his hands as he searched intently for any signs of distress.

He counted the seconds, her pulse, her breaths, until her eyelids flickered.

She shifted.

So soon?

"Nora?" He leaned in, touching her dry, cold skin.

She panted softly and looked at her arm. "You did it?" Relief tinted her strained words.

"Only two ounces," he admitted. But she was speaking again. Something she hadn't done for two hours. His head hummed with unformed questions.

Nora gave a small nod and closed her eyes. "More. Aunt. Pritch…" Her dry tongue crackled in her mouth, and she gave up attempting speech.

"I will," he promised. "How much?"

"Six," she whispered.

Six ounces? Too much. He'd kill her. But when he took her pulse, he found it slowed to one hundred beats per minute. Still far too high, but at least countable. He couldn't deny the marked change. How could such a small amount…

Fumbling with doubt, Daniel filled the entire syringe— four ounces of solution this time. The cut edges of the vein stuck together, the thick blood clotting faster than usual. Trying to ignore Nora's sharp intake of breath, he reopened the wound, exploring until the blood began to run again. "Please tell me you know what you're doing," he begged as he inserted the tip

once more and reluctantly released the clear fluid into her fal-
tering body. Nora shivered as the liquid traveled into her arm.

After several long minutes, she shuddered and then sighed,
the muscles of her face loosening.

"Nora!" He jumped forward, fearing she'd taken her last
breath.

"Better," she mouthed. And then: "Give me something to
drink."

CHAPTER 41

NORA PEELED HER EYES OPEN SLOWLY, PERPLEXED BY THE thin light coming through a window on the wrong side of the room. She closed them and tried again, giving her mind a moment to orient.

It didn't work.

"You're awake." The strident, out-of-place voice jarred her.

Nora focused on an unfamiliar peach silk comforter covering her narrow bed before turning toward the sound. "Aunt?"

Her identification was correct. Aunt Wilcox herself was alive and resting in the next bed. But this was no hospital ward.

"Where are we?"

"The nursery. Insulting, I know. Daniel thought he could care for us better in here since there were two beds and a water closet. Your Mrs. Phipps just left to get more towels."

Nora shifted her body—a mistake. Her muscles whined from cramps and disuse. "What nursery?" Aunt had no children.

"Mine, of course," Aunt snapped. "You were talking when Daniel and Dr. Croft carried you in. I thought you'd remember."

"Horace is here? And Mrs. Phipps?" The details were as disjointed as a jigsaw puzzle scattered across the floor. She dug into the recesses of her mind, remembering the sensation of being lifted and the sound of groans. Were they her own?

"They've all been here since yesterday. And Sarah."

"Yesterday?"

The door swung open, and Mrs. Phipps's lined face emerged from behind a tower of towels. "Nora!" She threw her bundle into a chair and whisked to Nora's bed, her hand cupping Nora's chin. "Thank God! You've been asleep for more than twenty-four hours. I wanted to wake you, but *that man*…"

She only used that moniker for Horace, and only at his most irksome. Nora almost laughed, but her sore, groggy head forbid it. "What's happened?"

"She doesn't remember," Aunt said, her voice tainted with annoyance.

"I suppose that's for the best." Mrs. Phipps tipped Nora's face with gentle fingers, assessing. "You look better," she conceded, "but Daniel should examine you right away." Her brow tightened as the corners of her mouth turned down. "If your mother-in-law hadn't come to us, we would have never known where you were. What did you—"

"Latta's solution." Nora squinted, forcing order in her mind. The ice storm. The quill pens…

Mrs. Phipps halted. "According to Daniel, that's all you would say when he found you. Do you remember?" Her stern disapproval didn't match the tender touch of her hands, smoothing Nora's hair.

"A little," she half lied. It was as vague as a muddy dream.

Mrs. Phipps anointed Nora's dry lips with a drop of olive oil, spreading it carefully. "I'll go wake Daniel now. He just sat down to eat a sandwich and was asleep in less than three bites. But that only makes sense, I suppose, considering he's been awake with you for two nights now without closing his eyes."

"Two nights?" Before Nora could finish her question, Mrs. Phipps hurried out, leaving Nora's confounded gaze nowhere to go but to Aunt Wilcox.

Aunt rolled her eyes. "You apparently put some mixture in my vein that saved me, so Daniel did the same for you. We've both had it done several times now." She gave her bandaged arm a disdainful glance and sighed. "Bruised as a beaten dog." Her voice dropped. "Daniel says I owe you my life."

Nora couldn't keep pace with the steady flow of information and had to wait with closed eyes for her head—or the room—to stop spinning. "I didn't know you were ill. I was coming to apologize." That much, she remembered clearly. She'd had a headache and nausea on her way over—most likely the beginnings of cholera. Stupid to mistake it for pregnancy symptoms.

"Perhaps we both should. I—" But Aunt Wilcox got no further. Daniel blundered into the room, stumbling on the rug in his haste.

"Nora?" He caught her up, kissing her forehead and groping for her wrist at the same time. He took her pulse and assessed her color before she could even murmur his name. "You have color in your face again." He pinched her arm, watching the skin creep back into place. "Better."

She was glad he didn't kiss her mouth; it had never tasted so foul. He pulled back the silk bed cover, revealing an unfamiliar flannel shift.

"I'm not sure this is warm enough for you," he said. "There might be a better one left behind by some maid—"

The word shook her, knocking something else to the forefront of her jagged, jostling thoughts.

"Where's Miss Pritchard?" There were two beds here, but Daniel could have put in a third. There was space for one next to the window, and if he'd wanted his patients close together…

"You haven't soiled this bed at all. The towels are clean. Can I help you to the water closet?"

He must have been too caught up to hear her question, and indeed, he didn't trouble to wait for her answer before lifting her into his arms and pulling her close against his chest.

"You don't need to…" she began, but it wasn't the truth. She could barely focus her eyes or speak. Walking anywhere was out of the question.

Mrs. Phipps hovered at his side, putting a nervous hand on Nora's arm.

"You can help me wash her up after," Daniel said to the housekeeper, who nodded, appeased.

Cholera left one with very little dignity.

As soon as they finished, Daniel returned her to the nursery. Mrs. Phipps helped Nora rinse her mouth with rose water until the fishy tang of old vomit and dry tongue washed away. "We'll leave your hair until tomorrow, when you're well enough for a bath."

Nora touched her head with a frown. "My hair?"

"Never mind." Mrs. Phipps waved her off.

It must be horrid. Even worse with Aunt Wilcox observing only feet away. The woman must have sensed Nora's distress.

"Well, we can't walk into our own graves and reemerge still looking presentable," she pointed out.

Instead of laughing at her quip, Daniel dropped his eyes, grief shrouding his worn face.

"It was that bad?" Nora whispered.

No one met her gaze. "For a bit," Daniel informed her shoulder, unable to raise his eyes any higher.

"I'll wake Horace and let him know she's past the worst," Mrs. Phipps said in the brisk tone she used to redirect wayward conversations.

"Please don't." Nora took a labored breath. She understood exhaustion. "Let him sleep. He'll see me when he wakes." She looked at Daniel with apologetic eyes. "I'm tired, too."

"Of course you are." He leaned forward, this time his kiss lingering on her forehead, leaving a circle of warmth pressed into her cold flesh. "But you should have broth first. You can doze until I come back with it."

She sank deeper into her pillow after they left, relieved to be free of questions and words. She needed to piece together the tattered fragments of the last days.

"What day is it?"

"Sunday," Aunt Wilcox answered more gently. "The twenty-third. You didn't miss Yuletide."

She'd arrived Friday afternoon. Her brow contracted with bleak memories of the first night: struggling to nurse Aunt and Miss Pritchard, finally collapsing on the floor when the cramps and evacuations overtook her.

"Is Miss Pritchard—"

"Daniel got here just in time," Aunt interrupted. "You were far gone."

Nora recalled the ice-coated world into which she'd sent her mother-in-law to fetch him. "Sarah saved us."

"I suppose there's praise enough to go 'round." Aunt sniffed. "Daniel's a fine doctor." She paused, her jaw clenched. "But you seem to know a few things even he did not." It was a difficult concession. Aunt's lips barely allowed the words passage.

Torrance's treatment. The infusions of Latta's solution.

"I was lucky," Nora admitted. "Experiments fail all the time. But the article sounded plausible when I read it."

Aunt grimaced, visibly galled to be part of any medical experiment deemed only *plausible.* "Be that as it may, I've had time to think while you slept. Daniel says your midwives are running the hospital in your absence." Aunt trailed her neat hands over her bedding. "I may have been hasty in my opinions."

Nora hesitated, but if she was ever going to speak her mind, surely there was no better time than now. "They won't be allowed to help much longer. Not if the colleges ban them."

Aunt waited so long to reply that Nora feared the conversation was spent. Then: "Agnes didn't live."

The words slammed into Nora's aching head. "Miss Pritchard?"

Aunt nodded slowly, turning away and fixing her gaze on the ash-stubbled coals in the hearth. "Agnes was my nursery maid, barely older than I was. She came with me when I married Colin. I only called her *Pritchard* when others were with us. She was always Agnes to me."

Guilt seared up Nora's chest like heartburn. She'd never given Pritchard the transfusion, thinking the uncomplaining woman was doing well enough to avoid the risk. And then, when Agnes must have been worsening, she'd been too ill to reach her.

"We decorated this nursery together. Agnes had a knack for it. But the children never came. And six years after we married, Colin drowned."

Nora froze. The formidable woman she'd feared for months was a grieving widow, convalescing in a gaily decorated grave-yard of shattered dreams. She'd known the same heartache as Julia.

"I didn't know," Nora whispered.

"That was long ago," Aunt replied gruffly, inhaling a fresh breath of courage. "But I'm quite broken up about Agnes." Aunt's cheeks burned red with determination as she fought back the emotion behind her stiff words.

"I wish I could have helped her," Nora admitted. "I should have done—"

"You were dying yourself. Like a good number of doctors have. But you were right. If the midwives were trained to nurse, and one had been with Agnes…"

A careful attendant could have made the difference. But… "Dr. Adams won't allow it if he has his way. He's gathered hun-dreds of signatures. He's already petitioned MPs."

"Leave Dr. Adams to me." Aunt spoke with the force of a lineman hammering steel spikes. "That man left me to die. I believe he owes me a favor."

———

"Broth," Daniel announced, returning with a tray, his mother close behind.

"Thank the Lord," Sarah said as she looked between Nora and Aunt Wilcox.

Her mother-in-law had never before looked relieved or happy to see her. Nor had she ever imagined Aunt allied with her cause. Nora wasn't entirely sure she wasn't still delirious.

"I'll help Fenella, and you feed Nora," Daniel's mother ordered him, her usual authority restored with her clean clothes and combed hair. "I've found a plain cook willing to start tomorrow," she informed Aunt. "And your father is bringing Joan now that the danger is past."

"No party," Aunt murmured as Sarah laid out her tray and handed her a fine napkin. "No one from high society will set foot in here for weeks after hearing the foul disease was in this home. How did it get here, Daniel? In Mayfair?"

The rumble of a cleared throat halted them all as they turned toward the doorway. Horace crossed his arms imperiously, his shabby coat straining against his wide shoulders.

"If any of us knew that, we'd be wealthy beyond mention and wiser than Solomon." He stared at Nora with fathomless eyes. "I've never once been sick with cholera, even though I've been exposed to thousands of patients. And Nora's been ill to the brink of death twice now."

She didn't miss the tightness in his voice or the exhaustion in his face and limbs.

"I didn't know I was ill when I decided to come," she defended herself meekly.

Daniel nodded. "It comes on fast. But you're still with us, and that's what matters."

Horace's thick white eyebrows shot upward. "Didn't know?

Truly? No headaches? No change in appetite? You didn't think to anticipate the weather? Did you even check my barometer?"

Nora never checked Horace's barometer, no matter how many times he admonished her.

"I had other things on my mind—Aunt Wilcox and the patients and—"

"And her pregnancy." Daniel's mother set down a china bowl of broth and stepped closer, the shadows of the half-open curtains obscuring her face.

They hadn't yet mentioned it. Nora tried to swallow, but her dry, burning throat barely allowed it. "Yes," she admitted.

Sarah wrung her hands. "I don't know what has gotten into young women these days. Climbing mountains. Trekking through tropics. And you, nursing patients almost to death while carrying my grandchild." She frowned in confusion but not anger.

"You nearly helped yourself to the grave." Horace grunted as he took a heavy seat on Nora's bed, half landing on her leg. He didn't ask permission before he pulled at her lip, checking her gum color. "Still too pale. Why didn't you get me when she woke?" he chided as he pinched with his fingers, making it impossible to reply.

"Because you're an old, tired man." Mrs. Phipps scowled.

Nora released a breath of laughter. Too many people had crowded into the nursery; her head ached from their movements and voices.

"Confusion?" Horace asked. "Disorientation?"

Nora closed her eyes. "A bit."

"To be expected," he mumbled.

In the darkness of her closed eyes, Daniel spoke up. "It's time to take them both back to private rooms. Aunt can't rest with us checking on Nora endlessly, and neither is in danger any longer."

"Anything's better than this arrangement," Aunt grumbled. "This room smells damp, and I hardly fit in this tiny bed. Tell Agnes—" The careless sentence broke, and she fell silent, pressing her lips together. After a long moment, she tried again. "I'll need someone to arrange my things."

Daniel found words first. "Mother can help you. Would you like to walk or have me carry you?"

Aunt grimaced. "Don't be foolish, Daniel. I'll take my cane. Get my wrap."

Fifteen minutes later, Nora was situated in a room with a thick Marseilles quilt stitched with such an intricate pattern of fruits and flourishes that looking at it made her dizzy.

"Your color's looking better every minute," Daniel said, sitting gently beside her. "I truly thought I might lose you."

"Like Miss Pritchard." Nora let her head delve deeper into the down pillow, as if she could find a spot where the memory didn't stab so painfully. The cotton pillowcase smelled of lavender sachets. "Your aunt is heartbroken."

"Not as heartbroken as I'd be if we'd lost you." Daniel rested his forehead against hers and she closed her eyes, his closeness better than medicine.

The door creaked quietly on its brass hinges, and they both turned to find Horace hovering. "I want to listen to the child."

He stepped over the Turkish rug slowly, his blue eyes clouded with worry.

Nora reached for her stomach. "Horace, it's too small," she started, but he'd brought his best stethoscope. She'd forgotten she was talking to a man who'd once pressed his head so close to a termite mound to hear their movements that he'd gotten one in his ear. If anyone could hear her little one, it was him.

"Have you felt anything?" he asked as he approached.

Nora shook her head, aware of the worried set to Daniel's brow. "I can't remember the last time I felt it. But I can't remember much of anything." The blur between reality and imagination grew fuzzier by the moment—like a dream receding just after waking. Horace gave Daniel such a fleeting and guilty look that Nora raised her chin in alarm.

"What?" She tried to read their averted glances. Her muddled head cleared just enough to sense deception. "Why can't I remember anything properly for two days?"

Mrs. Phipps stood mute in the dark corner of the room, her stillness testament to emotions too large for movement or speech.

Nora's heart quickened. Had she been entirely comatose? If so, it was all much worse than she'd imagined. Her hope for the baby faded with each second of silence.

Daniel squeezed her fingers in his warm grip. "You were having such severe cramps I couldn't keep up. Not even with the syringes of Latta's. Do you remember the first night I was here?"

Every memory came more as a sensation, a burning in her intestines, a sound of wailing. She remembered nothing but

red and black bursts of pain and Daniel's voice hovering somewhere outside time. "Nightmares," she murmured.

Daniel nodded in somber agreement. "You didn't sleep at
all that night. You improved immediately after the transfusions,
but you'd sink again after an hour or two. Toward dawn, you
had a fit and—" His lip gave an almost imperceptible shake, and
he cut off. He took a breath as if building strength to conclude
the story. "It was Horace's idea. He got here in the morning and
decided what we needed to do."

"What?" Nora squinted, trying to read Horace's cloaked
expression.

"Give you ether," Daniel finished.

"I've been anesthetized?" The strange quality to her memories, the lost days, made sense now. "For how long?"

Horace quirked his lips and looked away. Probably hoping
she'd give up if he ignored her.

"Horace," she demanded.

"We kept you on a light dose on and off for the past twenty-
seven hours."

"Good Lord," she whispered.

A small sob escaped Mrs. Phipps, and she turned to the
wall.

"Intermittently," Horace defended. "Whenever you grew
too fitful, we gave another small dose."

"You could have stopped my heart."

The strain of the last two nights revealed itself in the red
lines of Daniel's eyes and the new wrinkles etched across his
temples. "It nearly stopped mine." Unshed tears glossed his
lashes. "But your cholera wasn't responding to anything other

than the Latta's, and we'd worried we'd watered down your blood too much already—"

"It worked," Horace pointed out, pink spots appearing on his cheeks. "Your intestines were entirely stripped. But whenever you slept, the evacuations slowed. It gave your body time to recover. You were losing the war, Nora."

No wonder her head ached. Twenty-seven hours of ether. She might never have a clear thought again. "How often did you have to administer it?"

"Every two to three hours," Horace answered. "But for one stretch, every thirty minutes."

They'd all been through hell, then.

Nora caressed her stomach. "So the baby most likely…"

Daniel took her hand, gripping tight.

"There's been no bleeding at all," Horace reassured her. "That's the best sign. But I'd like to listen."

Daniel grasped her hand, tight enough to pinch her emerald wedding ring against her weak fingers, the stony promise on her flesh more consoling than uncomfortable.

She nodded permission, and Horace undid several buttons on Nora's shift to place the stethoscope on her bare skin. Her belly bulged even more visibly since losing so much weight the last two days. She closed her eyes, seeking inwardly for the minute sensations of movement as Horace repositioned the stethoscope. "Your heart is still too fast, Nora. Ninety beats per minute when you've done nothing but sleep."

She inhaled through her nose, as still and quiet as possible. "I'm just worried."

"It was racing so fast we worried it would stop. Usually, the ether suppresses the heart too much, but for you it was barely enough," Daniel revealed, the horrors she'd slept through creeping into detail. "When I first arrived, you spoke coherently. And for a bit after the first infusion. But a few hours later, I thought you wouldn't make it."

"No more talking," Horace ordered, shaking the stethoscope at them.

As he pressed his ear to the hollow instrument, his expression slipped far away, beyond the walls of the room and the glistening icicles dressing the window, beyond the reach of cholera or even the grave. Nora knew that look like she knew her own face in the mirror. He was searching for sound, for movement, for discovery, for life.

"Anything?" Daniel finally whispered.

Horace came back to them, landing his troubled blue eyes on Nora's. "Not yet. But that doesn't mean—"

"I know." She knew precisely everything it meant and didn't mean. In this strange region of waiting, her child was neither dead nor alive, neither lost nor found. Nothing, until they knew for certain.

"But you survived." Horace lowered his brow, as if to rebuke her trembling lip.

She nodded bravely, pretending a courage she didn't feel.

"Did I do the right thing? Using the solution?"

Horace put the stethoscope in his pocket, the wooden instrument projecting absurdly from his coat. "It didn't kill you. That's one thing. I'd never have dared pour anything into your veins."

"But is it viable?" Professional curiosity nudged against the threatening grief.

"Seems to be," he conceded. "But advisable?" He frowned. "Questionable, I think. Can't build a protocol from only two patients." His face softened, his uneven whiskers climbing down his aging jaw. "But it appears to have given you just enough time. The maid was the only one who didn't get the infusion, and she's quite dead."

Nora ignored his insensitive assessment. "And the ether?" she asked. "Would you repeat that?"

Daniel stood and turned away, as if the memories and her eager questions were too much to bear.

"Desperate measures, my dear," Horace concluded, also observing Daniel's strained patience. "It's time for you to eat and sleep a real sleep. Not a drugged one."

"But, Horace," she insisted, "our experiments worked." His with the ether, and hers with the transfusion. "You saved me again."

He frowned at her the way he used to when she was being precocious as a child. He sighed and rubbed his resigned eyes. "Considering you prescribed the Latta's, this time, child, you largely saved yourself." He cleared his throat. "You are no longer in danger, so I'm taking the carriage home to help the midwives overnight. But I'll be back in the morning."

The world froze like a painting as Horace paused in the middle of the room, a thoughtful shadow of a smile in his eyes, each line of his face suddenly as familiar as if she were the one who had sketched them into place.

She saw for the first time the shapeless state of his old jacket, hardly more than a dishrag with lapels and pockets. And she saw the man within it—his clenched hands hiding brilliant fingers that knew life and death by mere touch. Grief and gratitude burned through her frozen limbs.

"I love you," Nora whispered.

Horace's face quirked, his eyes tightening at the corners before he nodded gently.

A tear dropped like a hot cinder on her cheek as Horace lumbered away quietly.

Daniel wiped her tear away, blinking back his own. "If we have lost our child—"

"We don't know for certain. So let's not speak of it yet," Nora finished. The necessary words and thoughts were too heavy for hefting.

Don't think of it now.

Daniel put his head down on the thick blanket covering her stomach. This was the closest he'd ever come to their baby. She'd known the child from the inside, but he only from a distance.

"But I didn't lose you." He sighed, the words filled with something too much for words, like holding a mountain in his hand. Impossible.

"I thought I'd be immune." She murmured her awkward apology and touched his uneasy brow. "It was horrible for you, wasn't it?"

Daniel hated the question. She could tell by his silence. And that was how she knew…

"It was far too close, Nora. Are we fools to do this?" He turned toward her with a plea in his eyes. "Do we carry on? How can I let you go back into such danger?"

Nora pictured Magdalena and knew what her mentor would say. If only she could be as convincing. She dipped into a deep well at the center of herself, drawing up a bucket of unshakable certainty.

"Whatever comes, we keep our post. We didn't choose this work because we were curious or restless. We are called to this." Nora ran her thumb over his warm hand. "We stay."

CHAPTER 42

NORA WRAPPED HER FAVORITE LAP QUILT TIGHTER around her shoulders, comforted by the faint smell of soap mingled with the peppermint salve she used liberally on her patients.

"You look content," Julia said, plying her embroidery in Horace's chair.

"Because I'm home," Nora said. "I don't think I could have taken another day at Aunt Wilcox's."

"I thought she apologized." Julia pulled her pink thread taut.

"She did. And demanded I be catered to hand and foot. But she wanted Horace and Daniel to check for the baby every hour, and I…" Nora swallowed. She'd found no report of any kind of treatment for Julia's scarred uterus, so talking about her own pregnancy was too cruel a topic for her friend. "I didn't want to."

Julia dipped her chin. "Do you know anything yet?" she asked quietly.

Nora shook her head, diverting her eyes to the stuffed falcon on the mantel. She disliked the way the color had seemed to drain from the feathers with the passing years.

Just this morning, she'd overheard two housemaids

discussing her pregnancy in whispered asides. Pregnancies were lost as a matter of course, but this morning she'd noticed some spotting, and she hadn't felt any conclusive movements. Her stomach was still restive and unsettled. Though she'd told herself she could bear losing this child without histrionics, speaking her fears aloud was impossible.

She inhaled, the warm air assaulting her empty lungs. There wasn't room for this grief and breath at the same time.

"Is Ruth with patients? I wanted to hear how the Fletcher family is doing." She'd discuss any case but her own.

Julia obviously understood Nora's need to escape the conversation. She laid down her embroidery hoop and stood, smoothing her blue dress. "I was just thinking I needed to stretch my legs," she fibbed. "I'll find her and send her in."

When the door closed, Nora tilted her head back, taking in the solitude, almost the first she'd had all week. It had taken a Herculean effort to convince Daniel to leave the house to visit his patients today, and he'd insisted on going for only a few hours.

Now she was hiding in the study to escape Mrs. Phipps's attention. Nora hadn't comprehended the strain Mrs. Phipps had been under, until the tiny woman knocked into a plant stand yesterday while bringing Nora a compress, sending the Amazonian mandevilla sprawling across the study floor. The usually restrained housekeeper had struck out with her polished boot and kicked a shard of the broken pot under the desk, declaring the delicate plant blossoms an "infernal nuisance."

After that, Nora had closed her gaping jaw and swallowed the bitter tea Mrs. Phipps kept supplying without any complaints.

Even the nights didn't give Nora a moment to drop her tears or rehearse her worries in private. All through the sleeping hours, Daniel pressed himself close to her, his hands closed over her stomach, as if his protective hold could keep their child from slipping away into the shadowy beyond.

Nora wanted to believe his strong fingers held such power, but fables weren't helpful now.

"Nora?" Ruth pushed open the unlatched door, the lamplight in the windowless room throwing her sensible face into relief. There was comfort in knowing Ruth had attended hundreds of mothers who had not only birthed children but also lost them. She was a specialist in meetings and partings.

"Close the door," Nora requested, pushing her blanket away and making room on the sofa. "How are the patients? And the Fletchers?"

"We lost Donald last night."

Nora flinched. Their youngest son, with a shock of white hair, only two years old.

"But the rest of the family is recovering well," Ruth reassured her as she took a seat. "They were all equally ill, but we lost only one of the six. I think it's the transfusions. We're losing fewer when we can give enough solution in time."

Nora nodded, trying to be pleased. "Any doctor would be pleased with that percentage."

"And any midwife would be heartbroken," Ruth rebutted, her tight bun pulling her lined eyes. "Your friend Mrs. Trimble is taking it the hardest. She was especially attached."

Nora ran her eyes across the marble fireplace. Julia hadn't told her, probably to spare her. "I know it's been chaotic the last

week, but you ran the hospital as well as any medical student,"
Nora began, but Ruth sniffed.

"Don't insult me."

Nora huffed. "I stand corrected. Much better than medical
students."

Ruth nodded prim approval. "You don't sound overjoyed."

"I am," Nora countered. It wasn't a lie. The women she'd
trained had run a full hospital with minimal oversight for two
weeks and tended the patients with skill and acumen. It filled
her with pride. Or would, if she had room to consider it. Nora
closed her eyes, a tear sneaking out without warning. "I started
spotting this morning."

Ruth didn't move for several interminable seconds, not even
a muscle in her rigid face. "I'm sorry."

Nora's brave chin collapsed. "Then it's over?"

Gruff hands closed around Nora's jaw, forcing her head up.
"Spotting is the most expected thing in the world. It means
nothing on its own." Ruth's brown irises blazed defiantly.

Nora nodded as best she could with her chin held captive.

"You know several mothers feel their children very infre-
quently until late pregnancy. Or if they do, the baby must be in
the perfect position. Your child could be in the middle of your
womb jumping like a grasshopper as we speak." Ruth released
her but lowered her face to mere inches from Nora's.

Grasshopper. Such a cheerful creature. A perfect nickname
if…

"How much longer do I wait?"

"You just survived the near impossible. Give the poor babe
a day or two more of grace."

"I'm scared," Nora whispered. She'd admitted it to no one, but she couldn't lie anymore.

Ruth took Nora's hand, the touch reminiscent of Magdalena's firm grip. "I lit a candle for you at church on Christmas Eve. If the Lord child could survive the trip to Jerusalem and be born in a byre, then your child can survive his winter journey as well."

Nora fought the old, unbidden memories crowding her mind, of a dark room with dishes strewn across the floor, puddles of sick half-soaked into the rugs, and a terrifying mound on the floor that had once been her grandmother. "I'm worried I gave up on miracles the day my entire family died in front of me." The bleak, brittle voice couldn't be her own. Nora didn't recognize it.

Ruth looked at her as severely as Magdalena would have. "You certainly did not. The day you performed your first surgery or attended your first birth, or last week when you saved Fenella Wilcox—"

"Her maid died," Nora argued. Hope was too scalding to swallow, no matter how frozen her soul.

"And two of you lived." Ruth glared at her with loving eyes. "If I told you I'd had the same result, you'd be pleased with me. Just because everything isn't a miracle doesn't mean one doesn't show up occasionally."

Nora's head grew too heavy with fear and sorrow to keep upright. She pressed it onto Ruth's shoulder, her eyes wet. "And if I have lost the child?"

Ruth rubbed her back hard enough to hurt the skin. "Then you'll know the sadness that many of us have felt. I lost two."

Nora squeezed her eyes shut, a flash of anger rising at the

circumstances, at Ruth. It wasn't that she was wrong, but that she had the nerve to be right. This suffering wasn't new or unique.

Ruth pulled Nora's resisting body close and rocked her.

"I didn't take care of myself," Nora confessed as tears dripped into her mouth, mingling with the salty words. "I didn't take care of my own child."

"There, there," Ruth answered in melody, over and over. "There, there."

After years of training, the anatomy tomes, the lectures, and debates, no one had discovered a more helpful answer than that.

CHAPTER 43

FEELS A LITTLE BETTER NOW?" NORA GLANCED UP AT HER patient, a child of nine or ten, carried to the clinic by an older brother after a draft horse had trod on her foot.

The girl nodded her tear-streaked face.

"Keep still. I'm just going to move the ice," Nora told her, and slid the chunk to the lateral edge of her foot, where the bruising and edema were most noticeable. She suspected at least two fractured metatarsals, so the application of ice and tight bandaging would help. "Ruth?"

"Everything's ready," Ruth assured her. "Will you—"

"No, you do this one," Nora said, for Ruth was adept at binding. Her wrappings were neater than Horace's—before his stroke.

Truthfully, Nora was fortunate to have the chance to treat this girl at all. The men were all gone, and over Mrs. Phipps's protests, Nora had run to help, despite her promises to stay off her feet and leave the patients to the others. It had been four days of spotting. Nothing Nora did now would make much difference.

"Mrs. Doctor," a timid voice interrupted from the threshold. The new maid pushed her head around the door. "There's a woman to see you. Urgent."

"Ruth, I'll be back in a moment. Keep on just like that—loose enough to accommodate for more swelling, but tight enough to push some of the blood away from the wound." She turned to the pale girl and her worried brother. "It will feel much better in a few days. You're being very brave." She smiled at the girl, waiting until she got a small, watery grin in return before she slipped from the room.

She hurried up the steps, curious what woman had urgent business with her. Just as she stepped into the grand hall, Aunt Wilcox spun around to face her, a filthy, tattered carpet bag at her feet that certainly didn't belong to her. Nora couldn't reconcile the fastidious woman willingly touching such a thing.

"What are you doing out of bed?" Nora asked. "It's only been a week."

Aunt Wilcox narrowed her eyes at Nora's clinic apron, loosely tied to accommodate her thickening waist. "Long enough. You know as well as I do, there's nothing the matter with me. Yes, I'm thin and easily tired, but I'm more likely to expire from boredom than anything else. If you're fit to tend patients, then I—" She pinched her lips together. "There was an emergency at Whitecross Street Prison, and one of my friends—the president of our society—brought me this." She gestured toward the moth-eaten bag. "I think you'll agree this matter can't wait for me to finish a languid convalescence."

A sound emanated from the depths of the dirty carpet bag, and Nora jumped. Something living—certainly not a wombat. Nora threw a startled, questioning look at Aunt Wilcox before rushing forward and peering inside. It held an infant, wrapped in an expensive cashmere shawl. Nora lifted the undersized baby, cataloging the mustard-tinted skin, the tightly wound fists, and the crinkled skin around the eyes. Hours old, maybe.

Nora threw her eyes to the carpet bag once more. "Who—"

"Mrs. Sandish was doing a prison inspection when she found her. She was born yesterday afternoon, and her mother died in the night. Mrs. Sandish said the devils who run the place were waiting for someone from a workhouse to collect her. Apparently, no one could be bothered to rush her to a doctor."

Blood loss, fever. Stroke. Nora knew the most likely culprits of death in childbirth. But a prison birth could mean the baby was diseased, syphilitic, blind…

"They left her in this bag for hours, Nora. If Mrs. Sandish hadn't happened to be there today—"

"Has she eaten—" Nora pulled back the shawl—Aunt's favorite—taking in the clumsily tied umbilical cord and the surrounding skin. Red and inflamed. The baby girl was pitifully small.

Less than one day and you've already known hunger, death, and imprisonment.

"This way." Nora bolted down the stairs and laid the baby on the table as soon as they reached the exam room. This baby had the frail, deflated look of impending death.

"She won't survive, will she?" Aunt's hollow voice echoed with despondency—jarring to hear from such a domineering woman. "Mrs. Sandish lives close to me. She stopped to show me the poor child, and I convinced her to let me bring her to you right away instead of waiting for another doctor."

"That was wise. There isn't much time." Nora retrieved her stethoscope. The child wiggled feebly as she listened, repositioning the instrument several times. The lungs were too small and new for her to be sure of what she heard. Possible pneumonia. She may have swallowed amniotic fluid. "Who attended the birth?" she asked, already dreading the answer.

Aunt shook her head, the disappointment too heavy for words. The life of a prisoner was worth very little. Less than the price of a doctor, certainly.

If only Nora had been called yesterday, the mother might still be here. "Has she been nursed at all?" she pressed.

Aunt Wilcox clenched her hands against her dark skirt. "We know nothing except what I told you."

Then most likely no food at all. The mother surely died before her milk came in. Nora shuddered, imagining a dirty, hard floor covered in blood. "Ruth! I need you—as soon as you can!"

Ruth appeared half a minute later, her face morphing from mundane to shocked as she took in the pitiful sight.

"A orphan from the prison," Nora explained, her courage lagging as she tried and failed to coax the baby's eyes open. "What do you suggest?"

Ruth ran her fingers over the infant's head, sounding the fontanel. "Keep her warm. Give her some sugar water until I get back. I'm getting Ellie this minute." Ruth was gone before she finished her sentence, sending the instructions down the echoing hall.

Nora worked with a nearby wet nurse for such emergencies. Ellie Nugent had ten children and a healthy supply of milk and good humor. This child needed both after her deplorable start.

Nora unfolded portions of the blanket to reveal small

sections of the baby's body while still keeping her warm. Her wrinkled foot didn't respond when Nora brushed her finger from heel to toes. Only once did the baby crack open her yellow-tinged eyes, still stained with newborn blue.

"Jaundice and asthenia—"

"I don't know what any of that means," Aunt snapped.

"It means she's weak and her organs aren't working as well as we'd wish," Nora explained. "But if she pulls through, it will be thanks to you and Mrs. Sandish." Nora squeezed the tiny feet to stimulate blood flow. "I'd rather she be irritated and upset than groggy." And then, realizing her opportunity: "I teach this to all my midwife students. You can do this while I get a warm blanket and a poultice. Just—gently. And you can put a nappy on her." Nora grabbed a cloth and safety pins and dropped them on the table before hurrying to the dispensary.

The putrid smell of sweat and blood clung to the child. Nora hurriedly scraped together a paste of charcoal, lavender, and warm milk until it was the consistency of soft clay and wrapped it in cheesecloth. The charcoal would draw out the impurities and the lavender would soothe.

When she returned to Aunt Wilcox, Julia was standing at Ruth's side, anxiously watching Ruth sponge the complaining child.

"I ran into the maid on the front steps. She told me about the baby." Julia hadn't removed her hat yet, and it shadowed her troubled eyes.

"She's in the best hands now," Nora reassured her, though she had to bite her tongue when she saw Aunt's crookedly applied nappy.

Not the worst job I've seen.

"I sent the maid to get Mrs. Nugent." Ruth gestured at the tiny girl. This was no simple case. "Did you start the sugar water?"

"Not yet. I made a poultice to keep her warm," Nora said, holding up the cheesecloth package.

"Good. I changed my mind," Ruth announced. "If we do keep her here, we'll need milk she can drink between Ellie's visits. I'll tell Cook to get goat's milk and show her how to mix it into the sugar water."

"Will that work?" Julia asked.

"Usually." Nora put her pinkie into the tiny mouth to check for sucking reflex. The child resisted, unsure what to do.

If only I had milk. But that required a child first. Nora tried to push away the sudden threat of tears as she took the almost weightless infant into her arms. She'd never felt anything softer than the thin, dark hair atop the little head, still damp from Ruth's sponging.

As she ran her finger along the mottled cheek, a minute thrum shook Nora.

She turned her wide, startled eyes to Ruth, who was discussing the cost of wet nurses with Aunt Wilcox. After pushing the baby into Julia's surprised arms, she pressed her palms to her own stomach.

"Nora?" Julia's eyes widened with fear.

"What's the matter?" Ruth demanded.

Nora shook her head, listening, feeling.

"Is Nora hurt?" Aunt clutched Ruth's arm, her voice climbing.

"Did the strong bleeding start?" Ruth's stern eyes swam with worry.

Nora shook her head, shushing them all.

Another flutter.

Nora exhaled a broken breath, scrambling for a chair and collapsing into it. She was already crying, her hands wet when she pulled them from her eyes. "The baby."

"Yours?" Ruth spoke in urgent shorthand.

Nora nodded.

"You felt it?" Julia asked breathlessly.

"Yes." The most beautiful word. It soared out of her mouth and swelled in the morning air.

"Are you certain?" Ruth insisted.

"I've never been so sure," Nora promised.

Aunt's mouth gaped, wordless.

A small twist in her middle, a part of her body she'd never felt before. It could only be one thing. Nora closed her eyes, unable to bear the flood of relief that poured over her and stole her breath. *Grasshopper.*

"Dear God," she prayed, unable to even utter the thanks that came next due to her breathless sobs. The only other word she managed was, "Daniel."

~

It took ten minutes to stop crying and wash her red face, her smile bursting from behind the washcloth every time she looked in the washstand mirror. In that short time, Ellie Nugent had arrived, settled into a rocking chair, and managed to extract the baby from Julia's protective hold. After several coaxing attempts, the exhausted child latched on her breast. The baby had a weak suck and a reluctant swallow, but she was feeding.

Julia never took her eyes away from the baby's twitching cheek, hovering as she sat in a chair pushed up next to Ellie. Nora could almost see the ache of her empty arms and the longing to regain the helpless bundle.

She watched the commonplace miracle of new life, only half-aware of the conversation around her. She was counting the hours until she could tell Daniel, unsure she'd survive the wait. Mrs. Phipps would be back from her shopping trip soon. At least she could relieve the bursting happiness by telling her.

Nora even caught Aunt dabbing the corner of her handkerchief to her eye. Now they both stood in silence in the corner of the room, Nora rubbing her curved belly over and over.

Aunt sniffed beside her, shifting awkwardly. "You must think me neglectful."

Nora drew her eyebrows together. The infant's condition was hardly Aunt Wilcox's fault. "Whyever—"

But Aunt continued, "I haven't paid your bill."

"Bill?" Nora laughed as she caressed her stomach again. "What bill?"

Aunt frowned. "For attending me in my sickness."

Nora dropped her hand in surprise. "I would never charge you, Aunt."

"I thought as much," the woman concurred with a curt nod. "Which is why I have planned to show my gratitude in another way."

"Another way?"

Several yards away, the baby choked on the rich rush of

milk, coughing and releasing the breast. Mrs. Nugent wiped up the dribble of milk with her skirt and started again with coaxing words. Aunt diverted her eyes, most likely uncomfortable with the rough brown nipple in plain view.

"An ongoing contribution to your hospital. You are doing valuable work." Aunt's hand smoothed the cuffs of her sleeves. "Enough to hire the women you've trained. Mrs. Franklin is an admirable midwife. Heaven knows they must all need steady employment. And we need them." Her clipped words couldn't hide the emotion.

Nora turned away from the sight of Ellie wiggling the baby's chin to convince her to suck harder. "I agree. But you already give so much to your other causes."

"You made me your cause." Aunt Wilcox exhaled and looked away, the words costing her. "I will make you mine."

Nora blinked, unsure whether to protest again or accept and give thanks. As she deliberated, she pressed her hands to her stomach, bolstering her courage. Best to grab the iron when hot.

"Did you hear that, Ruth?" she called.

Ruth turned to her, blank-faced.

"As of this moment, Aunt Wilcox is patron of this hospital. She's going to help fund it."

No one moved. Mrs. Phipps frowned so deeply with confusion that Nora hurried on before Aunt grew insulted. "I told you about the conversation we had when we were convalescing and now…" Her voice dwindled.

Why didn't anyone say something congratulatory? Nora wished she was close enough to covertly give one of them a pinch.

Ever polite, Julia found her composure first with a dazed, "Oh."

Beside her, Aunt's eyes narrowed to slits.

"That's wonderful," Julia said, shaking herself from the shock. "Mrs. Wilcox, how generous of you." At last, she remembered to smile, and the spell binding the others into stunned statues broke as she beamed.

"I can hardly believe it," Mrs. Phipps fumbled, attempting to turn it into a compliment by elevating the last syllable.

Nora laughed at their astonished faces. It seemed miracles came in threes: her child, this orphan, and now Aunt's funding. But why stop there?

"Ruth, as founder of this hospital, I'd like to offer you the paid position of head nurse and midwife."

Mrs. Phipps's hand flew to her open mouth.

Julia threw her arms around Ruth before the woman managed to take a breath. Her reticent face rippled with minute signs of disbelief and joy.

"Well," Nora prodded with a grin. "Do you accept?"

Ruth nodded several times, blinking fiercely. "Gladly," she said, her voice unsteady.

Nora admired her control. She embodied Horace's maxim to never let yourself be caught off guard. "I'll do it gladly," Ruth answered.

A harsh throat-clearing silenced them all. "Very well, but will that baby live?" Aunt's voice sharpened to her usual briskness.

Julia's head jerked to the little one, her celebration cut short as her blue eyes swelled with distress.

Across the small room, Ellie pretended not to hear as she increased the volume of her humming and the vigor of her rocking.

As if in answer, the baby girl lifted one weak arm and rested it on Ellie's warm breast.

"I like to bet on long odds." Nora touched her stomach again. "She looks like a fighter to me."

———

Nora adjusted the blanket over her lap one more time, deciding the best position for her arm to appear casual, unrehearsed. She must tame her smile…

Daniel had promised to be gone no more than three hours, and it was over two and a half now. Her ears strained so hard for the sound of his voice or footsteps that her temples began to twinge.

Thumbing a book, she pretended to review tropical plants of the equatorial regions until at last the door budged. She sucked in her cheeks, schooling her lips, her heart jumping sideways in her chest.

Daniel stepped in slowly, haggard and burdened. *Had he looked that way this morning?*

His forehead wrinkled. "Your color is better."

No doubt from her happy flush. She needed to calm herself or she'd ruin the moment.

"Are you warm?" He approached, his hands still damp from washing, and felt her cheek.

"No." She patted the empty spot beside her. He'd already changed clothes, as he always did after cholera visits, and she wanted to press her face against his clean, soft waistcoat. "I just missed you."

"I missed you as well." With a quiet groan, he lowered himself onto the worn cushions, his tense muscles loosening as he collected her closer. He released a long breath.

For once she didn't want to ask about his visits—the protocols or treatments, who lived or didn't.

"You will not believe who came to clinic today," she began.

His eyebrows lifted.

She plunged into the entire account of Aunt and the orphan in the carpet bag. It took a quarter hour to dole out the details and satisfy his questions. She gestured and laughed, glad for the excuse to vent some of her pent-up excitement.

"You have money for your hospital and a salaried staff." Daniel grinned in pride and shook his head. "Amazing. But pleasing my aunt—that's a feat for the history books."

She nestled her head into his neck, burrowing in as if she never intended to leave, and inhaled the familiar smell of soap and medicants. Her lips found the spot against his throat where his pulse fluttered.

She'd not gotten far enough in her imagination to rehearse the actual words—the best way to tell him. Nor did she need to know yet, because his mouth found hers, his lips tasting of relief. He kissed her until she understood. He'd held her pain for so many days, wishing for the hour her smile would reappear. Fearing it never would.

Releasing his lips, she drew back several inches. "Something else happened today." She didn't muster enough volume, and the words cracked. Instead of speech, she took his hand and guided it to her waist, watching him as she placed it below her belly button, wishing her skirt wasn't so thick so he could reach her bare skin.

He froze. She saw him trying not to guess, waiting for her next words.

"I felt it," she whispered.

His eyes widened, flexed at the corners as if in pain. She knew he couldn't let himself believe until…

"More than once," she reassured. "I'm certain. Our baby's alive."

The breath fell out of him as he closed his eyes.

She thought she'd be too giddy to get through the announcement, but now she found her throat too closed and her eyes too hot. The misery that sloughed from his face fell into her stroking hands. She'd had no idea how much it hurt him.

"Alive," he breathed, his cautious hands finding her waist, as if frightened to disturb the fragile life.

"I'm sorry," he whispered.

The last words she expected.

Before she could ask, he pressed on. "For every minute we were at odds. For pushing against each other instead of together."

She inhaled, unsure how to best wipe away the debris of the past months. "I am, too. But it's done now." Her forehead creased. "Isn't it? You're not angry if I practice—"

He kissed her right where a worried line always burrowed between her eyebrows. "It is. Never again."

He increased the pressure of his fingers against her stomach, sounding the depths for some movement. "What does it feel like?" he asked.

Nora had never noticed how bright the gold rings in his eyes could shine when he was happy.

She laid her hand over his. "A grasshopper."

CHAPTER 44

Nora doubted the efficacy of closing the front door between visitors; they knocked urgently every thirty seconds, demanding entry from the wet, frozen wind. But it wasn't the weather that made them rap so eagerly. Daniel had two new cadavers—one with a malformed heart and another withered from cholera. He'd promised to reveal their newest cholera treatment and planned to have Nora lecture on the particulars of transfusing Latta's solution into patients' veins. Nora had known the lecture would be popular, but not to this extent. She stood at the front door, politely greeting the old doctors who at least pretended decorum and laughing at the students who paid their entry fee by shoving wrinkled notes into her hand and raced each other through the great hall to the surgical theater.

She watched in amusement as one young man nearly slipped on the marble floor and wheeled his arms in erratic circles to stay upright while his fellows mocked him. She was about to call out in pretended sternness to slow down when a sound behind her made her turn back to the cold, open door.

Aunt stood pink-cheeked in the cold, her back stiff and erect as she tapped her cane over the threshold. Nora swore she used it only emphasis, not balance.

"Aunt!" It was too late for society calls with the sun sinking toward the rooftops. "What a surprise." Her handsome carriage decorated the plain street, the driver bundled in a ridiculous amount of fur.

"I was going to check on the child," Aunt announced, "but I saw the advertisement for the lecture in the paper this morning, and I thought I'd look into that as well. I never endorse a program until I have fully inspected it."

Nora squinted, taking in Aunt's silk gloves and fine dress. "I don't think you understand. It's a dissection," Nora warned. "Not simply an academic discussion like at Marylebone."

"I know," Aunt said, stepping inside and closing her umbrella with a snap. "I've toured every prison in London and many more besides. I think I can manage one doctor's lecture. The notice never said 'doctors only.' It said you and Daniel would both be speaking." Aunt looked in vain for a maid or footman to take her cane and coat.

Nora quickly took her fur and hung it beside Daniel's finest. "But I'm sure you wouldn't enjoy this—"

"I've sent you money for six students, and I would like to see how you will educate them," Aunt repeated, undeterred. "It seems those young people are looking forward to it." The excited cries of the running students echoed against the tile floors and high ceiling.

Nora grimaced. "Daniel wouldn't want you to—"

Aunt waved his name away. "I paid for his schooling as well. It's time I saw what I got him into."

"Aunt, wait." Nora quickened her steps through the grand hall, trying to stay in front of the determined woman. "Couldn't I arrange a different lecture for you? Please?"

"Nora, if you want my money, you must endure my presence occasionally."

"No. It's not that. I love your company." They both paused. She'd gone too far. "Only, please feel free to leave if it disturbs you," Nora ended feebly. "The students can be a raucous bunch."

The edgy flock of medical men moaned as Nora elbowed them aside to make room for Aunt as she escorted her to the front row, where Ruth and the other midwives waited with notepads and pencils.

"We came an hour early for these places," one student protested as Nora motioned him to move back a row, his face too young for anything but scraggly tufts of an incomplete beard.

"And I run this hospital," Nora shot back. "If you'd like a place at all, I suggest you show some manners and move back a row."

An older man jabbed a finger toward Aunt Wilcox. "I can't see over the peacock tail on her head."

Before Nora could warn the man who he'd just insulted, Aunt turned, her face a good six inches beneath his but void of any fear. She reached up and unpinned her hat. "I am happy to remove my peacock tail, sir." The man's expression grew sheepish and embarrassed as she continued, "Perhaps next lecture, you will cut your curly mop shorter for those behind *you*."

Several of the students laughed as the man ran a self-conscious hand through his hair.

Daniel hurried over, alarmed by the disturbance. "Aunt? This is a surprise."

Nora caught his sleeve, turning him toward the marble-topped demonstration table so she could murmur to him without being overheard. "She showed up and insisted on watching the lecture since she's paying for the new students."

Daniel blinked twice. "I suppose there's that. Did you—"

"I warned her," Nora affirmed. "She won't be dissuaded."

"I'll speak to her." Daniel shot his cuffs and made his way to his aunt's side. Nora thought he might have better luck changing Aunt Wilcox's mind—but she wasn't counting on it.

Time to begin. Tucking away her watch, Nora walked to the center of the theater floor. It felt a bit more like a gladiators' arena this afternoon, ringed with a crowd of rowdy faces. She had to start her sentence three times before everyone settled enough to listen. "I believe I can trust everyone to behave decorously, with Mrs. Wilcox attending as a special guest and patron of the hospital." She gestured to Aunt, and the men who'd complained shifted in their places, abashed. "I believe we are ready."

The men leaned forward, eyes fastened on the sheet-draped cadaver. Behind it, Horace smiled benignly, laying out his tools. Only Nora caught the amused gleam in his eyes as he winked at her.

She swallowed a groan and exchanged a nervous glance with Daniel. She knew already they were in for a spectacle, but Horace was clearly indicating that he planned to show off for their unexpected guest.

He did just that, embellishing his dissection with stories that sent a chilled silence over the room. When Aunt finally left—she stayed to the bloody end—she fanned her pale face and stated baldly, "I don't believe I will attend anymore," with one hand fumbling at her poised throat. "But I will send the money this week."

The library felt smaller when crowded with five, the low flames of the fireplace casting a pleasant glow over the eclectic assembly. Julia sat in her customary pose, elegant and upright in the corner of the sofa, with Harry's sleeping head in her lap.

Nora occupied Horace's favorite wing chair, a pile of forgotten papers and books tottering on the floor beside her. Even though the lecture had finished hours ago, she was too jittery to read. Mrs. Phipps filled another armchair, sewing spilling over her lap. Even the zebra wore a particularly satisfied expression. Only Daniel paced aimlessly, as usual, the same way a seabird spins in widening circles when searching for land.

"That was the largest lecture we've ever held," Mrs. Phipps ventured into the silence. "Eighty-eight pounds in one day."

Harry's eyes opened as he gave a low whistle. "Eighty-eight attendees? Absolute mayhem. Were there really that many doctors?"

"Mostly students," Nora corrected. *Not doctors yet.* "You saw the lecture hall. It looked like a crowd at a boxing match."

"Heart dissection and a new cholera treatment both in one afternoon. They got their pound's worth." Daniel thumbed some of Nora's Italian books as he passed the shelves. "That show with Aunt Wilcox was worth the entrance fee alone."

The tired circle of friends smiled simultaneously—small, secret grins of relished memory.

Empty champagne glasses littered the library now, as they all drank in the memory of the day's victories. The only one missing from their rare quiet evening together was Horace.

He'd stayed in the lecture hall, refusing to join them until he'd prepared the half-dissected cadaver for day two of his demonstration. After word traveled in taverns and clubs tonight, they'd have to turn people away tomorrow.

Nora pictured the open, lifeless body on the table as Horace carefully unsealed the pages of the human tome, reading in the flesh the story of organs and arteries—of life. She wondered what he was saying to the corpse as he toiled on, now that she knew he spoke to them. Perhaps something about hollyhocks or poison ivy.

"They have to close the charity cemetery soon," Daniel mentioned as he nursed his glass of wine. "It was supposed to last another decade, but the cholera filled it prematurely."

"We're still in the thick of it, with no signs of slowing. They'll stack the bodies two deep and make it stretch a bit farther," Harry said with forced indifference, but Nora knew that many of his own patients rested there, and the thought of bodies discarded unceremoniously on top of their resting places bothered him more than he'd ever admit.

"I've said for months we should relocate. You know Horace is itching to take that offer from Kew Botanical Gardens," Mrs. Phipps grumbled. "Richmond has very little cholera."

"Impossible," Julia pronounced. "Horace would never leave London, or this hospital." For a woman who'd been horrified by Horace when she first met him, she sounded relieved to keep him now.

"Thousands of botanical specimens from every jungle and mountaintop in the world?" Daniel rolled and stretched his shoulders. "If anything could tempt him, it's that."

"Not to mention every odd creature the Linnean Society drags in," Nora added. "Good heavens, he'd try to get his hands on everything venomous and toxic. He's still begging for electric eels." No one in Richmond would practice enough restraint with Horace. The brilliant man still needed help not killing himself in his scientific excitement.

"Poison frogs or not, it would be slower paced than what he does here," Mrs. Phipps argued. "And whatever he says, his heart is still weak."

Nora bit her lip. She'd spotted Mrs. Phipps in the audience today, frowning anxiously as Horace chirped enthusiastically about malformed valves and weakened ventricles and enlarged organs. The cadaver had the same condition he did—angina.

"Why don't we send him off for a season to get it out of his system?" Harry suggested. "We could spare him for a few months. Maybe the worst would have passed by then. You could even go with him, Mrs. Phipps, to ensure we get him back in one piece."

Laughter broke the tension.

"And trust you children to run this house?" Mrs. Phipps's raised eyebrows made them all laugh harder. "Julia is the only trustworthy one among the lot of you."

"And Mrs. Trimble will be preoccupied." A deep voice boomed from the doorway. They all jerked around to see Horace, his arms filled with a blanketed bundle. "Mrs. Phipps is right. You could no more spare us than the tides can spare the moon."

"We thought you were still working," Harry said, sitting up. "What are you doing with the baby?"

"Do you think it takes me hours to prepare for a lecture?"

he huffed. "I've been examining this one in her cot. I took a good listen at her chest," Horace announced. "It's worse than we thought."

Julia's hands twisted. She'd been the most devoted attendant since Aunt Wilcox brought the child in last week, even placing the girl's cot in her own room at night, emerging in the mornings with bleary eyes and nervous questions. But despite her care, there was undeniable fluid in the newborn's lungs, and Daniel had warned them not to get too attached.

"What's wrong with her?" Julia gripped her embroidery hoop like a life rope.

Horace gave her a level stare, fathomless, bracing. "She's orphaned."

Julia stammered, "I—I know that, but what did you find—"

"The lungs are quite clear now. The poultices and warm wraps have worked."

Harry sat up, exclaiming with surprise, but Horace waved him back.

"It's her heart."

Nora held her breath, her hurrah cut in half. She'd missed something. She hadn't heard any murmurs or irregular beats. "Her heart?" she asked, tamping down nausea. They'd spent the whole afternoon discussing why nothing could fix a defective heart.

"It's broken," Horace continued. "She's lost her mother. There's nothing more dangerous for a child than losing the will to live." Horace stepped forward with the too-small bundle in his arms. "She's past the pneumonia, but she's not strong enough to be taken to a foundling home."

"Then we'll keep her longer," Harry offered. "Mrs. Nugent gives her plenty of milk every day, and we have the goat's milk—"

"Play nursemaid?" Horace lifted the corner of his lip in disapproval. "With your schedule? You don't know how much trouble a newborn makes."

"It's not playing," Julia shot back, her voice scolding. Her eyes glistened defiantly in the lamplight. "And she's no more trouble than burn patients or amputees or cholera or diphtheria—"

"And then what?" Horace demanded, cutting her off.

"Then?" Harry asked, perplexed.

"Would you throw her back like a fish once you get her well?" Horace asked. "Mrs. Phipps was horrified when I proposed that with our last orphan."

Nora narrowed her eyes.

Horace approached Harry and held out the child, folding back the mint-green blanket to reveal her sleeping face. "She shouldn't be our patient."

"Please don't send her away," Julia pleaded. "Not until—"

Horace held up his hand, stopping her. "It seems a simple calculation for anyone with half a brain. A child with no parents. Parents with no child. She shouldn't be a patient. She should be your daughter."

Harry's already pale face grew starkly white against his orange beard.

Horace pushed the child closer. "True, she's not a very lovely specimen, but she's the only one we have to choose from currently."

Julia yelped, "What do you mean? She's beautiful."

Nora—who knew Horace better—couldn't hold back a wince. He was such a clumsy meddler.

"A daughter?" Harry whispered as Horace transferred the sleeping baby to his arms. It took a moment to tuck her into place, and Harry looked at Nora for confirmation he was holding the little patient correctly.

"I can't promise she'll survive," Horace remarked offhandedly. "She's as scrawny as—"

"Survive?" Julia finally leaped to her feet as if jerked from a dream. She tucked the blanket under the infant's chin with shaking hands. "She'll live to be older and stronger than you," she declared with eyes as fierce as Horace's before she softened her tone. "Don't tease."

A smile so small only Nora caught it flicked across Horace's face, quickly replaced by a sober frown sent to Harry. "I wasn't teasing. Truly, she's weak. You have to prepare yourself—"

Julia's hand went up inches from Horace's mouth, blocking the words. She looked only at the fragile girl. "She's perfect."

They were all on their feet now, crowding forward.

Harry at last caught his wife's eye, his own face stunned and blank. "What do we…" he asked Julia with strangled words. "What if she—"

Julia's expression was more tortured than triumphant. As she struggled for words, Horace laid a heavy arm on Nora's shoulders, his skillful fingers firm and sure. She looked into his aged face, expecting to find more tired lines, but something animated his sharp eyes in a way she hadn't seen since his stroke. Nora closed her grateful hand over his.

"You're sure it would be legal? That no one will come for her?" Julia asked through trembling lips.

"My solicitor will take care of it," Horace offered. "I'm quite sure this child has no rich grand-uncle waiting to claim her. She was left to die in a prison."

"And I could keep her? Always?" Julia's eyes raked over each of them, begging them to confirm for certain. Mrs. Phipps's wet eyes were answer enough.

"The thought of taking in an orphan had crossed my mind." Harry's husky whisper nearly undid Nora. "In theory. But we still hoped—"

"She still doesn't have a name," Julia whimpered. "I wonder if her mother called her anything before she—"

"Holly?" Mrs. Phipps offered.

They all turned to her.

"She was born Christmas week."

"I've never heard it used as a name," Nora admitted, thinking of the glossy leaves and crimson berries. "But I like it."

"Holly?" Harry tried the word on his tongue as he waited for Julia.

"Holly," Julia whispered. "It's lovely." Her head dipped, her small nose grazing the baby's.

Horace slid his hand from Nora's and paced to the zebra, resting his arm on Enzo's striped rump. "But don't let emotion cloud your judgment. You can't be overly hasty. She's just an urchin, perhaps endowed with questionable morals. Are you certain you want her?" he asked, a strange tilt to his mouth.

Every eye turned to the old man in varying degrees of

outrage. He drummed his fingers against the stubbly hide. "I'll be the first to warn you—orphans bring more than their fair share of trouble and expense," he said as Holly stirred and mewed in Harry's arms. "Nora nearly bankrupted the entire household with this little hospital of hers. Now midwives and students are always underfoot, on top of the clinic—"

Daniel scoffed and circled Nora's waist, the strength of his arm sending a cascade of warmth down her spine. "Horace, I think your other little acquisitions cost far more than bandages and quinine, if you're worried about ledgers," he rebutted, pointing to the zebra and a fossil of some ancient bird beside a pickled Honduran bat floating in a jar of alcohol. "I suggest you stop buying specimens."

Mrs. Phipps huffed in agreement.

"I do," Julia choked, one tear hanging on her cheek as she ignored their exchange. "I want her very much. Holly Trimble."

At the sound of his surname attached to the baby, Harry blinked several times. "Holly Trimble," he repeated.

Julia pressed the soft head into her neck, holding the fragile baby against her chest. "Can we? Harry?"

Nora half wanted to flee the room and leave them alone in the staggering moment, but she was too selfish. Her stomach quivered with suspense as Harry swallowed several times, his face shifting through emotions too quickly for Nora to anticipate his next words.

"You heard Horace. It sounds as if orphaned girls can be ruinous." He tried to complete the joke, but his voice caught and ended in tears, which he wiped away as they all waited.

"A daughter," Julia breathed.

Harry could only nod as he closed his arms around his wife, the child buried between them.

Horace cleared his throat. "I wasn't finished." He paused, his limitless eyes locked on Nora. "Despite the risks—" His voice snagged. "Speaking purely as a scientist, I must recommend the experiment. The results, thus far, are promising."

CHAPTER 45

W ELL, I CAN'T SMELL THE SICKNESS," RUTH ADMITTED, appraising the copious arrangements of pink and purple hyacinths overtaking every bedside table and windowsill in the crowded ward.

Nora snickered. Though Julia strictly avoided the cholera patients to protect Holly, the new mother still found ways to make her presence known—immaculate linen smelling of lilac, lemon, and starch, and now bouquets so abundant Ruth wrinkled her nose in dismay.

"I can slip a few upstairs later. But it looks like the little ones like them." Nora nodded to a pair of children strong enough to climb off their cots and inspect the blooms. They'd be going home soon.

"I don't want the new nurses to think this is a flower market," Ruth justified. "We must keep it scientific." She tilted her chin defiantly, a slant of pride.

Nora grinned. "Science with a woman's touch," she countered, watching one boy pluck off a soft, bright blossom. "Just like you taught me in the birthing room."

"Taught each other," Ruth corrected. She turned stern eyes to Nora. "But don't think your niceties will get you in this room."

Nora lifted her hands in surrender. "I only came to peek."

She hadn't crossed the forbidden threshold, but a glance at the only unoccupied cot was enough. They'd lost another patient this morning. The cot wouldn't stay empty long; the steady flow of sick women and children streamed so quickly that Nora didn't even recognize all the patients anymore.

She now kept herself to the clinic rooms, treating injuries and noninfectious complaints, as well as attending births. Thankfully, at six and a half months, her belly hadn't expanded to the impossible proportions of some of her patients, and she could still maneuver easily. "I'll be in the clinic if you need me." She watched the other midwives as they buzzed through the ward, skillfully dosing and feeding patients.

They won't. They know what they are doing.

The hopeful scent of early-March air and Julia's blooms followed her down the hallway, where she found Daniel in the dispensary grinding salt crystals to a fine powder.

"Horace says powdered dissolves faster in an emergency. If someone needs Latta's," he answered before she could ask.

Nora gave an approving nod. "Reasonable."

"Well, it's good he still has a little reason left. He asked me this morning how large a cage a caracal would need."

"A what?"

"Some African cat with tufted ears, according to him."

"Heaven help us," Nora groaned as she sidled close to see his progress. The salt shimmered like snow in the stone bowl. Almost the consistency of flour. "He told me someone's sending him the skeleton of a rhinoceros. At least the front half."

Daniel paused and shook his head before he resumed grinding. He mumbled something incredulous about Horace and the "back half" that made Nora laugh even though she caught only a snip.

Rooting through the open cabinet, she found a small bottle of powdered opium and the sugar canister. She was almost out of throat lozenges, which was the only thing that calmed Meg's coughing fits. Nora doled out the meager amounts onto her miniature brass scales, humming as she measured the grains, her shoulder brushing Daniel's.

His left arm wandered as he worked, looping absently around her waist and resting on her swollen stomach. He stroked her belly without realizing—a mindless habit.

Deep in her middle, the little stranger groped for a more desirable spot, the movement no longer the light spring of a grasshopper, but the hardy thump of a baby hare.

Surely Daniel felt it.

Nora smiled as his lips lifted almost imperceptibly.

But still, there was work to finish. The churning pestle kept rhythm against the mortar, tapping out a clear and steady heartbeat that sounded to Nora like her favorite promise—tomorrows after tomorrows after tomorrows.

HISTORICAL NOTE

After writing three books featuring Nora, Daniel, Horace, and the motley crew at Great Queen Street, Regina and I can no longer describe our interest in nineteenth-century medicine as anything other than an obsession! So, thank you for coming along for the ride. It has been such an adventure for us.

For those who haven't read *The Girl in His Shadow* or *The Surgeon's Daughter*, we'll give a brief recap: Nora is not a real individual, though we were inspired to write her based on the lives and experiences of female scientists, surgeons, and physicians in the same period.

We've cheated a little. The first qualified English doctor presenting as female was Elizabeth Garrett Anderson, and she was licensed in 1865. But the University of Bologna (and some other institutions) were licensing and training midwives, female physicians, and surgeons (though most Bologna trainees were routed into obstetrics practice) long before Dr. Anderson tricked the college into approving her license by concealing her gender in her application.

Anna Morandi Manzolini took over her husband's work as an anatomy professor at the University of Bologna following his death in 1755, though she worked alongside him for many years before that. Celebrated throughout Europe for her knowledge and skill, her wax replica models are still on display (you can see a video of me touring one such exhibit on our Instagram page). Dr. Maria Dalle Donne received her medical degree in Bologna in 1799 and taught midwives at her home for thirty-six years.

Elizabeth Blackwell was born in England and moved to the United States, where she was the first woman in the United States to attend medical school. Her admission was put to a vote before the students of the Geneva Medical College of New York. The men cheerfully voted in the affirmative, thinking their professors were playing an elaborate joke. She got the last laugh when she graduated the very first of her class. Her sister, Emily Blackwell, was the second woman in America to earn a medical degree. In fact, Elizabeth enrolled in St. Bartholomew's Hospital in 1850, and would have brushed shoulders with Horace and Daniel if they were real people. She later established a medical school for women in London and mentored Elizabeth Garrett Anderson.

These women—among others—inspired us in creating Nora's character. We recommend turning to Gabriella Berti Logan's excellent article, "Women and the Practice and Teaching of Medicine in Bologna in the Eighteenth and Early Nineteenth Centuries," to learn more about them. The article is available for free via jstor.org.

Horace is also a historical composite drawn largely from the lives of Dr. John Snow (of Broad Steet–pump fame) and Dr. John Hunter. Please see our note in *The Girl in His Shadow* for more about these two men and the sources that inspired us.

We'd like to focus here on two things particularly relevant to this story.

First, cholera and transfusion therapy. Cholera is a terrifying disease, and the outbreak in this book really did unfold as we describe, beginning with the case of a single sailor in September of 1848. All told, 14,137 cholera deaths were recorded in London in 1849. Although many doctors recorded observations and posited theories and treatments, none were backed up (and grudgingly accepted by some) until the 1854 epidemic, when Dr. John Snow mapped Soho cases, linking them conclusively to contaminated water extracted from the Broad Street pump. Because of this discovery, Dr. Snow is credited with the invention of epidemiology.

Although earlier guesses and theories had already come tantalizingly close—in 1656, Athanasius Kircher posited that bubonic plague was caused by "little worms" in the victims' blood, and Ignaz Semmelweis was proselytizing unsuccessfully for handwashing in 1847—the world would have to wait for the work of Louis Pasteur, Joseph Lister, Robert Koch, and Kitasato Shibasaburō to embrace and employ germ theory. (Forgive us for neglecting to mention other contributors—there are many!)

The main thing for our book is, in 1849, no one really knew what caused cholera or what to do about it, so patients died when all anyone had to do to save them was to keep them hydrated. Symptoms (especially diarrhea) were so violent and rapid that the infected were dying of thirst.

Of course, keeping patients hydrated wasn't easy. Transfusion therapy had been attempted before for cholera and other illnesses, but the technique (back then, it's debatable whether you could truly call it a science) was random, careless, and dangerous (no germ theory yet, remember?).

But transfusion therapy had been used successfully by some doctors to save cholera patients. We were transfixed by an article by Mr. Torrance (yes, that part is real) describing the transfusion of Latta's solution to his cholera patients and their rapid recoveries. His article, "Cases of Epidemic Cholera, Treated by Transfusion," was published October 9, 1844.

Incidentally, Latta's solution is named for Thomas Latta, who is credited for introducing saline solution methodology. He transfused cholera patients in the earlier 1832 epidemic (which killed Nora's family) while working at the Royal Infirmary in Edinburgh. Torrance heard a rumor of Latta's success, tried it with his patients, and published his findings, which allowed us to write about Nora, Julia, and Horace reading them.

Again and again, as we researched and wrote these books, we've been amazed how many times a "discovery" is repeated before there is widespread change. Many scientists contributed to germ theory, cholera treatment, and the development of anesthesia and epidemiology. Many women had to push before closed doors eventually opened.

Which leads us to our second focus: Nora and the midwives. Unfortunately, advancements in science, while mostly improving care, led to increased restrictions on women, who were barred from nearly all universities and professional organizations. New laws, designed to protect the public from shamsters and quacks, led to stiff punishments for practicing midwives. The campaign against British midwives, led by doctors, was very successful in the nineteenth century, which is kind of hard to credit, if you've watched any *Call the Midwife*. But we digress.

As depicted in our book, the appropriation of women's

health care by men in the name of "licensing" became more and more extreme, leading to the passing of the Offences Against the Person Act 1861 (four years before the licensing of Dr. Elizabeth Garrett Anderson, if you recall). This law (which covered a wide variety of offenses) allowed midwives—or individuals purporting to be midwives, which, sadly, was not a rare occurrence—to be criminally charged for performing abortions or for failing in a complicated birth. Convicted women were imprisoned in gaols like those described by Aunt Wilcox, sentenced to hard labor, and even transported.

Happily, we know this social swing didn't last. Today, most of us will consult many women professionals, in and outside of health care, and we lobby alongside friends to protect our health care rights.

It's interesting to look at how the Offences of the Person Act aligns with the career of Dr. Elizabeth Garrett Anderson. Four years after the bill passed, she began her career in London. Dr. Elizabeth Garrett Anderson founded her own hospital for women and children. (Yes, we drew from her life extensively in creating Nora's.)

That hospital became England's first female medical school. Dr. Anderson had three children and never gave up her medical practice. She became Britain's first female mayor and was a prominent advocate of the female suffrage movement. Her daughter, Louisa, also became a doctor and surgeon.

Dr. Louisa Garrett Anderson founded the Women's Hospital Corps during the First World War. As a member of the Royal Army Medical Corps, she ran the Endell Street Military Hospital, which treated over fifty thousand soldiers.

Lastly, the 1902 Midwives Act mandated the licensing (and training) of midwives as recognized, skilled, and valued health professionals.

Jaima Fixsen

Edmonton, May 2025

READING GROUP GUIDE

1. Though Nora Beady is now a licensed physician in nineteenth-century London, she still faces many obstacles when practicing medicine, namely in the treatment she receives from her male counterparts. In what ways did Nora face prejudice throughout the novel? Did you find any parallels between her situation in the nineteenth century and today?

2. At the time of the story, what was the role of the midwife in medicine, and why did many people want to put restrictions on their profession? Were you surprised by this piece of history?

3. When the cholera outbreak begins, Nora makes it clear that she will continue helping patients, even if she puts herself at risk. Why did her family not want her to treat cholera patients? If you were in Nora's position, what would you have done?

4. Nora is one of the only women working in medicine in the nineteenth century and, throughout the novel, is determined to bring more women into the field. How did

Nora plan to do this, and what did the public have to say about it? Were you surprised by any of the characters' reactions, especially the ones close to Nora?

5. At the end of the novel, Nora tries an experimental procedure to save both Aunt Wilcox's and her own life. Why was this so risky during the nineteenth century, and how did Nora change the treatment of cholera? What would this procedure be called in modern medicine?

6. When Nora sees Mrs. Franklin deliver a child at the beginning of the story, she states that they might have "things to teach each other." What skills does Nora learn from the midwives, and what skills does she teach them? Why was this important to the story? Then, discuss a time when you learned an important skill or lesson from someone that may have surprised you.

7. Throughout the story we get to see medical cases and procedures that really happened during the nineteenth century. Did any of the cases surprise you? Did you catch any medical treatments that we still use in modern medicine?

8. Nora and Daniel are newly married and, though they love each other, face many challenges that threaten to tear them apart. What problems did they face, and how did they overcome them? Do you think working in the same profession as your family and friends can be difficult?

9. To gain support for her medical practice and for the careers of the midwives, Nora makes a compromise with Daniel's Aunt Wilcox, someone with a lot of power in the social circles that influence the medical world. What was that compromise, and how does it change Nora's career trajectory? Have you ever had to make a compromise or sacrifice to a major goal in your life? If so, why?

10. The themes of resilience and hope permeate the story. Discuss all the ways resilience plays a vital role within the narrative, especially to Nora's character. Then, think about what resilience means to you. Discuss a time you remained resilient in the face of adversity.

A CONVERSATION
WITH THE AUTHORS

You explore big historical topics within the story, one of them being midwifery and its pivotal role in medicine. What inspired you about this piece of history, and why do you think it's important to portray it in fiction?

Midwives were an intriguing facet of society caught between tradition and rapidly progressing science. They had long done things a certain way, but with the introduction of new medical advancements, midwives were seen as obsolete and even dangerous. Despite the criticisms of contemporary physicians and surgeons, midwives were a comforting and authoritative presence during the frightful hours of childbirth with services affordable to even the poorer classes, which saved many lives. However, they were not required to have any standardized knowledge of anatomy or disease. Though many midwives had learned techniques superior to doctors of the day, they could not effectively or scientifically advocate their points or defend their methods. I would argue it was not wrong for doctors to want to establish standards for safety, but far too often the physicians of the day discarded the wisdom and techniques of midwives that would have benefited their patients and their profession as a whole.

We believe the story of midwives is important to tell because they are an integral part of the history of medicine and of women. From ancient times, they have been present in the most crucial moments. Midwifery is the one area of medicine where women not only found and kept a foothold but dominated over their male counterparts. They have been figures of courage and fortitude, running toward crisis and protecting the givers and receivers of new life. I don't think we can tell the story of humanity without talking about the women who helped bring so many people into the world.

From the cholera epidemic to Victorian-era medical procedures, it's clear how much research was done to create such a rich portrayal of this time in nineteenth-century England! What does your research process look like? Was there a specific topic you found really interesting this time around?

We had to be torn away from our research and reminded to actually return to writing! The research was so riveting that many times I've cried or dreamed of the case studies I've read. We have pored over and through medical journals of the day, often getting stuck on names for procedures or medications that sent us digging deeper for understanding. There are several medical scenes we wrote that did not make the final editing cuts but remain in our consciousness as important developments for our characters. Many times we have spent days away from our keyboards as we hunted down a medical detail that did not matter to the story at large but mattered greatly to us. We did not want to lie to our readers in the smallest degree. When a doctor reported he used a "very dilute solution of the plumb. acet., two grains to the ounce of aqua rosa" we had to begin the tedious mission of ascertaining what in the world that meant so we could accurately portray it! Deciphering medical abbreviations no longer in use is a maddening and fascinating task. (In this case, plumb. acet. is short for Plumbum aceticum, or lead acetate. So basically, it was a prescription for poisonous lead salts mixed with rose water. At least it smelled nice.)

Unfortunately, there was no topic I did not find interesting. It is another reason research took so long. I speak for Jaima and me when I say we could not help being pulled into the drama of medical history. Every case study in every medical journal is a riveting account of life, death, suffering, recovery, despondency, and victory. It has been the best reading of my life.

You've now written three novels following Nora Beady and her family and friends as she navigates life as a woman physician. What have you loved most about writing this cast of characters?

Horace. He has been a perpetual source of delight to both of us. We began this entire story with Horace—wondering what a surgeon of his personality and genius would do with a young ward like Nora. Every time he opened his mouth we laughed or were oddly touched. Writing his interactions with Nora and all our other characters has been a constant amusement. As we have come to know each cast member of our story, they have educated, entertained, and surprised us without fail. We are so grateful we are able to write characters who possess brilliance, moral goodness, humor, and contradiction. They have been complex and challenging and an utter joy.

As co-authors, what does your writing process look like?

How do you decide who writes what, and how might working together help aid in creativity?

The process of writing together is ever evolving. Sometimes it is determined by life circumstances and asking our fellow author to tackle a chapter while we attend to other pressing matters. Sometimes one of us has been deep in a particular area of research and is better equipped to write a scene. Sometimes one of us hits writer's block and hands the baton off to a fresh mind.

One of the most important aids for creativity is facing the unexpected, and that happens constantly with a co-author. Jaima will write something I didn't anticipate and my brain must jump to the challenge—just as we all do in real life. It keeps our characters three dimensional and unpredictable as they sometimes say or do something we never imagined. It is an ongoing pursuit in the great arts of improvisation, compromise, and psychology.

What books, movies, songs, or other media has inspired you and your writing, specifically the Nora Beady novels?

Jaima's answers will differ from mine, obviously, but I was most inspired by authors I read in childhood. Sir Arthur Conan Doyle and his notorious character, Sherlock Holmes, brought Horace to life for me. Holmes's mix of genius and social blindness helped me find Horace from the very first pages. The journals of Humboldt exploring the regions of the Amazon also gave me a glance into a truly superior mind. I was also influenced by Louisa May Alcott and her humorous renderings of Jo March. James Herriot and his hilarious and heartwarming medical tales of veterinary life shaped me forever as an author. I am grateful for every author who taught me how to tell the stories that matter, and how to make the stories I tell matter to others.

Nora is a strong, resilient, and hopeful main character. What do you hope readers will take away from her and her story?

The tenacious power of curiosity. When we are passionately driven to accumulate knowledge or skill, remarkable things happen. Horace, Nora, Daniel, and Harry are all hungry—starving, really—to peer beyond the limitations of their time. They are tormented by ignorance, and they see that same torment in one another. Together, they collect and share all that they learn. I believe that is why Nora was able to break through the conventions and customs of her time. Horace recognized a hunger in her he knew too well to leave unsatisfied.

I also hope readers recognize Nora's fight was not so simplistic or predictable as a struggle between women and men. Hers was a battle against ignorance that knew no limits of gender or age. There were men who opposed her and men who championed her. There were women who thwarted her and women who applauded her. And at times she stood in her own way and at times threw open all closed doors. This is a story of the broken, curving path of history that never did run smoothly for anyone. And above all, a story of the hunger that drives us to the brink of the impossible, and then, over the edge.

ACKNOWLEDGMENTS

We are dumbfounded as we look back over the last twelve years. This series has been more than a decade in the making, from research to writing to finding an agent and a publishing home. First, we want to thank our agent, Jennifer Weltz. She has been a tireless advocate and truthteller. When we had not yet fully realized a character or plot, she pushed us on, and we are so grateful. The entire team at Jean V. Naggar Literary Agency, including Ariana Philips and Cole Hildebrand, has championed Nora's journey and are the reason these books are translated into so many languages, delivering Nora's story to audiences around the world. We are thankful to Recorded Books for bringing Nora's voice to life in beautifully produced audio books.

To the incredible team at Sourcebooks, we cannot say enough good. There is not a single publisher who compares. The skill, care, and professionalism you've afforded us has made our story into an international bestseller. To our first advocate, Jenna Jankowski, we thank you for your incredible work and passion. And to Liv Turner, Cristina Arreola, Diane Dannenfeldt, Annabelle Harsch, Jackie Cummings, and Rachel Norfleet, we express our sincere appreciation.

To our families, who supported us patiently for more than

a decade while we researched surgeries—and perhaps discussed cholera and diphtheria too much at the dinner table—we are so thankful for your consistency and encouragement. You've been with us when we typed into the night, at book signings and presentations, and as we stumbled our way through public speeches. Your tireless cheerleading has made this surreal opportunity a true joy. We love you, each and all.

And lastly, to our readers, book club members, and reviewers—thank you! You have been generous in your support and in recommending our books to others. That is the only way a story survives and thrives. Without you, Nora, Horace, Daniel, and all the characters at 43 Great Queen Street would be shut away in dark pages, unknown and forgotten.

We wrote the words. You brought them to life.

Thank you.

ABOUT THE AUTHORS

Audrey Blake is the pen name for writing duo Regina Sirois and Jaima Fixsen, two authors who met as finalists in an online writing contest, started messaging and critiquing each other's chapters, and then writing together. Their books have been *USA Today* and international bestsellers, and *The Girl in His Shadow* was selected as the Summer 2022 Big Library Read. *All in Her Hands* is their fourth book together.

Regina loves history, literature, and nature, and calls Kansas home. Her novel, *On Little Wings*, received the 2012 Amazon Breakthrough Novel Award.

Jaima lives in Alberta, Canada. She loves reading, cycling, and her dog, Bruno. Her book, *The Specimen*, was a finalist for the Crime Writers of Canada Best Novel Award.

THE GIRL IN HIS SHADOW

AN UNFORGETTABLE HISTORICAL FICTION NOVEL
ABOUT ONE WOMAN WHO BELIEVED IN SCIENTIFIC
MEDICINE BEFORE THE WORLD BELIEVED IN HER.

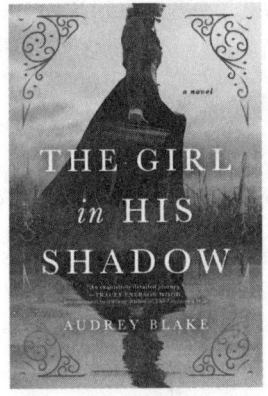

London, 1845: Raised by the eccentric surgeon Dr. Horace Croft after losing her parents to a deadly pandemic, the orphan Nora Beady knows little about conventional life. While other young ladies were raised to busy themselves with needlework and watercolors, Nora was trained to perfect her suturing and anatomical illustrations of dissections.

Women face dire consequences if caught practicing medicine, but in Croft's private clinic, Nora is his most trusted—and secret—assistant. That is, until the new surgical resident, Dr. Daniel Gibson, arrives. Dr. Gibson has no idea that Horace's bright and quiet young ward is a surgeon more qualified than even himself. In order to protect Dr. Croft and his practice from scandal and collapse, Nora must learn to play a new and uncomfortable role—that of a proper young lady.

But pretense has its limits. Nora cannot turn away and ignore the suffering of patients, even if it means giving Gibson the power to ruin everything she's worked for. And when she makes a discovery that could change the field forever, Nora faces an impossible choice: remain invisible and let the men around her take credit for her work, or step into the light—even if it means being destroyed by her own legacy.

Fans of *The Other Einstein* and *The Paris Library* will relish this riveting and empowering story about one woman's fight to follow her dreams and build a life—and legacy—beyond what is expected of her.

"An exquisitely detailed journey through the harrowing field of medicine in mid-nineteenth-century London."

—Tracey Enerson Wood, *USA Today* bestselling author of *The Engineer's Wife* and *The War Nurse*

THE SURGEON'S DAUGHTER

WOMEN'S WORK IS A MATTER OF LIFE AND DEATH.

Nora Beady, the only female student at a prestigious medical school in Bologna, is a rarity. In the nineteenth century, women are expected to remain at home and raise children, so her unconventional, indelicate ambitions to become a licensed surgeon offend the men around her.

Everything changes when she allies herself with Magdalena Morenco, the sole female doctor on staff. Together, the two women develop new techniques to improve a groundbreaking surgery: the cesarean section. It's a highly dangerous procedure, and the research is grueling, but even worse is the vitriolic response from men. Most don't trust the findings of women, and many can choose to deny their wives medical care.

Already facing resistance on all sides, Nora is shaken when she meets a patient who will die without the surgery. If the procedure is successful, her work could change the world. But a failure could cost everything: precious lives, Nora's career, and the role women will be allowed to play in medicine.

Perfect for book clubs and for fans of Marie Benedict, Tracey Enerson Wood, and Sarah Penner, here comes a captivating celebration of women health care workers throughout history.

> "This is an intense, suspenseful, and insightful read about the challenges both women and doctors faced in the nineteenth century... Our heroine rises to the challenge with courage and determination."
>
> —Historical Novel Society

THE WOMAN WITH NO NAME

OLDER, DIMINUTIVE, OVERLOOKED...SHE BECOMES ONE
OF THE MOST FEROCIOUS AND FEARED ESPIONAGE
AGENTS IN THE WAR AGAINST THE NAZIS.

World War II London, 1942. Though she survived the bomb that destroyed her home, Yvonne Rudellat's life is over. She's estranged from her husband, her daughter is busy with war work, and Yvonne—older, diminutive, overlooked—has lost all purpose. Until she's offered a chance to remake herself entirely...

The war has taken a turn for the worse, and the men in charge are desperate. So when Yvonne is recruited as Britain's first female sabotage agent, expectations are low. But her tenacity, ability to go unnoticed, and aptitude for explosives set her apart. Soon enough she arrives in occupied France with a new identity, ready to set the Nazi regime ablaze.

But there are adversaries on all sides. As Yvonne becomes infamous as the nameless, unstoppable woman who burns the enemy at every turn, she realizes she may lose herself to the urgent needs of the cause...

Based on a true story, *The Woman with No Name* is a gripping story of secrets, spies, and the women behind the Resistance, from *USA Today* bestselling author Audrey Blake.

"Resilience, courage, and bravery outshine the
enemy in this fast-paced, historical read."

—*Booklist*